The BOY WITH The PORCELAIN BLADE

Also by Den Patrick from Gollancz:

The Naer Evain Chronicles

Orcs War-Fighting Manual
Elves War-Fighting Manual
Dwarves War-Fighting Manual

The Erebus Sequence

The Boy with the Porcelain Blade

The BOY WITH THE PORCELAIN BLADE

DEN PATRICK

GOLLANCZ

LONDON

Copyright © Den Patrick 2014
All rights reserved

The right of Den Patrick to be identified as the author of
this work has been asserted by him in accordance with
the Copyright, Designs and Patents Act 1988.

First published in Great Britain in 2014 by Gollancz
An imprint of the Orion Publishing Group
Orion House, 5 Upper St Martin's Lane, London WC2H 9EA
An Hachette UK Company

A CIP catalogue record for this book is available
from the British Library

ISBN 978 0 575 13383 9 (Cased)
ISBN 978 0 575 13397 6 (Trade Paperback)

1 3 5 7 9 10 8 6 4 2

Typeset at The Spartan Press Ltd,
Lymington, Hants

Printed and bound in Great Britain by
Clays Ltd, St Ives plc

The Orion Publishing Group's policy is to use papers that
are natural, renewable and recyclable products and made from
wood grown in sustainable forests. The logging and manufacturing
processes are expected to conform to the environmental
regulations of the country of origin.

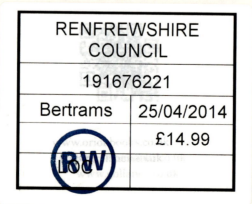

For Christine,
and for John.

Pain is a great teacher, Lucien.
PROFESSORE VIRMYRE

The kiss is to love as lightning is to thunder.
POPULAR LANDFALL PROVERB

The Great Houses of the Diaspora

ORFANI

Lucien 'Sinistro' di Fontein
lacks ears and confidence, lives with House Contadino

Golia di Fontein
a hulking brute, possesses tines that grow from his forearms,
lives with House Fontein

Araneae 'Anea' Oscuro Contadino
a fearsomely intelligent veiled young woman, never speaks

Dino Adolfo Erudito
a young Orfano of some pluck, lives with House Erudito

Festo Erudito
the youngest of the current Orfano

HOUSE FONTEIN

Duke Fontein
an elderly and conservative member of the nobility

Duchess Fontein
his notoriously bad-tempered wife

Maestro Superiore di Spada Giancarlo di Fontein
senior sword master, originally a commoner from the
Contadino estates

Maestro di Spada D'arzenta di Fontein
Lucien's tutor and long-suffering member of
Giancarlo's coterie

Maestro di Spada Ruggeri di Fontein
laconic, to say the least

Capo di Custodia Guido di Fontein
an ambitious fop and popinjay from a minor house

HOUSE CONTADINO

Lord Emilio Contadino
a viscount of middle age, yearning for prestige

Lady Medea Contadino
the viscountess, the soul of House Contadino,
diplomatic to a fault

Massimo Esposito
the viscount's indispensable aide

Rafaela da Costa
housemaid to Lucien di Fontein, a wise head on
young shoulders

Camelia di Contadino
cook, no-nonsense giantess of the kitchens

Nardo Moretti
messenger and loyal servant

HOUSE ERUDITO

Maestro Gian Cherubini
head of House Erudito, a voice of reason

Professore Falcone Virmyre
stern lynchpin of the teaching faculty

Dottore Angelicola Erudito
possessed of permanently poor humour

Professore Russo di Fontein
an ambitious and talented teacher

Mistress Corvo Prospero
whip-thin dance teacher and scourge of the ill coordinated

HOUSE PROSPERO

Duke Stephano Prospero
a stentorian barrel of a man with poor hearing

Duchess Salvaza Prospero
his much younger and often dissatisfied wife

Stephania Prospero
the image of her mother, a sharp wit and kind heart

Raul da Costa
a craftsman of rare skill

OTHERS

The Majordomo
the voice of the king, Steward of Demesne

The Looking-Glass

HOUSE FONTEIN ANTECHAMBER

– *Febbraio* 315

Lucien di Fontein stood in the antechamber waiting, feeling his pulse quicken and his mouth go dry. It was always the same before a testing. His breath steamed on the air. This part of the castle lacked heating, and he was grateful for his vest, dress shirt and frock coat. He clenched, stretched and clenched again his nearly numb fingers, chiding himself for not requesting gloves. He made a mental note to obtain calfskin fingerless ones. Assuming of course he lived out the rest of the day.

The room was a simple affair. Behind him stood tall double doors. Ornate black iron hinges lent the aged wood a severe solemnity. A pair of matching doors loomed ahead, a portal to the training room beyond. Two pews, narrow and uncomfortable, ran down either side of the chamber. A faded flag in the scarlet and black of House Fontein had been left in the corner, the fabric providing a feast for the moths. Latticed windows let in pale autumnal light, throwing a diffuse net shadow over the interior.

A lone pot plant grown monstrous and a full-length looking glass were the only other decorations. Biology was not his forte, although he suspected the growth was poisonous in some way. The looking glass reflected a man-child of eighteen summers, a grave expression etched onto his face. He had polished his knee-length boots to an impressive shine, the deep brown leather worn and sturdy. The buckles had been buffed to a honey-coloured gleam. His trousers and frock coat were of a blue so deep as to be mistaken for black in poor light. He was particularly taken with the fine embroidery on the lapels, a repeating motif of vines and leaves. The buttons had been made from shark teeth on his insistence. Virmyre had told him the creatures regrew their teeth many times over the course of their lives. The idea of renewal had appealed to Lucien, the possibility of attaining something once lost. He'd imagined the buttoner cutting his fingers to shreds on the awful teeth. Filing down the triangular shards into ivory discs must have been an ordeal – still, there were worse things in Demesne. Hoops of copper run to verdigris decorated the epaulettes of the jacket, just as he'd requested. Being Orfano he was expected to present a certain profile and had taken a fancy to sketching unlikely outfits when his tutors bored him. All in all he rather liked his new wardrobe; too bad it would see ruin at the hands of his opponents.

Worst yet, it might be the outfit he died in.

He was aware enough by now to know his obsession with finery was simply compensation. He couldn't change the way he looked. He hoped he might yet grow into a more aristocratic-looking young man. His brow was too heavy for his tastes, his eyes too deeply sunken, lips too thin. He felt rather stocky and squat, sulking for a month when he realised he would never be as tall as Golia. No matter. He'd be the better of Golia in other ways, ways that mattered. He raised his right hand to his hair. Thick, black, coarse hair that he'd let grow long against Superiore Giancarlo's wishes. And Mistress Corvo and a number of other teachers. He hesitated from lifting the swathe of black, not wanting to see the disfigurement beneath. And his nails. The newer staff thought him effete, or affected, or both. His nails matched his hair but he'd never once painted them. Angelicola had been unable to tell Lucien why his nails should be such a dismal hue. Nor had the belligerent *dottore* managed to decipher why Lucien bled clear fluid that turned pale blue after a few seconds.

It was the same for all of the Orfani: they hid their disfigurements as best they could. The deformities were an open secret among the subjects of Demesne in spite of the Orfani's attempts to appear normal. Lucien knew full well the common folk branded the Orfani witchlings – *streghe* in the old tongue. He felt the familiar sting of pique. His hand strayed toward the ceramic blade resting in its sheath on his right hip.

Lucien drew the weapon, holding it out in front of himself, the tip just inches from the floor, looking almost casual. Almost. He brought the blade up to his face in the fencer's salute. None of the Orfani were allowed to carry a metal blade. It was tradition, so they said. Only proven men or women could be trusted to carry such an expensive weapon. Metal cost money and could not be squandered on the young. Lucien didn't believe a word of it. Ceramic blades were just as difficult to produce, so he'd been told. Still, this blade was his, a constant yet silent companion. The weapon had a stylised crosspiece in the Maltese fashion. The hilt was bound in taut scarlet leather, worn soft by endless training. Three notches marked the leading edge, almost too small to see. The blade was the colour of bone and it pleased him, he'd chosen it especially.

'Which style will you fight in?'

Lucien spun and almost lunged. Dino gave an almost imperceptible shake of the head, disapproval etched on his lips. He was dressed in sober grey.

'Trying to get yourself killed?'

The boy shrugged and pushed out his bottom lip. His hand rested casually on his own blade, but there was no suggestion of drawing. The Orfano bore a certain fearlessness in his grey eyes despite being six years Lucien's junior.

'You'll make a fine assassin one day if you keep sneaking around like that.'

'So they tell me.' Another shrug.

Lucien sheathed his blade. 'Is there something you need?'

'Thought I should wish you luck,' replied Dino. 'We've not spoken for a while.' His eyes showed nothing; he folded his arms and slouched against the wall.

'Virmyre sent you, didn't he?'

The boy nodded. Lucien felt no need to fill the silence that followed. Dino let it spool out between them until his curiosity snagged a question from his lips.

3

'Any idea who you'll face? What style?'

Now it was Lucien's turn to shrug. Rumours of his intended opponent had been scarce, unusually so considering gossip was currency in Demesne. He still didn't know what awaited him beyond the doors of the training chamber, whether it was to be a fight to first blood or to the death. The one thing he could depend on was Maestro Superiore di Spada Giancarlo. The *superiore* administered every testing. A sour tang flooded Lucien's throat. His palms began to sweat.

Maestro di Spada D'arzenta had been Lucien's primary teacher, an even-handed but reserved man in his mid-thirties. He taught in the *stile vecchio*, a single blade in the leading hand, the empty hand for balance.

Superiore Giancarlo taught *spada e pugnale*, attacking with the sword and parrying with a dagger in the off hand, although his opinions were sharper than both. Lucien had endured a dozen lessons by the *superiore*. Eleven lessons too many.

Maestro Ruggeri didn't waste time on opinions, if indeed he had any. Ruggeri simply taught. There was the correct way or the incorrect way, no praise, no chastisement. Ruggeri favoured the cloak and sword.

'Well, the pleasure was all yours,' mumbled Dino, interrupting Lucien's thoughts, but there was no real bite to his sarcasm. The younger boy edged toward the door, made to let himself out.

'Dino.'

The boy turned, mouth set, a flat line holding something back.

'I'm sorry. For that night.' Lucien cleared his throat, 'After *La Festa* when you were with Stephania...'

'Well, it's done now.' Dino shrugged again, a slow blink of those grey eyes. A touch of sadness about them perhaps. 'What happens if you fail today?'

'I'm not sure,' replied Lucien, 'Shame and embarrassment certainly. Perhaps success leads to some position in Demesne. I don't know what failure will bring.'

'They say Golia may join the *Maestri di Spada*.'

'All I ever wanted was to be part of House Fontein.' Lucien

chewed his lip, regarded the hilt of the sword. 'And now I'm here at my final testing, and I don't know what I want.' A weary breath escaped him.

'Don't fail,' said Dino. 'And don't die.'

The younger Orfano flicked a lazy salute and was gone. Lucien stood in the chamber remembering the bitter morning after *La Festa*. How he'd felt responsible for Stephania coming to his chamber somehow. Ridiculous of course. Regret coiled around him like mist. The doors behind opened again and he resisted the urge to draw his blade in response. The history books of Landfall were littered with feuds between the houses. The Orfano were not immune to such internecine violence, despite being under the nominal protection of the king. Assassination had been a currency paid out all too keenly in earlier decades.

Anea slipped into the room unescorted. Lucien realised he was holding his breath. As ever she wore her veil: midnight-blue fabric covering the bottom half of her face. Tiny bronze discs and tassels decorated her forehead, suspended from a headscarf of white. Her dress, a matching midnight-blue, was tightly fitted. The sleeves were elegantly slashed to show the white blouse beneath. Her skirts were of an impressive volume, almost floor length. She reached into her sleeve and Lucien's hand drifted to his blade, he dropped back a step. Anea caught the motion, holding out her hand, placating. She drew a palm-sized leather-bound book from her dress and searched for a particular page.

Just three years younger, nearly matching him in height, he guessed she was wearing her heeled boots, buttons running to the ankle in neat precision. Her blonde hair had enchanted the houses when she had first arrived on the steps of House Contadino. She looked up, caught him with her piercing green eyes, proffered the book to him. Her exquisite script curled and ran across the page:

I know things have been difficult between us lately but I wanted to wish you luck. Keep your wits and your feet. Don't let him talk down to you.

Everyone knew Anea, the silent Orfano. Araneae Oscuro

5

Contadino by birth, Anea on account of hating her full name. It was tradition for Orfani to petition a house for adoption at sixteen. They took the name of whoever they lodged with in the interim. Anea was, if rumour were to be believed, the most fiercely intelligent Orfano in a hundred and fifty years.

'Thank you,' he replied. 'I should have spoken with you since *La Festa*, but I've been busy training.'

Anea took a moment to scribble another message in the book, a pencil appearing from nowhere in her clever fingers.

And with the wedding plans? It seems you are destined for great things, provided you survive the day.

Lucien read the note, then glanced at her, unsure if he was being mocked.

'The wedding isn't set. No formal offer of marriage has been made.' He struggled to maintain a polite tone of voice. 'I'm still undecided.' This last an escaped stray thought. Demesne had been aflame with talk from the ruling nobles to the farmers in the fields. There could be few in Landfall who didn't know of the potential pairing.

Anea's eyes narrowed above the veil, her pencil resumed its scratching in the book, the strokes more hurried. Lucien waited, flinching as she thrust the book at him.

You'd be a fool not to marry Stephania. What else is there? Marrying into one of the great houses is your most prudent option. A political marriage could give you a degree of safety.

'Safety? What do we know about safety?' Lucien curled his lip. 'We're protected by the king's own edict, yet we live our lives in fear of poison and fire, blade and maul. Some safety. Do you really suppose a political marriage will change anything? For you? For me?'

Anea stared, green eyes hard like jade. Tears formed but refused to brim over. Lucien immediately regretted mentioning the fire. Clearly the memory of that particular night burned all too brightly in her mind. She scribed another message, agitation obvious, her handwriting now jagged.

You're pathetic. You don't even have the sense to save yourself. Even after everything that's happened.

She snatched the book back from his fingers before he could

respond and swept out of the room, not bothering to close the doors behind her. Lucien sighed. He made to close the doors, pausing a second to watch her march down the hall, passing from darkness through pools of lantern light and back again. Her heels rang out on the stone floor, fading into the distance as she passed deeper into the castle, back to her studies in House Erudito.

The antechamber was silent again. Now he could press on with the business of clearing his mind, letting the noise and confusion of the day quieten. Dino's visit had provided some measure of closure, Anea had only reminded him of a situation that was all but inevitable. Thoughts came to him, roiling waves breaking on the shore. The anxiety in his stomach rose and fell, his breathing continued slow and steady. Superiore Giancarlo was on the other side of the doors, waiting for him in the training chamber. Giancarlo and all of his towering disdain. Lucien pushed the thought away and kept breathing. Maestri di Spada D'arzenta and Ruggeri would also be there. This was a more welcome thought but he turned it to one side all the same. Quite why Anea had suddenly appeared was a mystery. Images of her leather-bound book and angry green eyes filled his mind. He reined his concentration back, setting aside the curious visitation. The anxiety within dwindled. He breathed, immersed in the sound of the wind howling around ancient towers and weathervanes.

His thoughts strayed to Rafaela. She'd been conspicuous only by her absence these last few days. Their paths crossed less and less, it seemed.

Back to concentration, back to a clear mind. The tension moved out of his gut now, lurking in his shoulders and at the backs of his knees. That was to be expected. He remained standing, kept breathing. The doors to the training chamber opened, yawning wide, creaking on ancient hinges.

'Are you ready to be received?' said a deep voice. Lucien raised his face, eyes hard.

'I am ready to be received.'

Lucien stepped into the chamber beyond, chin pulled in tightly, staring out from under his brow. His fingertips rested

7

on the hilt of his blade. Two final diversions raced across his mind before the testing began. The first was of gloves for his icy fingers, the second was of Rafaela.

2

Ancient Tales

HOUSE CONTADINO

– Settembre 306

It was a day of many firsts, but Lucien always looked back on it with a feeling of disquiet. The soft innocence of childhood had been snatched from him that day; things would never be the same again.

He'd started his physical training just after his eighth birthday. The Majordomo had taken to visiting his rooms once a week. The small talk was strained, sparse from the boy, dry from Demesne's warden. The seasons were on the change, ushering in winter with the shrieks of night-time storms. The days were an endless susurrus of leaves caught in autumnal winds. Lucien wondered if the castle would ever be warm again. He'd have happily stayed in bed until spring, nestled among sheepskins with the fire banked up. He'd not thought it strange to have his own apartment back then. It was all he had ever known.

The Majordomo entered the sitting room without knocking, as he always did. Lucien glowered at him, setting aside the oversized book of fairy tales. He'd been roused from his bed early that day, taken from sleep by nightmares. The book had been a comfort in the early hours of the new day. The armchair was a small fortress about him. He slunk from it like a reluctant hound, immediately wishing he hadn't. The Domo was tall in a way that was uncanny in Demesne, perhaps seven feet of ashen robes. His deeply lined face remained hidden under a heavy cowl, only his great chin jutted out, like some work of masonry. A purple rope served as a belt, holding together the many folds of fabric that comprised his attire. Skeletal hands extended from voluminous sleeves, the skin on them stained parchment, busying themselves attending to the fire. Lucien stood rooted to the spot, unsure of etiquette, dread seeping into him for no discernible reason.

The Majordomo was the voice of the king, that shadowy recluse lurking at the centre of Demesne like a spider in its web. The four houses, and all of the houses minor, paled into insignificance when placed alongside the power and influence of the Domo. And here he was, banking the fire with desiccated hands, nails dirty and cracked. He spoke in a tired drone, like the buzzing of insects, enquiring about Lucien's studies. He looked ridiculous, hunched down at the hearth – the quality of his robes marked him out as beggar, certainly not anyone of substance. Lucien answered in single stunted syllables, chewed his lip, folded his arms.

'And Professore Virmyre is teaching you well, I trust?'

'Yes, and Maestro Cherubini too.' Who was far easier to talk to than the stern and unreadable Virmyre.

'And Maestro di Spada D'arzenta speaks very highly of you.' Just for a second there was the shadow of inflection. Lucien wondered if this was some slight or sarcasm.

'That's good,' he breathed, willing the gaunt collection of rags out of his apartment.

The hooded official finally left, staff beating out a slow percussion on the corridors. Lucien wasted no time finding himself a blanket to nestle under, snug again in the high-backed armchair. The life of an Orfano was a lonely one; he'd nearly finished the book of fairy stories when the next visitor arrived.

She leaned on the doorway, arms folded across her chest. Her hair was untied, thick corkscrews of rich dark brown falling about a heart-shaped face. Her hazel eyes were filled with what Lucien thought at the time was amusement, but would come to realise was tenderness. It was Rafaela's day off, but she looked much as she always did. She wore a cream blouse, rucked and ruffled where it met her black bodice, tightly laced. Her skirt was a rare shade of scarlet, the colour of cheap wine, and her lips. Buttoned boots peeked out from the demarcation of her hemline, heels adding inches to her height. At that time Rafaela was fifteen or thereabouts; the first blush of womanhood had taken to her well. She had neglected to wear her apron, sending out a clear signal she was not present at Demesne to perform duty.

'Ella. I wasn't expecting to see you today. What are you doing here?' He set the book aside and kicked off the blanket, becoming tangled in it a moment before finding his feet.

'Come to find my charming prince, of course. What are you reading?'

'Oh, just some nonsense for children.' He shrugged.

Rafaela laughed and shook her head.

'You are funny. The things you say. Come on, I'll take you on an adventure and you can hear a much better story. How about that?'

'Won't we get into trouble?' he said, glad to be released from being alone.

'Not much.' She smiled at him. 'It'll be fine.'

They left Demesne and Lucien was wide-eyed with excitement and more than a touch of fear. He'd not set foot outside the brooding collection of stones before. The towers reached into the sky, pointing at pale blue heavens. The last of the stars were fading and the moon remained only as a chalk smudge. The squat bulk of the *sanatorio* stood apart from the castle proper, with gargoyles flocking the roof, staring after them as they retreated into the countryside. Rafaela had dressed him in peasant's attire when they'd reached the kitchens of House Contadino.

'It's a disguise,' she explained. 'Today you are not Orfano; today you can be a normal little boy. We'll call you Luc.'

'I'm not a *little* boy, I'm eight,' he replied affronted and wishing he were already nine or even ten. He couldn't even imagine what it must like to be ten. Incredible, most likely. He'd probably have to start shaving when he reached ten.

Cook Camelia had given them apples, watered-down wine, a good cheese and some bread past its best. She spoke quietly to Rafaela in that voice the teachers used, seemingly below the range of children's hearing. Perhaps he'd learn how to talk like that too when he grew up.

The wind whipped about them and Rafaela concentrated on driving the cart, the mule plodding, perhaps less than walking speed. The countryside stretched away ahead of them, orderly hedgerows and drystone walls marking boundaries and paths. In the distance a copse of cedar trees clustered together, swaying at the dictates of the weather. Birds broke from cover in a commotion of wings and sleek bodies, flying in formation, wheeling about high above. They swooped and climbed, turning back to retake perches among the whispering trees. Lucien pulled the knitted skullcap down, clutching at the simple jacket he wore.

'Make sure you keep your hat on all day: it's cold,' said Rafaela. Lucien nodded, thinking this an obvious thing to say.

'Where are we going?'

'We're going to the Contadino Estate. It's where I grew up, where my family live.'

'Is your father a farmer?'

'No. Not everyone who lives on the Contadino Estate works the land or fishes the sea, just as not everyone who lives on the Fontein Estate is a soldier.'

'That's what I want to be. I want to be adopted by House Fontein when I'm sixteen.'

Rafaela laughed, her hazel eyes twinkling, 'And I'm sure you will be, if you practise with your blade and don't spend windy days reading fairy stories.'

Lucien blinked a few times, not sure if he was being chided or not.

They continued onwards, the cart creaking and rocking on the road, which was in good repair. They passed a small huddle of buildings, shuttered against the wind, smoke dissipated in a pale grey plume above the chimneys. Lucien spotted some boys playing outside, ragged-looking things, pinched and dirty. Their clothes were a uniform blend of dark grey and smudged brown. They wore no shoes, their feet pale underneath the mud that clung to them. Lucien said nothing and looked down at his boots, grateful for the thick socks he wore.

'Why aren't those boys at school?' he asked.

'Because their parents can't afford it, most likely.'

'What do you mean, afford?'

'It costs money to send children to school, and not everyone has enough. Some people struggle to feed themselves.'

'Who pays for me to go to school?'

'Well.' She paused. 'The king, I suppose.'

'And where does he get his money from?'

'The king takes money from the people. Taxes.'

'Even from people who don't have enough to eat?'

Rafaela nodded.

'Even from people that don't have shoes?'

Another nod.

'I don't think I understand taxes,' mumbled Lucien against the wind.

'Few people do,' said Rafaela, concentrating on the road ahead.

Finally they came to a building. Based on its size, Lucien guessed it was a barn. Moss had grown up one side of the structure, creeping across the stacked stones and feeble mortar of the bottom half. The top was constructed entirely of wood, caulked with flaking white plaster.

'This is a strange building,' whispered Lucien, not knowing why. Rafaela smiled at him and jumped down from the cart, unhitching it from the mule.

'What makes you say that?'

'Well, half of it is made from wood.'

'Not everyone can afford a castle made out of stone, little prince.'

'So it's about money? Again?'

Rafaela smiled and nodded.

'Everything is about money.'

'Then why have I never seen any before?' he asked.

'The rules don't apply to you; you're Orfano.'

She tied the mule up and made sure it had access to water, then held out her hands to him.

'Come now, jump down. I want you to hear this.'

They entered the building and Lucien struggled to breathe. Inside were close to thirty children, ranging from six to twelve years old. He'd not seen so many before, certainly not children who were anything but scullions or pages. Even in the training rooms of House Fontein the number rarely rose above fifteen of Demesne's privileged noble young. The children in the barn sat at small tables, chatting to each other and reading aloud from books. Some noted down single words on scraps of parchment and took them to a wooden board where they pinned them up. Most of the children had shoes, but their clothes were well worn and often threadbare.

Rafaela rested a hand on Lucien's shoulder, holding him against her. She was taller than him back then. He looked up at her, forcing a nervous smile.

A woman attired all in black clapped her hands twice. The children became hushed, folding hands neatly in front of them. Some couldn't quite direct their attention to the teacher, instead staring at the girl and the shivering boy who had just arrived.

'Today we have a special treat. Mistress Rafaela has come to speak to you. As many of you know, Mistress Rafaela works at Demesne, but once she attended this very school. She learned her words just as you now are learning yours.'

The schoolteacher nodded politely to Rafaela, a small smile stealing over her thin lips. She was a severe-looking woman, her black hair scraped back into an unflattering bun. She had an abundance of forehead and rather beady eyes. Lucien was glad she wasn't one of his tutors.

Rafaela ushered the children to one end of the schoolhouse, where they variously wriggled and bumbled about, managing to cram onto a broad, slightly mangy rug. Lucien perched on a corner near the front, not straying far from Ella. The children sat beside him and said nothing. They stared with owlish expressions or ignored him altogether, some more interested in the contents of their noses.

'Hello. My name is Rafaela, and this is my little friend Luc.' She indicated Lucien and he swallowed, felt himself blush.

'I've come to tell you a folk story today, and perhaps some history too. The problem is this all took place so long ago no

14

one quite knows what happened for sure.' When she spoke loudly Lucien became aware of a pleasant timbre to her voice he'd not noticed before. Usually, when she was about her work at Demesne, she spoke in a respectful hush.

'All we have is the story, and I will recount it as well as I can. Are you all comfortable?' Ella smiled as thirty heads nodded; excited squeals escaping in anticipation of what was to come. Outside it began to rain, the drops drumming lightly on the wooden shingles above, the dull pattering providing a backdrop of sound.

'A long time ago, perhaps three hundred years ago now, there were three great ships. They set out from a land a long way from here. Many, many miles. The ships carried people, dozens of people, even hundreds, and these people came looking for a new home. However, the ships were undone with bad luck. The captains, who were very old when the voyage began, died one by one. The first died in his sleep, the second captain collapsed while checking the maps. The last captain despaired. The ships had stumbled into a great storm, and it were as if many days had passed since anyone had seen the sun. In fact, many crew members on the ships were beginning to believe they were shrouded in constant night. When the storm reached its worst, the winds howling and shrieking like hungry ghosts, the last captain passed away. The crews of the three great ships were distraught, but the captain had seen a glimmer in the darkness before he died. With his dying words he gave orders to sail toward the blinking light. The glimmer was in fact a lighthouse, made to warn sailors that the coast was unforgiving and rocky, but the crews did not know this. Due to the storm's great power, and the fact the crews were much diminished without their captains, the ships were wrecked.'

Rafaela paused. Outside the schoolhouse, the wind had picked up. Lucien could well imagine how frightening it must have been to hear that dire sound under darkness, perhaps feeling the ocean crashing against the cliffs. Behind him the children were rapt in silence.

'All was not lost. By some great stroke of providence, the ships were not sundered on the cliffs, but instead washed up on the beaches of an island. Almost all of the people on the three ships had been asleep, lulled to their beds by the constant night of the voyage. Many of the sleeping travellers were saved by soft blankets when the ships ran aground on the shore of the island. The crews however were not so lucky.'

Rafaela raised an eyebrow at this, before giving a sly wink to Lucien. A few of the children mumbled to each other about the fate of the crew and shivered at the thought.

'Eventually the storm blew itself out, exhausted and spent. Blue skies revealed themselves, but the people in the ships slept on, because there was no one to wake them.

By chance a clever and powerful man was out walking along the coast that day. He spotted the three ships, now wrecked on the beach, and took it upon himself to wake the people.'

Lucien fidgeted. The press of bodies behind had made him hot. He noted the schoolmistress had built up the fire. Sweat prickled under his woollen cap. He did his best to sit still for Rafaela, not wanting to be a nuisance.

'The clever man did not wake everyone all at once, for he only had so much food to share. He woke some and they made the first farms together. He woke some more of the slumbering travellers and they built the castle we now call Demesne. The clever man worked ceaselessly, until all the people on the ships were awoken and then he declared, "I am your king. You would not be alive if it were not for me, would not have farms to tend nor shelter from the rains. I am your king and I ask for your loyalty."'

A few of the children on the rug smiled, others looked smug. They were beginning to understand what they were being told and were making sure their peers knew that they had made the leap of logic.

'Of course the people could not argue with such a thing. They divided themselves by function: the most talented with wood and metal formed House Prospero, the fiercest became House Fontein, the most skilled with the land, House Contadino, and life went on. Eventually the clever man, whom everyone now called the king, became sick and retreated into the castle. He couldn't tell the people his clever secrets, or share his wisdom with them, so he created House Erudito.'

This would explain why Erudito had no ruling family, and was instead governed by a board of directors, decided Lucien.

Rafaela smiled at her audience and the Orfano smiled along with her. He was at once entranced by her storytelling and unbearably hot. He slipped the woollen cap down from his head and balled the material up in his fist.

'And that is how we come today to live around the great walls of Demesne, and why the king never shows himself at *La Festa* or at parades. Now, who has questions?'

Lucien felt someone shift behind him and a knee in his back, not hard, but it surprised him all the same. He turned, coming face to face with a boy his own age holding up his hand limply. The boy had sandy hair and dull green eyes. He needed his nose wiped. There was an expression of absolute horror on the boy's face. Lucien looked around, noticing the same look seep through the crowd. Each face was caught up in it, a rictus contagion. Lucien became painfully aware all the children on the rug were staring at him, and had drawn back, revolted.

'Yes?' said Rafaela, her voice wavering with uncertainty. The sandy-haired boy flinched, his eyes flickered to her.

'I have a question.'

'Please.'

'Why doesn't your friend Luc have any ears?'

3
The Shattered Blade
HOUSE FONTEIN
– *Febbraio* 315

Lucien entered the testing chamber, a circular room fifty feet across. Thick candles sprouted at intervals, waxy fungus grown on ledges in the wall. Daylight spilled in from portholes high above, a chill draught on his skin like a phantom's breath. A dais rose from the floor on the opposite side of the room, bearing the face of the king in profile, like a discarded giant coin. Giancarlo stood on the platform, arms crossed over his barrel-like chest, brow furrowed. Three narrow standards provided a backdrop. The flags were divided diagonally into two colours.

Lucien regarded the material as it swayed gently in the draught. Red like dried blood, black as any tar, the flags bore no crest or symbol. He'd longed to wear those colours, the colours of House Fontein, for so long, a yearning now eroded by contempt. House Fontein: few in number and yet wildly self-important. The double doors Lucien had just passed through boomed closed behind him, snapping his attention back to the task at hand, away from the bitterness in his heart.

On his left-hand side, a dozen feet above the smooth granite tiles, was a recess in the wall. D'arzenta and Ruggeri looked down from the balcony above, two stern presences barely lit. Lucien allowed himself a moment of eye contact with D'arzenta. The *maestro* shook his head almost imperceptibly, signalling his unhappiness. Lucien felt cold sweat break out under his arms and across his back. Ruggeri stood statue still; if he had any opinion on the format of the testing he did not show it.

Lucien wasn't sure what he was seeing at first. He'd expected Giancarlo to make things difficult, but this beggared belief.

Three common folk stood huddled together in irons next to the dais. The men looked thin and dirty, their eyes hollow. The rags they wore were soiled with their own foulness.

He turned his attention to Giancarlo, the *superiore*. A broad slab of a man, Giancarlo possessed a wide face and heavy-lidded eyes. A fencing scar ran down his right cheek, parting the olive complexion with a dark exclamation. His hair was cropped and unfussy, deep brown and yet to show any grey. As ever, he wore his uniform, tan leather britches and a battered jacket reinforced with studs. His boots were immaculate, a product of novices currying favour. Two sashes in house colours were tied around his left arm displaying his allegiance, the statement redundant. All knew of Giancarlo's unflinching loyalty, the favourite son of House Fontein. Another deep red sash was wrapped twice around his waist, marking him out as the *superiore*.

Lucien struggled to keep his expression neutral. There were few people in all of Demesne he wanted dead, but Giancarlo's name was top of the list and underlined for good measure. Lucien gripped the hilt of his sheathed sword and forced out a calming breath.

It was then that he recognised one of the prisoners. Franco was in his late fifties and owned a large orchard on the Contadino Estate. The cider he produced was very popular across Demesne's many hamlets and farmsteads. His forearms were like great hams from fetching barrels; iron-grey hair fell to his shoulders, now lank and greasy from imprisonment. Lucien liked him very much, even grooming his ponies on occasion in earlier times. Franco had always managed to make Lucien feel like a regular boy, never putting on the airs and graces required to interact with the Orfano. Many were the times Franco had rescued him from misery with a kind word.

'Why are they here?' said Lucien quietly.

'They're criminals,' replied Giancarlo. 'It has been decided that they can go free if they face you in single combat.'

'To first blood?' said Lucien, feeling a chill in his veins.

'To the death.' Giancarlo's face was stony.

Lucien's lips twisted in a sour approximation of a smile. He'd long known Giancarlo would stoop to any depths to unman him – he'd grown accustomed to it – but this was beyond the pale.

'I'm a student of the sword, not an executioner. This is a farce.' Lucien's eyes locked on Giancarlo. The *superiore* stared back unperturbed. Lucien thrust out his chin and crossed his arms.

'Golia had no such reservations when he tested three years ago. Still, if you'd rather cling to ethics I can fail you right now. And these wretches can return to a slow death in the oubliette.'

A novice appeared from behind Giancarlo in House Fontein livery, one of the Allatamento boys. His tunic was overlong, the cream hose sagging. He couldn't have been more than fourteen summers, already gangly and awkward with the onset of puberty. He fussed at the farmers' irons with a key and unlocked the three prisoners, scurrying back to Giancarlo's elbow, where he waited with anxious eyes. He looked ridiculous in contrast to the threatening bulk of the *superiore*.

The captive farmers rubbed feeling back into their wrists and ankles. They glanced at each other, eyes haunted with unease. Giancarlo pulled his blade from the scabbard, advancing toward one of the men. He looked to be in his mid-twenties and gazed at the *superiore*, incomprehension frozen on his face. Giancarlo muttered something to the man, handed over the weapon and withdrew with an expectant look.

Lucien swore under his breath. Ten tests, beginning at age eight, continuing each year until eighteen. Failure at any point could mean expulsion from House Fontein. Only Lucien's title had prevented his ejection before now.

Refusing this final test would mean a mark against him for all time, as both student and Orfano. He really didn't want *that* particular reputation dragging at his heels. Giancarlo would damn him with a loss of status and a significant dwindling of prospects.

The farmer advanced, the tip of the sword shaking, weaving in the air before him. Not any sword but Giancarlo's own blade. The *superiore*'s slight did not go unnoticed.

'What did he do?' said Lucien, ignoring his opponent. Gian-carlo frowned.

'That is not important. Only the fight is important.'

'What was the crime?'

Giancarlo sneered and said nothing.

With his opponent on his right side Lucien crossed his left foot behind, turning and drawing his sword, striking in one fluid motion. There was no need to look directly at the target. His peripheral vision was more than adequate for such a blow. The man ducked under the sword's reach, then backed away breathing heavily, visibly shocked with the speed of the attack. Lucien followed up, feinting high. His opponent's eyes went wide with fear, throwing an awkward parry in front of his face, lurching back from the waist. Lucien winced as his own ceramic blade hit the steel of Giancarlo's sword, the *superiore* had stacked the odds steeply. The ceramic stayed true and Lucien realised his opponent had forgotten his feet. Lucien's next strike came low at the exposed front leg, then pulled his blow at the last moment to avoid contact with the kneecap. The farmer attempted a clumsy counter, and Lucien ducked beneath it, then withdrew three steps.

'I could have immobilised him. The fight is mine. There's no need for this charade to continue.' Lucien struck Giancarlo with a wintry look. 'Release him.'

The *superiore* scowled back but said nothing.

The farmer sneaked forward while Lucien was distracted with Giancarlo. The blade clattered from Lucien's hastily prepared parry and bounced up, opening a small cut on his shoulder. Lucien snarled and swore. Stepping back he let forth an angry bark and unleashed an overhead blow, a hammer strike, knocking his opponent's blade downwards. Lucien knew first hand how demoralising this manoeuvre was. Golia was all too fond of exactly that style of combat. He remembered numb fingers and an arm too sluggish to respond. Lucien had not wanted to hurt the man, but was struggling to contain his pique.

Too bad.

Lucien struck again, made contact with the farmer's right

arm. He spun back on himself, lashing out again to connect with the farmer's left arm. Lucien feinted low, striking high with the bone-coloured blade before the man could mount a defence. There was a wet smacking sound and the farmer crumpled to his knees. A choked sob reverberated through the training room. Lucien stood over his opponent breathing lightly. No blood had spattered the tiles. The farmer checked himself in shock and wonder. Lucien had used the flat of his blade to batter his opponent into submission. He was bruised, certainly, but unbloodied.

'Finish him,' grunted Giancarlo.

Lucien resheathed his sword with a flourish, then folded his arms.

'Finish him yourself,' he replied.

The *superiore* was behind the farmer before he'd regained his feet. Lucien stared at him, unable to believe what was happening. A knife appeared like a conjuration in Giancarlo's hand, a twist, a jerk, and then the farmer was face down on the floor, clutching at his throat. Deep red fluid grew in a pool around him. Lucien stared aghast, barely able to breathe. The farmer made a last pitiful wet cry and expired. Lucien stared up to the balcony, where Ruggeri was carefully inspecting his fingernails. D'arzenta looked away with a creased brow.

'*Figlio di putana*,' whispered Lucien, knowing he could be failed for insulting the *maestro superiore di spada*.

The Allatamento novice ran over and dragged the corpse to the side of the room, struggling with the weight. Lucien scowled at the lack of dignity, then concentrated on making his hands stop shaking. The novice mopped up the blood and none could ignore the taint of voided bowels on the air. The clatter and clang of the mop and bucket was a crude and unpleasant din in the silence following the farmer's death. Finally the chamber was ready for the second test.

'Knife fight,' was all Giancarlo said. The novice scuttled forward, equipping the second man with a short blade, then withdrew. Even across the room Lucien could tell it was a well balanced weapon, the hilt wrapped in deerskin. Lucien laid his sword on the dais with reverence. He looked up to find Giancarlo gazing down intently. Neither of them spoke.

It was unusual but not unheard of for students to be tested on the knife. It wasn't regarded as a noble weapon but a crude tool for thugs and petty thieves, the domain of desperate women and assassins. If Giancarlo had wished to insinuate something through his choice of trials then he was making his message admirably clear.

The man circled Lucien and regarded him with cool grey eyes. He was weatherbeaten, olive-skinned with a large aquiline nose. His right eye bore the purple-yellow of severe bruising. The knifeman's left hand extended forward, fingers spread wide, the knife held up next to his face in his right hand, ready to be thrust into unprotected flesh. His knees were bent slightly, weight over the balls of his feet. Lucien hadn't conceived there might be dangerous criminals in the lands surrounding Demesne. He quickly revised this opinion.

The punch from the left hand caught him off balance. Clattering into his jaw and knocking him to one side. There was a twinge of panic as he realised how quick his opponent was. Lucien purged the feeling, holding a picture of Virmyre's most admired sharks in his mind. Deadly, implacable, attacking without reserve or hesitation.

Lucien slashed across the man's torso, making him leap back, then directed a backhanded blow with the hilt of the weapon, cracking it across his opponent's nose. Blood spilled in a torrent; the criminal stumbled and swore. Lucien attempted to kick his feet out from under him, instead walking into a wild swipe that opened the right breast of his jacket. The flesh beneath remained whole. The man grinned, his teeth a foul shade of yellow. He launched in with a series of staccato jabs, using the point of the blade to drive Lucien back across the chamber. On and on, his attacker pressed forward, not pausing for a second, each thrust faster and more ferocious than the last. He punctuated the knife thrusts with strikes from his left hand. Lucien batted the blade aside with his knife held in a reverse grip, watching the knifeman's left hand warily. Much more of this and he'd be up against the wall.

A split second, a realisation. The man had overextended himself. Lucien bent his knees, punching with every ounce of force in his body. Using the blunt handle of the knife he mauled the man's ruined nose. The criminal howled in pain, staggering back, blinking away tears. The farmer, if indeed he had ever been a farmer, slipped on the spattering of blood from his own nose. He hit the ground with a muffled yelp, his right hand concealed by the weight of his body. He attempted to stand, then exhaled noisily, an awful shiver running through the length of his body.

The training room pitched into silence.

'Get up!' roared Giancarlo, who cuffed the novice soundly across the back of the head. The novice ran forward, in turn giving the criminal a generous boot to the ribs. The man didn't flinch, a deadweight. The novice looked to the *superiore* with an edge of rising panic on his face. Giancarlo approached and rolled the body over. The man had fallen on his own blade, betrayed underfoot by his own slippery blood.

'This at least you have managed to get right, bastard boy,' said Giancarlo eyeing Lucien. 'Let's see if you've really got the nerve to wear the sashes of House Fontein.'

Lucien stepped forward to the dais to retrieve his cherished blade. Giancarlo calmly laid one boot down on the scabbard and folded his arms. A cruel smile twisted on his lips.

'You'll not need this. The last fight is hand-to-hand.'

'What?' said Lucien, outraged. No testing had ever been conducted in such a way. 'I have to kill a man with my bare hands?'

'If you think you can manage it,' sneered the *superiore*. He knelt down and collected Lucien's blade, drawing it slowly. 'After all, there will be times when you don't have a sword to rely upon.' Lucien stared open-mouthed in horror. Giancarlo hefted the weapon above his head, then brought the bone-coloured blade crashing down onto the granite floor. The blade flew apart, shattered into uncountable pieces.

Lucien felt the fury grow behind his eyes, at the back of his neck, coiling in the muscles of his torso like reptiles. His fingers curled into claws and then he was lunging forward.

D'arzenta shouted something from the balcony, but the sound came from a great distance, drowned out by Lucien's rage. The smirk on Giancarlo's face gave way to uncertainty. Lucien grasped him by the jacket, mashing his forehead into the nose of the *superiore*. Giancarlo collapsed with a muffled thump, blood streaming down his chin.

For a few seconds no one in the chamber moved. D'arzenta and Ruggeri stood leaning over the balcony, faces frozen with shock. The Allatamento boy cowered, keen to be away from the furious Orfano. Franco sidled to the wall, flattening himself against it, perhaps hoping he would be forgotten. Lucien stood at the edge of the dais, the remnants of his blade scattered all around like bone fragments. His hands were shaking but his anger had fled.

Giancarlo dabbed at his face with blunt fingertips, regarding the blood on them. He looked at the bright fluid for a few seconds and laughed.

'Striking the *superiore*. This is ... unforeseen.' He stood up and Lucien backed away from the dais, hand straying to his knife.

'Not only am I failing you, but I'm petitioning Duke and Duchess Fontein to strip you of your colours.' Giancarlo's eyes glittered coldly. 'You'll be forced to change your house name.'

Lucien tried to swallow, struggled to breathe. He'd delivered to Giancarlo everything the *superiore* could have hoped for short of dying. Everything Lucien had worked for, all he'd dare dream of, swept away in one moment's insanity.

'In fact, I'm taking this further,' growled Giancarlo. 'I'll petition all of the houses for your immediate expulsion.'

Lucien staggered back a step as if he'd been struck. He totalled up the votes. Against him, Duke and Duchess Fontein, Lady Prospero and the *capo de custodia*. Golia most certainly. In his favour, Lady Stephania, if she was allowed to vote. Dino perhaps. Unknown: Lord and Lady Contadino, the Majordomo, the directors of House Erudito. Would Anea stand by him or simply abstain? Worse still no student had ever struck a *maestro* in all of Demesne's history, much less a *superiore*.

'Why don't I save you the bother and just leave,' he whispered.

'Oh no, I'm going to enjoy this.' Giancarlo grinned through blood-rimmed teeth. 'I'll see to it your name goes down in Demesne's history books as the most wretched Orfano that ever existed.'

Lucien turned and walked out of the chamber, the sound of his boot heels too loud. He struggled with the door, pushed through into the antechamber, then away into the dank corridor beyond. All that followed him was silence.

4

Festo's Arrival

HOUSE CONTADINO KITCHENS

– Ottobre 307

Lucien leaped out of bed, eager to spend a few hours practising before his testing with Superiore Giancarlo. His first test, the previous year, had been unremarkable. He'd passed largely at the charity of Ruggeri and D'arzenta, eliciting a sneer and nothing more from the belligerent *superiore*. Lucien had noticed that Giancarlo's school were heavier in the shoulder than other students. They wore their hair cropped close, like the *Maestri di Spada* who trained them. Giancarlo's school was a mix of students from the lower classes, or else the second or third sons of noble families. At best they could hope for commissions among the guards of House Fontein. They were a far cry from the bravos trained by Ruggeri, or the gentlemen duellists tutored by D'arzenta. Giancarlo wasn't a teacher you respected, they said; he was one you feared.

Lucien regarded himself in the looking glass, adopting a stern demeanour. Certainly he could benefit from some additional muscle. A lean-limbed slip of a boy looked back from the oak-framed mirror. He hoped he'd be bigger next year, after he turned ten. Some boys remained small until they turned sixteen or seventeen, then sprouted suddenly, surprising everyone. These thoughts weighed on him with increasing frequency. He shivered in the cool morning air then flicked his fringe back from his face. His black hair had grown long in the year since Rafaela had taken him to the Contadino Estate. Since that awful day at the schoolhouse.

Why doesn't your friend Luc have any ears?
He recalled the words all too often.

He dressed himself in his practice clothes before belting his blade and checking himself in the mirror once more, keen that his disfigurement remained hidden. He waited for Rafaela to appear on her morning round. The long-case clock in the hallway chimed eight, audible through the stout oak door of his sitting room.

Still no Ella.

He didn't want for a nanny but no one had brought breakfast. And there was the fact he'd not spoken to anyone since dinner the previous night. Sharing the top table with Lord and Lady Contadino should have been a pleasure, but instead proved awkward. The nobles had a duty of care to him, though he was not their son and there was sparse affection. All interaction was bound up in formality and reserved in the extreme, conversations stunted on the rare occasions they flourished. The Contadini had their own children to dote on, and so Lucien would sit at the end of the table, slipping away as soon as etiquette allowed.

Still no Ella.

He fussed at his sword belt, checked himself in the mirror one last time, then set off on the long walk to D'arzenta's practice chamber. Disappointment dogged his steps, a rumbling stomach his only companion. The Majordomo had also failed to make his customary appearance, but this fact was largely unheeded by the armed boy stalking the corridors of the castle.

Rafaela was not alone in being unavailable to him that day. D'arzenta took ill barely twenty minutes into practice, blaming the damp climate of Landfall for setting off his racking cough. The pale *maestro di spada* gave his apologies and departed, wheezing his way down the curving corridors of House Fontein, leaving his student alone. Outside the wind howled, rattling the windowpanes. Lucien continued his forms, concentrating on cut and slash, thrust and riposte, making his footwork meticulous. Spine straight, chin tucked in, knees bent ever so slightly, weight on the balls of his feet. D'arzenta's words repeated in his mind like a whisper, chanted over and over.

Tempo. Velocità. Misura.

Finally he gave in to pique, swearing at the absent adults.

Angry at Rafaela for not greeting him, cursing the Contadini for being aloof, sneering at D'arzenta for his weak lungs. Was there no one in this damned edifice that would keep him company? He slunk out of the practice room clutching the hilt of his blade, a sour gaze reflected from the looking glass near the door. He chewed his lip a moment.

It wasn't until Lucien reached the kitchens that he became aware of the quiet inhabiting House Contadino like an elderly guest. He'd managed to walk off the greater part of his petulance, arriving at his destination in a curious state of mind. Camelia was there, humming to herself contentedly, her only companion a small boy sitting on the kitchen table. He gnawed mindlessly on a crust of bread and butter. The kitchen was a cavern of a room, packed full of blackened pots and pans of every dimension. Barrels and bins of produce littered the sides of the chamber. A selection of knives hung from hooks at the far end, glittering coldly in the autumnal light. It was tradition he be ushered out upon arrival, the porters griping there was little enough room without an Orfano underfoot. He'd not seen the kitchens so empty before. The room so often filled with industry did not suit being abandoned.

'Where is everybody?'

Camelia flinched and dropped a potato, before stopping it rolling under the table with a deft foot.

'*Porca misèria*, Lucien. You scared me half to death!' She was a large woman, tall with a hearty hourglass figure, blessed with a head of corn-blonde hair contrasting with deep brown eyes set in a broad honest face. Camelia was taller than some of the men in Demesne but didn't stoop to soothe their vanity.

'Sorry, I just... It's strange seeing the kitchen so empty.'

'Everyone has gone to help at House Erudito. It's their turn to host *La Festa* this year. I'm looking after little Dino here and making some gnocchi.'

Lucien crossed the kitchen, trailing fingers along the smooth wood of the long table. The room smelled of flour and a soothing chord of woodsmoke, oregano and other herbs he'd yet to learn the names of. Onions and garlic hung from hooks in the wall, someone had placed wild flowers in a cracked vase on the dresser, a tiny riot of blue and red petals. Camelia's blouse sleeves were rolled up and she was grating potatoes into a large bowl with gusto.

'Why do we have it?' he asked.

'*La Festa?*' Camelia smiled. 'Well, it's a custom – we have it every year. And it gives Duchess Prospero a chance to wear one of *those* dresses.' Lucien knew full well what she meant and coughed a barely concealed laugh into his fist. Camelia straightened a moment and stretched her back, then regarded Lucien with a curious look.

'We celebrate the harvest and give thanks that we have enough to eat. Don't your tutors teach you this?'

'Why don't we have a party to thank the farmers of House Contadino instead? Wouldn't that be, I don't know, more appropriate?'

'Appropriate!' Camelia broke into a wide smile. 'You sound more like noble's son every day.'

'But it would, wouldn't it? For the farmers,' he pressed.

'*La Festa* isn't just about crops and harvest, it's about being grateful to the king for finding us, for waking us from the deep sleep, for building Demesne for us. If it weren't for him you and I might never have been born.'

Lucien paused to consider this for a moment.

'So what do the mimes and performers have to do with it then?'

'They just add a sense of occasion. You know, fun. Don't you like them?'

'I think they're a nuisance,' he replied, crossing his arms over his chest.

'Well, there's many that might think you a nuisance too, young man, so mind your manners.'

Lucien looked around the kitchens a while before letting his gaze come to rest on Dino. The boy looked at Lucien from under a heavy brow, continuing to worry the scrap of bread he was clutching in cherubic fingers. Lucien had never seen a child so small, so young.

'How old is he?'

'Dino? Why, he's all of three, or thereabouts, we don't know for sure because he's ...'

'Orfano.' Lucien took a step back, regarding the boy anew. He had dull grey eyes and soft brown hair. He looked completely unremarkable, could have been any child from any estate. Lucien pouted a moment, frowning at the small boy, the innocent usurper, before realising Camelia was watching him.

'Don't go gaining the wolf, or I'll turn you out of here with a broom handle.' She put one great hand on her hip. 'And you'll not get any dinner tonight.' She gave a sigh and rubbed her forehead with the back of her palm, smudging flour onto her face.

'Does he have any ... ? You know. Does he ... ?'

'Yes, I know what you're asking.' She raised her eyebrows. 'I wouldn't be surprised if he doesn't grow those awful spines from his forearms like Golia. He also has trouble with his eyes.'

'Trouble? How so?'

'The place where your tears come from ...'

'Ducts,' supplied Lucien, a rare flash of biology coming to him. Virmyre would be proud.

'Yes, well, they don't work. Dino's tears are blood. The poor little thing. Fortunately he's a stoical boy and isn't given to crying too often. We have to keep giving him milk and ground beef to build him up.'

Lucien scrutinised the infant some more. He'd not met any Orfani other than Anea and Golia. Everyone knew of the reclusive Orfani who lived with House Prospero, but he'd never bothered to learn her name, just as she'd never bothered to leave her apartment. He imagined her in an attic somewhere, talking to herself in a made-up language.

'That said,' continued Camelia, 'he reminds me of you in a way. You used to sit right there when you were his age, good as gold, staring at folk, oh so serious.' She smiled at Lucien kindly and he reciprocated with a touch of embarrassment. Camelia had always been someone he'd gravitated to. He invariably ended up lurking in the kitchen, getting in the way or peeling potatoes for want of an excuse to remain. Better busy in the kitchens than alone in his apartment. She'd sat through the night with him a few times when the pneumonia was on him, and sometimes to read to him, which no one else did except Rafaela.

'I suppose you've come down here for gossip and tittle-tattle,' said Camelia after a moment.

Lucien leaned on the kitchen table, one hand resting under his chin. He looked at her blankly.

'Surely you've heard?' she asked. 'A new Orfano was found outside of House Erudito. They're saying it's lucky he survived the night. It was dreadful chilly under the stars on those stone steps. They're calling him Festo.'

Lucien shrugged. D'arzenta hadn't mentioned it.

'There's quite a fuss over who will look after him,' continued Camelia. 'Someone suggested Duke Prospero adopt him. *Porca misèria*, can you imagine? It took them an hour to get Duchess Prospero down off the ceiling.'

Lucien wondered where the Orfano materialised from but knew better than to ask. He'd received more than his share of stern looks for making such enquiries in the past. He pushed the tip of his thumb into the corner of his mouth, testing how sharp his teeth were. He thought back to when he was three and found his memories of those times sparse, the few available to him cloudy and indistinct. Something didn't quite fit.

'Ella hasn't always been my nanny, has she?'

'What makes you say that?' said Camelia.

'Just a feeling. I mean, she's much too young. She would have only been seven when I was a baby.'

Camelia grinned and paused a moment, regarding the growing pile of shredded potatoes. She set down the grater with a clatter.

'I see those lessons are paying off.' She rested one hand on her hip and looked down at him. 'Rafaela's mother died when you were just four – it was she who looked after you when you first came to us. She was a lovely lady. Kind and patient. Rafaela looks just like her. Uncanny it is. Sometimes Rafaela walks through that door and, well, it's like her mother never passed on. Of course, you're probably too young to remember.'

Camelia wiped her hands on a cloth.

'Rafaela had been raised to see the care of the Orfano as a great privilege. She petitioned and schemed and argued for the right to keep on looking after you. She'd always helped her mother, you see?'

'And they turned me over to a eleven-year-old girl? Just like that?'

'Not exactly.' Camelia broke some eggs and fetched a large wooden spoon from a dresser further down the kitchen before continuing. 'You just about screamed the place down for about a month. You were unbearable. In the end they gave in to Rafaela. She was the only one who could do anything with you. I thought Mistress Corvo was going to throw you out of the window one night. *Porca misèria*, you were a noisy thing.'

'Where's Ella today?'

'She's at home. Her sister is ill.'

Lucien blinked a few times. Ella had never mentioned a sister before. Suddenly he realised there was a whole side to Ella he knew nothing about. He was embarrassed to realise he'd never thought to ask.

'Sister?

'Yes. She's called Salvaggia, about your age.'

A bang and scrape in the corridor broke Lucien from his introspection and he suppressed a shudder. It came again with a constant even rhythm, growing louder with each iteration. A cowled figured emerged from under the pointed arch of the doorway, darkness releasing him into the well lit kitchen. The Domo turned his seemingly blind gaze toward them and approached, staff continuing to tap out the dull percussion of his stride.

'Lucien,' he droned in his flat voice, the head bobbing in the slightest imitation of a bow. Technically the Domo outranked everyone in Demesne barring the king, but he always nodded to the Orfano. 'I had not expected to find you here.'

Camelia stepped forward and slipped one arm around Lucien's shoulders, pulling him close to her.

'Isn't he growing up to be a fine young man?' she said. Lucien thought he detected a note of challenge in her words. The Domo simply stood in front of them, not saying anything.

33

Behind them Dino smacked his lips and continued gnawing on the bread.

'He is indeed growing up,' said the Domo, the flat line of his mouth betraying nothing. His eyes were, as ever, hidden in the deep shadow of the grey hood.

'I dare say he'll make a fine addition to the castle.' Camelia squeezed him, but Lucien could not drag his eyes from the looming presence that filled the kitchen. Another awkward pause and then the chief steward spoke again.

'Perhaps he can be of some help. It occurs to me there may be a job he could perform admirably.' And then the Domo turned abruptly, drifting from the kitchen, the hem of his dour robe sliding over flagstones, the staff resuming its plaintive clatter.

'He's a strange one,' whispered Camelia. 'They say he's older than sin and twice as ugly.'

Lucien sniggered, caught himself for a moment, then resumed laughing anyway.

'What do you think he meant? About performing a job, I mean.' Lucien chewed his lip, suddenly anxious.

'Who knows what goes on under that hood. Best not to wonder at it.'

'What will I do when I grow up, Camelia?'

'I'm not sure.' She narrowed her eyes a second, hands resting on her hips. 'I've always known about the Orfano, but Golia was the first I'd ever seen. People say there were more back in older times. Then you came along, and Anea, and Dino. And now we have Festo.'

'But why?'

'I couldn't say. And we're told not to ask.' Camelia smiled, stifling a laugh behind one flour-dusted hand. She was looking at Dino, who was holding out a soggy crust of bread to Lucien.

'Looks like you've made a new friend.'

Lucien nodded, noticing Dino's shy smile.

'Don't you have somewhere to be? I'll be in just as much trouble as you if your teachers find you down here.'

'My testing isn't until later.'

'Well go and practise then, for goodness' sake.' She sighed. 'You'll be the death of me, Lucien Contadino.'

34

He shrugged awkwardly. He'd always hated that expression. He didn't want to be the death of anyone, certainly not Camelia. She pulled him close, kissing him on the forehead, before shooing him out of the kitchens. Dino waved, at Camelia's insistence, dropping the crust of bread on the floor in the process. Lucien waved back and headed through the arch, into the labyrinthine corridors beyond, and on to his testing.

5

Camelia's Tears

HOUSE CONTADINO KITCHENS

– Febbraio 315

Lucien walked down the corridors of House Fontein, hearing his own footsteps in a daze. A few novices noted his slashed jacket, opened at the shoulder and across the breast. They avoided him, not wanting to speak with a *strega*, the bastards of Landfall. He heard their whispering as he walked on. Speculation had been rampant in the run-up to the testing, but they could not have dared imagine Lucien's expulsion. Word of his failing would find its way into every corner of every keep by nightfall. The women of House Prospero would chatter breathlessly from behind fans in well-appointed salons, while the *professori* of House Erudito would shrug and grumble in lecture halls laden with dust and age. Even now, the many novices and adepts of House Fontein's three schools would be delirious with the telling and retelling of such disobedience. The least of the novices would be bullied into running to other houses, spreading the word and bringing back new details, fabricated or exaggerated. Few would care. Only the members of House Contadino might spare him sympathy. They knew him best, for better or worse.

Onwards he walked, into the chiaroscuro lamplight of King's Keep, gliding dreamlike through the circuitous corridor linking the four houses. The wide passage was windowless, supported by thick columns, making it a claustrophobic nether world. Artisans from House Prospero hurried past, clogs sounding on the flagstones *toc toc toc*, aprons flapping at their knees, calloused fingers thrust into deep pockets. Scholars from House Erudito ambled toward private lessons for Demesne's privileged few.

The *professori* looked indistinct in their black gowns, pale faces standing out in the gloom. Some small few regarded Lucien with barely concealed distaste. Nothing new. Messengers bore scraps of parchment and lofty expressions, each trying to outdo the others with self-importance and pomposity. They stared each other down through white-powdered faces, pouting past beauty spots. They rushed as if the very stones of Demesne depended on their messages being delivered. Lucien was too stunned to give them one of his customary glares. The guards on the gateways mumbled to each other, shooting wary glances as Lucien approached. He barely noticed. His expulsion would mean an end to the indignities of Demesne.

Thirteen years of schooling. Almost daily education in blade and biology, classics and chemistry, philosophy and physics, art and, very rarely, assassination. He had been given the best of everything in Demesne as set down by the king's edict, even when he'd not wanted it, which had been often. Now he would be bereft of everything, all thanks to Giancarlo. Worse still, Franco would be consigned back to the oubliette. The whole affair had been as pointless as it was futile. Lucien groped at the hilt of his bone-coloured blade and found the scabbard empty. He remembered the ceramic weapon shattering, shards exploding across the floor of the practice chamber, just as his life was now sundered into parts across Demesne. Lucien chewed his lip and fixed his eyes on the flagstones in front of his feet, walking mechanically. The candles guttered and flickered around him, making the way ahead unclear, threatening to drown him in Demesne's deep darkness.

Finally he returned to House Contadino, his feet leading him back of their own accord. He tried to swallow and found his throat thick and uncomfortable. He was being thrown out. Exiled. He, an Orfano; the very idea of it.

'Lucien? What's happened? You're as pale as a ghost.' Camelia stood before him. He was standing in the kitchen. Several other cooks, maids and porters looked up from their labours, nudging each other and speaking in low voices. The news had not raced ahead of him, it seemed.

'Are you hurt? Your jacket...'

'I'm fine,' he said, his own voice sounding distant. 'Small cut on the shoulder,' he added. It occurred to him he was still bleeding, but it was something unremarkable, as if it were happening to someone else.

The staff continued their work without a word, weaving between one another, vying for space on the long table. Lucien was no stranger to them, not always welcome but tolerated. He knew they thought him spoilt and privileged, just as he was aware there was an unspoken competitiveness between the staff of the four houses.

He may be Orfano, but he's our Orfano was the maxim. The nobles whined and complained about having the unwanted foundlings attached to their houses but couldn't resist lapses of proprietorial braggadocio. The staff aped their attitudes in their own, less nuanced, fashion. Some even pretended to like him. Fewer still actually did, like Camelia.

Lucien had eavesdropped enough to know the staff had nicknames for the various witchlings. Time spent listening at doorways had revealed Golia was 'the lug', unsurprising on account of his great size and apparent dull-wittedness. Lucien had received the less insulting 'Sinistro' on account of his left-handedness. Dino was referred to as 'little Luc'. Nobody called Anea anything other than her name, which itself was a shortened version of her birth name. And there was the woman who lived with House Prospero, the nameless recluse. Festo had yet to earn an epithet, still too young.

'Well you can't stand there all day,' said Camelia. 'You'll get blood all over my floors for one thing. And you look like you're about to pass out. Can someone get him some coffee? *Porca misèria.*' She was doing her best not to sound flustered. She was doing well. 'Come on. Time to see Dottore Angelicola.'

Lucien looked at Camelia, confusion crowding his features. How had he come to be here? Hadn't he been going to his apartment to collect his things?

'Camelia . . . I'm going to be exiled.'

'What?' The cook stared at him, eyes narrowed not comprehending.

'I'm going to be exiled. I struck Superiore Giancarlo.' The

industry of the kitchen slowed. People were straining to hear. Somebody at the back of the room dropped a metal ladle which clattered on the floor. Lucien's mind recalled his shattered blade – he flinched at the thought of it.

'Well, isn't that sort of the point?' said Camelia. 'You didn't kill him?' She swallowed. The silence in the kitchen was absolute. 'Lucien, tell me you didn't kill him.'

'No. But he tried to make me kill people. I refused. He smashed my blade.' Lucien delivered each word without emphasis, as if he were mumbling in his sleep. 'Then I hit him.' His gaze was locked on a point only he could see. In his mind he saw the criminal collapsing onto his own knife. That terrible shudder passing through his body, impaling himself after slipping on the bloodied flagstones.

'I'm sure it's just a misunderstanding,' said Camelia, but she couldn't keep the uncertainty out of her voice. By now the entire kitchen staff had gathered to listen, forming a wall of white jackets, caps clutched in anxious hands.

Into their midst came the Majordomo, towering over everyone. He looked more grim than usual, cheeks and chin almost grey beneath the heavy cowl. A quartet of flies circled him lazily, nestling within folds of fabric the colour of wet ashes. Lucien wondered if the garment was held together with cobwebs and dust. The Domo grasped his staff of office in a skeletal hand, the veins thick and vulgar, his nails frayed and chewed. The porters and cooks shrank back, as if afeared he might spread some nameless contagion. All except Camelia, who stepped forward and placed one arm protectively around Lucien's shoulders.

'Lucien. I have been informed of the situation,' said the Domo in his dull monotone. 'Most regrettable.' Lucien stared up at him. A tiny spark of the rage he felt for Giancarlo kindled in his soul.

'I imagine you're delighted,' he whispered harshly.

'Nothing could be further from the truth, Lucien,' replied the Domo. 'No Orfano has ever been exiled. Something I hope to address this very moment. I will persuade Superiore Giancarlo to drop his petition.'

Lucien stared at the Domo. The darkness under the cowl was total, shielding the man's eyes. Only the flat line of his mouth gave away any emotion, and there was precious little of that.

'Liar,' hissed Lucien. 'You want me gone. You offered me a chance to fit into your grand scheme and I refused. *Vai al diavolo*. And Giancarlo with you.'

The cooks nearby flinched at this. Some had already slipped away, out through the side door from where they fled to other houses, keen to share the unfolding scandal. The Domo let out a breath; his grip tightened on the staff; the flies took to wing, agitated.

'Lucien, you are upset—'

'Upset? I'm a good deal more than just upset. What happened to first blood? And when did the Orfani become the executioners of Landfall?'

'It is regrettable,' the steward droned.

'Regrettable? We're killing common folk like cattle now, are we? Just so *nobili* can pass their testings?'

Several staff in the kitchen struggled not to stare open-mouthed at Lucien's tirade.

'He was determined to fail me, no matter how well I fought. You think I lack the stomach to kill?' He stabbed one finger forward. 'You're wrong.'

The Domo said nothing, grimace deepening.

'One day you'll need to make good on all the secrets you're harbouring,' sneered Lucien. Suddenly his shoulder was throbbing with pain. The Domo remained motionless. The remaining kitchen staff receded further away, gazes averted, busying themselves at the other end of the room. The Domo opened his mouth to speak just as a messenger in House Fontein livery came through the kitchen door.

'You are requested in the grand hall of House Fontein, Majordomo,' panted the youth. He'd run directly from Giancarlo no doubt, who even at this moment would be marshalling support for Lucien's expulsion. The Domo paused, then turned and followed the messenger.

40

Camelia laid her hand gently on Lucien's shoulder, then pulled him close. Tears tumbling down her cheeks.

'*Porca misèria*, Lucien. What will you do?'

'I'll leave. But first I need to find Rafaela. Do you know where she is?'

'She's at home. With her father. Her sister's birthday is soon, possibly today, I think. She asked for some time off.'

Lucien growled a curse. He turned, making his way out of the kitchen.

'Lucien, wait. I'll bring you some food. For the road.'

'Thank you, Camelia.' He turned to her under the arch of the doorway, trying to smile but failing. He swept his gaze over the kitchen one last time, then stalked away into the dark corridors of House Contadino.

His ascent up the spiral staircase left him feeling weak, or perhaps it was the blood loss. Lucien opened the door to his apartment, looking over the deep armchairs where he'd spent so many winter's nights, deep in sleep, deep in books and occasionally deep in conversation. Not nearly enough of the last. Pale grey light filtered in through the latticed windows. Outside promised chill winds and a threat of rain. He dragged fingertips across the spines of cloth-bound books. All were neatly ordered on custom-built shelves, the elegant craftsmanship of House Prospero. He turned his back on the sitting room and entered his bedroom. Warm clothes were pulled from a trunk and the bottom of his closet; thicker boots were pulled on. A waxed greatcoat he'd never worn was dragged out and tried on for size. He winced as the wound in his shoulder snagged and complained. He looked hideous, but it would have to do

'Vanity is always the first casualty of survival,' he mumbled before gathering up more items, small clothes mainly, stuffing them into a pillowcase. He swore as he again realised his sword was gone. The scabbard empty on his hip. A hollow vessel.

'Headbutt, eh?' It was Virmyre, pale blue eyes giving away nothing, his features glacial. The *professore* was famously as emotional as a rock. Virmyre leaned against the door frame with arms crossed over his chest, his black robes hanging like the folded wings of a great raven. He ran a hand through his black hair, shot through with stark white, then yawned expansively. 'Not exactly in the syllabus, is it?'

'Never was any good at following the rules,' said Lucien. 'Improvising always came more naturally.'

'I had hoped we'd trained you to make your arguments in a more articulate fashion. Perhaps this failure is mine,' said Virmyre, hand straying to his beard.

'He set me up,' growled Lucien. 'He wanted me to kill people.'

'You must be aware, Master Lucien, a sword isn't just for show. What point in training you if you've not the will to use it?'

'True enough. But I'll not earn my place in Demesne killing farmers. Aren't we supposed to give people trials?'

'Only the *nobili* get trials,' said Virmyre; 'the commoners get—'

'Murdered?' Lucien eased himself out of the slashed undershirt, wincing. Transparent blood was weeping from his shoulder, turning blue after a few seconds.

'Yes. Murdered.' Virmyre let the word hang between them, then nodded.

'I thought it was supposed to be a testing, not an execution.'

'Giancarlo has a limited vocabulary; perhaps he muddled the two.'

Lucien shook his head, lip curled at the mention of the *maestro di spada*.

'So tell me,' continued Virmyre. 'You didn't give up your values today, even when forced, even when provoked, so who really failed?'

'True enough, but I'm not being tested on my values,' said Lucien. He inspected the wound and a wave of nausea overtook him.

'When word gets around regarding what you did, about what you refused to do, I'm sure Giancarlo will be forced to reconsider failing you.'

'Giancarlo not only failed me, he's expelling me. I'll be lucky if I can even leave the Contadino Estate.' Lucien slumped down on the bed. 'I'm a failure, I always have been.'

42

'You're not a failure, Lucien,' said the *professore*.

'My days out there are numbered. Golia will come looking for me, backed up by others. They'll come by night and I won't see the following dawn.'

'Have you considered bleeding to death?'

'Trying it right now. How am I doing?'

'Admirably, I'd say. Although I don't have a great deal of experience in such things.'

Lucien grinned at his deadpan mentor, shook his head.

'How am I supposed to beat him when he comes? I'm no match for that sort of strength.'

'Then you'd best be smarter than him. I've not spent the last thirteen years letting you grow up to be a dullard. You can't beat Golia with strength, so outwit him.'

Lucien slung the jacket onto the bed and ignored the throbbing in his shoulder. One of these days he'd repay Giancarlo in kind for every scar he'd ever inflicted. He looked up, eyes narrowed.

'What is it?' said Virmyre.

'Someone's coming.'

Sure enough, footsteps from the corridor outside gave away the *dottore*. The grumbling man entered the sitting room without knocking before poking his head into Lucien's bedroom.

'I was sent for,' he said simply. Angelicola was a shambles of a man. Permanent stubble and wild wiry grey hair conspired to make him look unkempt. The navy-blue doublet and britches he wore were out of date, thick with dust and dandruff on the shoulders. Threadbare elbows gave way to ragged sleeves. His boots were scuffed and long past polishing, his shirts were always rumpled and horribly stained.

'Cook Camelia said I was to attend you. You've been injured, apparently. You look all right to me.' He blinked small furious eyes under bushy brows, his overlarge aquiline nose making him look older than his forty-nine years.

'Master Lucien was wounded at his testing,' said Virmyre, 'I'd like you to very carefully tend to him. Clean and stitch the—'

43

'I don't need to be told how to do my job by a *professore*! I actually *work* for a living.' He swayed slightly and Lucien caught the slightest hint of wine, even across the room.

Virmyre drew himself up to his full height, just a fraction taller than the ill-mannered *dottore*, and unfolded his arms. His jaw clenched and Lucien saw him take a long slow breath before trusting himself to speak. When he did the sound was low and controlled.

'I think you forget yourself—' his pale blue eyes were wintry '—and, more than that, you forget whom you address.'

Angelicola blinked a few times and opened his mouth to speak, then thought better of it. Something passed between the two men and Lucien saw regret pass across the aged *dottore*'s face like a fleeting shadow.

'Now stitch Lucien up,' said Virmyre, 'before I lose all patience.'

6

Via al Diavolo

HOUSE FONTEIN TESTING CHAMBER

– Ottobre 307

Lucien was unaware it was customary to arrive fifteen minutes early to a testing. A stricken-looking novice was pacing back and forth when he finally arrived at the antechamber. He was an older boy, possibly sixteen. The ghost of a moustache hung on his top lip. His cheeks had broken out in a riot of acne.

'Where in nine hells have you been?'

'Maestro di Spada D'arzenta was ill this morning. I was in the kitchens with Camelia. And Dino.' Anxiety clenched at the pit of his stomach.

'In the kitchens?' The older boy sneered.

'D'arzenta didn't say anything about—'

'You'd better get in there,' grunted the novice, 'and hope he doesn't fail you immediately.'

'No one told me – it's not my fault.'

He thought back to the previous year's test with Ruggeri. D'arzenta had been with him every step of the way, and there'd been no chance of being late.

The novice stalked off, his scabbard slapping against his leg. Lucien flicked his fingers from under his chin as he'd seen the older boys do.

The doors to the training room were open, waiting for his entrance. Students were expected to present themselves in formal dress for tests, although Lucien couldn't understand why. The clothes would invariably get spoiled, slashed open or, worse yet, bled upon. The tailors of House Prospero had taken to making spare sets of sleeves for jackets, leaving the stitching loose at the shoulder. It had saved them a lot of time

45

over the years. Lucien wore a suit of charcoal-grey, with black leather riding boots and a thick leather belt. A simple white cravat completed the ensemble, managing to make him look paler than usual. He caught sight of himself in the mirror and wondered what Superiore Giancarlo would say.

The circular training chamber stretched away from him. He seemed to himself an insignificant detail in the great space. Three banners were fixed to the wall above the dais, one for each of House Fontein's three schools. Giancarlo, Ruggeri and D'arzenta stood stony-faced and serious beneath the banners. Light bled in weakly from overhead windows, outmatched by clusters of candles flickering on ledges built into the walls. The quiet strangled all sound in the room, becoming a ponderous weight that crushed Lucien's hopes. To stop them shaking he pressed his hands to the seams of his britches.

None of the other novices or adepts was present in the chamber except one. Carmine was roughly the same age as Lucien. He stood at one side of the chamber with a smirk playing on his lips. Where Lucien was slight, Carmine was sturdy. His light brown hair was cropped close in the fashion of all Giancarlo's students. Lucien had not sparred against Carmine before and there'd been no chance to study the boy's footwork or judge his form. His attention was brought back to the *superiore*, who was feigning boredom.

'*Tempo. Velocità. Misura.*' Giancarlo beat his scabbard against the palm of his hand, a dull slap accompanying each word.

'The essences of a duellist, Lucien. And yet you come to me late, slouching along the corridors like a chambermaid, no doubt. Looking as if you fell from your wardrobe.' Giancarlo sighed theatrically, then kicked the wooden stool at his feet across the room at Lucien, who jumped out of the way. Not fast enough. The seat struck his shin and he hopped about a moment, looking at his examiner, incomprehension clouding his eyes

'Sit, bastard child!' bellowed Giancarlo. His voice was like a thunderclap. Lucien swallowed, felt himself tremble. No one had ever spoken to him that way. He righted the stool, not taking his eyes from the *maestro di spada* as he lowered

46

himself onto the seat. He allowed himself a glance at D'arzenta, who had hooked his thumbs over his belt. His knuckles were chalk-white, mouth a flat line, cheeks pinched. He looked ashen, clearly not recovered from the morning's coughing fits. Ruggeri was his usual self, an unremarkable-looking man with the dark features and olive skin so common among the people of Demesne.

'So, Lucien,' boomed Giancarlo, his voice filling the chamber easily, 'it seems your teacher tolerates your idiosyncrasies.' He was advancing across the circular room. 'I, however, do not.'

Lucien realised Giancarlo had held his hands behind his back until that point. He had thought the *superiore* was affecting a patriarchal pose, but it was deceit. Giancarlo's right hand bore long scissors, not unlike the shears Lucien had seen used by the tailors of House Prospero. Black enamelled handles entwined Giancarlo's walnut-brown fingers. The blades champed together with a steely scrape.

'The problem is this, Lucien.' The *superiore* grabbed his hair roughly; Lucien suppressed a yelp. 'The Orfani are supposed to be examples to the four houses.' Lucien sat up straighter on the stool, his hair yanked upwards. 'Better educated.' There was a grate of metal on metal, then a fluttering of black hair fell past his eyes.

'Highly trained.' Another snip, another flurry of descending hair.

'More fearsome.' Again the slice of scissoring blades. Lucien closed his eyes.

'More intelligent.' *Slice.*

'Attired perfectly.' *Snip.*

'Turned out in a manner befitting a gentleman.' *Scrape.*

Vice-like fingers held his head firm as tears tracked down his cheeks. He couldn't explain the sensation, only that he felt shrunken somehow. Smaller and terribly self-conscious.

'Now. That is a vast improvement, and you may actually be able to see who you are fighting. Not so much with that ridiculous fringe, I imagine. I nearly mistook you for your nanny when you walked in.'

Lucien found himself on the floor, the stool kicked out from under him. His elbow had gone numb, smashed on the granite tiles. His cheeks were aflame with embarrassment. The shock disorientated him. From his sprawled position he caught a hint of movement in the unlit gallery above, but could not see who lurked there.

'Begin!' bellowed Giancarlo.

Lucien staggered to his feet, struggling to draw breath. The blade edged from his scabbard with difficulty, his arm unresponsive. He willed feeling to flood back into the numb limb but it remained dull and painful. It was a ceramic blade of course, as for all novices. Matt black like the older boys carried with a hilt bound in soft leather stained red.

Carmine had advanced quickly, then paused a moment, confused by Lucien's strange grip. There wasn't a single student in Giancarlo's school who fought left-handed. Lucien used the moment to lunge in, the tip of his blade aimed straight for the boy's breast. Carmine batted it aside clumsily. The shock rang along Lucien's blade and rattled his still numb elbow, nearly prising the weapon from his grip. He backed off, breathing deeply, desperate for sensation to flood back into his arm. Carmine did likewise and circled, passing foot over foot, moving around him clockwise. Lucien was put in mind of the sharks Professore Virmyre admired so much, circling before closing in for the kill.

Carmine thrust again, keen to win Giancarlo's favour and draw the Orfano's blood. Lucien threw up an ill-prepared parry, almost fumbling the angle and letting his opponent's blade snag on his jacket sleeve. He stepped back, hoping to free himself but instead inviting Carmine's boldness. Giancarlo's novice stepped forward, a low thrust towards Lucien's knees, lips drawn back from his teeth. Lucien sidestepped, breathing hard, a jagged edge of adrenaline making his hands tremble. Carmine followed up with a slash directed across his face, and Lucien's attempted strike manifested as a graceless parry. At least it had broken the larger boy's momentum. The opponents stepped away from each other, regarding each other. Lucien cursed under his breath. He had hoped he would be better than this. Or not so hopelessly outmatched.

Carmine came for him, feinting slow for his front leg, before turning the attack into an awkward slash across his eyes. Rather than try and block, Lucien dropped to one knee, mashing the pommel of his blade into his opponent's crotch. There was a strangled cough, then Lucien kicked Carmine's leg away. The clatter of his blade hitting the polished flagstones filled the chamber; a muffled thump came after as the boy followed it down. Lucien stood over his opponent and extended the black blade in first position. The tip hovered inches away from Carmine's throat.

'Yield.'

Carmine acquiesced, a surly and shocked expression frozen onto his features. Lucien held the pose a moment longer before holding out a hand to help him up from the floor. Carmine collected himself and stood without assistance, avoiding eye contact with the victor.

'*Vai al diavolo*, you *strega* bastard,' he whispered.

'Well, at least I didn't rip your jacket,' mumbled Lucien. Carmine failed to not clutch at his britches, eyes bright with tears. Giancarlo turned to D'arzenta and frowned a moment, then regarded each of the duellists. Icy seconds passed.

'I hope that was improvisation,' said Giancarlo to D'arzenta, 'and you've not taken it upon yourself to include an unwelcome addition to the syllabus.' D'arzenta began to say something, then struggled to contain a fresh round of coughing. He withdrew to the wall, where he steadied himself with one hand. Giancarlo sneered at student and teacher alike before fussing with a crate at the back of the room. He pulled out a buckler and strapped it to his forearm. The *superiore* turned, looking sternly at Carmine before inclining his head to one side in a brief nod. Carmine retired from the centre of the room with a stiff-legged walk that would have been comical in other circumstances. Lucien was too distracted by the wisps of his own hair decorating the flagstones to notice the boy's departure. So much black hair, and a year in the growing. A year trying to cover up his hated affliction.

Why doesn't your friend Luc have any ears?

A good question.

49

'So, Lucien, you have proved you are the match of your peers, even if you are somewhat unorthodox. Now I'd like to see how you fare when the odds are against you. It may so come to pass you will have to fight opponents better armed and better armoured than yourself. You will have to deploy all your learning and all your wit to overcome them.'

The *superiore* held up the buckler. A small shield, it was just over a foot across, perfectly flat, and had been polished until it gleamed. Lucien shivered. He could see himself in the reflection, a badly made scarecrow that no amount of finery would disguise. His hair had been savaged and lay in scraps over his scalp. The puckered red holes of his deformity looked even worse than he remembered, contrasting with his pale skin, matching his red-rimmed eyes.

'Begin,' bellowed Giancarlo, but the sound came as if from a distance. Lucien's eyes were haunted by the reflection on the buckler. Up close the instructor seemed a giant, not just tall but broad as well, his every step measured, each move self-assured, crowding down on the Orfano just as the silence had when he entered. Lucien prised his eyes from the mirrored buckler, looking to D'arzenta for some clue. The *maestro di spada* stood, left arm clasped across chest, his right hand clamped to his mouth, eyes like flint.

Lucien was shunted back. Giancarlo had slammed the buckler into his shoulder. He would not get another warning like that. The Orfano looked down at the *superiore*'s footwork, trying to decipher which way he might move next, then met his eyes, looking for some signal or tell. Giancarlo raised the buckler and Lucien caught sight of himself once more, ragged and pathetic, ridiculous without the camouflage of his hair.

A strike descended, and Lucien's own blade met it, largely on instinct. He backed away from the *superiore*, eyes darting between the strands of hair on the floor and his reflection on the buckler.

D'arzenta surrendered to a round of coughing that left him bent double, hand pressed against his lips. He was positively grey. Lucien backed off a few more steps, distracted by the wet rasping sounds. When the blade came he barely saw it. A jolt, and then a flood of sensation in his shoulder indicating he'd been struck.

He stepped back, looking aghast at the ripped fabric of his jacket sleeve. The cut was above his bicep, crossing the top of his arm. Slowly the jacket became sodden with the pale blue strangeness that served him as blood. A tide of dizziness swept over him and he swallowed with a dry throat. D'arzenta stepped down from the dais, mouth open with shock. Ruggeri had turned away and was making to leave. Everyone moved with a dream-like languor. Lucien looked up at Giancarlo, who was sneering with disgust.

'I'm failing you, Lucien. Your attacks, when you attack at all, lack vigour. Your concentration is worse still. Perhaps if you built on your footwork you might make a half-decent fighter, but I really rather doubt it. I wouldn't trust you with a spear, let alone a sword. You're the worst Orfano student ever to have lifted a blade.'

Lucien didn't hear the rest. The ground pitched and rolled under him, then he was rushing down to meet it, flinging up his good arm to protect his head. He rolled onto his back and stared up at the gallery, where Anea looked back from the shadows with an unreadable gaze. She stood slowly and sneaked away from her place of hiding.

'You call this being ready, D'arzenta?' grunted Giancarlo.

The ashen *maestro di spada* said nothing, kneeling down at Lucien's side, hands pressed to the wound.

'This is pathetic,' sneered Giancarlo before turning on his heel.

'*Vai al diavolo*,' Lucien whispered, and then nothing.

7

Over Rooftop, Under Moonlight

DEMESNE

– *Febbraio* 315

Lucien woke to find Virmyre standing over him, a grave expression haunting his face. The wounded shoulder throbbed, his thoughts came slowly, torpid and unhurried. It was dark outside and the lantern on the dresser made a chiaroscuro of the *professore*. The sound of murmuring voices came from the adjoining sitting room, muffled by the closed door.

'What's going on?' said Lucien, throat hoarse.

'That idiot *dottore* gave you a sedative. A very strong one. You've been like the dead all day. I was beginning to wonder if you'd ever wake.'

'It's late?'

'Yes. Very late. And if you're found in Demesne after midnight they'll throw you in the oubliette.'

'They wouldn't dare,' replied Lucien, swinging his legs over the side of the bed. There was an unpleasant twinge in his shoulder. 'Exiling me is one thing, but the oubliette?' He felt his anger rise, but also a pang of fear. Giancarlo had proved he was capable of anything.

'I think we're long past the dictates of etiquette and history,' replied Virmyre.

'Who's next door?' Lucien asked, gesturing with a brief nod of his head. He stood and reached into his closet, beginning the unhappy job of selecting clothes for the road.

'Master D'arzenta, Dino, Camelia and Massimo.'

'What?' Lucien turned to Virmyre. 'Why are there so many?'

'We barricaded the door to stop Giancarlo's men entering the apartment. He was going to have you arrested in your sleep.'

Lucien blinked a few times wordlessly. The *professore*'s face gave nothing away. Only his pale blue eyes showed his concern.

'*Figlio di puttana*. Angelicola is going to be the death of me.' Lucien resumed packing. 'This is ridiculous,' he muttered testily. He pulled on a heavy greatcoat. It was waxed and had a sturdy high collar. He'd never worn it before, thinking it bulky and crude.

'Why is Massimo here?' said Lucien suddenly. The boy was Lord Contadino's personal aide and was regarded by him as indispensable. It was rumoured he received private duelling lessons from Ruggeri.

'Lady Contadino decided she wanted a witness here if anything were to befall you.' Virmyre cleared his throat. 'No one in their right mind would move against Lord Contadino's page. And D'arzenta is armed of course. There's not many who'd be quick to move against a *maestro di spada*, even at a time like this.'

Suddenly a booming sound came from next door, accompanied by muffled shouting.

'What now?' hissed Lucien. Virmyre opened the door a crack, peering through into the sitting room. He flashed a warning glance at Lucien, then closed the door, turning the key in the lock.

'Giancarlo has returned. It must be midnight. Quickly, through the window. No time for goodbyes.'

The sound of shouting increased from the next room. Lucien thought he could hear Camelia crying. D'arzenta was calling out in his most superior tone. He imagined he could hear the rasp of steel as his sword came free of the scabbard.

'*Avanti*, Lucien,' said Virmyre. 'If they've brought axes they'll be through the door in minutes. Let's not give them anything to find.'

Virmyre crossed to the windows and opened them. It had finally stopped raining and a full moon shone with harsh intensity from inky skies. The stars looked muted by contrast.

'I can't do it,' said Lucien quietly.

'You don't have much choice. Climb up to the roof. I'll meet you in the House Erudito courtyard. I'll have a horse saddled, but you're going to need to give me some time. Come on now, quickly.'

Sounds of dull chopping issued from the sitting room. D'arzenta was swearing at the top of his voice. Virmyre held out a hand and gestured impatiently. In three quick steps Lucien was across the room and perched on the windowsill like a huge raven. The bulk of his bag lay in the small of his back, the strap straining across his shoulders. He realised he had no scabbard resting on his thigh, the reassuring weight of a sword painfully absent. He turned to Virmyre breathing hard, steaming in the night air.

'What the hell is going on?' he whispered.

'Chaos,' said Virmyre. 'Now go.'

Lucien's fingers sought the gaps in the masonry, gingerly grasping coarse networks of ivy root, not trusting them to support his weight. His feet slipped and struggled to find purchase; his wounded shoulder complained spitefully. The walls of Demense were still slick and treacherous with the day's rain. Underneath and far below men scoured the perimeter with lit torches and spears. Raucous voices carried through the gloom; muffled cursing could be heard from the surly guards. Lucien climbed up, whispering incredulously to himself as he went, shocked by the unfolding consequences of his final testing.

So consumed with the climb was Lucien that he forgot Anea's room was located two floors above his own. He glimpsed her through a gap in the curtains as he squatted on her windowsill to give his wounded shoulder a rest. Anea was tearstained and tired, folded in on herself on the couch. Professore Russo was comforting her, one arm holding the girl close. The Orfano girl was scribbling something in her book. Lucien felt tempted to knock on the glass and say goodbye, but just as he did so a corresponding knock sounded at the door, drowning out his own summons. Russo opened the door and stood at the entrance, arms crossing her chest and looking down her nose. There was a moment of conversation, and Russo's temper flared, her hands going to her hips, chin thrust out defiantly.

Insistent shouting came from the other side of the doorway, increasing in pitch and intensity. This would not end well.

Lucien began to climb again. He wondered if there was a single room of Demesne that was safe tonight. The minutes stretched as he pressed on, relying on his right arm, his left almost useless except to steady himself. The rooftop overhang above was visible, signalling the end of his climb. His limbs felt like lead and perspiration leaked down his neck from his pallid brow. Angelicola's concoction had slowed him, perhaps even inured him to his plight. Now, so close to the end of his climb, he realised how much danger he was in. A fall from this height would end any escape before it had even begun.

With a grunt he pulled himself onto the uneven rooftop of House Contadino. It was a landscape of tiles and shallow sloping angles. The other keeps that made up Demense were of roughly the same height. Long-forgotten weathervanes rusted beneath the stars, encrusted with moss and guano.

Lucien calmed his breathing, feeling his heart beat strong and steady in his chest. Far below, the men with torches continued their restless search, becoming bored or frustrated. Lucien rose shakily to his feet and set off toward the centre of Demesne, toward King's Keep. Its two towers jutted up near the middle of the roof, slumped against each other like drunken lovers, upholstered in ivy which fluttered in the weak breeze. No light shone from their windows, each one a darkened eye. The moon made the rooftop unreal and dreamlike, a monochrome vista of tiled slopes and sinister statuary.

He was halfway across the rooftop of House Contadino when a flicker of movement made him turn. Distracted, he lost his footing and fell, winding himself on the slippery tiles. His left shoulder sang with pain, settling into a droning ache. There was grit in his mouth, metallic and sour. He lay there for long moments, trying to suck the night air into lungs that refused to obey. Lucien listened, straining to hear footsteps in the darkness, but no one appeared. After a few anxious moments he pushed himself to his knees, wheezing with the effort, his ribs bruised. There was someone up here with him, he was sure of it.

The Orfano looked around with caution, then began again,

taking care with each step; he could ill afford another fall. He was close to where House Contadino merged into the King's Keep when the figure sprang on him. Lucien threw one arm out to ward off his attacker and tried to sidestep.

Too late.

The impact lifted him from his feet: he landed on his back with a thud, the bag of clothes slung over his back breaking his fall. He gasped with shock all the same. A hooded man pressed down on him, sour breath coming in gasps. Searching fingers sought Lucien's neck. He tried prising his attacker's hands away, but it was futile. In desperation he pushed his hands under the hood, attempting to gouge an eye, but his thumbs could find no purchase on the shadowed face. His attacker responded, squeezing harder on his windpipe. Lucien was beginning to black out when he remembered he wasn't completely unarmed. The loss of his sword had preoccupied him, but he had other weapons.

Lucien bucked his hips, forcing the strangler to one side, allowing him to bend his leg. His hand snaked down to the top of his boot, sliding the knife from its concealed sheath. Darkness blurred at the edges of his vision. And he thrust into the hooded man's neck. There was a moment's stillness. His attacker shuddered, then issued a dreadful cough. Lucien felt something hot and wet on his face. The man slumped to one side, clutching at the blade lodged in his throat with tremulous hands.

Lucien stood over him, realising his attacker looked smaller in death than he had in life. Had he ever been a man? Was he a child, living rough on the rooftops? There was a final shudder and then stillness. Lucien drew the blade out of his attacker's neck, cleaning it on the dead man's clothes. His garments were old and weather worn, stained with bird droppings, rough stitching from hasty repairs. The jacket was held together by a rope faded to grey. He had no boots, thin feet blackened with grime. The skin on the corpse's hands was calloused and wizened. No child then, but someone much older. Someone who had clung to life with a steely tenacity. Lucien felt a wave of relief; infanticide was not a sin he could live with. This death alone was weight enough on his conscience.

Finally Lucien noticed the man's nails. Not trusting what he was seeing at first, then fervently hoping it was some trick of the night or an accumulation of dirt. The man's fingernails were black, his toenails the same. Not the deep brown of mud and soil, but a rich and lustrous black, like a beetle's carapace. Lucien regarded his own fingernails and shivered. The man had been an Orfano.

Lucien emptied his guts, heaving the contents of his stomach into one of the many gutters that criss-crossed the rooftop. He took a moment to compose himself then slumped to his knees, shivering in the moonlight, giving thanks the hood had fallen over the corpse's face. He could well do without the accusing stares of dead men.

At one time this man had lived in Demesne too, just as Lucien had. He'd most likely have been educated by House Erudito, fed by House Contadino, outfitted by House Prospero, trained by House Fontein. Just as Lucien had. He'd have attended *La Festa* and trained to dance with Mistress Corvo. He may have even lived in the very same apartment Lucien had grown up in. Now this nameless Orfano was a forgotten casualty of a rooftop brawl.

No one would come looking for him, a luxury Lucien envied him for.

Lucien pushed himself to his haunches, steadying himself with his free hand, the other still clutching the dagger, adrenaline far from spent. He shuffled forward and reached for the hood, intrigued yet simultaneously dreading what lay beneath the mean fabric.

A rude exclamation issued from behind him. Lucien flinched, falling back, finding himself staring into the beady eyes of a jet-black raven. Lucien rolled over and gained his feet, swearing loudly, heart hammering in his chest. He dusted himself off, realising it was a hopeless endeavour. Blood had splashed across his coat, gleaming dark and red. He rinsed his face with rainwater from a meagre pool. A sudden pang of regret lanced through him. He'd spent that morning bending his will to *not* killing people, only to find himself covered in the blood of a nameless assailant. An assailant who had shared all the pain of being a *strega*. Someone who had borne all the crushing expectations of being an Orfano. A hated foundling. A feared witchling.

'I'm sorry,' Lucien said in a whisper to the corpse. 'I'd have given you my coat if you'd only asked.'

The corpse remained silent, face shrouded, hands still reaching toward the gaping wound which had spilled his life so quickly, blood tar-black in the moonlight. The raven perched on one dirty foot of the corpse and glared at Lucien balefully. Thunder rumbled in the distance like a protestation. More heavy weather was approaching from out at sea. Lucien frowned and moved toward King's Keep, forcing the bested Orfano from his mind.

The twin towers of the King's Keep stood before him. Lucien circled them, worried that a light would appear in one of the many darkened windows, imagining guards of House Fontein swarming up the many staircases of Demesne. He was so preoccupied that the cupola's presence caught him by surprise. He very nearly walked into it. It was octagonal, though its corners had been rounded, each side a large arched window. Tawny light filtered up from below. Lucien held his breath and dared himself to look down. Beneath was the sanctum of their mysterious monarch, home of the reclusive ruler.

Nothing stirred.

The room appeared to be a laboratory. Eight workbenches formed a hollow octagon, each in disarray, cluttered with glass containers full of opaque fluids or piled high with old books. Strange slates made of black glass collected dust, while silvery medical instruments sat in velvet-lined cases. The walls were hung with sheets of fine paper yellowed with age and covered with formulae and diagrams. One in particular depicted a crudely drawn tree. Lucien was so fascinated that he almost failed to notice the Majordomo enter. The hooded figure stood, head bowed in reverence, hands grasping his staff. A tiny movement of the cowled head indicated some conversation was occurring, the other speaker remaining unseen. Moments passed and then the Domo was gone, grey robes trailing floors thick with dust.

Lucien couldn't bear to move, curiosity burning, before it occurred to him that Virmyre would be waiting. He fled across the rooftops toward House Erudito with a chill in his heart. Something about that room had felt very wrong and he was grateful to be away from it. Fortune smiled on him then in the shape of a long disused tower with winding wooden steps. He descended into House Erudito, clinging to the shadows, using servants' corridors and stairwells far from the main junctions. Hesitant and cautious, he worked his way toward the courtyard, toward Virmyre. And his freedom.

But Virmyre was not the only one lying in wait for him there.

8

The Uninvited

Lucien woke with his heart pounding in his chest. He ran trembling fingers through his hair, reassuring himself the black strands had grown back. A year had passed since his failed testing with Giancarlo. The wounds of that event were not confined to his flesh and had been slow to heal. Outside a gale shrieked and moaned, gusting around the towers of Demesne. Rain drummed against the window, a constant percussion on the glass, trailing away in rivulets. He pulled the sheets up around himself as if the bedclothes might insulate him from his fears. Something banged in the wind – an unsecured shutter perhaps? He wriggled down under the blankets, his heart returning to a more restful pace.

He'd done his best to be less than a shadow during the last twelve months, not venturing to the other houses for anything more than lessons. His absence from House Contadino's kitchens was greeted with relief from the surly porters, although Camelia clucked and fussed as if he were her own. His fleeting visits were irregular; the words he managed to utter much the same. Lucien's contact with people was largely restricted to his teachers, fellow students and Ella. His evenings were spent alone, perching on wide windowsills. He'd gained entry to an abandoned tower of House Contadino. His favourite companions were forgotten books taken from the House Erudito library. The Archivist Simonetti tried to engage him in conversation every so often, but the Orfano pared down his responses, not inviting anything more than pleasantries. Frequently disappearing for hours on end, Lucien would arrive at his rooms just in time for dinner, clothes ghosted with dust and cobwebs.

The wind howled with renewed ferocity. The sound of wood creaking and slamming in the gale filled his senses. There would be no rest while the storm raged. Cursing under his breath he kicked the sheets to one side, leaving his bedroom, padding into the sitting room beyond, naked feet on cold tiles. The sky was a deep and impenetrable black, the light of the full moon held hostage behind hulking clouds. The source of the noise was obvious. One of the windows was open, swinging wildly at the wind's insistence. It was a mercy the panes of glass had not been shaken out of the soft metal lattice. The last thing he wanted was a coterie of surly artisans trooping into his rooms come the morning.

He crept over to the window, practically blind in the dark. Leaning out he pulled the shutter closed first, then locked the window after it. He pressed his fingers to the chilly glass, checking each pane remained in place. This was not a night to lose sleep. Tomorrow was his second testing, this time at the hands of Maestro di Spada Ruggeri. D'arzenta had quietly confided there would be no repeat of last year's humiliation, but his words had failed to calm Lucien's unease. His hand strayed unconsciously to his black ragged tresses.

Something shuffled and scraped in the darkness. Lucien realised he was unarmed and cursed himself. He edged to the dresser blindly, one hand held out in front, stubbing his toes on solid mahogany. Numb fingers fumbled around, trying for matches. A yellow nimbus greeted him. The lamp took the flame despite his shaking hands. He peered into the gloom, holding the light before him, daring not to breathe. No cloaked assassin detached himself from the darkness to plunge a blade into his chest. Not that he was a difficult target – he'd just given away his position, and with no weapon to defend himself.

'Regard Lucien!' he called out, a bitter smile scarring his lips, 'The poorest Orfano in Landfall. More witless than a dullard, more clumsy than an ox, and likely to get slashed open by Maestro di Spada Ruggeri in just a few hours' time.' He bowed

61

theatrically, rose with a mocking wave of his hand and blew sour kisses to an imaginary audience.

The imaginary audience squawked, the call raucous.

Lucien started violently, dropped the lamp, scrambling to retrieve it. A string of uninventive curses escaped his lips, turning to thanks as the lamp stayed alight. Something in the darkness had called to him. He stared into the dimness of his sitting room, eyes straining, took a wary step forward. He'd taken to discarding his sword in the armchair of late, causing Ella to make pointed comments about how he treated his gear. Perched on the hilt of his blade was a great raven.

Lucien had not seen a raven up close before. He found himself surprised at the bulk of the dark bird. It fussed and flapped, extending its wings, before settling down and regarding him with a steady gaze. There was a great age and weariness in those black eyes, Lucien thought. The raven called to him again and Lucien fled to his bedroom. He dressed quickly, throwing on a cloak before surrendering his rooms altogether.

The long-case clock in the corridor had stopped. He could not guess at the time, but yearned to be free of his uninvited guest. His yearning was then replaced by desperation to be free of Demesne too. He drifted through House Contadino, no destination in mind, lingering at junctions and on staircases. After a time he found himself at the Contadino kitchens and then outside, through a concealed side door. He pressed on, grateful to find the storm departed. Dawn was insinuating itself across the horizon, revealing a day of pale greyness: indistinct clouds to the east, heavier, darker clouds to the west, retreating like slovenly bravos tired of taunting. Lucien crossed the rain-slicked grass, feeling blades of dull green swish and whip at his boots. He looked around in the predawn and his eyes settled on the squat presence of the *sanatorio*.

It had been there all his life. No one spoke of it of course. He noticed adults did their best to avoid even the sight of it: a collective blindness, a shared denial. The building was apart from the four houses that clustered together around King's Keep, yet made of the same stone, the same deep red tiles adorning the roof. The edifice consisted of one large circular tower, six storeys high. A spindly sister tower leaned against its north-eastern side. Buttresses embellished the base of the larger building, while hunched stone figures leered down from the roof. Suddenly Lucien knew exactly where he wanted to be.

It didn't take long to climb. The side of the *sanatorio* facing Demesne was decked in a riot of ivy, the many windowsills providing hand- and footholds despite being narrow. Lucien enjoyed climbing. It made sense to him on a level that nothing else did. Not swordplay or conversation. Not chemistry or art. Certainly not Demesne itself. There was just the steady precision of movement and the feeling of accomplishment when you reached the summit. There was no competition, merely terrain. There was no failure, only falling.

He emerged on the roof of the *sanatorio*, looking around at his new fellows. Each was as tall as he, variously grinning or gurning, looking manic or pained in its stony way. Some were winged, most had tails. Lucien was fascinated, studying each one in turn, running his hands over the pointed ears, or tracing the tips of horns. He dared himself to push fingers into fanged mouths, snatching them away as if the gargoyle might suddenly snap down. The watchers' tongues were silent, furred with moss and guano. He wondered how he'd missed such sculptures before, revelling in the uniqueness of each of them. It began to rain again, not as heavy as before, the heavens no doubt exhausted by the earlier storm. The landscape stretched away before him, the woodland at the back of the graveyard swaying silently in the dying wind, ancient oaks beside languid willow. Roads wound themselves between fields and hedgerows, stands of proud cypress following the gentle rise and fall of the island of Landfall. Slumbering farmsteads sent up traceries of smoke, exhalations from fires burning late into the night.

Eventually he tired, squatting down next to one of the brooding presences, regarding Demesne. His home. A landscape of rooftops and towers lay ahead of him, crumbling masonry and dirty windows. Out of sight were courtyards and rose gardens, fountains clogged with leaf mould, statues embraced by ivy. Forgotten cloisters linked old rooms now carpeted only in dust. Bedrooms beyond counting, pantries and kitchens. And somewhere within the castle were the four great halls of the four great houses, each vying with each other for decor and taste. At the heart of it all was the circular keep of the king, their mysterious benefactor, saviour of their souls.

If he even existed.

Lucien snorted to himself. Probably just an old man given to ranting, weak enough to soil himself yet too strong to die. He sneered, becoming another gargoyle on the roof of the *sanatorio*.

Faint at first. So faint he thought the wind had resumed its mournful din. Then louder, unmistakable. He gripped himself tightly. There was genuine fear and helplessness in that tone. He looked down between the curving stone keeps of House Contadino and House Prospero – he knew a direct gateway to the King's Keep nestled between them. The triumphal arch, that was how he'd heard it described. The king would have visitors from the estates arrive at these portals, weighed down with gifts and tribute. This was over two hundred years ago, back when the king would still see people, before he became ill. So Virmyre had said one day after class.

The wind blew harder, ushering another gust of raindrops. Lucien shivered. He could feel the rain coming through the fabric of his cloak, his shoulders damp. The Majordomo emerged from beneath the triumphal arch, hood pulled over his face as ever, covering his unseen eyes. Voluminous sleeves flapped and trailed in the wind as dew clung at the hem of his robes. It was strange to see him from this angle, so far above. He looked less imposing, furtive even. The great oak staff looked more fragile, as if it were just kindling pressed into service. It was then that Lucien noticed Superiore Giancarlo, attired in a black cloak that reached his boots. The *maestro di spada* gripped a girl. Lucien swallowed and felt himself shrink back against the statue beside him. The girl was blindfolded, gagged. Her wrists were tied. Even from this distance Lucien could see they were red raw where she had chafed herself trying to be free. She stumbled and fell, refusing to get up. The Majordomo stopped, said something to Giancarlo, the wind snatching the words away. The stout *maestro di spada* attempted to drag the girl to her feet but she remained resolutely prone.

Lucien fingered the hilt of the dagger under his cloak, mind racing, trying to understand the scene below. Incomprehension etched itself across his brow, a crawling panic edging up his spine, forcing the air out of his lungs. The Majordomo gestured urgently with one cadaverous hand. He'd raised his voice, but Lucien still failed catch the commands issued.

Giancarlo dragged the girl up by her hair, cuffed her twice and lifted her over his shoulder. He advanced toward the *sanatorio*, distaste evident on his features.

'Some privilege this is . . .' Lucien strained to catch the rest of the words, damning his deformed ears. Giancarlo continued walking in the wake of the Majordomo. They would be at the doors of the *sanatorio* itself in just moments, six storeys beneath his very feet.

'I'd never have taken the position if you'd told me about this business before you made me *superiore*.'

'We serve at the pleasure of the king.' The Majordomo's voice was a bored monotone.

'I don't think I care too much for the king's pleasure,' grunted Giancarlo.

'Not the pleasure you might assume; he seeks only to practise his science.'

They were right below Lucien now, knocking on the iron-studded double doors of the tower, waiting in the chill wind. The captive wriggled on Giancarlo's broad shoulder, moaning weakly through her gag. Lucien tried to guess her age, certainly not more than twenty. Younger than Ella, but older than Anea. He clung to the statue feeling numb and helpless, as cold as the stones of the *sanatorio* itself.

'There is much more to this than just you and I, Giancarlo. Not a one of us would be here without him.' The Majordomo stood with both hands clutching his staff in front of him.

'If anyone finds out there will—'

'It is a small price to pay, no?' interrupted the Domo.

And then the doors to the *sanatorio* creaked open. Lucien nearly slipped, engrossed in the conversation between the two men, craning his neck over the edge of the tower. He saw Giancarlo enter as the Majordomo looked around. The occupants of Demesne slumbered on, peacefully ignorant of the unfolding event. The many people of the estates were tucked up in their hamlets and villages, too far away to see the abduction. Lucien gasped. *Abduction*. The word sat in his mind and curdled, a foul and unbidden thing. He was witness to something unnatural.

A roof tile underneath Lucien's boot moved just as the Domo disappeared from view, a horrible grating sound. Lucien flinched, edged back. The tile loosened then plunged over the edge. He stared after it, eyes wide, paralysed with disbelief. Had they closed the doors to the *sanatorio* yet? Would Giancarlo come to the roof to investigate? The questions tumbled over themselves as the tile continued its descent and the light on the horizon broke through the cloud, the first sliver of sun.

The tile impacted on the stone steps of the *sanatorio*, shattering into numberless pieces, an explosion in terracotta and umber. Lucien could never be sure how loud the sound really was, but to him it was as if the universe ended. A flock of birds took to wing, the sharp crack rolling across the farmland surrounding the castle. He imagined it shaking raindrops from tree branches, rattling glass in windowpanes, rousing babes to wakefulness.

The doors groaned on their hinges and Lucien froze. Six storeys below him the Majordomo reappeared. The narrow face under the hood regarded the fragments at his feet, then the cowled dome angled upward. Lucien dared not move for fear of freeing another slate. It was in that moment Lucien realised he'd never really seen the Majordomo's eyes before. The ancient official always kept the heavy edge of his hood drawn low. Those speaking with him would see the tip of his nose and nothing above.

Lucien waited, watching the narrow chin beneath the sombre hood, the old man's gnarled hands clutching his staff. For the tiniest fragment, like a sliver of time itself, Lucien was sure the Domo knew. His chest began to hurt; he'd forgotten to breathe. The Domo turned to his left and then right before going on his way, one foot idly pushing fragments of tile to one side. Lucien remained huddled against the gargoyle, eyes pressed together tight, waiting for someone to emerge on the roof.

No one did.

There was hell to pay when he eventually appeared at the House Contadino kitchen porch that night. The sun was descending and the day, such as it had been, was ending.

'Lucien, you're soaked through and you look like death. Where have you been? They had every guard in Demesne looking for you.' This from Camelia, who had taken him to his rooms and then insisted on shooing Giancarlo, Ruggeri, D'arzenta and Virmyre away. Lucien had looked on incredulous as the simple cook gave each their marching orders. No mean feat.

'You can shout at him after I've made sure he doesn't have pneumonia.' They'd not liked that. All of them protested except D'arzenta, whose face showed only concern. Giancarlo complained with his usual vigour, but Camelia remained unperturbed.

'I said *after*,' she boomed. 'You're in House Contadino now, so behave yourselves. That is all, gentlemen.'

Lucien shivered in his cloak, looking miserable.

No sooner had the irate teachers left than Rafaela barged into his apartment, her deep-brown hair tangled and windswept, boots muddied, skirt spotted from the road. Lucien had never seen her look furious before, but he saw it then. Her nostrils flared, her jaw was set. The silence stretched between them, then snapped.

'I've spent all day traipsing along cliff paths, checking you hadn't fallen in the ocean.' She paused to gasp, but this broke and became a sob, 'Twice we thought we found a body washed up on the shore.'

Tears appeared at the corners of her eyes. She dashed them aside with the back of her hand, trying to marshal anger now fled.

'One of the guards broke his wrist climbing down the rocks,' she said, voice unsteady, 'only to find a sheep's carcass tangled in seaweed.' She paused again, her anger coming back to her.

'Have you any idea how many people have been worried about you?' Her red-rimmed eyes confirmed there had been at least one.

Camelia knelt down next to him and pulled off his sodden garments.

'He's not said one word since he got back. Wherever he's been, whatever he's been up to, well, it's fairly shaken the words out of him.'

Lucien thought it peculiar that Camelia spoke about him as if were not there. She stood, spiriting his clothes away, departing for the kitchens, where water was being heated. Rafaela threw a blanket around his shoulders. He was grateful to be free of his nakedness as much as the warmth the blanket provided. He pulled on small clothes as if in a dream before Rafaela led him to the sitting room and lit the fire, casting concerned looks back over her shoulder. Lucien perched on the couch, glassy-eyed and unspeaking.

'So, are you going to tell me where you've been hiding all day? I've heard of one or two Orfano who wanted to miss their exams before, but nothing like this.' She sat down next to him, one arm slipping around his narrow shoulders, the other hand pushing his fringe back from his face, hazel eyes full of concern.

'You're shaking like a leaf,' she whispered.

'I...' The word lodged in his throat as if he might choke on it. 'I saw something.'

Rafaela's eyes narrowed.

'Tell me, Lucien. Tell me what you saw.'

'I...' He faltered, sickness uncoiling in his gut, his breathing ragged. He was remembering, remembering the gag, the blindfold, the sound of her voice. Remembering his own inaction, his disbelief, his fear. He saw her lying in the long grass as Giancarlo struggled to lift her.

'I believe I may be able to help,' droned a voice from the door. Lucien shuddered, recognising the dreadful monotone instantly. Rafaela stood and bobbed a curtsey, a look of confusion and curiosity on her face. She glanced at the dishevelled form of Lucien and back to the Majordomo.

'It seems Master Lucien has had quite an ordeal.' She smiled blandly.

The blanket fell from his shoulders as he stood, before making his way to the armchair where the raven had settled. The armchair where his blade rested in its scabbard. It called to him now. He drew the weapon in one fluid motion, pointing the tip at the Domo. He caught sight of himself in the full-length glass near the door. Ashen-faced, naked but for his small clothes, ridiculous, like drowned vermin.

'Get out of my rooms. Right now. I don't want you anywhere near me.'

The Domo remained, unperturbed by the blade that had appeared at his throat. His robes were dry now, not the dew-drenched attire of that morning. The hood still obscured his eyes. Then he stepped back, bowed and departed. The only sound in the room was the crackle of burning wood in the hearth. The tip of the sword wavered: Lucien's arm ached from holding it. Rafaela took it from him gently, prising the hilt from his chilled and trembling fingers.

'What happened, Lucien?' Her voice was the sweetest whisper. He turned to her, the words sticking in his throat.

'I had a nightmare. When I woke up there was a big raven.' He swallowed. 'It came through the window last night. I ran away, and then I was too scared to come back.'

The lie didn't make sense, even to Lucien, but it would have to do. There was no telling what the Domo would do if he feared his secret compromised. Better to keep that dark truth from Rafaela's ears, else she might fall victim to abduction. Her ignorance might be all that kept her safe.

9

A Stallion Aflame

HOUSE ERUDITO

– Febbraio 315

Lucien emerged into the moonlit courtyard warily, his breath steaming in front of him. He still clutched his dagger, blood staining the creases between his fingers. The iron stink of it repulsed him, so different from his own. There was a bitter taste he could not rid himself of. The wound in his shoulder continued throbbing, the pulsing of his heart providing a rhythmic counterpoint.

The night sky was smudged with ash-coloured cloud. Stocky barrels lurked in the corners of the courtyard holding a vigil, while a cart missing a wheel waited for an artisan's attention. A selection of buckets lay discarded around the base of a well, waiting for the dawn, when they would be pressed into use again. The stables stood on the far side, a feeble light escaping from above the door. Nothing moved; a cemetery hush weighed on him.

Lucien fretted. If Giancarlo's soldiers had chopped down the door to his apartment there was a good chance the encounter could have descended into combat. Virmyre, D'arzenta, even Dino could be dead this very moment.

He shivered, making his way on silent feet around the edges of the courtyard, remaining in shadow, not daring to walk out in plain sight. This was his life now, existing at the edges, fearing danger at every corner. He pressed on, eyes restlessly roving over every door, each portal threatening to disgorge soldiers at any moment. Soldiers all too keen to spill the blood of the troublesome witchling.

The courtyard remained silent.

The stable was home to around twenty horses, including Lord Contadino's splendid black stallion, a much-admired thoroughbred. Lucien slipped in through the doors and pulled them closed. The wooden bar slotted into the metal hooks, preventing any unwelcome guests. The warm smells of straw and manure greeted him, not unpleasantly. Two battered lanterns spilled yellow light down the center of the stable, revealing the only visible occupant. A scrawny stable boy lay in a heap of blankets with a sheepdog curled up around him. He opened one bleary eye toward Lucien, then closed it and rolled over. An empty jug lay discarded in the straw, relieved of the small beer inside. A few of the horses whickered, eyeing Lucien with interest.

'Virmyre?' he whispered, not daring to call out. The *professore* appeared from one of the stalls. He was his usual unreadable self, although his hair was a mess.

'What happened back at the apartment?'

'Never mind that,' growled Virmyre, 'What in nine hells happened to you? Are you hurt?'

Lucien realised he must look terrible, covered in the outcast Orfano's blood.

'I was attacked on the roof.' He paused to chew his lip. 'There was someone up there. Living up there, I think. He attacked me.'

'Are you hurt?'

'Just bruises. I . . . I had to kill him.'

'Were you seen? Were you heard?'

'No. He was alone up there.'

Lucien pressed fingers to his neck, remembering the constricting grip of the Orfano, then the awful sound of the man dying with a blade lodged in his throat.

'Where's this horse? I'd better make my exit before things become worse.'

Virmyre took a saddle down and placed it on a roan horse that looked at Lucien with large bored-looking eyes.

'So I'm going to be a horse thief in addition to being an outcast?'

71

'No. This is my horse. Now it's your horse. He's called Fabien. Try and look after him. Or find someone that can.'

'But you don't ride.'

'I used to, back when my wife was alive. I keep meaning to go riding again, but...'

Lucien stood in the dimly lit stable watching Virmyre attach the bridle and fasten the straps, feeling overwhelmed by the older man's generosity. A knock at the door startled both men and they ducked down into the stall. Lucien pulled his knife free of its scabbard an inch before Virmyre laid a hand atop his and gestured he calm himself. The stable boy huffed and grumbled, shrugging off the blankets, pushing himself to his feet reluctantly.

'Who's there?' he called out in a rough voice thick with sleep.

'It's me, Camelia.' The lad shrugged and lifted the bar from the door.

'This is a stable, not a common room,' he grunted sourly. Camelia calmly cuffed him about the head, then pushed a small jug of cider into hands.

'Mind your manners, you little beast.'

The stable boy resumed his pose amidst the many blankets. His dog yawned and regarded the newcomer, tongue lolling from an open mouth. Virmyre led the horse out of the stall as Camelia gave a sob and hugged Lucien to her fiercely. The sound of her distress threatened to undo Lucien's resolve. He felt his throat grow thick while his eyes prickled with tears.

'What...?' said Camelia, 'Why are you covered in blood. Look at you. *Porca misèria.* You look like death warmed up.'

'I'm fine. I ran into some trouble. I'd better go before I cause any more.'

'Too late.'

It was Dino; he'd appeared at the stable doors like an apparition, dressed in black with only his pale face catching the meagre light. He clutched a sword cane in his hand with white knuckles, his expression grave.

'Golia is heading this way. He'll be here any second.'

Camelia tied a sack to the saddle and grasped Lucien's head, planting a kiss on his forehead as silvery tears tumbled down her broad cheeks. Virmyre tried to lead Fabien out into the courtyard, but the horse stubbornly refused to move. It swung its head from side to side, making a dreadful noise. Other horses in the stables called out in answer, as if aware of Lucien's plight.

'What's got into him?' asked Lucien.

'They're here,' hissed Dino. He drew the slender blade from the cane and stepped out into the courtyard, only to come stumbling back in moments later, nose bloodied. He collapsed in the straw and stared up, ferocity blazing in his eyes.

Golia filled the doorway with his bulk, sword drawn, a cruel smile sketched on his vulgar lips. Three years older than Lucien, he was a slab of man, shoulders hunched unnaturally and heavy with muscle. His neck was almost as broad as the crude bulb of his head. He wore his black hair in a close crop, the way all of Giancarlo's school did. Golia hulked over all of Demesne's inhabitants with the exception of the Majordomo. As ever, he wore a hooded voluminous tunic in the black and scarlet of House Fontein. Wicked spines sprang from his forearms, extending back to his elbow. People whispered they were poisonous, a rumour Golia had not discouraged. The Allatamento novice from Lucien's testing accompanied him. The boy lurked behind House Fontein's favourite Orfano, struggling to see past. Golia pointed one hand at the stable boy and stared at him.

'Be somewhere else,' he grated.

The boy complied, grasping blankets and cider jug, slinking out into the courtyard followed by his faithful companion.

'Lucien was just leaving,' said Virmyre. 'It would be unfortunate if anyone prevented him.'

Golia made an unpleasant hacking sound. Lucien realised he was laughing. He'd not heard it before and had no wish to again.

'What do you intend to do, Professore?' said Golia. 'Bore me to death with one of your lectures?'

Virmyre snatched up a nearby pitchfork and calmly extended the tool in front of himself, the twin tines gleaming in the lantern light.

'Leave this alone, Golia.'

'I'm afraid not. I'm under orders from Superiore Giancarlo. Sinistro is to be arrested.' Golia smiled at Lucien. 'And if he'll not come willingly . . .'

And then the Orfano lunged forward, lashing out with his blade. Camelia gave a shriek, falling as she tried to retreat.

'Get on the damned horse!' hissed Virmyre before lunging forward. Golia parried the strike from the pitchfork casually, sneering back at the *professore*. Lucien clambered up into the stirrups, almost missing his footing. Golia had moved into the stable now, grinning at Lucien as he closed with Camelia. The Allatamento novice pressed in behind him, clutching a blade in both hands. Lucien cried out impotently and caught his breath. Dino dashed forward, chin dark with his own blood, eyes shining with fury. He parried Golia's strike with the slender blade, turning it to one side. Golia followed up with another, but Dino slipped back and sketched a deep slash across the back of his opponent's hand. Golia swore, thrusting forward, but the younger Orfano danced away, kicking Golia in the knee, eliciting a grunt. A heavy backhanded swipe resulted in Golia's blade lodging in the wooden wall of the stable, but Dino had already ducked under it and rolled forward. The novice dared to step from Golia's shadow a moment, but there was no one within reach to attack. He hopped about from one foot to the other and paused.

Camelia scrambled back on hands and knees, Virmyre helping her to her feet. They didn't dare to take their eyes from the fight between Dino and Golia, who even now was wrestling his blade free. The horses in the stalls stamped their feet and whinnied, clearly rattled. The smells of fear and pungent sweat misted the interior of the stable. Fabien backed up, away from the melee, clearly unsettled by Golia. It was not uncommon for creatures to be skittish or antagonistic in the presence of *streghe*. Golia in particular never failed to unnerve them.

Virmyre stepped forward as if to sweep the hulking Orfano out of the stables with a broom. The pitchfork bobbed back and forth in a series of jabs. Frustrated, Golia held his ground and struck the haft of the fork with a backhanded blow of his sword. Suddenly Virmyre found himself wielding nothing more that a stick. The head of the fork shot across the stable, clattering against the side of the stall, narrowly missing Dino.

Golia grinned. The advantage his, he hefted his blade up for one of his characteristic hammer blows. Only a brute like Golia could reduce the art of sword fighting to such crude strikes. Lucien feared for the *professore*, waiting for the blow that would surely cleave him from collarbone to sternum. Virmyre could only watch, frustrated at his lack of a weapon.

Golia's blade reached its apex and connected with a lantern high overhead. The glass shattered with a crack and the whole device pitched backwards, tumbling down, igniting like a comet.

It landed on the shoulders of the Allatamento boy, still lurking in Golia's shadow. The boy released an inhuman howl as the burning oil splashed over him. Golia looked aghast, confusion creasing his slab-like features. The stable was filled with the scent of burning hair. Then, inevitably, the smell of scorched flesh. The novice, screaming like the damned, fled across the courtyard, pitching himself down the well in frantic desperation. For a moment his agonised howl intensified. There was a muffled splash as he finally reached the bottom of the shaft, then silence.

Everyone in the stable stared after the young noble in shock, then Golia turned, still blocking the door.

'You'll pay for that, Sinistro,' he grunted, not noticing the flames licking around his boots. Virmyre called out as the fire took hold. Lucien beat his heels against Fabien's sides and the horse shot forward, then stalled as Golia blocked the way. The roan, finding his hooves surrounded by fire, reared up and lashed out. Forelegs smashed into Golia's bulky shoulder, almost lifting him from his feet. The *strega* staggered back into the courtyard, losing his footing and crumpling to the ground, sprawled across the cobbles. His sword skittered from his hand, far from reach.

Virmyre was doing his best to escort Camelia from the infernal scene. They emerged into the cool air of the courtyard clutching each other, wide-eyed with shock and struggling with lungfuls of acrid smoke. Virmyre's sleeve was smouldering.

Inside, Dino ran from stall to stall, unfastening the catches and urging the now terrified horses out of the blazing stable, now far beyond redemption. Dino coughed and retched, the fire threatening to overtake him at any point, smoke making his eyes smart.

Lucien urged the panicking Fabien into the courtyard, where the horse wheeled and stamped. He'd never been much of a horseman so could do little but cling on, bending down close over the horse's neck. He prayed he wouldn't be thrown onto the cobbles and stamped on by metal-shod hooves. Golia crawled away, keen to be spared a similar fate.

Into this devastation came a full unit of guards, spilling from doorways brandishing halberds, the officers shouting with swords drawn. They were a cacophony of blind obedience, caught up in the fervour of hunting a hated *strega*. Virmyre and Camelia found themselves surrounded by surcoats, breastplates and helms.

Viscount Contadino's perfect black stallion erupted into the courtyard, the jet horse looking newly arrived from hell itself, wreathed in yellow and orange flames and shrieking. The doomed creature raced across the yard and out through the gates, into the dark, quiet countryside, where it receded from sight like a lantern growing small in the distance. Everyone looked on, shocked into immobility. Lucien felt his blood turn icy.

'The madness is upon us all,' grated Virmyre. The spell broke and the guards rejoined their purpose, but less sure of themselves now. Virmyre shouted and harangued them. The stable roared and spat with great sheets of flames, falling in on itself with a dreadful groan. People were appearing at the windows overlooking the courtyard, calling out in dismay. Presiding over everything from a balcony high above was the hooded figure of the Domo. Lucien pressed his fingertips to his chin and flicked them at the gaunt spectre, then put his heels to the horse's sides. He squeezed his knees together and hoped he wouldn't slip.

How Lucien got past the array of halberds was pure fortune, helped in no small part by wildcat slashes and threats from

Dino. The younger Orfano trailed curses, blade dancing in his hand. Lucien managed to control the roan, pleading in hushed tones lost in the melee. Fabien headed out of the courtyard, keen to be away from the din and clamour. More people had emerged from Demesne, attempting to quell the flames with a chain of buckets. In the morning they would wonder at the corpse they found in the well shaft, and declare the entire night cursed.

Lucien glanced back over his shoulder, unable to tear his eyes away from the unfolding scene, even as Fabien carried him into the safety of the countryside. Standing in the centre of House Erudito's courtyard was Dino, bloody tears tracking down his pale, perfect face, his chin smeared with more of the same. He raised his sword to a vertical position before his eyes in salute. Behind him were Virmyre and Camelia, holding each other close, glad to be alive amid the turmoil. Maestro Cherubini was clucking around them, dressed in a satin nightgown. The guardsmen provided a backdrop of halberds and the scarlet and black of House Fontein. Some pursued him as far as the gates, shouting for his return, others busied themselves putting out the fire. Golia had dragged himself to his feet, spending a moment to glower at Dino before retreating back into the darkness of Demesne.

Lucien struggled to gasp down air as Fabien pounded the road, dark trees looming ahead of them, the stars above glittering coldly. He cursed himself for his inaction. The woodland near the graveyard rushed to meet him and the horse galloped freely, on and on, hooves like thunder. Lucien wondered at what had passed, dismay and shock buffeting him, regret and remorse threatening to drag him from the saddle.

Lady Allatamento would be hearing word of her son's death, while Giancarlo would learn of Lucien's escape, and somewhere in the deep darkness of the night a stallion had burned to death.

10

The Blind Quartet

KING'S KEEP

— Febbraio 309

Lucien had done his utmost to avoid the Majordomo in the five months since witnessing the abduction. He realised he was most at risk of an impromptu audience when alone in his apartment and lowered his profile to the point of invisibility. Lucien restricted himself to familiar groups and safe locales after the episode at the *sanatorio*. Anything to steer clear of another confrontation with the gaunt shade of the king's will. There was the cruel weight of the Domo's secret to bear and a lack of anyone to tell. Who if any would believe him?

The House Contadino kitchens had been his first refuge, the porters and cooks surprised at his reappearance. Camelia was delighted of course, although she took pains to hide it. He'd applied for additional lessons from Maestro di Spada Ruggeri, in part to make amends for missing his testing, but also from a genuine desire to improve. It also placed him within House Fontein, where the Domo rarely appeared. He spent as much time in the library as possible, even helping Archivist Simonetti. Other times he lurked around Professore Virmyre, offering his help as a laboratory assistant. Lucien's scheme paid off. He'd not been cornered by the hooded old man since that dreadful night, the events of which were still etched into his mind, painfully and precisely, revisiting him in dreams with impunity.

'I can't get over the change in you, Lucien,' said Rafaela one morning. He was attempting to clamber out of his nightshirt without appearing naked. He'd recently become very self-conscious in front of his nanny. So self-conscious in fact he'd stopped using the term nanny altogether, instead settling for 'maid' when forced to use a title at all. When they were alone together she was simply his Ella.

'Well, I just thought, seeing as I've failed the last two testings, I need to attend more lessons.' He flashed her a smile. 'Obviously I'm not a natural with the blade, which means I have to work harder at it.'

He'd spent days rehearsing this justification and felt suitably pleased he'd had the chance to use it. Rafaela arched an eyebrow at him. He couldn't decide if it was incredulity or something other.

'Hmm. I'm not sure where this new Lucien has come from, but I think I like him.'

'Not new, just, I don't know . . .' he floundered, looking away embarrassed, searching for a shirt.

'You should make sure he stays. It would be a pity if he vanished before we could get to know him properly.'

He blushed of course. He was always blushing these days when Rafaela spoke to him. She was seventeen now, and he never quite knew what to do with himself in her presence. Technically she worked for him, but she was also there to discipline him when he forgot his manners. The relationship was baffling. The only person he had attempted to discuss it with was Professore Virmyre. A thoroughly bad choice as it turned out. Virmyre had coughed into his fist and suggested he talk to Camelia, and they'd drifted into an uncomfortable silence.

'So, what does today hold for young Master Lucien "Sinistro" Contadino?' She curtseyed with mock solemnity, then flashed a taunting smile.

Sinistro, his new nickname, given to him by Master Ruggeri on account of his left-handedness. Lucien was ambivalent about the epithet, but the name had taken on a life of its own. The other students at class had adopted it immediately, thinking it vexed him. They'd been disciplined repeatedly for using the word *strega* in class, but that didn't stop them inventing a battery of other pejoratives.

Perhaps it was just as well. Lucien didn't consider himself an Orfano. Poor with the blade and unremarkable at many subjects, 'singularly unspectacular' had been Superiore Giancarlo's latest rebuke. He could reinvent himself as Sinistro, become more than the sum of his abysmal testings and ragged reputation. As Sinistro he could rise above being 'the boy who ran from the raven'. Lucien was tied to incompetence and insecurity; Sinistro didn't have to be fettered by such labels.

'I've got the day off,' he replied cheerfully, having negotiated his way into his britches without loss of dignity. 'Think I'm going to practise some forms with D'arzenta. After that Professore Virmyre said we should attend a lecture by Dottore Angelicola. They say he has a corpse to dissect.'

'And I suppose you're dying to see it, you grotesque child.'

'Virmyre says it's biology. I have to go. I think it's disgusting actually.' He wrinkled his nose and grimaced.

'Mind that the *dottore* doesn't dissect you. You know how he is about Orfano.'

'It's fine. My scalpel is bigger than his.' Lucien drew his sword with a flourish and sketched out a few thrusts and parries. Rafaela rolled her eyes.

'And after that?'

'After that I'm going to help Camelia out for a bit. We're having gnocchi tonight.' He grinned. The prospect of spending the afternoon in the kitchen pleased him no end. Rafaela said nothing, smiling at him warmly. He continued dressing himself, tucking a knife into the top of his boot and concealing another within his jacket, recent additions to his armoury at D'arzenta's insistence.

He was careful to leave his apartment the moment Ella did, for fear the Majordomo would appear, like the dreadful raven, as if from nowhere. He checked himself briefly in the mirror by the door, content his long black hair hid his deformity. He'd even consented to let Camelia cut off the worst of the split ends, making him look halfway respectable.

Lucien locked the door to his apartment and strode along the corridors, jogging down stairs, arriving at the junction where House Fontein connected to King's Keep. The guards nodded to him more from duty than respect. Lucien flicked a lazy salute in a way he knew infuriated the career soldiers.

They muttered between themselves and tried to ignore him.

'You could use a shave,' he drawled and went on his way, knowing the guards would be flicking their fingertips from under their stubbly chins behind his back.

The centre of King's Keep was a largely unknown quantity. Each of the four houses adjoined the central structure, linked to each other by a poorly lit corridor that ran the circumference of the keep at ground level. There was the usual stifling bureaucracy of the gate guards, who insisted on doing searches. They had nothing better to do after all. Gate duty was seen as punishment among the soldiery, given to those too lazy, too incompetent or too old to be effective. Outbreaks of corruption would occur every now and then, only to be rooted out by Giancarlo. The guards were, in truth, as decorative as gargoyles but much less useful. No one really believed that inter-house squabbles would escalate into assassination. Only the Orfano were watched closely, and Lucien tired of the suspicious gazes lingering on his every step.

The grand corridor of the King's Keep was also the main artery into the king's own chambers. Doors fully twelve feet high towered over passers-by, leading to the heart of Demesne. The passage itself was ribbed with buttresses supporting the outer wall. Lucien imagined being inside the hollow chest of some giant petrified snake. It was here, in this dank gloom, that Lucien saw the Majordomo.

And he was not alone.

Behind the hooded figure were three women and a man, all wearing fine clothes, tailored in the same cut, the style antiquated. All were elderly and bore traces of dusty neglect. There was a perverse formality about them, as if they were ancient quadruplets whose parents still dressed them, twee and yet sinister. All wore tar-black spectacles which reflected the lamplight. Lucien crept closer, his curiosity outweighing his desire to flee the lurching presence of the Majordomo.

Hiding in the shadow of one of the corridor's buttresses, Lucien studied them. Each of the bespectacled strangers had a hand extended to rest on the shoulder of the person in front. The foremost rested her hand on the Majordomo's shoulder, creating a sombre chain of seemingly sightless individuals. Each clasped a violin in their left hand, surprising since instruments were such a precious rarity in Demesne. Lucien furrowed his brow in confusion, forcing himself against the cold stone, desperately hoping to avoid detection. The Majordomo busied himself at the doors to the King's Keep with an unusual two-pronged key. Some mechanism inside the lock churned, followed by the sound of grinding. Metal chains rattled from behind the thick wood. Lucien waited, suddenly much too warm, heart beating loud in his ears.

The doors opened inward, their ancient oak grating on the flagstones until they came to rest with a shudder. The Domo led the blind quartet into the king's chambers, his staff tapping and rasping on the stone floor, its amber headpiece winking in the gloom. Lucien stared after them, his pulse racing, not daring to breathe. The corridor was deserted. He set off, closing the distance between his hiding place and the cavernous entrance at a flat run. The rattling of chains greeted him, loud and fast. The mechanism had been released. And then the doors swung shut, booming closed in his face. Lucien hit the wood and bounced back, his pride receiving the greater wound.

'Fine,' he muttered, resuming his spot next to the buttress. He glowered at the offending portal, wondering who else had been privileged to pass beneath the ancient arch. A few people passed by, eyeing him warily, but none challenged him. Being Orfano, he could generally do as he pleased.

It was impossible to gauge how long he stood there. The darkness combined with the muted music made Lucien feel as if he were outside time itself. He found himself floating, anxieties and curiosities holding him in place, becalmed on an ocean of worry.

The doors grated inward again, hinges groaning, the grease on them long dried to a black crust. The Majordomo appeared, an ashen shade, his amber-topped staff clasped in his hand as ever.

'I had wondered if you might still be here.' That bored flat monotone. Lucien stepped out of the shadows, slouching insolently.

'I want to see the king,' he said, thrusting his jaw out, trying for a pugnacious mien. His fingers trembled and sought the comfort of his blade, the worn leather of the hilt reassuring.

The Majordomo started laughing, a horrible thing. Wheezing wet exhalations filled the passage until the tall figure coughed loudly, folding at the waist. The laughing, if indeed it had been been laughing, was replaced by a dreadful hacking. The Domo held out a hand to steady himself on the wall, then regained his composure. Lucien stepped closer, his hand still clasping the hilt of his blade. The Domo reached beneath his robes. Lucien nearly drew on instinct, the urge to unleash his blade almost painful to resist. The emaciated long-fingered hand brought forth a handkerchief. Lucien sighed and stepped back, tension draining out of him. The Domo dabbed the corners of his mouth a few times.

'Are you ill?' Lucien felt like an idiot the moment the words took shape.

'Old. Ill. Name me the difference.' The Domo was more phantom-like than ever in the gloom.

'How old *are* you?'

'It becomes so difficult to count. Not more than a hundred and one by my reckoning.'

Lucien took a step back, a sneer coming to his lips. He was positive the Domo was telling the truth. He'd been mocked enough to know the distinction between sincerity and sarcasm.

'I assume I can share this little secret with you,' droned the Domo. 'After all, you kept the business at the *sanatorio* to yourself, no?'

'I didn't tell a soul,' Lucien whispered. 'I guessed you'd kill anyone who knew about it. I can't stop you killing me, but you don't have to hurt anyone else on my account.'

The Domo paused to consider this for a moment. His hand dabbed the corners of his mouth with the kerchief again. He nodded slowly, and an insinuation of a smile stole over his parchment-like lips.

'Perhaps you have a sharper mind than I gave you credit for.'

'You hurt anyone on my account and I'll see you dead.'

Lucien's hands were trembling freely now, equal parts fury and cold fear.

'And possess some measure of conviction too, it would seem.' Another ghost of a smile from the Domo, this last a definite mockery.

'Why are you so old? Why don't you die like other men?' asked Lucien, sounding affronted.

'Curious too.' The Domo wheezed once before continuing. 'The king. He has magics from a time long ago. A time before we washed up on these shores. He can alter people to his choosing. Make them live longer, encourage certain attributes. I may be over one hundred years old but I feel no older than fifty-five.'

'Why the coughing then?' Lucien pressed.

'I am ill. The king can do many things, but he is far from expert on diseases. Especially his own.'

The Domo resumed coughing, more violently this time. His staff clattered to the floor, the sound reverberating down the corridor. He reached out a withered hand for the wall, already beginning to fold in on himself. Lucien caught him as he fell, struggling under the weight. It was unnatural one so thin could weigh so much. Lucien lowered him to the ground as delicately as he could, grunting with the effort. He stood there waiting for help. None came. The shadow of an idea scuttled across Lucien's mind, the dagger beneath his jacket sang to him. It would be the work of seconds. He thought back to the night on the *sanatorio* roof; the sound of the girl resisting Giancarlo still haunted him. Mere seconds, a sharp knife, and the king's steward would never again spirit away the helpless.

A procession of troubling thoughts trampled the urge to kill: where would he conceal the corpse? Would he be a suspect in the murder? Would Giancarlo continue the abductions in the Domo's absence? It was too much for one Orfano to take on, or so he told himself.

Lucien struggled under the weight of the man, dragging him to House Contadino past startled gate guards to a small sitting room. There was no one there of course; all the servants who rested here were at their tasks. Lucien was sweating freely as he hefted the long-limbed bulk of the Domo onto a couch. Once this had been a windowless storeroom. Dilapidated furniture had been given a new lease of life by house craftsmen. A particularly hideous candelabra dominated a scuffed sideboard. Lucien lit the candles, grateful for the warm light that infused the room. He turned, seeing the form of the Majordomo sprawled across the couch, chiding himself for not killing the *bastardo*. He most certainly deserved it for the part he had played outside the *sanatorio* that night.

Another idea slithered into his mind, unwelcome but difficult to resist. Lucien peeled back one of the Domo's voluminous sleeves to find short spiny growths extending from his forearms, flattened backwards, running toward the elbow. Lucien forced down a surge of panic. Golia and Dino had the very same spines.

Bile soured his throat as he lifted the heavy cowl of the robe, forcing it back above the line of the Domo's nose. He fell back with a cry, his scabbard catching a low table awkwardly. Unsure of what he had seen, he crawled across the carpet, lifting the hood once more. There were human eyes, but all were small and mismatched. Lucien counted six of them scattered across a high forehead and felt his stomach turn. The Domo's eye sockets were just two twisted indentations. The man had a narrow face, his chin and nose pointed, skin leathery and deeply lined.

Something happened to the Domo's chest just as Lucien was about to withdraw in revulsion. It came again, a twitching movement, like something stirring in sleep. Too great a movement to be the rising and falling of breath. And there was the smell. An unwholesome scent permeated the room, not of unwashed flesh, rather the sweet tang of rot. Three flies drifted in lazy spirals above the Domo. Lucien looked toward the door, plucking at his lip with forefinger and thumb. He knelt quickly, retrieving a knife from his boot. It was simple quick work to cut open the fabric. Starting under the Domo's chin, Lucien split the garment to the navel, sawing through the rough weave. He dropped the knife, holding the back of his hand to his mouth. His stomach protested and he ran to the side of the room, heaving into the bucket of firewood.

For long shaking seconds he stood, bent over double, hands clutching his knees, trembling with the force of his unease. Cold sweat sprang out across his brow.

'And now you know what I am.'

'Hardly a surprise,' grunted Lucien. 'I can't believe I didn't realise sooner.' The acid foulness of vomit stained the air between them.

'You and I are much alike, Lucien.'

'No, we're not. We're Orfano, and that's where the similarities end.'

The Majordomo had recovered himself, the cowl pulled down over his many eyes, sleeves smoothed down over his forearms. He held the cut fabric of his robes together with a massive fist.

Lucien's curiosity could brook no further silence.

'What were you doing with that girl?'

'Ah, the girl.' The Domo bowed his head a moment. 'Her mind had fled. She was a danger to herself and her family. That is why we have the *sanatorio*; it is for the sicknesses of the mind. The king has no jurisdiction there; he deals only in the flesh.'

'She was suffering from madness?'

'Yes. It is an unfortunate side effect of this island. The damp settles on weak lungs while the winters unsettle the mind.'

'So, so you weren't ab—' Lucien paused. Remembering the harsh texture of the gargoyles beside him. How Giancarlo had cuffed the girl into submission. The rope burns on her slender wrists.

'Abducting her? No.' Another grim smile from beneath the cowl. 'But there are many in Landfall and Demesne who are ashamed of madness.' The Domo sat forward, pressing his fingertips together. His fingernails were ragged and chewed. 'They fear the diseases of the mind are contagious. This is not the case. People fear things they do not understand. This is why we take people at night.'

Lucien said nothing, not sure what he was hearing. The Domo fetched up the knife from the dusty floorboards, then stood, towering over Lucien. He offered the hilt toward the boy.

'There is no need to be afraid, Lucien. I am sorry if you have been worried by this thing.'

Lucien took the knife, not returning it to the sheath in his boot. He turned the blade over in his hands, looking at the inscrutable darkness beneath the cowl of the Domo.

'And if I succumb to madness?'

'Then I'm afraid you'll go to the *sanatorio* too, although I find that outcome unlikely. Both your spirit and your mind are too strong, Lucien.'

The steward turned his back and passed through the doorway, leaving Lucien wondering how much truth, if any, he'd just been told.

11

The Macabre Machine

THE CEMETERY

– Febbraio 315

Lucien awoke on the cold floor of the mausoleum, just a dozen feet away from the final resting place of Stephano, sixth and longest-reigning Duke of Prospero. A flag lay atop the sarcophagus, a neatly folded triangle of purple and black. The house had flourished under Stephano's guidance: craftsmanship had reached new levels of wonder, old methods refined, the prosaic now meticulous. Goods and artefacts commanded prices impossible to imagine just a decade ago. While Stephano was most certainly a buffoon in the public realm, he was a canny operator in his office. Few who left that room could claim the better part of any bargain struck. There was little House Prospero had not been able to achieve when combined with his wife's hungry ambition. The duchess had brought a battery of schemes and plans to the wedding bed, not discounting a wealth of rumour and scandal. Never overburdened with chastity, it was told Salvaza counted Duke Emilio Contadino among her conquests, which made her marriage to Stephano all the more intriguing. Jealous members of other houses would sneer the word *mercantile* behind their hands, a pejorative for the newly rich. House Fontein had been forced to strike up an alliance in order to retain some standing. Contadino on the other hand had been relegated to a house of farmers and dullards. Some whispered that Lord Contadino's reduction in influence had been a vengeful scheme long harboured by Salvaza Prospero. One did not bed her without some cost or consequence, it would seem. Lucien tried to imagine what it would be like to marry into that empire of commerce, being wed to Stephania.

Small chance of that now he was outcast. His goal was not one of attaining status, but simply surviving. Beyond that he simply wished to see Rafaela one more time.

An unkindness of ravens heckled outside the mausoleum, their voices carrying over the windless skies. Lucien shivered and felt ridiculous. The graveyard was barely twenty minutes' ride from Demesne. The complete darkness of the countryside had made escape impossible. He'd ventured beyond Demesne's environs just a handful of times, and always by daylight. The poor visibility, combined with a lack of destination, had delivered him here. The sepulchre was a welcome refuge, shielding him from the night and the questing gazes of House Fontein.

He pined for hot water and soap, for plush towels and freshly baked bread. A curse escaped his lips as he pushed himself to his feet. His bruises grumbled, making themselves known across his back, writhing pain on his ribs. His shoulder had resumed its familiar dull ache. The rain, so prevalent these days, was absent, leaving a sombre but unthreatening grey sky. The sun itself was no more than a wan white disc at the edge of the world. He'd need to leave now if he were to escape the search parties sent by Giancarlo.

Head bowed, he approached the vast sarcophagus of Duke Stephano, laying one hand on the chilly stone. He thought about the night of *La Festa*.

You'll take care of her, my boy? Tell me you'll take care of her? the duke had all but begged, drunk and farcical in a powdered wig.

Tell me you'll take care of her. You two have a chance I never had. You're the same age. Don't make the mistake I did.

Lucien felt a powerful pang of regret. He'd not made the same mistakes as the duke, but had created an entirely new catalogue of failures.

'I'm sorry,' he said, kissing his fingers and laying his hand gently on the corner of the sarcophagus. He turned his back and chewed his lip, ignoring hunger pangs.

The cemetery was a study in stillness. Mist ghosted around headstones strangled with bindweed. Mourning angels presided over the scene, hands pressed together in reverence. The statues had been sculpted from the same dark grey stone as Demesne itself. A path of white gravel neatly bisected the tangle of dew-slicked grasses. Other mausoleums hunkered nearby, coated in moss, spattered with guano. Wrought-iron gates decked with tenacious ivy led to the road. And his escape.

The ravens called out in boisterous rude greeting, drawing his attention to the stand of trees beyond the cemetery wall. It was here he'd tied up Fabien, out of sight and sheltered from the worst of the downpour.

Lucien retreated back into the cover of the sepulchre.

A thin wisp of smoke wound its way into the skies, a single tendril drifting above the trees. Someone was cooking nearby. *But who cooks in a graveyard?*

He gathered up the sack of food Camelia had given him and unsheathed the dagger from his boot. The trees whispered, confiding to each other as the Orfano set out toward the telltale plume, dew soaking his boots. Lucien climbed the wall easily, one handed, not wanting to trouble his left shoulder. He pressed on, fighting his way through a weeping willow, the limbs clinging and dragging at him like an intoxicated lover. All around were the trunks of dead trees swarming with woodlice; spiders picked their way across the woodland floor, beetles marched across leaf mould. Miniature life teamed and floundered. The ravens above had fallen silent or taken to wing. He was just moments into the woods when he stumbled across the discovery, able to do nothing but stare in disbelief.

In front of him was a filthy man crouched by a mean fire pit. Fabien, Virmyre's beautiful roan, lay on the ground, its throat a ragged wound, as if a large stake had punched a hole through the creature. The leaves nearby were splashed with congealing crimson. The roan was missing a foreleg, now sizzling over the meagre flames. The smell of blood was overpowering.

'You bastard! You killed my horse.'

The man turned to him, saying nothing. Any further rebuke from Lucien died on his lips. He shuddered, stomach knotting, a thick surge of bile in his throat. Two sets of eyes, one pair below the other, stared back. One of the four was an odd blue, the rest three shades of unwholesome green. He looked to have lost his teeth, his lips forming a puckered arsehole below a broken blunted nose. The skin around his eyes and neck was deeply lined, his head bald and massive.

This creature was old.

Suddenly Lucien understood why the fire was so poor. The man had no hands. His wrists extended to black points, sharp and shiny, not unlike his own black fingernails. The right limb was splashed with gore, clearly the source of the roan's demise. The grotesque didn't move, only blinked and shivered, chest rising and falling, each exhalation making the sphincter of his mouth tremulous. He was stripped to the waist, skin raddled with discoloration, bruise-purple and jaundice-yellow. Four atrophied arms extended from his broad chest, hanging across his stomach. Each terminated in a withered child-like hand.

Lucien recalled the day the Majordomo had collapsed, re-membered the horrors hidden beneath the ash-grey robes. The Domo and the wretch who crouched in front of him had much in common.

Lucien cut four skewers from some wood. He passed them over the flames a moment, burning off splinters, then ran the skewers into slender cuts of the dead roan. He took a moment to bank the fire up. Finally he set the meat above the flames. The toothless man watched with jealous fascination, his many eyes lingering on Lucien's clever fingers. They waited beneath the trees as Lucien thought of the Orfano he'd killed on the rooftops of Demesne. He'd not been given the chance to feed that starving wretch but saw no reason the man before him should go hungry.

The meat sizzled, browned. Lucien gave the man a skewer, which he struggled to grip between the two pinions of his misshaped limbs. The flaccid ring of a mouth stretched open to reveal mandibles which tore and worried the horse flesh. Lucien looked away, unable to eat or even speak. After a few moments came a wheezing rasp. The grotesque was pointing an appendage at the remaining skewers. Lucien passed another and deliberately looked away, struggling to conceal his revulsion. Gratitude welled up in his chest as he studied his own fingers.

Always a symbol of his difference, a source of embarrassment, they were now cherished in a way he'd never considered.

Lucien stood and busied himself, removing the saddle from the still-warm body of his short-lived mount.

'Not like I was much of a horseman anyway,' he mumbled. 'Still, you deserved better than this, Fabien.'

He snatched a glance over his shoulder as the grotesque kept eating. How many more of his kind had been made outcast, hidden away on this windswept isle? How many had been too twisted and warped to serve any purpose? Lucien tugged and fussed with the saddle, performing a quick inventory of his possessions. A gentle tap on the shoulder brought him around sharply, his dagger clenched in his left hand. The wretch shrank back, a manoeuvre that looked as redundant as it was ridiculous; he had to be over six and half feet tall.

'Sorry. You startled me.' Lucien looked at the roan. 'You shouldn't have stolen my horse. I would have given you food. You mustn't steal horses.' He felt absurd, doubting the wretch even understood. He looked up into the mismatched eyes, studying the strange topography of a face wrought hideous.

'You're an Orfano, just like me. And this is how they treat us. Forced to live in graveyards and dine on horse meat.' He regarded the roan. '*Porca misèria*. Virmyre will kill me for this.'

Lucien shook his head, wondering how far it was to the next town. The deformed Orfano loped away, then turned, a wheezing sound escaping the crude ring in his face. He waved the cruel spikes of its arms in agitation. Lucien realised he was being beckoned.

The track through the copse of trees was indistinct. Branches had been cut back long ago but since grown anew. The yellowing grasses had been trampled underfoot. Brambles conspired to entangle. Lucien followed, keeping his distance, not re-sheathing his dagger for fear of the destination. Suddenly the rude path ended, and they were at the edge of a clearing. Weeping willows formed the edges, while older oaks towered over all, shedding leaves as winter approached. Coarse grasses grew to chest height, now yellowed with the advance of the season. Not a clearing, Lucien realised; it was in fact a second cemetery. The *sanatorio* was monstrous for being in plain sight, but the secret graveyard affronted Lucien more. Unease constricted about him, but the faint sting of curiosity also piqued.

The headstones were simpler here. No angels watched over the resting dead, no elaborate crosses decorated the rows of graves, and there were certainly no mausoleums. Lucien spent long minutes resting on his haunches, reading inscriptions. He knelt and scraped moss and guano from where chiselled details had been obscured. The other Orfano stood mute, expression unreadable, seemingly rapt with Lucien's investigation.

'There must be nearly sixty graves here,' said Lucien, as much for his own benefit as for his new companion. He was still undecided if the huge Orfano understood a single word.

'And I'll bet they're all *streghe*. Every one.'

Lucien kept reading, advancing from grave to grave, then doubled back and rechecked his earlier findings. The wretch scratched at himself and looked around, wishing to be back at the fire perhaps. And the horse meat. He hummed to himself tunelessly, an unkind dirge from his ring-like mouth.

'They're born every three years on average,' offered Lucien. 'They die at various times, presumably due to complications from their deformities.'

Lucien eyed the wretch and wondered how he'd survived so long.

'Or perhaps due to more direct action.'

The wretch gave an excited hoot, loping back to the path they had emerged from. The wind exhaled and set the willows to whispering. A raven called out, remaining hidden from view. The sun had continued its shallow climb while he'd been here, lost in the details of the dead.

Someone approached, and not alone.

Lucien collapsed down behind a gravestone, waiting, feeling cold sweat in the small of his back. His throat was suddenly dry. The silence of the secret graveyard was broken only by the beating of his heart.

The Majordomo appeared at the entrance to the clearing, carrying a body. Lucien's eyes widened with horror. The wretch scampered in the Domo's wake, subservient, trailing him like a favourite hound. Lucien's panic mounted as he realised the Orfano could give him away at any moment, bounding over and drawing the attention of his master.

Instead the wretch began to dig with the spikes of his arms, Lucien's presence apparently forgotten. The Orfano loosened the surface of the ground, then used both limbs in concert to lift the earth. The Majordomo let the body slump to the ground without ceremony or care. Lucien stole a glance from his hiding place, face pressed against the gravestone. The corpse was familiar to him. His hooded assailant, so keen to throttle him in the gutters of the rooftops, now dead by Lucien's desperate attack. Seeing the corpse in the dawn light gave new fuel to his shame. Time ground on all too slowly, fraying Lucien's nerves. He dared to think of sneaking away, but chose stillness over stealth. The Domo had always been preternaturally efficient at detecting him. The wretch continued digging, his breathing becoming more laboured, his wheezing more pronounced. Lucien squeezed his eyes shut, praying the Majordomo was too preoccupied with the burial.

There was a break in the work and Lucien risked another glance. The Domo had grasped the slain Orfano and was depositing the corpse in the crude grave. The wretch loped about, excited hooting escaping the ring of his lips. He dropped to his knees and looked up at his master expectantly. The Domo produced a loaf of bread, placing it between the deformed man's limbs. This was how the wretch survived, Lucien realised. Another pawn in the Majordomo's great game. Another cog in Demesne's macabre machine. Lucien clutched himself, drawing his knees to his chest. Small wonder the Domo's influence extended beyond the castle walls. Lucien doubted that any corner of Landfall was free of his unholy jurisdiction.

A sharp snap broke the stillness, ravens gained the skies, exploding from the trees in a flurry of black wings. Lucien pressed his face against the gravestone, one eye straining to see what had happened.

'No more need for you, my friend,' said the Domo. 'The endgame is upon us, for better or worse.' He turned and disappeared among the trees, back along the path, staff holding back branches. Lucien willed himself to stillness, certain Demesne's steward would return at any moment.

The skies lightened, the disc of the sun became visible over the tops of the trees.

Lucien stood, satisfied he was alone, clutching his knife, for all the small protection it might afford him. He approached the grave cautiously, well aware of the sight waiting in the rude earth. The slain Orfano and the gravedigger lay together in a twisted embrace. In life they had most likely never known each other. Now they had been discarded callously into the same grave.

Lucien made his way back to the fire pit, now smouldering weakly, stamped out by the Majordomo, no doubt. He retrieved the saddle, slung it over his good shoulder with a grunt. Flies buzzed about the corpse of the slaughtered roan, gorging themselves on the congealing blood. Spiders and their various cousins in the order of insects had joined the gathering, already returning the horse to earth in tiny increments.

'Virmyre is going to kill me, assuming no one else does first.'

Lucien froze in the shadow of the cemetery wall as two House Fontein guardsmen appeared at the gates. The men looked bored and unhappy, their halberds dull in the flat light. The scarlet and black of their uniforms were more subdued than usual, mud-spotted from the road. No guard would relish hunting down a highly trained Orfano. The guards were merely a deterrent, bullies kept in line by tyrants.

Lucien swore as one happened to look up and spot him. Disbelief gave way to anger, and they clutched their weapons more tightly. Lucien turned on his heel and ran, struggling under the weight of the saddle, cursing his luck. Or the lack of it. He longed for a scabbard and a blade at his hip, feeling naked without them. Behind him stifled shouts, the clattering of men in breastplates scaling the cemetery wall. Lucien ran, feet tumbling over themselves. The branches of the copse conspired to hold him back, roots foxing his steps, leaving him sprawling. He emerged from the copse in a tangle of limbs, some of them his own. He took a moment to pick himself up. A surge of elation.

The dull scar of the road cut through the land among patchwork fields and ragged hedgerows. Farmsteads clustered at junctions in the distance. Lucien turned and listened, hoping the guards had given up and turned back to Demesne, reporting to their betters.

It was a short-lived hope.

The guards emerged, muddied and red-faced, exhalations steaming on the chill air. One was missing a helmet, spewing curses and indignation. Their eyes fell on him and Lucien ran, with only the open road ahead of him and nowhere to hide.

12

Diplomatic Intervention

MISTRESS CORVO'S STUDIO

– Settembre 309

Mistress Corvo, his dance teacher, was a woman in her late fifties. Unmarried and always attired in black, she was emaciated and wizened. Despite this she was possessed of a vigour that few within Demesne could match. Lucien surmised she sucked the marrow from children's bones to sustain herself. There could be no other explanation. He'd said as much to Rafaela, who'd chided him when she finally stopped laughing.

'You should be grateful you have the luxury of such lessons; there's many that don't,' Rafaela told him one morning.

'Have you ever learned?'

'To dance?'

'Of course.'

'When would I find the time?' She shook her head, then set down a pile of fresh bedding on the chest in his bedroom. 'Between keeping this place and helping Camelia I barely have five minutes to myself.'

'I hadn't thought of that,' he replied, feeling a twinge of guilt. 'Maybe I could ask Mistress Corvo to—'

'That's a sweet gesture, Lucien, but there's no need.'

He'd felt curiously raw following her refusal.

'Lucien, will you pay attention!' His focus snapped back to the gaunt dance teacher in her studio at House Erudito. He couldn't shake the feeling: there was something unseemly about her. No one that thin and corpse-like should have so much vitality. She was given to grinning inanely in the presence of nobles, resembling an awful skull, hair gathered up in a bun at her crown. Thick blue veins ran through her hands and up her age-spotted arms. Technically she was part of House Erudito, on account of her status as a teacher, but she spent the greater part of her time clucking around Duchess Prospero. She doted on the duchess's daughter Stephania, a regular attendee of her classes.

Mistress Corvo treated Lucien no differently to how she treated any other student, which is to say she castigated him in the most caustic language available.

'Lucien, another blessed hour in your presence. And to think, I could be teaching a dozen young ladies to walk like princesses.' She rounded on him, slapping and prodding him into posture. 'Instead I'm teaching an ape to walk. Never let it be said I do not suffer for my art, no?'

'No, Mistress Corvo,' he managed from gritted teeth.

'There are some men who are fair of feature and move with beauty. You are not one of these men, Lucien. Nor will you grow into one, I think. Still, we must work with what we have.'

Lucien hated the dance studio: full-length mirrors greeted him at every turn. Mistress Corvo insisted he tie his hair back during lessons. While this did not reveal his missing ears, he could not find any peace. His self-consciousness manifested with greater intensity with each passing year. Now eleven years old, he wondered if he could bear to make it to his teens. He squeezed his eyes shut to be spared his reflection for a second, took a breath, then set his gaze on the withered teacher

She had been especially exacting of late, abandoning their work on a tarantella to teach him a rather more sedate gavotte. He'd not minded. The constant rattle of the tambourine with its effete ribbons, so essential for the tarantella, had tested his nerves. She'd even foregone her attempts to make him do ballet, much to his relief.

'I can't bear it,' she shrieked one afternoon. 'You're beyond incompetent. You make the incompetent look graceful. I'd rather teach servants.'

'Maybe you should, and stop torturing me with this horrible shit,' he muttered. Not quietly enough, as it turned out. He'd been barred from lessons for a week and forced to help muck out the stables. Not much of a punishment, as he rather enjoyed it.

Now he was learning to dance with a partner, and he suspected he knew why. Noble children were often called on to dance with each other at *La Festa*. The idea of performing like a trained dog mortified Lucien. The dance teacher had icy-cold hands, and Lucien recoiled from touching her. Her breath was strangely odourless, and being so close to her filled him with disgust. He never embraced anyone except Camelia, who occasionally swept him into a bear hug.

'I see no reason you shouldn't learn some court dancing now that you're eleven,' snapped Mistress Corvo. 'A boy like you will be quite sought after next year.'

'Only if I grow some ears,' mumbled Lucien sourly.

'What?'

'Ah ... I said, "I hope I get taller next year." '

Mistress Corvo squinted at him, opening her mouth to say something, then thought better of it.

La Festa del Ringraziamento was the one time of the year the Orfani were officially gathered together in the same room. Twelve months from now he'd be made to dance with an empty-headed noble's daughter, probably a halfwit from House Allatamento. Golia would be there, glowering at Giancarlo's heels like a wolfhound. Anea would put in the slightest of appearances. She stayed as long as etiquette dictated and not a minute longer.

Lucien hated *La Festa*. He loathed that moment of walking through the double doors, being announced by the steward of the house, only to find himself staring back into the dismissive faces of courtiers and pages. Worse still, he never knew what to say, either to his peers or anyone else. He'd be fussed over by some teachers and blanked by others. The nobles of the four families would try to outdo each other in their finery, duelling with sharpened slights and veiled put-downs.

Duchess Prospero would wear a gown that would reveal more than it concealed, and would flirt with and tease anyone who caught her eye. The more elderly duke would get slowly fuddled on strong wine, before stumbling to his rest. Their daughter Stephania would lead a procession of noble girls, all whispering spitefully behind their fans.

Duke and Duchess Fontein, on the other hand, would mark out one corner of the hall as their sole domain. Those breaching the threshold would earn sour looks and barbed compliments for their pains. Even Ruggeri and D'arzenta shunned their company, but Giancarlo would remain by their side, ever the faithful retainer.

Lord Contadino would endure the night but take no pleasure from it. It was common knowledge he preferred the comfort of his privacy. His wife would charm the various guests and earn the admiration of the courtiers anew. Often she'd sing, unaccompanied, to rapturous applause.

Maestro Cherubini would be found presiding over a great flock of teaching staff from House Erudito. The *professori* would do their best to act as a collective charisma deficit. Some called them eccentrics; Lucien called them embarrassing.

Messengers and aides of every stripe and persuasion would haggle and threaten and cajole for an invite to *La Festa*. If only Lucien could palm off his invitation on someone who wanted it. Small chance of that. No Orfano had ever missed the event – it would be a scandal should he fail to attend. And yet Lucien couldn't find it in himself to care this year. Superiore Giancarlo had declared his testing would be held three days prior to *La Festa*. All his thoughts were turned to scissors, stools and humiliation.

Lucien waited in the antechamber of the training room, bent double at the waist, struggling to draw breath. He feared he would lose the meagre breakfast he'd picked at just an hour earlier.

'Just nerves,' Ella had said. He'd not replied, blushing furiously. Being nervous at all was bad enough; in front of Ella had increased his shame sevenfold.

'You'll be fine,' she soothed, brushing his epaulettes with a firm hand before straightening his cravat.

'I don't care about "fine". I just want to pass this year.' He rubbed his shoulder, remembering where Giancarlo had injured him at the second testing. She squeezed his hand, concern glimmering in her eyes.

'Just do the best you can. That's all anyone can ask.'

'Giancarlo doesn't care for my best.'

She sighed, then stepped forward, soft lips brushing his cheek. Lucien was suddenly breathless. The scent of her hair, of her skin, while subtle had struck him like a hammer blow. The gesture had arrived unbidden and he was blushing furiously in response.

'Be careful, Lucien.' Her voice was just above a whisper, eyes now downcast, worry evident in the set of her shoulders. She retreated from the antechamber, drawing the doors shut behind her. Lucien waited, chewing his lip, the heat of hers still burned on his cheek, a sun-warmed touch that lit him like a candle. Thoughts of the impending test crowded in on him, stifling the wonder of Rafaela's affection. He swallowed on a dry throat, not able to meet his own gaze in the floor-length glass. Anxiety ambushed him: he worried he'd arrived late or even confused the day. Did anyone await him in the training chamber? Might he be able to return to his apartment? Would he see out the day unbloodied?

Finally he was summoned.

The circular training chamber was now familiar to him, the three identical banners of House Fontein the only respite from the grey walls and flagstones. Giancarlo indicated he sit on a rough wooden stool provided by a scurrying novice. There were a good number of them present this year, all of them from Giancarlo's school. They variously sneered or primped themselves, looking haughty and superior. D'arzenta stood to one side, cold and furious, head bowed as if in great concentration. He knew what was coming, just as Lucien did. Maestro di Spada Ruggeri stood on the dais, occasionally glaring at the students when they became too boisterous. Behind everyone, leaning against the far wall with his arms crossed, was Golia. He looked more thuggish that usual, his blunt features impassive.

Giancarlo began to lecture the students on practicality and appearance, ignoring Lucien entirely. Then he brought forth the scissors, brandishing them like a short blade. He turned to Lucien as if noticing him for the first time.

'Ah, Master Lucien. You arrived on time this year. Small wonder you arrived at all.' Giancarlo turned to his students, who sniggered on cue. The *superiore* continued his lecture on the virtues of appearance while shearing off the longer sections of Lucien's hair. The scissors cut especially close to the sides of his head, laying bare his disfigurement for all to see. Lucien sat, not hearing the words only the steady steely scrape of the metal blades. His upper lip curled with hatred. A single tear tracked down his cheek before hitting his chest, now covered in slivers of coarse black hair.

He'd expected this. And Giancarlo was more thorough than he had been the time before, taking his time to shear every lock

'Now, Lucien. Now you are ready to fight. Like a man, I would hope, rather than a boy masquerading as a woman.'

All the adepts and novices laughed at that. All except Golia, who simply looked bored. If any emotion crossed his features then it was one of irritation. D'arzenta caught Lucien's eye and nodded almost imperceptibly. Lucien dried his eyes on the sleeve of his jacket and felt a calm descend on him.

They'd spent many hours training for this.

The *maestro superiore di spada* and the student took their positions, Giancarlo strapping a shiny buckler to his left forearm, just as he'd done before. He gave Lucien a fencer's salute, a mocking grin fixed on his tanned face. Lucien caught sight of his own reflection in the surface of the buckler. His black hair had been ravaged completely. When offered a shield of his own, Lucien flicked fingers from beneath his chin, glowering at the novice who held it.

'Well, well, it seems your etiquette is the equal of your swordplay, Lucien,' sneered Giancarlo. 'Perhaps I can carve some manners into you.' Another round of laughter from the boys, and then the fight began.

Giancarlo opened with very basic attacks, smiling as Lucien threw up the correct parries and ripostes. Lucien pressed in, only to be turned aside by the buckler. The sight of his reflection drew his eye, the distraction costing him a slash across the ribs, ripping fabric but not the flesh beneath. Giancarlo grunted in satisfaction, then renewed his assault, thrusting at the Orfano's chest. Lucien struggled to turn the blade aside in time, feeling the point score him deeply. His shirt became damp, but he couldn't tear his eyes from the *superiore* to see how much blood he was losing.

'Perhaps now is a good time for you to quit, Master Lucien?'

The pack of novices brayed and heckled, cheering on Giancarlo. A few dared to boo before finding themselves sent out by D'arzenta.

The pain of his wounds called out to Lucien – an irresistible song but not one of defeat. One of fury. The Orfano launched a series of deft strikes, slashing high, low, high, low, thrust, altering the tempo of each attack as he went. His gaze was fixed on the *superiore*, no longer daunted by his reflection. Giancarlo's mocking expression changed to one of surprise, then concentration. All eyes followed the fighters, every breath in the chamber baited. The *superiore* batted aside a thrust with the buckler, managing to parry the following strikes. He'd given ground and was backed up against the far side of the circular room. A cruel smile stole over Lucien's lips; the watching novices were silent, ashen-faced and incredulous.

Then Giancarlo counter-attacked, wiping the smirk from Lucien's face, threatening to disarm him. A few of the adepts glanced at each other, knowing full well the *superiore* was using moves far above Lucien's syllabus. The Orfano fell back under the onslaught, throwing up parries where he could, dodging back when he couldn't. Then Giancarlo's blade snagged Lucien's forearm, opening a shallow cut. The Orfano stifled a curse and retreated, the biting sting all too familiar. Giancarlo had height advantage, reach advantage, and was undeniably stronger. He was all but implacable. Lucien surrendered more and more ground to the *superiore* until there was nowhere left to go. The wall was at his back, just inches away.

Giancarlo grinned, hefting his sword above his head, bringing it down like a hammer strike. The novices gasped. Giancarlo had disarmed Lucien. Worse still, the Orfano's ceramic blade had fractured as he had parried. The weapon tumbled from numb fingers, shattering on the granite floor, breaking apart in three distinct shards of polished black.

Across the chamber D'arzenta pressed one fist to his mouth. The students were rapt, keen to see the pale blood of the Orfano spilled. Giancarlo stepped in smoothly, kicking Lucien's feet out from under him, shoving him down onto the polished floor of the training chamber with the buckler. Adepts and novices around the chamber winced, jeered or gestured with down-pointed thumbs. D'arzenta looked on with narrowed eyes. Giancarlo could have stopped there, his point made, his victory assured.

But he pressed on.

Lucien had been expecting all of this – the stool, the scissors, the rampant unfairness. He'd expected to be barged to the ground by the larger man. Expected Giancarlo's blade to open his flesh.

Giancarlo swept the blade down at the supine boy, eager to add to his scars. And his shame.

Instead the sword chimed like a bell, blocked by a thick steel dagger. Lucien had smuggled the forbidden weapon under his jacket, fully aware he would be failed for using it. It barely mattered. Giancarlo's eyes widened in confusion, then narrowed in contempt.

'Orfano are not permitted to bear steel weapons. I'm failing you.'

Adepts and novices around the chamber stared open-mouthed. Giancarlo withdrew and sheathed his sword.

'And I will petition for your exclusion from further lessons. Such disobedience will not be tolerated.'

The boys on the dais were caught up in a frenzy of whispering, incredulous that such a thing should occur. D'arzenta stepped down and began to protest in a loud voice. Ruggeri endeavoured to silence the students. Lucien wanted to mash his fist into every face of every one who had dared to laugh at him. But most of all he wanted to hurt Giancarlo. He wanted him dead. The chamber was filled with the sound of outrage and disbelief; only Lucien remained close-mouthed, consumed with fury at being cast out from his lessons at House Fontein.

Three great detonations sounded, silencing everyone.

All eyes turned to the balcony above, where the Domo stood.

'This is no testing at all,' said the ancient steward. 'There will be no expulsion.'

'You don't dictate to m—'

Giancarlo was cut off by another impact of the staff, booming from the floor of the balcony. It were as if the Domo had summoned thunder.

'I *will* dictate as the king sees fit, you will carry out the king's wishes, or I will find someone else who can.'

Giancarlo looked up at the Domo, impotent with fury, then swung a hate-filled gaze at Lucien. The Orfano approached, closing with the *superiore* until only a hand's width separated them.

'*Vai al diavolo*,' whispered Giancarlo.

'You first,' replied Lucien, 'and don't even think about cutting my hair again, you piece of shit.' These words loud enough for Giancarlo's ears only. Deathly quiet filled the space, dense like smoke. The students were aghast, some blinking, others open-mouthed in surprise, gaping like landed fish. Golia grunted something. He pushed past the smaller boys, shouldering through the larger ones, exiting through the door at the back of the chamber. Some flinched, others swore, all called after him with angry bravado.

Lucien looked up at House Fontein's novices and spared a look at the balcony. The Domo had departed as silently as he'd arrived. And then the Orfano was gone, sweeping out of the training chamber, kicking the doors open as he went.

One year later he'd do the very same thing at *La Festa*.

13

Master Esposito

THE EASTERN ROAD

– Febbraio 315

Lucien had not known about the road that ran behind the cemetery until the moment he broke free of the weeping willows. He hoped the road led somewhere useful, or at least somewhere less dangerous. He ran, feeling the weight of the saddle pressing down on his shoulder, the sack of food slapping and catching on the back of his leg. He was struggling to believe his luck could turn quite so sour. Losing his horse had been unthinkable, being discovered by the Majordomo even worse.

The two soldiers gave chase in a half-hearted manner. The lower orders of House Fontein were far from specimens of physical perfection, more given to standing and glowering than hunting down enemies of the king. Red-faced, the men floundered and collapsed under the weight of their weapons and armour. They would undoubtedly return to Demesne, pretending they'd not seen Lucien. Better this than admitting their failure to Giancarlo.

Lucien had escaped. Or so he thought.

He pressed on along the road, grey sky unremarkable, the wind tugging at his coat and teasing his hair. The landscape rolled to the horizon, undulating in gentle swells, hedgerows and sturdy stone walls edging the fields. Here and there a cluster of cypress trees broke the panorama. Lonely farmhouses wheezed chimney smoke into the sky. Lucien set his mind to the walk ahead, ignoring the chill that crept through his bones.

Lucien was unsure how many hours passed, only that his legs grew more weary. Then two dots appeared on the horizon behind him, quickly joined by a third. They were undoubtedly from Demesne. Lucien pressed on, resisting the urge to look back over his shoulder. He walked calmly so as not to arouse suspicion. Small chance of that, he decided. Few folk in all of Landfall owned saddles. Fewer still wore blood-spattered raincoats. He surrendered to the need to see his pursuers and turned. Mud rose behind them, kicked up by horses approaching at a gallop. Definitely three of them now.

A cluster of buildings lay ahead, just a few miles out of reach, snug in a gentle depression. Blue-grey smoke dissipated above thatched rooftops. It looked peaceful, as if the inhabitants might still be at their rest. Lucien envied them their cosy beds and their quiet lives.

The horses were audible now, their hooves beating a subdued thunder on the track, the sound pressing against the back of his skull. If he were anyone else he could at least attempt a bluff, to claim he was a blacksmith or an artisan on his way home. As an Orfano he was immediately recognisable. Anonymity was the province of other people.

Closer now, so close he could think of nothing else but being trampled. Iron-shod hooves smashing his ribs and snapping his spine. He wondered if they would even try and apprehend him, or simply choose to cut him down as they rode past. It would be the work of seconds. They could drag his corpse back to Demesne and parade it in front of Giancarlo. They'd be rewarded with promotions, favoured with positions for life. The tension increased, balling his hands into fists, his throat becoming dry. He dared himself not to look over his shoulder.

Keep walking.

The drumming of hooves.

Keep. Walking.

The first rider shot past him, the horse skidding to a halt, then rearing up on hind legs. It was lathered in sweat and steaming in the chill air. The rider looked back at Lucien and grinned spitefully. He nodded to his companions, who remained behind Lucien, their pace slowed to a trot.

'Lucien "Sinistro" di Fontein,' crowed the rider, some jackass nobleman who had forgotten his origins, adopted a few years earlier from a minor house and now a favourite of House Fontein. He fairly reeked of braggadocio and self-assurance, twenty years old and reputed to be a capable swordsman. Lucien had pointedly refused to learn his name. Not much of a victory, but Lucien would take what he could get.

'What do you want, you odious horse cock?'

Perhaps the swordsman thought Lucien would turn himself in without a fight, cowed by being outnumbered. He was in for a bitter disappointment. Lucien relished the chance to serve it up to him.

'Superiore Giancarlo demands that you return to Demesne this instant. You are to stand trial for arson at the request of House Erudito, and also for the killing of Viscount Contadino's horse.'

'Well, that's difficult,' replied Lucien.

'Why so?' said Horse Cock.

'Well, firstly, I'm an Orfano. Strictly speaking, I don't take orders from anyone. I acquiesce at my discretion.'

'What does "acquiesce" mean?' grumbled Horse Cock, now thoroughly aware the conversation had slipped from his control.

'It means I do what I like, when I choose to. Only the king and the Majordomo can command me to do anything. And then only directly. Perhaps if you'd spent longer at your etiquette lessons you'd know this. Now, the second reason I can't come back to Demesne is because I'm outcast.'

'Outcast or not, Superiore Giancarlo has ordered it,' croaked Horse Cock.

'That really doesn't sound like my problem,' said Lucien, enjoying himself immensely.

'But Superiore Giancarlo—'

'Can go fuck your mother for all I care.'

Horse Cock bristled. He nodded to one of his companions. It stood to reason he was too much the snivelling coward to take action himself. Lucien heard the grate of metal on metal, the unmistakable sound of a blade rasping from its sheath. He turned, flung the saddle he carried into the face of the chestnut mare which had approached close behind him. The beast floundered to one side and staggered, confused. The rider struggled to exert control, curses escaping his lips as he pulled on the reins. Lucien followed up, stepping in on nimble feet. He had to get the timing exact or he could expect to lose his head. At the very least he'd be struck in the face. The rider had already committed to a downward slash, blade descending. Lucien stepped in closer, the smell of horse, leather and oiled weapons strong in the air.

This was the telling moment. It all hinged on this one desperate gamble. His wounded shoulder protested, but he was only dimly aware of it through the intoxicating flood of adrenaline. Reaching up with both hands he caught his attacker's wrist, twisted his body and heaved with every ounce of his strength. The rider sailed over his head, then clattered to the ground along with his blade. The chestnut mare fled back along the road at a mindless gallop, free of its burden. Horse Cock and the remaining rider drew blades, wheeling their mounts. Shock was now etched onto faces that had borne arrogance just seconds before. Lucien stamped on the fallen rider's head, snatching up his blade from the road in a heartbeat. He felt the strange weight of metal and its promise of death; no longer would he be contained by the fragility of a ceramic blade. A surge of excitement ran down his spine and he switched his concentration back to his opponents. They were swearing and cursing him loudly.

Lucien realised he was laughing and tried to stop himself.

The first of them, he was unsure which in the chaos, trotted in and swung a blade. He ducked beneath the flashing steel, remaining low, then spied an opportunity. Lucien lined up his strike, taking a moment to dodge the pounding hooves. There was a split second he was afraid he might eviscerate the beautiful white mare, but his training and concentration held fast.

The deed done, Lucien dived forward, rolling and rising to his feet in one smooth motion, sword held in a reversed grip. The riders turned their mounts, trying to avoid trampling their unconscious companion. Horse Cock advanced shouting incoherently, blade held high. Spittle flecked his lips and rage lit him from within.

And then the nobleman slid off his mount, saddle and all, landing with a stifled yelp.

Lucien sniggered and flourished his new sword.

'How the mighty are brought so low. A tragedy.'

Cutting the broad leather strap that buckled under the horse's stomach had been a master stroke. The mount, now free of its overbearing master, trotted to the side of the road and began to nibble on the grass.

Horse Cock stood on shaking legs, sucking down air into reluctant lungs. The fall had winded him badly. He stooped to retrieve his sword. Lucien watched him and waited, affecting boredom.

'You *streghe*. You think you're so much better than everyone else, better than us,' spluttered Horse Cock. 'Well, I'll give you a lesson that pathetic D'arzenta never could.' He charged toward Lucien, fury written across his face, quickly changing to confusion and frustration. Betrayed by a twisted ankle, he was off balance and he knew it. The parry he threw up was weak and after the fact. His head was separate from his chest before he even hit the ground.

Lucien had barely moved.

The corpse shuddered slightly and lay still except for the viscous throb of fluid jetting out of the neck. Crimson pooled on the muddy track. The remaining horseman stared at the corpse of his fallen companion and grew pale. The hand holding his blade shook, and it looked as if he might drop it. Lucien flicked his new blade to one side: a trio of red droplets spattered the road. He cleaned the dull metal, feigning disinterest in his last opponent.

'Tell the *superiore* I am Lucien 'Sinistro' Esposito from this moment onward. If he wants me back at Demesne he can come and find me himself. Tell him to stop sending errand boys. And tell him he'll have to kill me before I attend any charade of a trial.'

The horseman nodded mutely. Awkward seconds passed, and he turned his horse, trotting off the way he'd come. Lucien watched him recede into the distance, disappearing around the trees. Finally he was alone again on the dirt road with only the clouds for company. It was then the adrenaline left him – he almost staggered with the intensity of it. Something was wet inside his sleeve. A surge of panic and he was shrugging off the coat, fighting down the crawling sense of unease. The pain in his shoulder increased its pitch. His shirt was wet with clear blood, now turning light blue. He felt faint, darkness crowding the edges of his vision. The stitches had torn during the fight, the decapitation costing him deeply. It had been an attack born of instinct, but ultimately unnecessary. Now he was left with the painful consequences.

He sat down at the side of the road and stared at his boots, willing himself to get back up. His vision wavered.

Then came the darkness.

It was the rain that saved him. The cool drops returned him to the conscious world. He ran his tongue over wet lips and let out laughter verging on hysterical. Standing was its own unique torture, his limbs all fighting to cramp at once. He struggled to attach Virmyre's saddle to the white mare, which had miraculously remained nearby. The creature was a docile sort. Lucien wondered if the mount could sense his desperation and had decided to give him an easy ride out of pity. He collected up the sack of food and both the swords. He then stole Horse Cock's jacket because it was a fashionable cut and he couldn't help himself.

'Some habits die hard,' he muttered as he struggled to pull the garment from the headless corpse. The other fallen rider chose this moment to wake up and stifled a sob. Lucien reckoned the swordsman had broken his collarbone judging by the way he gasped, cradling his arm to his chest. Lucien walked over, helping him to his feet roughly. The swordsman winced but remained standing. They stared at each other for a few moments, Lucien well aware of his opponent's injury. He hoped he looked more threatening than he felt. He could ill afford another fight.

'Your horse ran off,' said Lucien, indicating the road behind them. 'You'll need to walk back.' He returned to the white mare and threw the looted jacket over the front of the saddle.

The swordsman stared at him as if he were unhinged. His expression blossomed into fully fledged horror as he recognised his friend lying in the road. The head lay off to one side, gawping at the horizon.

'Don't kill me,' whispered the broken man. 'I'm unarmed. You wouldn't kill an unarmed man, would you?'

Lucien threw the man his sword, pommel first so he could catch it. An action the noble bungled spectacularly. He stooped to retrieve the blade from the road, crying out in pain as he did so. Lucien guessed the break must be grave indeed. The rain continued to fall and Lucien wondered where he'd find Rafaela. He'd never learned where she lived, aware of her faint embarrassment when the subject arose. He turned to find the swordsman brandishing his weapon and raised an eyebrow in response.

'Go home. I'm done with killing people today. I gave you the sword back as a mark of respect, not that you deserve it.'

The swordsman didn't flinch.

'I have orders,' said the man in a pleading tone.

'I said go home. You've broken something. Even Giancarlo can't punish you for that.'

The man was wet through now, scarlet and black tabard no more than wet rug. His hair was plastered to his forehead, rain running into his eyes.

'You should probably get Angelicola to look at your shoulder,' said Lucien before mounting the white mare. He took care to haul himself up with his good arm, gritting his teeth through the pain. The swordsman continued holding his *en garde* position. Lucien couldn't be sure but thought his lips were turning blue.

'You're an idiot. Go home before the pneumonia is on you.'

He turned the horse, heading away at a trot, the stolen sword a satisfying weight on his hip.

The day ebbed away as the motion of the horse attempted to lull Lucien to sleep. He'd never taken to riding, but the previous night's lack of rest and his injury conspired to make him drowsy. He rode on. The wind and the rain leached the warmth from him until he could barely keep his eyes open. Soon it was all he could do to stay upright in the saddle. He dismounted with care, but his legs gave out as his boots found the road. Suddenly he was staring up at the sky, a sky flecked with winged black shapes high above. His eyelids pressed down, seductively heavy.

14

The Rosewood Box

THE GREAT HALL OF HOUSE FONTEIN

– Ottobre 310

A year had passed since Giancarlo had been publicly humiliated by the Domo. Lucien's slashed forearm had scarred nicely, the wound across his ribs almost faded. Only his hair had failed to return in a suitable fashion. While not short, it failed to hide the puckered holes of his ears sufficiently. He'd grown taller since turning twelve that year and additional lessons with the blade had put wiry meat on his bones. Camelia was forever bringing extras to his apartment 'seeing as you're shooting up now'. He was glad of the food, and the company, ravenous for both in equal measure.

The last two weeks had perhaps been the happiest of Lucien's life. This year, for the first time ever, he had passed his testing with a respectable mark. Ruggeri had been the lead examiner, and for reasons known only to himself had passed the hapless Orfano. Lucien couldn't be sure if he'd warranted the pass on his own merits, or if Ruggeri was playing politics. D'arzenta assured him of the former, although Lucien was aware of rumours that indicated otherwise. Rumours that centred on the influence of the Domo.

La Festa had begun well enough that year. Lucien had expected whispers and stares to follow him and had not been proved wrong. Demesne had spoken of little else since the Domo's intervention. Many wondered if Lucien had been singled out for some special attention. He enjoyed the notoriety and was content to leave everyone guessing. The *superiore* stood in the corner of the House Fontein hall, sharing quiet asides with his duke. Golia lurked nearby, larger than ever in his fifteenth year. Lucien wondered if the older boy would ever stop growing.

Rafaela appeared through the crowd, a new shawl of turquoise pulled about her shoulders. Her hair fell in loose ringlets about her face, a hint of blush on her cheeks.

'Are you enjoying it?' he asked.

'I find all this tiresome, to be honest,' she replied, not taking her eyes from the room full of guests. 'The staff work flat out for three days, all so the courtiers and *nobili* can enjoy themselves for six hours. If you can even call it that.' She sighed irritably. 'Look at Lord Contadino. He looks as if he'd rather be mucking out the stables.'

'Maybe he would. The stables are less full of dung than some of this lot.' He flashed a grin, and Ella gave a disapproving shake of her head, failing to stifle the smile that crossed her lips. Now nineteen, she had passed the threshold of adulthood, leaving him to feel small and ridiculous, longing to be older.

'I see you've worn your blade,' she said, a further hint of disapproval in her tone. He'd worn it in spite of etiquette. The year had been peppered with ugly fist fights, usually during lessons at House Erudito. And knives had been drawn one night when he'd been returning from the library.

'Well, you never know who you'll meet,' he replied, 'and we are in House Fontein. Not exactly friendly territory.'

He didn't trust any of Giancarlo's students, knowing full well they might corner him and seek satisfaction. A few of them leered over at Rafaela, lascivious as they were obvious. Lucien felt the urge to call them out.

'Ignore them,' she murmured.

'They shouldn't behave like that.'

'No, but then you don't always behave well either.'

'True, but it's never at your expense.'

She smiled at him. 'Are you going to grow up and be my knight protector?'

He couldn't be sure if she was mocking him, but a smile pushed itself onto his face all the same.

He shrugged. 'Maybe.'

Rafaela stifled a yawn and then made her excuses.

'I have to be up early tomorrow, and I've still yet to get home. Do you think you can keep out of trouble for the rest of the night?'

'Me?' He adopted an injured look. 'Trouble finds me; I never sign up for it.'

Another shake of her head, another smile, and then she turned on her heel and was gone.

Few of the partygoers welcomed him with open arms. Lucien hovered at the edges of conversations. What could he possibly have to say to other children? They didn't train for two hours a day with the blade, only to have sit through hours of tutoring on mathematics, politics, chemistry, poetry, etiquette and so on. The Orfano stood resolutely apart from the nobles' children, not that there was anything mundane about *them*. Every one could recite where they stood in the order of succession. Each knew the old feuds by rote.

Duke Prospero's daughter Stephania stood amid a coterie of fawning hangers-on. She gazed at Lucien from behind her fan, her look neither warm nor disparaging. This in itself was a curiosity, as few in Demesne bore anything less than polarised opinions, especially when it came to the Orfano. She was the image of her mother, with the same proud bearing and olive skin, same abundance of black curls piled atop her head. The girls around her whispered as he looked over. A blonde girl in a green dress said something which provoked laughter, but was quickly silenced by Stephania. Lucien turned away, keen to put distance between himself and the comments. There was no need to hear the insults; he could imagine them all too keenly.

It was then that the mimes entered, made up in white, wearing carnival masks with long noses. There were seven of them, each attired as a noble of the four houses. A rotund man in a toga smiled beatifically over the shoulder of Maestro Cherubini. The head of House Erudito smiled back, masking his discomfort with a gulp of red wine. The mime minced and swooned, tiny swan wings wobbling, a gauche halo above a bald pate. Aides and retainers laughed as the mime imitated the mannerisms of the *maestro*. Cherubini winced with discomfort and absented himself from the room.

Two other mimes were dressed in clothes more fitting for *La Festa del Ringraziamento*, but wore muddy boots and bore turnips. They closed in on Viscount and Viscountess Contadino with a bow-legged gait. Lady Contadino's imitator had thrust two of the bulky vegetables down the front of her gown, which she rearranged, much to the mirth of the bravos who had crowded around her. She curtseyed with faux modesty. Lord Contadino's mime drew a stem of corn from his cap and adopted a fencing posture, earning him an unforgiving glare. It was well-known that Emilio Contadino hated his nickname Prince of Farmers.

If Lord Contadino was irritated then Duchess Prospero was aghast. A man dressed in drag tottered across the hall, a great commotion occurring at his breast. His head was piled high with deep brown rope and sackcloth, a crude imitation of the duchess's own tresses. Halfway across the hall the mime adjusted his costume and two suckling pigs wriggled out, leaving him breastless and deflated. The room roared with laughter, while a fake Duke Prospero, a ruddy-faced buffoon in a powdered wig, bumbled around, bumping into pretty girls.

Duke and Duchess Fontein received an easier ride. Far from being mocked they were actually feted. Their doubles performed an intricate *pas de deux* that involved wooden knives painted silver. When finally the performers finished, Lucien was glad to see the back of them. While he had no love of the ruling families he also disliked public humiliation. A pastime he was all too familiar with.

Lucien's boredom leached the remains of his good humour. He managed to last some thirty minutes of tedious banter and awkward silences. Finally he slunk off to the shadow of a great pillar, one of six holding up the lavish ceiling. Fat marble cherubs hovered above, pathetic wings on their backs decorated in gold leaf. It was from here he watched the party ebb and flow. The chandelier shed amber light onto the assembly below, lords and ladies chatting in their finery, mainly avoiding topics that might revive simmering vendettas. Some were sounding out political marriages or making allies in houses not their own. Aides and staff made free of the wine, making ill-judged amorous advances.

Lucien felt a tug at his sleeve, gentle but insistent. He looked down to see Dino staring up, eyes grey and earnest. He'd seen the boy only rarely since first being introduced to him in the kitchens of House Contadino. The younger Orfano was six now, neither slight nor rotund. There was something familiar about him that Lucien couldn't place. He held hands with a smaller boy, who sucked on his thumb beneath a thatch of straw-coloured hair.

'Hello, Dino. Are you well?'

Dino said nothing, managing a furtive nod. A small grin creased his features, making him look impish.

'And who's your friend?'

Dino grinned but offered no answer.

'Would it be . . . Festo?'

Another nod, but still no reply.

Festo could only be three, and clung to Dino happily, contentment shining in his green eyes. Women nearby clucked and smiled, enchanted by the younger Orfano in their finery. It was then that Lucien noted the wooden sword tucked into Dino's belt, the blade painted silver, the hilt wrapped in fine leather.

'I don't suppose they've started you on your weapons training yet. Whatever anyone tells you, stick with Ruggeri and D'arzenta. Giancarlo's an ass.'

Dino continued to smile. It was then that Lucien noted how long his hair was. Strangely out of fashion for Demesne, not unlike his own hair had been before Giancarlo's shearing. The boy's attention was directed elsewhere, and Lucien followed his gaze. Sure enough, Golia loitered on the far side of the hall, arms crossed over his chest, the broad square of his chin thrust out in silent challenge. Lucien flipped a lazy salute, then ruffled Dino's hair affectionately. He knelt down so he was eye to eye with the younger boy. Festo removed his thumb from his mouth and favoured Lucien with a smile.

'That dullard over there is the most dim-witted Orfano in all of the king's wicked creation.'

Dino giggled.

'If there's one thing you must be sure of, Dino, it is not to turn out like him. Understand?'

Dino grinned and giggled some more, grey eyes now filled with mirth. Festo added his own chuckle to the sound, the act one of imitation rather than real amusement. Across the hall Golia bristled and glowered, aware he was being slighted. Eventually the hulking Orfano busied himself at the buffet table, amassing a plate fit to feed three.

It was then, standing in the shadow of the pillar, that Lucien again noticed Stephania's clutch of girls. They had drawn closer and were whispering among themselves, discussing something salacious, no doubt. They fell quiet when they noticed him staring. So he thought. In fact they had noticed an artificer, who had appeared unannounced.

'Master Lucien.' It was an old man he'd not seen before, bald with pale skin. He had kindly hazel eyes that reminded him of someone. The man was not attired in finery. He wore a leather apron that marked him as a craftsman, a member of House Prospero. Weathered hands with many callouses clutched a rosewood box. It had been polished to a perfect finish. Lucien noticed the craftsman's wooden clogs. They looked especially crude compared to the finely cobbled boots and shoes of the nobles who were gathering around. Lucien felt himself turn ashen. He had no wish to be the centre of attention, and yet here he was again, as if on stage.

'Forgive my intrusion,' the craftsman said in a smoky baritone, 'but I took the liberty of fashioning these for you.' The craftsman opened the box, the lid neatly hinged with fine brass. Lucien's eyes widened and he felt a thrill of surprise run up his spine. He struggled to swallow. Inside the box, resting on scarlet velvet, were two ears crafted from palest porcelain. Lucien shivered and looked up at the craftsman.

'For me?' he managed, his throat thick, regretting the words as they left his mouth. No one else in the room wanted for ears.

'Please, Master Lucien,' the man smiled, 'let me attach them for you.'

Seconds passed as he fixed the prostheses. The artificer was so close Lucien could smell the red wine and old tobacco on him, smell the leather and horsehair, wood shavings too. He didn't mind at all, almost trembling as the ears were attached to his head by means of a soft metal band across the top of his skull.

'The band is almost invisible, hidden by your hair,' whispered the artificer. Finally he stepped back, inspecting his handiwork with a critical frown. A page had appeared with a small looking glass, which he offered to Lucien respectfully. Lucien took the glass with a trembling hand and regarded his reflection. The nobles and scholars around him nodded agreeably. Others simply waited to see his reaction. The room was filled with a hush of expectation.

'I modelled them after my daughter's ears. She's about your age, you see.'

There was a burst of laughter from the bravos.

He had girl's ears affixed to his head – that would take some living down. Older boys in the crowd looked on smugly, while the girls whispered and joked behind raised fans. Duchess Prospero gushed her admiration while her husband nodded his great bald head. Lucien blushed but said nothing, ignoring everyone, concerned only for the reflection that stared back. He looked absurd, of course. The porcelain looked nothing like his skin tone. The metal band that pinched at his scalp looked crude and ugly against his hair.

None of that mattered.

His scars were covered up. Who cared if the ears looked peculiar? It was far better than parading around with scab-red holes on each side of his skull. Lucien shook the man's hand warmly, not wanting to let go. Wanting to hug him despite the gross breach of etiquette.

'Thank you. I'll not forget this. You must tell me your name.'

'Ah, that's not important, Master Lucien, only that you enjoy the work.'

'No, I mean it. If there's anything I can do. I am in your debt, master craftsman.'

'Not a master, but very pleased to be of service all the same.'

Lucien barely had a moment to savour his gift before Mistress Corvo appeared through the crowd, a black-clad revenant. Sour looks in her wake told of her impatient elbows and none-too-subtle shouldering. She clapped her hands twice at the side of her face, staring into the throng, imperious.

'And now,' she glanced around trying to look impish, her rictus-like grin anything but, 'Lucien will dance a gavotte.'

Several boys sniggered openly and were cuffed by the adults present. Lucien looked at the floor, hoping for an earthquake. Mistress Corvo took his hand in her own icy claw, giving further credence to Lucien's theory she might actually be dead. Before he had the chance to object he found himself in the centre of the hall facing Anea. He stared mutely at Mistress Corvo.

'Just like we've practised, Lucien.' The dance teacher grinned, a skull with waxy parchment plastered to it.

Lucien's stomach turned to ice. Anea was just nine. A child. He was being made to dance with a child in front of his peers. Any reputation he'd gained by passing his recent test was about to be diminished by this curious arrangement. They began, nervously pacing through the first steps before finding their confidence. Lucien allowed himself a sideways glance. Anea wore a cream gown featuring a black frill along sleeves that reached her wrists. Not a frill after all, he would realise later, but many loops of soft thread. They quivered with each step and every movement of her arm. Her hair was swept into an immaculate golden plait. She glided across the room with a noble air quite at odds with her age. A cream veil with black gauze covered the lower half of her face, vaguely web-like. Her ears had been pierced since the last time he'd seen her, each bearing a tiny amethyst rose.

'Did you know about this? About dancing with me?' A sullen whisper from Lucien as they faced each other before resuming the steps side by side.

A reluctant nod in reply.

'You could have warned me.'

She shrugged in response and continued gliding through the stately yet intensely boring dance. Lucien managed to get through the routine with only two hesitations and no missteps. He was glad of this at least. He would do well not to displease Mistress Corvo again. The last notes of the music died and Lucien let himself enjoy a sigh of relief.

The sound of polite clapping, then the snag of her sleeve on his epaulette. Her wrist was snared, the angle awkward. She flinched, then panicked, lifting her arm. Her fingers brushed one of the porcelain ears. The metal band had lost some of its grip during the gavotte and the prosthetic fell, hitting the floor with a heartbreaking crack. The room fell silent, save for one gasping girl.

Lucien looked down. The pale ears looked small and pitiful on the polished slate grey flagstones. Neat fractures ran across them, and the lobe of one ear was quite separate. Lucien didn't meet Anea's gaze. He couldn't bring himself to look at her. Instead he slunk out of the jacket, sleeve by sleeve, leaving her still attached to the offending garment. He stalked away, hand gripping the hilt of his blade, knuckles white. The crowd parted, men stifling objections, bravos coughing unkind remarks as he left. Women tottered on heels, stumbled on the hems of dresses in their haste to avoid him. Anea remained in the middle of the room, shocked and shrunk small, an apology frozen in her eyes. Low and mocking laughter came from the back of the hall. This from Golia. D'arzenta rounded on the brute and backhanded him into silence.

Lucien kicked open the double doors with one booted foot. They rattled on their hinges, leaving only Anea's muffled sobs to fill the room. Mistress Corvo flapped about the girl, not knowing what to say, almost stepping on the broken ears.

15

By Ravens Watched

TERMINIELLO FARM

– *Febbraio* 315

Tap. Tap tap.

The sound came like the first raindrops of a storm on a windowpane. Lucien felt the soft darkness dragging him back into the snug folds of sleep. His limbs were leaden, his breathing regular, each intake soothing him back toward unconsciousness. He paid the interruption no mind, the sound seeming far away.

Tap. Tap tap.

The same sound, regular, measured. His eyelids fluttered, a shift of his body, a half-hearted moan. He was blood-warm, a pleasant soporific heat, a welcome change to the late-winter chill he had known for hours. His mind fumbled at the edges of memory – the previous night spent in the mausoleum of the nearly deaf Duke. It seemed ridiculous. Why had he slept there?

Tap. Tap tap.

No rain ever fell with such precision. Shouldn't there be a howling gale to accompany it? Shouldn't there be winds shrieking around weathervanes? His childhood was littered with such nights, yet none were so vividly remembered as the night he'd fled to the *sanatorio*. The night the raven had invited itself to his sitting room.

Tap. Tap tap.

Hadn't he been going somewhere? Hadn't they sent people after him?

Eyes open now, yet heavy with the promise of sleep if not for the insistent noise. He took in the golden interior of the kitchen, oil lantern burning with a flame turned down low. The light was a bulwark against the wintry gloom outside. Knives hung from iron hooks, blades well used and bright from sharpening. A table occupied the centre of the room, four chairs ordered around it neatly, simple and functional. Fire smouldered in the grate beneath a mantelpiece empty of affect or decoration. This was not the Contadino kitchen. Or any kitchen in Demesne.

Tap. Tap tap.

Lucien shifted his gaze to the window. A silhouette of a dark bird greeted him, framed against grey light. He could feel the single corvid eye on him, willing him awake. He looked down and pulled away the thick blanket. Tied tight against the shoulder wound was a new bandage. He lay, supported by threadbare cushions, trying to piece together the last few hours. The hilt of the stolen sword caught his eye, called to him in the silence, scabbard and belt hanging from a hook on the sturdy door. His jacket was folded over a chair. He still had his britches on.

Tap. Tap tap.

The familiar smells of garlic and flour drifted on his senses, bringing with them reminiscences of Camelia. And Rafaela. Lucien swung his legs over the side of the divan, naked feet seeking flagstones. A surge of nausea ran through him from gut to palate as he tried to sit. The room swayed, spun and stilled itself. A grunt of frustration

'Do not be so keen to rush to your death. Stay awhile.' A voice from beyond the nimbus of the lantern cracked like aged parchment.

'I feel terrible.' He wasn't exaggerating.

'We gave you a preparation to fend off the pneumonia. One can't lie in the road with rain on your face without *conseguenze*. And the wound, of course.'

Tap. Tap tap.

The raven spread its wings but did not depart.

'I need to go,' Lucien croaked, throat dry. The nausea had passed now.

'Need. Want. So many never learn the *differenza*.'

'Where—'

'This is better. Where are you? At last the mind awakens.'

He'd tracked the voice to its source, not much more than a bundle of rags occupying one armchair in the far corner of the room. A large bald dome, a slab of a chin covered in whispery grey growth. Eyebrows white and shaggy. Lucien squinted into the darkness.

'Where am I?'

'A mile from where my grandsons found you. You attracted a *grande* audience.'

'Audience?'

'*Corvino.*' The old man nodded his great head in the direction of the window. 'They drew up in a black circle all around you.'

Tap. Tap tap.

'Persistent, no?'

Lucien eyed the raven, which still hunched on the sill, then turned back to the patriarch. His eyes had grown accustomed to the light, revealing more of his host. The face was deeply lined but yet to collapse to time's ravages. The eyes that looked out from it gazed into the middle distance, milk-white and cloudy. His hands were clubs of pale wood in his lap, knuckles overlarge, fingers curled tight.

'What happened to your eyes?'

'They betrayed me a long time ago, along with my legs. I don't suppose you see such imperfections in Demesne. The frailties of the mind safely stored in the *sanatorio*, the physical ones hidden in high towers.'

Lucien looked down at his nails, shiny and black like beetle carapaces.

'There's some would say I'm far from perfect.' He smoothed his hair down over an absent ear.

'Imperfection,' said the old man in his dry-as-dust voice. 'And yet there is one who prizes the Orfani above all things.'

'Perhaps they prize Golia, but not me.' Lucien's mouth twisted with bitterness. 'You found me in the road half-dead. Remember?'

'There are always casualties.'

'What do you mean, "always"?'

'Ah, the young! Always so convinced their problems are

125

unique in nature and unique to themselves. You think Landfall has not seen variations of these events before?'

The patriarch held up his hands and extended his fingers, his palms toward his face. It took him some time. Lucien thought it a strange gesture. It was only when he'd finally extended the gnarled digits that Lucien understood. The man had the same-coloured nails.

'You're Orfano,' breathed Lucien.

'Once. I was much like you. Learning my lessons, learning the *spada*, learning *politica*.'

Lucien had always known there were older generations of Orfano, but the unspoken rule had persisted: one did not ask questions. The past remained unknown. He'd had to make do with snippets and teases of information for so long.

'Tell me, tell me everything.'

'This is good. The mind has truly awakened.' The old man paused and cleared his throat, hands now returned to pale clubs resting in his lap. 'It was different in my time. All of us twins. They said the generation before were triplets, the generation before that quins. We knew we were being trained to rule. Some of us suspected we were destined to lead one of the houses, others hoped to take the throne. The *nobili* knew this. And they despised us for it. They turned each of us against each other, just as the king turned the houses against each other. We were schooled in *vendetta*, obsessed with slights and affronts.'

'How many of you were there back then?' Lucien was rapt, the confirmation of the unsubstantiated was intoxicating.

'Nine. Twins for each of the four houses; House Allatamento had a half-blind runt. No one expected him to last, certainly not the Domo.'

'You knew the Domo?'

'Of course. He was much younger then, but no less devious. He hoped some of the crop would survive to maturity, make a play for power. Some even spoke of marrying into the four houses, but it was not to be.'

'Go on,' urged Lucien.

'Some killed each other. *Duelli* took their toll. We were all half-mad with retaining our honour. *Assassini* came for others, often the knife, sometimes poison. Blood spilled, lives lost. And now you, Anea and Golia begin the same dance, each another step to oblivion. And the *musica*, it grows faster, no?'

'You forgot Dino.'

'No, I did not. He is already dead.'

'You can't know that.'

'He will not survive. It makes no difference.' The old man shrugged.

'He will survive,' grated Lucien, a faint stirring of anger coming alive in his breast.

'If he has any sense he will flee, just as I did. I came to this place when I was sixteen. I married a maid from Demesne; we had *bambini*. Now there are only my two grandsons.'

'Where is the rest of your family?'

'Dead. Of course. Taxed into submission, taken by fevers.'

'Couldn't you call for a *dottore*?'

The man wheezed, his mouth breaking into a bitter curve, cracked lips becoming a sneer.

'You think Demesne cares one shit for the farmer? You are as naive as you are rash.'

'There wouldn't be a Demesne without the people, without farmers.'

'There will always be Demesne.' The old man grunted and his head bowed, thick eyelids covering the rheum of his unseeing eyes. Lucien wondered if he had succumbed to sleep.

'How did it happen?' Lucien sat forward. 'How did you escape?'

'In a wagon. In a barrel on a wagon. I spent the night hiding while fires raged on the upper floors. It was terrible. Everyone was awake, extinguishing the flames. You could taste the panic. The previous Duke Fontein . . .' The old man coughed, sucked down a breath. 'He had five men scour Demesne. By this time there were only four Orfani left. Two died in their beds, the other was run down as he tried to flee the castle. Cut down in the night like a thief. The Domo could do nothing – all his plotting, all his schemes, all his bribes. Nothing. I waited until dawn and chanced on the *compassione* of those who had served me. In the end, *compassione* saved me. It is *compassione* that people do not like to speak of. They think it a weakness. Never turn your back on *compassione*; to do so sends you along a road few return from.'

Lucien remembered his own flight from the castle, the Erudito stables consumed with flames, Viscount Contadino's horse the same. The panic, the sickening feeling of unfolding chaos like a stormy sea. And despite all of this he found he missed the place.

'Do you regret not staying?'

'Many times.' The old man forced a smile, a faded, tired thing.

'Why?'

'The Domo, he offered me a chance, a chance to succeed him.' The old man paused, his mouth remained downturned. A wheeze. 'Imagine the power.'

Lucien nodded. It was a fantasy he'd entertained all too often over the years since the Domo had collapsed in the King's Keep. The voice of the king, the new Majordomo. No one would question him. Pure authority, but at what price? There was something maddening about it, a thought that settled like a bird, sharp beak picking at the thought over and over.

Tap. Tap tap.

'With that power,' the old man wheezed, visibly tiring, 'we would have been rich. Not counting *denari* to buy firewood and going hungry in the winter. That power,' he whispered, 'I could have saved my *famiglia*. Imagine, me the Domo. *Dottori* would have fallen over themselves to attend. My daughter . . .' The words caught in his throat; the corner of one milky eye became wet. The tear tracked down his lined face to be lost amid the white of his beard. 'And now, nothing. The same *patetico* charade. The players change, but the game is always the same. Death and ambition. And for nothing.'

Lucien eased himself off the bed, testing his legs, not convinced they'd bear his weight. He stood, taking a breath, feeling the strength return to him.

'What will you do?' said the old man.

'I don't know. If I go back they'll kill me. If I stay away, they'll kill Dino, Anea too most likely. I need to find Rafaela, stop her from returning.'

'A girl.'

Lucien smiled. 'A girl,' he agreed.

'That was why I left Demesne, to protect a girl,' said the old man, a ghost of smile stealing over his lips.

'I thought you said you hid in a barrel?'

'I did, but in the months that followed many staff that served Orfani disappeared. Some retired to the countryside and were not seen or heard of again. It was only because my staff fled with me they were spared. We all took different names. No one came to look for us. The four houses bury their secrets completely.'

'All the four houses?'

'Only Contadino has some semblance of morality.' The old man shrugged. 'The other three are slick with the blood of murderous pasts. Go now, go to your girl. The other Orfani are not *bambini*, they will defend themselves if they are able. Perhaps in time they will find you.'

'Thank you for finding me, and your kindness,' said Lucien.

'Bah! What are grandsons for if not to bring back scraps from the road?'

'Scraps?'

'You were little more when we found you. An Orfano sleeping in the rain.'

Lucien smiled, just a scrap from the roadside.

'What should I call you?'

'Names?' The old man wheezed out a derisive laugh. 'What are names to the Orfani? A pretty thing to cast aside when we change our allegiances. Names do not interest me.'

Lucien turned up the lantern light and retrieved his jacket from the chair. His vest and shirt lay beneath. He shrugged them on, taking care with his shoulder.

'I'd rather call you by something, else I'll have to give you a name of my choosing.' He crossed to the door and fetched down the scabbard, started looping the belt around his waist. He drew a few inches of steel from the scabbard, reassured by the glint of the blade.

129

'You may call me Terminus. A fitting name. I am the end of my generation.'

'Terminus?'

'Yes. And I would have it that you come back, tell me what happens. Introduce this girl of yours. You will do that?'

'It would be my honour.'

'Good. Go now. And be careful. They have been looking for you.'

It was close to midnight when he finally found the cottage he was looking for. Three times he'd stopped to ask for directions. Once he'd been flatly ignored. The sky had cleared and he was able to guide the mare by starlight to his destination. His shoulder felt stiff, his backside had fared little better. He was bone-tired and famished.

The cottage itself was a single-storey affair; likely there'd be a bedroom in the loft. The roof was thatched and the windows all bore shutters, now closed against the night. No light escaped the dwelling. Lucien hoped he'd found the right place.

He knocked, the sound of his knuckles abrupt and loud in the night. No response. Not even the sound of grumbling and stirring from within. He drew back his fist to knock again and felt the sharp press of metal through his coat in the small of his back.

'How about you hand over that fine sword in its scabbard and then we'll have a chat,' said a voice in the darkness behind him.

'And supposing I don't?' asked Lucien, his tiredness and impatience getting the better of him. 'Do you have any idea—'

The blow was sudden and expert. Lucien sank to his knees and passed out in the mud.

16

The Cataphract Drake

THE CEMETERY

– *Novembre* 310

Lucien pulled his hat down, hoping it might shield him from prying eyes. Ridiculous of course; there was no one on the road to see him. He was wearing a long oilskin coat, like the teamsters had. Stealing it from House Prospero had been fraught with problems but he'd managed. Being only twelve, as he was, the coat was too large, but it served his purpose.

Three weeks had passed since *La Festa*, and there'd been no respite. Whispers followed his footsteps, people abruptly stopped speaking when he entered the room, girls laughed behind their fans. He'd never felt so self-conscious. Night after night he'd cursed his luck, cursed the porcelain ears for shattering, cursed Golia for gloating about it. At one low point he'd even cursed the unnamed artisan. Better to have not had the porcelain ears in the first place than suffer their loss so quickly. He'd wanted to blame Anea of course, but word reached him that she was sick with guilt. She'd spent two days locked in her apartment refusing to see anyone. Finally Professore Russo had gained entrance and persuaded the stricken girl to eat.

Lucien had returned from a lesson with D'arzenta to find broken ears drawn on the flagstones outside his apartment in chalk. The crude graffito had reappeared three days later after he'd scrubbed the floor clean. It was unbearable.

He'd packed saddlebags with some spare clothes, but the burden insisted on sliding from his shoulder. Not having a horse detracted from the disguise. The lack of a cart was also a problem, but he'd set out now and couldn't turn back. He chided himself for a fool and bowed his head against the wind.

'Some teamster I am,' he complained.

Half a sack of pilfered food bounced against the back of his leg. His arm ached from carrying it. He'd been up early to raid the kitchens, making his exit before the staff awoke. He wouldn't be getting under their feet again.

The wind picked up, making his coat snap and flutter. He clamped his jaws shut in an effort to keep his teeth from chattering. His destination was unknown; the desire to put Demesne firmly behind was all he needed. Perhaps they were looking for him already. Guards from House Fontein would be dispatched to check, sour complaints about searching for a spoilt *strega* on a winter's day. His thoughts turned to Rafaela. Instantly he regretted not leaving a parting note. Or an apology for Anea. Suddenly he worried the veiled Orfano would blame herself for his departure. He was so engrossed in musing about his torments and failures he almost missed the ravens.

There were over a dozen, all black as night except for their claws, which were mired in gore. He stared on and tried not gag, the bile in the back of his throat acrid and sharp. A cow lay dead at the side of the road. The carrion was being consumed in steely silence, beaks and beady eyes set fast on the flesh. Lucien wondered why they didn't squabble and fight like gulls. There was an uncanny orderliness about them.

'Better table manners than most of Giancarlo's students,' he grumbled.

Seeing so many of the birds froze him in his tracks. If they could do this to a cow then what was to stop them turning on a twelve-year-old boy?

Lucien shivered and backed away a few steps, resisting the urge to turn back to Demesne. Cypress trees shook, the oaks nearby clutching at the skies with bare branches. Wild grasses bent in the wind, pointing away from the brooding architecture toward the endless patchwork fields and occasional farmstead. He was close to the cemetery. The black gates were wide open, hanging on rusted hinges, taken over by bindweed and ivy. Lucien looked back to the cow, which stared back with hollow sockets. One or two of the ravens glared at him. They hopped forward and cawed, the sound unpleasant and loud on the lonely road.

With few choices, Lucien passed through the cemetery gates. The drystone wall, high as his head, did much to shelter him from the wind. He spent idle moments inspecting some of the more baroque statuary, before sequestering himself in a corner. He was glad to be free of the ravens' belligerent gazes. He could still hear them, calling out in coarse and unlovely shrieks. He imagined them mocking him.

There goes the boy without ears, too scared to pass the Corvidae on the road for fear we feast on his brains. What brains? Perhaps we'll feast on his fears, an abundant crop assuredly.

Small mercy the creatures couldn't speak, Lucien decided.

The morning dragged on as the clouds in their turn were dragged across the grey heavens. The sun was a white smear like a rheumy eye, and the wind continued gusting fitfully. Lucien worried at an apple, taking tiny bites only as a respite from the boredom. He ventured to the gates to discover the ravens still occupied the road. He slung the apple core at them in a moment of pique, earning savage stares. The black birds cawed outrage, flapped but refused to flee. Lucien resumed his position in the corner of the cemetery, resisting the urge to eat something else. He'd been up the whole night worried for his departure, now exhausted he was easy prey to slumber. Sleep overtook him in the deep silence of the cemetery.

The sound of boots crunching crisply on gravel woke him. His fingers were pushed into the warm darkness of his armpits. His feet by contrast were frozen, run through with pins and needles. He looked out from under the tricorn, wondering how to escape. To his surprise and relief Virmyre appeared, clutching a bouquet of lilies wrapped in a piece of black silk. The *professore* was wrapped up for the weather, a formal black riding coat and sombre grey britches making the reason for his presence clear. This was no casual passing. His hair was beset by the wind, whipped up around his crown or falling into his eyes.

Stranded by his own numbed feet, Lucien watched, hoping he might go unnoticed. There were plenty of hiding places, but there was small chance of passing through the gate unnoticed. Virmyre strode through the graveyard, past the unseeing gazes of stony angels, then turned away from Lucien. He picked his way through two rows of headstones before arriving at his destination. He knelt slowly, placing the flowers by the grave with care. Lucien watched, fascinated, curious to know who could inspire such devotion from the taciturn scholar. Virmyre remained kneeling for some time. Lucien couldn't tell if he spoke aloud or paid his respects in silence. The trees ceased their breathy whispering, their respect measured in silence perhaps. A calm descended on the windswept cemetery for the first time that day. Finally Virmyre stood. He turned neatly on his heel, returning to the gravel path. He was almost at the iron gates when he looked up and turned to Lucien.

'Good morning.'

'Good morning, Professore.' Lucien pulled himself to his leaden feet. He used the wall to steady himself.

'Lucien? Master Lucien, is that you?'

'Yes, Professore, it's me.' He tried to take a step forward but his legs disobeyed. He swayed awkwardly.

'Are you drunk, Master Lucien?'

'No, Professore. I fell asleep in the cemetery and my feet have gone numb.'

Virmyre considered this for a second, his hand straying to stroke his goatee.

'Sounds entirely reasonable,' he deadpanned.

Lucien hobbled closer, feeling his cheeks flush.

'And about to start a new career as a highwayman. How exciting. Mind if I join you?'

'Oh no, Professore. I'm not going to be a highwayman.'

'Pity. I could use some excitement.' Virmyre sighed. 'I shall have to remain a teacher then. So be it.'

'I... I suppose you're going to tell me off for hiding in the cemetery.'

Virmyre looked around, taking in the mouldering stones, regarding the tumbledown wall at the rear of the graveyard. The trees overhead resumed their muted conversation.

'Even you can't get into trouble here, Lucien. Unless you've discovered a way to antagonise the dead.'

'No, I wouldn't do that.'

'I'll take great relief in that fact when I shuffle off this mortal coil.'

Lucien felt increasingly ridiculous in the oversize coat. The wind snatched his tricorn from his head. He flapped about awkwardly before reclaiming it. They stood unspeaking as the wind continued to snare and pull at their coats.

'Who were the flowers for?'

'My wife,' said Virmyre. 'She died some time ago. Today is her birthday. I . . . always come. You must think me foolish.'

'No, no,' blurted Lucien, but in truth he was unsure what to think. 'I don't know any dead people.'

'I don't advise it. They're terrible conversationalists.'

For a second Lucien thought the *professore* might smile, but he gave a sly wink instead.

'How would you like to continue this conversation on the way back to Demesne? I'd rather not catch my death of cold visiting the cemetery. That's a touch too ironic, even for my taste.'

Lucien found himself agreeing. His predicament seemed markedly less bleak with the soothing balm of Virmyre's humour applied to it. And there was the small issue of having no idea where to go nor the horse to get there.

'Seeing as we're not going to be highwaymen, perhaps we can plan a career as pirates? What do you say?'

Lucien snorted a laugh and nodded with enthusiasm.

'We'd best start with a ship.'

'How large will it be.'

'Big enough for two, at least.'

They passed through the gates and Lucien wrinkled his nose at the ravens, still tearing at the fallen cow.

'Gah. I hate those wretched things.'

'Really?' Virmyre regarded the corvids. 'I find them fascinating.'

'But look at what they're doing.'

'Not a sight for the faint of heart, I'll grant you. I've not seen them eat carrion before. How curious.' Virmyre sniffed.

Lucien turned his back on the grim spectacle and they walked at a steady pace toward the grey bulk of Demesne. The *sanatorio* haunted the castle, a sentinel on the road before reaching the destination itself.

'How did she die?' His curiosity gnawed at him.

'In childbirth.' Virmyre clasped his hands behind his back, tucking in his chin. He regarded the road, concentrating on avoiding the worst of the potholes. The wind shrieked around Demesne and Lucien willed himself to stop asking questions.

'Couldn't Dottore Angelicola help?'

'He was unavailable. There was urgent business in the *sanatorio* that night.'

'I'm sorry.'

'These things happen,' said Virmyre. He looked away to the horizon.

'Do you ever wish you could just forget?' asked Lucien quietly. 'Forget painful things, I mean?'

Virmyre considered this for a while.

'Pain is a great teacher, Lucien. If you encounter pain, and remember that pain, then you stand a chance of avoiding it in future.'

'I wish I could forget about *La Festa*. And Giancarlo.'

'Some things can't be avoided.'

'Perhaps I'll invent a medicine that makes people forget things.'

'That already exists, Lucien. It's called wine.'

'No, I mean really forget.'

'What happens when you meet someone who can remember the thing you've forgotten?'

Lucien looked crestfallen. 'They remind you of it, I suppose.'

'Exactly. The truth has a habit of coming to the fore, even if we wish otherwise.' Virmyre looked up from the road and regarded the castle a moment before turning to his pupil.

'A rumour persists that there is a dungeon beneath Demesne, a dungeon where the water is knee deep. People say if the prisoners drink the water they lose all trace of their memory.

After enough time, and enough water, the prisoners even forget their identity, becoming dumb beasts.'

Lucien said nothing, chewing his lip.

'I sometimes wonder if House Fontein spend a few days in there each month.'

Lucien sniggered but kept his silence.

'Perhaps the Majordomo will throw you in this fabled oubliette, if you ask nicely.'

'I hope not,' mumbled Lucien. 'I'm not keen on the dark.'

'Few are.'

'Besides, I don't want to forget everything.'

'Then you must learn to not dwell on the past, as I have done.'

They continued up the road, anxiety fraying Lucien's nerves.

'Will I be in much trouble when we return?'

'I don't see why.' Virmyre glanced down at Lucien from the corner of his eye. 'You came with me to the cemetery. I was paying my respects to my wife. You offered to carry the flowers. I forgot to inform Rafaela. The trouble will rest on my shoulders. That's how it happened. Yes?'

'Ah. Yes, Professore.' Lucien smiled.

'Quite. Of course you'll need to lose that ridiculous outfit. But I can't be responsible for solving all your problems.'

Virmyre circled Demesne, taking Lucien in through the House Erudito courtyard. They disposed of the coat and saddlebags in the stable and made their way to Lucien's apartment.

Dino, Festo and Rafaela were standing in the sitting room chatting excitedly. A long glass case sat on a low table made from mahogany. On the floor of the case was a layer of sand three fingers deep. Driftwood occupied one end of the case, and a lizard perched on it with a haughty look.

'Lucien. There you are,' said Rafaela. We've been looking everywhere for you.' There was a flicker of annoyance in her eyes before she realised Virmyre was with him.

'He was quite safe, I can assure you. We took a walk around the castle.'

'Where did the reptile come from?' asked Dino.

'Drake. It's a cataphract drake,' supplied Virmyre. 'I heard about what happened at *La Festa del Ringraziamento*—'

'It's nothing,' said Lucien. 'I was ... I acted badly.' He shrugged and chewed his lip, thinking of Anea.

'Well, in any case, I thought you could use something to take your mind off the whole wretched business. And you're old enough to have a pet now.'

The *professore* reached into the tank and lifted the drake. The creature coiled itself, staring at Lucien from black-within-brown eyes as it gripped its tail between its jaws. The head was a blunt wedge, the body covered in armoured scales of dark olive and dun brown.

'He's currently curled in a loop to protect his soft underside. It's a defence mechanism. They're rather far down the food chain, but they've become adept at protecting themselves from larger foes. Myself in this demonstration.'

'I wish I could curl into a loop,' exclaimed Dino.

'Well, eat your vegetables, train hard, and anything is possible,' replied Virmyre.

'Loop,' repeated Festo and resumed sucking his thumb. Lucien laughed. It was the first time he'd done so since *La Festa*.

'What do they eat?' asked Dino breathlessly.

'Mainly worms and insects,' supplied Virmyre.

'Oh, that's disgusting.' Rafaela wrinkled her nose.

'Clearly you've never dined at House Erudito,' he replied.

'D'gusting,' added Festo and nodded with a grave expression on his cherubic face.

'Of course you'll need to feed him,' said Virmyre. 'I have some dead crickets. Or you can catch live ones, if any remain at this time of year.'

'Excellent.' Lucien grinned.

'Excellent,' repeated Dino.

'Crickets!' exclaimed Festo.

The *professore* lowered the drake into the glass tank, regarding the coiled creature a moment with unblinking eyes. Lucien pressed his nose to the glass. Gradually the drake straightened out, revealing itself to be around a foot long, perhaps a few inches more.

'He's amazing,' whispered Lucien, smiling at Virmyre. 'Thank you.'

'I'm glad you think so.' The *professore* straightened up and clasped his hands behind his back, suddenly looking very formal. 'I've written a list of instructions for you. You'll need to pay close attention. And you'll need to keep him warm. It's a good thing your room is south facing. Now I must take my leave.'

Rafaela left not long afterwards, taking the younger Orfani with her. Lucien watched them depart and turned back to the drake, speaking to it in hushed tones like a long-lost friend.

17

Blunt Questions

THE CONTADINO ESTATE

– *Febbraio* 315

'I tell you, they took the wrong one. Then they sent someone back for Sal.' The voice was gruff and spoke in the old dialect. It was the voice of a farmer, grizzled and sure, sounding not more than thirty years old to Lucien's ears.

'We can't know that for sure.'

'Leave this to me. I'll fix him. He'll sell his own mother to crawl out of here alive. *Figlio di puttana.*'

Lucien was bound, arms behind his back, ankles secured to the legs of the chair he was sitting on. A sack had been placed over his head, which let in vague light, nothing discernible. His head throbbed at the base of his skull; his shoulder joined in, complaining bitterly. Mud encrusted his face where he'd fallen in the yard, his mouth was dry and gritty with the taste of earth. The room smelled of woodsmoke, a faint tang of sweat underneath it. Lucien drew in a shuddering breath, trying to force the pain out of his mind.

'He's awake,' said the second voice. Older, perhaps wiser, this voice was more measured than the first. It would be this man that kept him alive. Lucien heard them approach, just a few steps, boot heels on floorboards. His captors could afford footwear at least.

'Where is she then, eh?' This from the younger man, who stood over him very close. Beer on his breath, cheap courage from a small barrel. A large shadow loomed beyond the gauze of the sackcloth.

'I'm sorry. I don't know who you mean. Look, about the sword. I realise I was being rude. You surprised me and—'

'Ah, sounds like we've got one of Demesne's dandies. Not so clever now, eh, your lordship?'

'Actually I'm not a duke; I'm an *Or*—' He didn't finish the sentence. A fist clubbed him across the jaw, snapping his head to one side. The chair tipped and tilted, then settled again with a scrape and rattle.

'*Porca troia!* You've got a smart mouth. Shame you're tied up, eh? Not so funny now, my friend, eh?'

'Where were you last night?' The other voice now, the older of the two, off to his left. The reasonable one, he hoped.

'I slept in the graveyard.' Another strike. His bottom lip split, a bright pinprick of pain. He felt blood drip down his chin.

'He asked you a question, funny man. Where did you sleep last night?'

Lucien felt his head spin and struggled to breathe a second. The truth sounded ridiculous to him, but it was all he had.

'I was made outcast. They threw me out of Demesne. There was a fire. I had nowhere else to go, so I slept in the House Prospero mausoleum.'

There was a pause as if they were weighing each word.

'This could take a long time,' said the elder.

'I can keep this up all night,' said the younger, mock cheerful. There came the sound of knuckles popping and cracking. Lucien strained at the ropes on his wrists. He was tied fast.

'Tell us about this graveyard then,' said the younger.

Lucien reached for the words, knowing they sounded untrue 'It was very cold. When I woke this morning I saw a fire in the woods. An Orfa— a man had stolen my horse and was eating it. He showed me a secret graveyard, behind the cemetery.'

'He's either mad or simple,' said the older voice.

'The secret graveyard was full of Orfano graves. However, that's just incidental. I was made exile and Professore Virmyre gave me his horse.'

'He's lying, eh?' said the younger. 'His horse wasn't ate; he rode in on that white one. Secret graveyards. He's full of it.'

'I know it sounds far-fetched. I'm having a very bad couple of days. If you let me go I'll help you find your friend, I promise.'

'Find our friend, eh?' roared the younger, '*Buco del culo!* You already know where she is. They've taken her to the castle. Just like they always do, eh? Then they lie about it and say the girl was mad, or the Unquiet Dead got her. It's always the same, and they always lie.'

The next strike wasn't unexpected. The younger man had worked himself up to a fury; the outcome was inevitable. Knowing the punch was coming didn't make it any less painful.

'It's not always the same,' said the elder. 'It's different this time.' And for a second his voice cracked with emotion.

'Let's take a moment,' said the younger. 'Come on. He's not going anywhere, eh?'

Lucien breathed a sigh of relief. Escape was not on the cards, no chance of that, but any reprieve from the beating was welcome. The door creaked and the men's boots scuffed and sounded on the wooden floor, receding, to be replaced by a lighter step. The gentle smell of roses filled his senses. The sack was taken from his head. Lucien blinked several times and found himself looking into the face of an angry blonde girl about his own age. Her eyes were deep brown, red-rimmed from crying. There was something familiar about the curve of her mouth. A heavy woollen skirt reached the thick worn leather of her wood-man's boots. Her bodice was a deep brown over a light green blouse.

'You might get out of this alive if you tell them what they want to know.' This in a low whisper. She grabbed his chin and wiped him down with a rag. The water was cool and welcome. His lips stung and he knew the dull ache in his face would be replaced by bruises of rich purple and black. He could feel the grit and mud being scoured away.

'What is it they want to know?'

'You need to stop being clever.'

'Stop? I'm not sure I ever started.'

She dipped the rag into the water and carried on cleaning him up. 'We know you're from Demesne. Why not just tell them.' There was something about her voice. She was too well spoken to be a farmer's daughter.

'Wait.' He couldn't believe he'd been so stupid. 'Someone's been taken, right? A girl?'

142

'Hardly a girl. My sister, as well you know.'

'Where am I?'

'You know very well where you are.' She scrubbed at his face some more. 'Why are you making this so difficult?'

'I'm looking for the da Costa house. I'm looking for a maid who works at Demesne.'

'That's not funny.'

'I swear to you. Please tell me where I am.'

The blonde girl glowered at him. Tears sprang to her eyes.

'You've no heart at all. The lies you tell! Better we kill you tonight.'

She stood, her chin thrown out with indignation, then grabbed the bucket of water.

'No wait—' was all he managed before she threw the contents over him. He felt his hair slicken and the final vestiges of mud sluice from his face. He gasped with the shock of the cold water, then there was a moment of silence.

'What did you say your name was?' she asked, voice suddenly calm, demeanor changed.

'I didn't get the chance. We skipped that part to get to the hitting. In the face.'

She grabbed his hair, ignoring his protests, lifting the long tresses where they covered the place his right ear should be.

'Oh, porca misèria,' was all she said.

Lucien watched her leave the room, trying to make his mind work. Something was right in front of him if he could only reach it through the fog of his pain and grasp it. He saw dust gathered in drifts in the corners of the room, firewood piled to his right, a hefty axe leaning against the wall near the door. A woodshed then. He hoped they'd keep hitting him with fists and not resort to the axe.

The two men walked back in. Lucien recognised the eldest immediately. He was bald with hazel eyes and the leather apron of someone who worked with his hands. Someone who worked for House Prospero. The blonde girl followed, her brow furrowed, wringing her hands anxiously.

'You,' said Lucien and the elder in unison, the spark of shared recognition flashing in their eyes.

'What's going on here then, eh?' said the younger. He was huge, barrel-chested, with a broad bat-like face and a snub nose. His eyes were like dull pennies. The barest traces of bruises could be seen on his knuckles, consequence of applying them to Lucien's face. Sandy hair stood out on his skull like stunted corn.

'You're the artisan who made my ears, the porcelain ears, back when I was twelve.' It was true. The elder man was the very same craftsman, his once-kindly eyes now red with grief. There were a good deal more lines on his face, which was paler than he remembered.

'Lucien?' said the craftsman to the girl. He shook his head, incredulous.

'I didn't recognise him with all the mud on his face,' she said, 'but when it came off...'

'Will someone tell me who in nine hells this fop is, eh?' said the younger.

'You've been beating the face of Lucien "Sinistro" di Fontein, you great arse,' said the girl. The man had the sense to pale. Even the workers in the fields of Landfall knew the names of the Orfani. More from fear rather than respect.

'Actually I go by Esposito these days,' said Lucien casually. 'House Fontein declared me outcast.'

'That doesn't mean he's not guilty,' grunted the younger man, 'outcast or no. He might still have done it. He's a *strega*, eh? They get up to all sorts behind closed doors. They say Golia eats live goats, and Anea can cast spells now.'

'Are you even paying attention?' hissed the girl.

'He's a witchling,' continued the man. 'Why are you making excuses for him? He's even more untrustworthy than the *nobili*.'

'Who *are* you?' said Lucien finally, his temper flaring. The cold water had sluiced away the muddiness of his mind. The big farmer made to lunge for him, but the craftsman laid one hand on his chest.

'I'm Raul da Costa, father of Rafaela and Salvaggia.' He indicated the blonde girl, 'who you've already met. And this is my son-in-law Gian.'

Lucien felt the pit of his stomach lurch and the room suddenly became unnaturally warm.

'They've taken Ella,' he mumbled, knowing instinctively he was right. The pieces all fell together at once. Raul and Salvaggia nodded mutely.

'Who is Ella?' said Gian, shuffling his feet.

'Ella. Rafaela. My maid?'

'We thought you were one of them,' said Raul after a moment of silence, 'come back to take Sal. It's always girls of eighteen that are taken. Never women of Rafaela's age.'

Lucien nodded, seeing the sense of it. He was all too aware of which girls were taken. They haunted his nightmares.

'It was your birthday a few days ago,' he said, addressing Salvaggia.

'Day before last,' she replied, her mouth twisting with sadness.

'I was asked to work late at Demesne last night,' explained Raul, 'asked to make more ears for you, they said. On account of you passing your final testing. I see now it was just a ruse.'

'It wasn't your fault, Papa.' Salvaggia laid one hand on her father's arm. The old man shook with anger.

'For God's sake, untie him, will you?' Raul growled. The farmer lumbered forward, busying himself with the rope, thick fingers fumbling at the knots.

'They took her last night,' said Lucien, his voice no more than a whisper. Salvaggia nodded.

'Last night.' He stood up, felt the room pitch slightly and took a moment to steady himself. He winced as pain spiked through his shoulder. Gian gave him a sheepish look. Lucien took a deep breath and exited the woodshed, finding himself in the living room of Raul da Costa.

Ella had grown up here.

It was small. Too small for three grown adults. A table and four chairs crowded together at the centre of the room; a well ordered kitchen was situated at one end. A ladder led up to the loft – he imagine a crowded space divided into two areas, simple mattresses, no beds. A small posy of dried flowers hung on the wall next to the window. A horseshoe hung from the door frame.

Lucien washed his face and inspected his wounded shoulder. In spite of everything it remained resolutely uninfected. He drank a mug of water, then another, feeling his weakness wane.

Salvaggia milled around, not knowing what to do. Gian lurked by the door to the woodshed looking deeply uncomfortable. The sword Lucien had stolen hung in its scabbard from a peg on the cottage door. He drew it and regarded the edge. He hefted the weight of it. So different to the ceramic ones he'd trained with all this time.

'Can you bind this up, please?' He indicated the wounded shoulder. Raul nodded and put a pot of water on the fire. Lucien wolfed down some bread and cheese while he waited for the water to heat up. No one spoke as Raul worked on his shoulder, the tiny cottage desolate with sadness. Salvaggia cleaned his split lip and added a dash of ointment to it.

'It's from Demesne,' she explained. 'Rafaela brought it.'

Lucien stood and shrugged on the jacket he'd acquired. It was a fraction too large across the chest. No matter.

'What will you do now?' said Raul finally, his voice a cracked whisper again.

'There's not much I can do. I have to go back to Demesne.' He belted the sword on his hip and looked at Gian. 'Go saddle my horse – I'll be right out.' Lucien turned to Raul. 'I'm going to get your daughter back.'

'Can I come with you?'

'Can you fight?'

The old man looked at him, a sour turn to his mouth, a single shake of the head.

'That's what I thought. Best you stay here.'

They followed him outside, watching him mount the white mare.

'I'm sorry about the . . . uh.' Gian gestured toward his face.

'Don't worry yourself with it. I'd have probably done the same in your place.'

'What if she's already dead?' said Raul, barely able to get

146

the words out. Salvaggia folded one arm around his shoulders protectively.

'She's not dead,' said Lucien, although in truth he was trying to convince himself. Moments later he was galloping toward Demesne, morning sun staining the sky visceral red as purpled clouds lingered on the horizon. Ravens watched him pass from bare tree limbs, eyes of jet tracking his progress.

18

Crossed Words, Crossed Swords

HOUSE CONTADINO KITCHENS

– *Augusto* 311

Lucien stood in the doorway leading to the kitchens of House Contadino, a mix of emotions surging through him. He'd spent a lot of time standing on this very spot during his thirteen summers. Usually he waited here until the porters were too busy to turn him away, then would accost Camelia, bringing her some bauble or fancy. Other times he sought tasks to keep him from his restless boredom. And his loneliness.

He was yet to form any friendships from his various lessons at House Erudito. The noble's sons were keen to stay apart from him. He'd lost track of the last time he ventured out of his apartment without a dagger concealed in his boot, and two of the *professori* had barred him from lessons for fighting. This had the somewhat negative effect of freeing him to pursue more lessons at House Fontein. The irony was not lost on him. Virmyre refused to eject him from class, even at the cost of losing other students, students with fathers who paid into the House Erudito coffers.

Lucien brooded on this as he stood on the threshold of the Contadino kitchen. The flagstones under his feet had been worn smooth by countless feet spiriting innumerable dishes to the grand hall by numberless waiting staff. Lines in chalk on the door frame marked his increasing height, but he was still a long way behind Golia, now sixteen and fully the size of a man. The top of the doorway arched gracefully to a point, the wooden door itself removed long ago, more nuisance than useful barrier.

Lucien stood, not slouching or leaning as he usually did, but almost hiding, flattening himself against the wall. Staff had downed tools inside the vast but cluttered kitchens to regard Dino with amusement. He was still young enough to escape the prejudices some castle folk had for the Orfani. Lucien furrowed his brow and chewed his lip. He wondered at what point people traded in *bambini* for *streghe*. What act of mental alchemy transmuted feelings of affection into distrust?

Camelia, Rafaela and the staff had crowded around the seven-year-old, admiring his new suit. The jacket and britches were a splendid shade of maroon with a stark white dress shirt and matching tights. A scarf of black was tied at his throat, and the boy's hair had been cut in such a way it remained long but did not look unkempt. Lucien scowled, smoothing down his own hair, which stuck up in all directions. He would need to get it trimmed soon, though the idea of letting anyone near him with scissors was abhorrent. Rafaela was laughing and clapping her hands with delight at some utterance from the younger boy. She was always radiant when smiling, a shimmer in her eyes that was difficult to ignore. Lucien swore under his breath. He simply could not fathom how a seven-year-old could captivate an entire kitchen of people.

'There you are,' said Rafaela brightly, a broad smile on her lips. Lucien tensed. She approached him. Her hair had come undone from her ponytail, loose corkscrews spiralling down each side of her face. Her skirt swished out behind her as she skipped across the room to him. Today she had chosen a demure powder-blue ensemble.

'We were just saying how much he looks like you when you were his age.' She wrapped an arm around Lucien's shoulder, pulling him close, then ushered him into the kitchen. He felt his cheeks flush scarlet.

'It's uncanny really,' said Camelia, favouring each of them with a warm smile. Dino stood in front of her, turning to face Lucien. He nodded, then flipped a lazy salute, adopting a relaxed posture, not quite slouching. Such a pose looked gauche and rehearsed on someone so young. Lucien would know, after all. He'd spent enough time smouldering in front of a full-length looking glass, affecting the same bored insouciance.

Rafaela stifled a laugh behind her hand and exchanged a knowing glance with Camelia.

'Seems they've got more than looks in common,' said Camelia. 'Right, come along. This venison won't roast itself. Back to work.' She clapped her hands twice. The kitchen sprang into life and some of the porters sighed and muttered as they stepped around the elder Orfano. Occasionally one would utter the word *strega* just loud enough for Lucien to hear. Even without ears he had no trouble discerning when he was being spoken about. Or when he was unwelcome.

Lucien resumed his spot by the door and realised Dino was no longer present. Somehow the boy had vanished amid the hustle of cooks and bustle of porters. A messenger entered by the side door, not more than eighteen years old, the same age as Rafaela. He wore House Contadino livery, soiled from the road. His tabard was frayed at the edges. Lucien guessed he'd inherited the garment from his father. Such roles in Demesne were passed down father to son and mother to daughter wherever possible. The messenger looked out of breath, his pallor suggesting he wasn't in the best health. The newcomer beckoned Rafaela close, whispered urgently. Moments later she was gone, hurrying out of the kitchens with the ragged-looking messenger, her shawl thrown around her shoulders in haste, face troubled. Lucien found himself desperate to know what had been said.

Puzzled, he slunk off to his apartment, trailing fingers over the rough stonework of the corridor walls, savouring the abrasion. He practised some exercises Ruggeri had set him before becoming bored. He discarded the blade in its scabbard on the armchair, still haunted by the spectre of the crow. None of the books on the crowded shelves offered him any comfort; the drake dozed in its glass case, and his deck was missing two cards, making any game of *solitario* futile from the outset.

Suddenly, the door to his apartment opened and Lucien leaped to his feet. Two quick steps and he was across the sitting room, curiosity verging on panic. His sword was already out of the scabbard before he'd even registered who stood in the doorway. The tip of the ceramic blade hovered inches away from a startled face

'Rafaela? I thought you were one of Giancarlo's thugs come to cut some new scars into me.' He forced a smile, then returned the blade to the scabbard with a flourish. Rafaela said nothing, hazel eyes downcast, no longer shimmering with amusement.

'What's happened?' he whispered. 'Did that messenger… did he hurt you?'

'No, that was Nardo.' Her mouth twisted, she stepped into the room and leaned against the wall, arms crossed over her stomach.

'Take your time,' he said, stepping close to her, one hand resting on her arm. She was trembling.

'Nardo is the twin brother of Navilia, my best friend. No one's seen her for three days, and House Fontein won't spare more than a handful of guards to look for her.' She sucked in a shuddering breath, and then the tears were streaming down her face as she shook with silent sobs. Lucien stared at her, frozen with surprise, before coming to his senses. He pulled her close without thinking, trying to ignore the warm scent of her hair. Suddenly he was self-conscious. The embrace was an awkward affair; she was still a few inches taller.

'I'll go and talk to the Majordomo,' he said earnestly 'Maybe he can put pressure on the *capo* to send out more men.' He doubted the Domo's acquiescence in light of what he knew. Rafaela nodded and blinked away tears, managing the slightest of smiles.

'Thank you. I'll come with you.'

'Perhaps it's better I go alone?'

She shook her head, one hand still clutching his arm.

The Majordomo had no quarters within any of the four houses and shunned the idea of an office. It was another point of interest on the castle's long list of curiosities: the ancient aide didn't appear to have rooms anywhere.

'Probably so he can't be killed in his sleep,' muttered Lucien.

'What?' asked Rafaela.

'Nothing. I was just thinking aloud.'

Lucien wondered if the Domo lived inside the King's Keep

itself. Perhaps the hooded dignitary haunted the corridors at night, keeping watch over the king's subjects.

They started in House Contadino. The kitchen, the sitting room, the grand hall, the granaries in the courtyard, even enquiring at Lord and Lady Contadino's quarters. In desperation they knocked on Anea's door, only to receive a hastily scribbled *I don't know*, written in her leather-bound book. She flashed angry green eyes at Lucien from above a black veil. She'd barely opened the ancient oak door, peering through the narrowest of margins.

They moved on to House Erudito, where the scholars, Maestro Cherubini in particular, proved unhelpful or simply obtuse. The staff drifted into oft-given lectures on nothing of import before Lucien lost patience. He took Rafaela by the hand, leading her back to the dim circular corridor of the King's Keep. The gate guards made none-too-subtle comments to each other, lascivious and hungry-eyed. Lucien flashed a warning look and the men fell silent.

'Doesn't it bother it you?' asked Lucien, nettled.

'Of course, but it's the rule not the exception.'

'Are there any exceptions?'

'Well, I've high hopes for you.' She nearly smiled but couldn't manage it. He squeezed her hand and she returned the gesture.

Next was House Prospero. Lucien and Rafaela crossed workshops carpeted in sawdust and through sewing rooms, before finding a knot of tailors who revealed the Domo had passed through just recently, requesting the finest seamstresses and tailors for an impromptu fitting.

They located the Domo in the last place Lucien could have ever hoped to go, one of many places he'd never visited in the sprawling edifice. The Majordomo was in Golia's apartment, in the heart of House Fontein. The guards here discarded even the pretence of respect, openly hostile. Two stood outside the apartment, the elder tensing to draw steel as Lucien approached.

'Maybe we should go back?' said Rafaela, squeezing his hand.

'We're here to see the Domo,' said Lucien, his own hand resting on the pommel of his blade in open challenge. The guard weighed his options and nodded for them to enter.

It seemed everyone was in Golia's apartment that afternoon, which made what happened next so much worse. Golia was standing on a low stool, his already looming presence now giant in the centre of the room. Two seamstresses and a tailor fussed around him, obviously irritated. None would give way to the other. They almost fell over each other, intent on their tasks like ravens fighting over a scrap of bread. Measuring and sizing, pinning scraps of fabric here and there, sketching with chalk. They grimaced polite smiles at each other while brandishing sharp elbows.

Mistress Corvo was there, smiling like a grinning skull, smoothing the hair at the back of her neck absent-mindedly with one hand. Her other hand was busy with a fan of stiff black card, odd and coquettish. She was talking to the new *capo de custodia*, who was much too young for the position. It was said his father, while not high in the line of succession of House Fontein, was fabulously wealthy. The new *capo* was famously attractive and had the mental capacity of a goldfish, according to Virmyre, who revelled in such character assassinations. Giancarlo stood to one side, regarding Golia like a fine sculpture. The *superiore* tossed asides to Ruggeri, who looked as if he might well cut his own throat to be spared the tiresome spectacle. Carmine skulked at the back but couldn't mask his boredom.

And there at the back of the room, standing against a wall so as to be out from underfoot, was the Majordomo. His head was more bowed than usual under the hood. Lucien wondered if he'd fallen asleep. The hem of his robe looked more ragged, the *tabaro* on his shoulders more dusty. Even his staff, a sturdy length of oak topped by a piece of amber, looked rough and unvarnished that day. He was a study in atrophy, as if all his years had abraded him. Standing next to the looming Domo, barely reaching the height of his waist, was Dino, still striking in his maroon jacket and britches. The young Orfano's eyes met Lucien's and he nodded gravely.

Lucien strode across the room, brooking no interference from the assorted flunkies. One of the seamstresses squawked and clucked at him. Rafaela trailed in his wake, managing to look both awkward and guilty, tear-stained and exhausted.

'Why in nine hells aren't you sending out more guards to look for this missing girl?' Lucien blurted.

'Lucien!' this from Rafaela, shocked. The room had turned as one to regard the unfolding commotion. The Domo roused himself, a shudder passing through him. A trio of flies took to wing, hovering above his head.

'Lucien?' He cleared his throat. 'What? What girl?'

'Navilia. She's Rafaela's best friend. No one's seen her for days.'

The room was silent now, the atmosphere prickling at skin like a heat rash. One of the seamstresses absented herself, shedding pins as she left. Lucien stared into the face of the old man. The Majordomo's mouth was set in a thin line. Salt-and-pepper stubble days old conspired to make him look particularly haggard.

'I wasn't aware of any missing girl,' said the young *capo*, a sneer etched onto his too-perfect lips.

'It is of no concern,' droned the Domo, phlegmatic.

'It's of concern to me,' replied Lucien, just slightly too loud. He turned to the *capo*. 'Maybe you could see your way to doing some work for a change?'

There was a sharp intake of breath from Mistress Corvo, and Giancarlo stepped forward, but it was Ruggeri who spoke first.

'Lucien, you forget yourself. You may be Orfano but you will give the *capo* the respect accorded to him by his rank.' Lucien held the gaze of his teacher for a few seconds, his brow creased, lips curling to a sneer. Had the rebuke come from Giancarlo he'd already have had his blade out of its sheath. Finally he looked down at his feet.

'Apologies, Capo de Custodia. If you could mobilise additional guards for the search effort I would be indebted to you.'

'There is no need, Guido,' rasped the Domo. 'She has already been missing for sometime. There is no point in deploying more men.'

Rafaela sobbed. Not a soul in the room could have failed to hear it. The tailor and the remaining seamstress stared at their feet, afraid to lift their gazes. Mistress Corvo had retreated behind the *capo*, pouting angrily. Giancarlo bristled, his blood up, but Lucien met his gaze and raised his chin.

The Domo drew himself up to his full height and began to exit the room, indifferent to the tension that swirled and eddied like a rip tide.

'I have matters that need my attention,' he said.

The last vestiges of Lucien's patience dissolved. He found himself holding a fistful of dusty fabric, dragging the Domo around to face him. The larger man stumbled, looking ridiculous as he tottered over the teenager. The wooden staff clattered to the floor.

'This is your work,' hissed Lucien. 'There's conspiracy at work and you're trying to cover it—'

He got no further with his accusation. He was flung bodily across the room into a table. When he staggered to his knees he found his tongue bleeding, adding to his chagrin. Rafaela had also fallen and was likewise finding her feet. Her eyes were dazed and she clutched one arm. Golia stood over both of them, grinning.

Lucien heard himself snarl and rushed toward the older Orfano, his hand going for his blade. Mistress Corvo screeched. The tailor passed out and the seamstress cowered behind the *capo*, clinging to his sword arm and preventing him from drawing his weapon.

Curiously, it was Dino who reached Golia first. The young Orfano charged, clutching a small dagger. Golia swung around, backhanding the boy to the ground with a club-like fist. Dino sailed back from the blow, crumpling in a heap on the floor. He twitched once and then remained still.

Ruggeri was already shouting at Golia to stand down while Giancarlo smiled. Both boys drew their blades at the same instant, Golia unleashing a series of strikes, blade held in both hands, no finesse. Lucien angled his sword to weather the storm, but the intensity of the attacks would not be parried for long. The ceramic blades fractured, then shattered altogether.

With the taste of his blood hot in his mouth, Lucien stepped within Golia's guard, mashing a fist into the larger boy's face.

Golia's head whipped to one side, but the larger Orfano displayed no evidence of feeling the blow.

Suddenly they were surrounded by House Fontein guardsmen, a ring of halberds levelled at them. Two veterans stepped between the duelling teenagers, parting them with shields. Lucien dropped the remnant of his blade with resignation; Golia spat blood on the carpet.

The Domo had left of course, and Lucien had got nothing for his troubles except the sight of Giancarlo's gloating smile. Lucien remained silent as the guards dragged him from the room. There would be consequences for this in the weeks ahead.

19

Demesne Revisited

THE *SANATORIO*

– *Febbraio* 315

Lucien was unaware of how long he'd been unconscious in Raul da Costa's woodshed. His wrists still burned from the rope, his neck felt stiff, complaining with each surge of the horse beneath him. He worried at the split in his lip with his tongue. The thought of Rafaela in the hands of Giancarlo and the Majordomo consumed him entirely, alternately filling him with dread or impotent fury. Worse still were the thoughts of what Golia might do to her.

Had she already been consigned to the *sanatorio?* he wondered.

The dipping of the blood-red sun below the horizon marked his second day as an exile from Demesne. The sky stained itself pink, darkening to purple and deepest- blue as the first stars revealed themselves. The road stretched out ahead dusty and endless. He'd pushed the white mare hard, only noticing his single-mindedness when he began feeling faint. He'd barely eaten in two days. Chiding himself for a fool, he stopped at the cemetery, where he whispered apologies to his mount. The horse steamed in the chilly air, sweat lathered like foam on the creature's pure hide. She looked almost spectral in the cemetery grounds. He offered her an apple, small compensation, he realised. Once the mare was calm, he threw a blanket over her and sated his own gnawing hunger with bread and cheese, now well past its best.

The hulking menace of Demesne waited on the horizon as he washed down his simple meal with wine. The *sanatorio* stood before it like a squat nightwatchman holding a vigil over the larger building. Slowly, more and more stars made themselves known. The night swallowed the last of the red and yellow brilliance from the sky. After a moment's hesitation he left the mare in the cemetery, watched over by the sculpted angels. He was confident there was no one around to steal her. Losing one horse was unfortunate; losing two would be unforgivable.

He hurried on deft feet, feeling the night settle around him like a favourite cloak. He was grateful for it. A mist had rolled in from the sea over the lowlands. It would protect him from unwanted gazes in the hours ahead. He was close to Demesne now, the scents of the place keen to him. Woodsmoke and rotting food, horse manure and wood shavings. The pungent odours of the tannery at House Prospero. The smells remained the same but there was a subtle shift to the mood of the prodigious edifice. The hairs on his arms stood to attention; a chill passed down his spine. If Demesne did have a gaze, then it was surely directed inward, preoccupied with history, lost to reverie and perhaps regret. Many of the arched windows were shuttered, others remained unlit. Those rooms that were illuminated showed no occupants. He was pleased to note the guards were not outside the walls. A handful patrolled the battlements and rooftops, thinking themselves unnoticed so high up. They stamped their feet, cursing bitterly about the wind. Some lit pipes, making themselves conspicuous against the night. Lucien took them all in with a hunter's eye. One by one he could dispose of them; en masse he'd be lost.

The Orfano ran to the *sanatorio*, pressing himself against the curving stone, his breath before him in small wisps. If Rafaela was in here he'd find her, even if he had to break the lock on every door to every cell. No sooner had he started to climb than he heard his name, harsh and insistent on the evening wind.

Not Sinistro, as the guards would call, but his real name.

He looked around, trying to locate the source. Sweat prickled at his brow, ears straining. Fearing discovery he flattened himself against the wall, willing himself to become just another patch of darkness. After a moment of confusion his eye was drawn to Anea's window. Russo was shaking a white pillow case at him, flagging frantically for his attention.

158

He ran, bent low at a sprint until he reached the familiar grey stone of Demesne. The burgundy ivy trembled in the breeze. He climbed without thinking, fingers mechanically seeking each handhold, feet seemingly moving of their own accord. His shoulder held fast under the tight bandage despite grumbled whisperings of pain.

Lucien arrived at the window and gazed inside. The sitting room was a wreck. The shelves had been thrown down, scattering the floor with leather-bound books. A few of the tomes smouldered in the fireplace, shedding a mean ruddy light. The oak door to the apartment was splintered and shattered. Whoever had wrought this destruction had also taken a sledgehammer to the furniture. Lucien imagined the old prejudices against *streghe* finding an outlet among the guards. Few were more feared than the silent and mysterious Anea. Golia at least could be understood – he was composed of brute force and cruelty – Anea was unknown and haughty, ever Demesne's enigma. The sacking of the apartment was total. Lucien opened the broken window and hopped down from the sill like a great raven. His boots crunched on broken glass; splintered wood lay all around. A vase lay in countless pieces, lilies cast across thick carpets soiled with mud, countless footprints of vandal guardsmen. He crossed the room, avoiding the wreckage, knocking at the bedroom door, still intact somehow.

'It's me, Lucien.' There was a pause, and then a key scraped in the lock. The door opened a fraction. Russo's incredulous, red-rimmed eye stared out from the gap.

'Why are you here?' she whispered.

'You summoned me – with the pillow case?'

'Did I? Oh, I thought I was someone else.' Russo opened the door. She was alone. Her jacket had been ripped at the shoulder. The corner of her mouth was bruised, a splash of blood dried at the corner, her customary purple lipstick now faded.

'You mean *you* thought *I* was someone else"

The *professore* forced a weak smile onto her face and blinked slowly.

'Russo? Who did this to you?'

But she was staring into the middle distance. She wrung her hands with a dreamlike slowness. A lantern on the nightstand behind gave a tawny light. She looked faint, insubstantial.

'Can you tell me what's going on?'

'Dino and Festo were found slain in their beds this morning and Anea's been arrested. I tried to stop them but...'

'What?' whispered Lucien, clutching the hilt of his sword, sickness yawing in his gut.

'We think Golia killed the other Orfani. Even the very young ones didn't escape.' Russo shivered and clutched herself. 'He's blaming you. You didn't do it though, did you?'

'Of course not! It's me, Lucien, I—'

'No one dares to contradict him,' she continued, 'in case they're killed too. Like Festo.'

'And Dino is really ...'

'Gone. All gone.' She stared at him with glassy eyes. 'Killed in his sleep.' A sigh escaped her and then she swept the dust from her riding skirt.

'Professore?'

'Oh, hello, Lucien. When did you get here?'

'You were telling me about Golia, and the Orfani.'

'Yes.' Her eyes snapped back into focus. 'No one knows what to think. We've barely heard from the Majordomo since all this began.' She began to cry. 'Giancarlo is never seen without at least four bodyguards.'

'This whole thing has the stench of a coup.'

Lucien walked to the window of the sitting room, gaze set on the *sanatorio*, shaking with fury, breathless with it.

'What will you do?' asked Russo, her voice no more than a cracked whisper.

'I'll go to the place where Demesne deposits all of its wayward unwanted women; I'll go to the *sanatorio*.' He turned to her. 'Stay here. Lock the door.' He surveyed the damage. 'For all the use it will do.'

The sound of booted feet came from the corridor beyond. Russo flinched instinctively, eyes widening with panic.

'Lock the door,' repeated Lucien, taking a deep breath. He turned to find two guardsmen in the ruin of the doorway, their tabards bearing the scarlet and black of House Fontein. The shorter of the two bore a sledgehammer, likely the perpetrator of the earlier damage. He was in his thirties and sported two days' worth of stubble and a broken nose. The taller of the two was a sour sort that Lucien recognised. Their dirty faces betrayed their shock at finding him.

'Hunting Orfani, are we?' said Lucien, his voice low. 'Looks like you struck gold.' He held his arms out at his sides, beckoning them in.

'We're just following orders,' grunted the shorter guard. 'Giancarlo said Mistress Anea was part of a plot against the king.'

'And that bruise on Professore Russo's mouth. Was that "following orders" too?'

The guardsmen looked at each other, but if either felt any guilt they didn't show it. They'd not miss the chance to strike at both an Orfano and an eminent member of a rival house; it was simply too tempting.

'And killing Dino in his bed? Was that just "following orders" too?'

The short guardsman looked confused, while the taller of the two blanched and gripped his weapon tighter.

'Don't know anything about that.'

'And what about me?' whispered Lucien.

'Well—' the shorter guardsman swallowed nervously '—you burned down the stable and set fire to Viscount Contadino's stallion. People are saying it were you that murdered the other Orfani.'

'And you're an exile,' added his comrade, but the strength behind the words faltered.

'That's right. I'm the hunted exile returned,' said Lucien. The taller of the two wilted, an perceptible slump of the shoulders. Lucien knew in that moment that they feared him. They feared him as an Orfano. They feared him as a swordsman. But most of all they feared him as an exile, no longer bound by Demesne's stifling protocols and etiquette.

The sword came free of the scabbard with a hiss. Lucien felt the tension flood out of him as the metal shone in the firelight.

A smile flickered across his mouth, opening the split in his lip. He savoured the pain, almost delirious with it. Glass crunched beneath his boots. He'd need to be careful or he'd lose his footing. He imagined D'arzenta chiding him quietly, just over his shoulder, out of sight. His breathing was slow and deep, anger and blood a hot roil in his veins. Dino, just twelve years old, killed in his sleep. He imagined the younger Orfano in bed, unable to defend himself. And Festo succumbing to a similar fate, all of nine years old, snuffed out like a candle. Shocked moments of wakefulness and then pain. Then nothing.

Lucien snarled, desperately wanting to hurt someone.

The taller guardsman fell back, attempting to level his halberd. A foolish weapon to use indoors, it was ill suited to close-quarters fighting. Lucien stepped past the point of the pole-arm, grasping the haft with his right hand and unleashing the full force of his hatred. The metal flashed in the darkness.

Once.

Twice.

Three times the blade fell in short brutal strikes.

The guard lay on the floor gasping, face split open, shoulder shattered, a dull gleam of sickly red leaking through the black fabric of his tabard.

'That was for Dino,' hissed Lucien.

The shorter guardsman dropped the sledgehammer and made to draw his sword, visibly shaken. Lucien swore. Only men of *sergente* rank or higher were given swords. This would be a harder fight. But only if the man could draw the blade from the scabbard.

Lucien lunged murderously to find the *sergente* ducking out of the room, backing into the unlit corridor. Committed to the strike, Lucien was off balance. The weight of his body and the momentum of his fury embedded his blade in the shattered door frame.

And held fast.

Lucien swore, felt his anger diluted by panic. The sound of the *sergente*'s sword escaping its sheath reached his ears. Lucien tugged feverishly at the hilt of the sword. It refused to move. The door frame shuddered, and a shadow moved in the corridor, black on black. Lucien stumbled away, losing his footing and rolling back over his shoulder as D'arzenta had shown him. The broken glass snagged and bit at his shoulder through the fabric. He regained his feet searching for a weapon.

The *sergente* surged through the door sensing victory, his blade held before him in a tight grip. His smug expression changed to one of shock as a burning book crashed into his face. Being a legal tome, it had considerable weight. Lucien continued pelting the *sergente* with burning books, ignoring the heat of his singed hands. Finally, the guard pressed into the room, heedless of the stream of fiery projectiles. He swung wildly, losing his footing on a shattered table. Lucien was already moving, stepping in close, past the arc of the blade, embracing the man with his right arm. They came together, close like lovers. The *sergente* looked back with stricken eyes, now realising the extent of his mistake. Lucien's dagger thrust into the hollow behind his jaw. He tried to speak but the words that escaped were wet and crimson. He convulsed once, shook again, Lucien clinging to him savagely. The guard tried a futile slash, but the fight had left him, just as life was fleeing him with each surge and gush of blood from below his ear. Lucien swore, angling the blade up into what he hoped was the man's brain. Another convulsion, another pitiful strike from the sword, no more than a dull slap. The *sergente*'s eyes became blank and he died silently, slipping to the floor amid the ruin.

Lucien stepped back, cleaning his dagger on the rich brocade of a torn-down curtain. He re-sheathed it in his boot before wiping his bloody left hand on his trousers. His heart hammered in his chest as he eased the sword from the door frame. Killing the two guardsmen had done nothing to cool his anger. He wanted more. He wanted to find those responsible for the murder of the Orfani.

A sound drew his attention back to the broken window he had entered through. A raven perched on the frame, taking care to avoid the shattered glass. The creature surveyed the scene with disinterest, then turned its back, pointing into the night with its great beak. Lucien crossed the room slowly. The large midnight bird remained on the sill, giving a raucous cry, then took to wing, swooping down toward the *sanatorio*.

'Rafaela, Anea,' breathed Lucien. Elsewhere in Demesne someone screamed. Lucien sheathed the blade, nurturing his anger, fearing he would simply curl up in defeat if it left him.

'Anger gets you so far and then it gets you dead,' D'arzenta had said to him.

Lucien hoped he was wrong.

20

The King's Insistence
VIRMYRE'S CLASSROOM
– Settembre 311

Lucien had spent much of the lesson staring through the arched windows of the classroom. Professore Virmyre was scribing in a large tome behind his desk, brow furrowed in concentration. The boys had been tasked with copying the table of elements into their own books. Lucien had given up even the pretence of transcribing the information. His mood had been uniformly sour during the six weeks since he'd come to blows with Golia. Even D'arzenta had excluded him from lessons. Lucien had spent much of the time in the kitchen, under the protection of Camelia's maternal authority; the rest he spent in the library, where Archivist Simonetti warned him to behave himself.

Lucien gazed out of the window, drowsing in the heat. People made tiny by distance were working in the fields. The sun was showing no sign of relenting, early autumn promising to be as stifling as high summer. It had been an airless sort of year, disappointing and frustrating in equal measure. He knew the number thirteen was unlucky; perhaps his fortunes and mood would improve come his fourteenth year. He hoped so.

The classroom had a high ceiling, its plaster and white paint flaking. The wall behind the teacher's desk was a vast array of shelves. Thick dust slept on ancient timbers crowded with curios and oddments. There were books in languages no one could decipher, jars of preserved body parts – many animal but a few human. There were diseased organs bloated with corruption and, more disturbingly, an urn full of ashes that Lucien had never summoned the courage to ask about. It was Virmyre's practice to make unruly students clean the shelves on occasion, but he'd abadoned this recently, preferring to make the entire class run a lap of the castle 'to work off excess exuberance'. Lucien found this enforced exercise pointless. Some of the boys simply idled and failed to return to the lesson; many gritted their teeth and ran doggedly. Lucien took it as a point of pride to beat every one of them, every time.

The Orfano closed his eyes and listened to the scratch and scrape of quills on paper. They sounded like rats clawing at panelling, like stray thoughts wanting to enter the recesses of his mind. Thoughts of Giancarlo scuttled while Golia gnawed at Lucien's nerves. His fears for the future swept about in a great swarm, and there was the ever present anxiety of his next testing.

His thoughts drifted to Rafaela, who had only recently come back to herself. The disappearance of Navilia and the fiasco in Golia's apartment had shaken her. He'd seen less of her since that day. She'd gained some additional duties that meant she lacked the time to lavish on one Orfano. Not that he minded; he didn't need looking after like a child. Still, he missed the opportunity to speak to her, the curve of her smile, her wit. He missed the informality of her banter and the small encouragements she offered when he felt low. Which was often in the silence of his room, even with the drake for company.

He too was busier these days. It was a small luxury that he could decide his own timetable, although he always sought Camelia's counsel. She did not comment that he implemented the majority of her suggestions, content to hear of his successes.

'You must do what makes you happy, Lucien. You have such rare opportunities,' she often said when not complaining about the great many duelling lessons he took. He was well acquainted with Ruggeri now, despite the uneven start to their relationship some four years gone. Cherubini and Russo also spared time for him, often coming to his apartment to tutor him.

Sitting there in the classroom, consumed by the sunshine, he realised how he was just going through the motions, un-sure of what he was trying to achieve. His aim of gaining the sponsorship of House Fontein was fading more with each passing year. He remembered his younger self, fascinated with the very idea of being ten years old and how exciting it would be. At thirteen he couldn't be more bored or apathetic. He didn't attend Ruggeri's lessons to gain access to House Fontein; he attended Ruggeri's lessons in order to survive.

A handbell rang from somewhere deep in House Erudito, and the boys looked up at Virmyre expectantly. Stools scraped on the wooden floorboards impatiently. A few daring souls were already beginning to pack their writing kits away. Two boys began an animated conversation. The *professore* did not look up from his labour.

'Just because I am old does not mean I am deaf, you insolent wretches.' Virmyre's rich baritone carried across the classroom easily.

The boys fell silent, some not daring to breathe. Just because the lesson was over did not mean they might not earn themselves a punitive run.

'Away you go, gentlemen,' said Virmyre, not bothering to meet their gazes, his pen continuing to scratch out a line of spidery script. 'Onwards to your destinies.' The stools resumed their scrape and groan; there was a clatter and a stifled curse as one boy dropped his satchel. Virmyre looked up and skewered the boy with a piercing glance but said nothing.

Lucien received a sharp elbow to the ribs as a larger boy by the name of Paolo passed him.

'*Figlio di troia.*'

He locked eyes with the curly-haired student and sneered, his lips twisting with distaste. The other boys stared on, wondering if the pair would fight. It would not be the first time.

'They say Golia will cut your head off and use your skull to piss in.'

Lucien said nothing, lacing his fingers in front of him but not looking away from the smirking Paolo, who was forced to break eye contact in order to exit the room. Detached and watchful, Lucien regarded his classmates leaving. Some pushing and shoving occurred, but the boys left the class quickly and quietly in the main.

The word *strega* drifted in from the corridor beyond and Lucien sighed.

Silence pressed into the room, almost tangible, a calming and welcome presence. Lucien sat, enjoying the motes orbiting each other in the thick shafts of extraordinary autumn light streaming through the windows. He wondered if the tiny particles ever collided with each other. No mean intention, just blundering into one another due to circumstances beyond their control. Not like Paolo and his intentional shove, more akin to his own missteps, inadvertent breaches of etiquette.

'Master Lucien,' Virmyre's rich baritone again, 'is it not strange that you've done your level best to be an unwilling student in my class for the last sixty minutes? And now, when the session is done, I find myself enjoying your august presence?'

Lucien smiled.

'It is strange, I grant you.' He stood, gathering his things and dumping them unceremoniously into his satchel, before approaching the platform on which Virmyre's desk stood.

'Do you think me lonely perhaps?'

'Not overly so, Professore.'

'Not overly?'

'No more than anyone else in Demesne.'

'Ah, the teenager has discovered his inner poet. Such sentiment in one so young.'

Lucien's mouth creased in a lopsided smile. Virmyre's chiding was legendary throughout Demesne, but he couldn't help but enjoy being the target.

'So, aren't we overdue for one of your youthful displays of boundary-testing?' asked Virmyre, setting down his quill. Lucien felt those cold eyes on him but stared back unperturbed.

'I'm sorry, Professore, I don't follow you.'

'Some scandal or flourish of shocking behaviour. I think you are overdue for some trouble or nonsense.' Just for a second Lucien thought the corners of Virmyre's mouth might turn up; instead the *professore*'s eyes twinkled with mischief.

'Wasn't the brawl in Golia's apartment exciting enough for you?'

'Had I known your intent I would have attended. It sounded—' a pause '—spirited.'

Lucien struggled to keep the smile from his face and shook his head, feeling ridiculous. He still couldn't believe he'd marched into Golia's apartment and accosted the Domo. He'd need to keep a tighter leash on his temper.

'It may come as a shock to you, Professore, but my actions lack any premeditated spite. I just have a particular gift for being in the wrong place at the wrong time.'

'And what happens when you find yourself in the right place at the right time, Master Lucien? Will you still rail against your elders and Demesne? What then?'

Lucien floundered, unsure what the *professore* was driving at.

'How will I know it's this right time you speak of?'

'Instinct. It's what sets you apart, Lucien. It's why you'll succeed where all the others have failed.'

Lucien's eyes narrowed, suspecting some sort of game or trap. Virmyre was seldom this talkative.

'Others? You mean other Orfani?' he whispered. Virmyre nodded, his brow creased intently

'How long has this been going on? This business with the Orfani?' asked Lucien, clutching the edge of the *professore*'s desk with both hands.

'How long do you think?' said Virmyre, stroking his chin with one ink-stained thumb.

'At least as long as the Majordomo has been alive, obviously,' Lucien replied. 'He may well have been the first of the Orfani, but I doubt it.'

'A reasonable deduction.'

Virmyre sat back and sighed, dropping his gaze. For a second Lucien took this for disappointment and assumed the conversation had come to a close.

'See the shark in the tank behind me?' said the *professore*. Lucien couldn't miss it. The specimen was not overlarge, barely three feet long, but it was the focal point of the various strangenesses Virmyre had piled on his shelves. The creature inside the glass tank was preserved in some foul-smelling yet clear fluid. Lucien stepped around the desk, past his teacher, and approached the body, trapped in chemicals and held in time. The skin was a faint and dappled beige with speckles of darker brown. The eyes were elongated and delicate. There was not an ounce of excess flesh on the slender form; every curve of every fin spoke of efficient movement. Virmyre turned on his stool, clearing his throat.

'Some sharks can increase their girth by two or three times. They make themselves larger to make predators think twice about attacking. It's an impressive tactic, one that must have evolved over a very long time.'

'Why are you telling me this?' said Lucien, his fingers pressed lightly against the glass casket, attention on the dead creature.

'Because you're not going to be able to adopt that tactic, Lucien. You're not going to be able to scare off the competition with a show of size or bravado. The shark in the tank is a cat shark, not dangerous, not large. It's Dino. It's Festo. Small, inoffensive, easily bested.'

Lucien turned to his grave teacher and waited for him to continue.

'Golia on the other hand is a great white. He is force and aggression, he is a perfect killer. I sometimes wonder if Golia is human at all.'

'And what shark should I be?'

'That I can't tell you. Some things you have to decipher yourself.'

Lucien turned his back on his teacher, pressing his fingers against the glass once more. The delicate eyes put him in mind of Anea, not piercing green like hers, but a pleasing shape.

'What of Anea? Is she to be a shark too?'

'She certainly has the intelligence for it. Did you know many sharks have a similar brain mass to that of the large land mammals. It's not impossible to theorise they might have admirable problem-solving skills, just like Anea.'

'Why do you admire them so?' Lucien looked back over his shoulder, noting the wistful look behind his teacher's eyes. He'd seen it before when discussing the very same topic.

'They're not slowed or weighed down by this construct we call morality. They act, they survive, and they're incredibly aware of their environment, of their surroundings. They are, for the most part, solitary too, which is something we have in common. They rarely stop swimming. Some scholars think they have to keep moving in order to breathe.'

'Breathe?'

'Yes, the act of water passing over their gills allows them to draw in a tiny amount of oxygen from the water. This constant movement, this restlessness, is another thing we have in common. And you too, Lucien. I see the shark in you, the restlessness, the hunger, the instinct. There are going to be times where you have to put aside the niceties and etiquette of Orfano life and become a killer. And you're perfect for it, but you don't see it in yourself. Or you choose not to see it.' Virmyre stood, clasping his hands behind his back. 'That's why so many of your teachers fear you: they know your instincts make you difficult to control.'

The word shook Lucien as if the *professore* had grasped him by the shoulders and performed the action itself. Control. Even the thought of it left a sour taste in his mouth.

'What is all this about?' said Lucien, gesturing vaguely, his curiosity aflame.

'You mean the scheming? The internecine nonsense that pervades these crumbling walls? The Domo's agenda for the favoured Orfani?'

'What else?' replied Lucien, 'It seems as if every effort of Demesne is bent toward the education of awful, spoilt, misshapen children.'

At last Virmyre smiled, but there was little warmth to it. 'That's a very telling and unique perspective, Master Lucien.'

'It's upon the king's insistence, isn't it? The Orfani are being trained for some role, some task.'

Virmyre stepped past him and bent from the waist, knocking one bony knuckle against the glass in which the cat shark was suspended. Lucien was well accustomed to these idiosyncratic twitches, but he was baffled why the *professore* would try and rouse a dead shark.

'And that Giancarlo is intent on encouraging vendetta between myself and Golia must mean we are in competition with each other,' Lucien continued.

'Very good, Master Lucien. Now keep going. Take the line of thought to its logical conclusion.' Virmyre gazed at the elegant creature beyond the glass.

'If the Orfani are in competition with one another then there can only be one role, one important position. Like the role of Majordomo.'

Virmyre turned to him, his face impassive, pale blue eyes grave. Lucien tried to swallow in a dry throat.

'Like the Majordomo. Or the king.'

Virmyre's hand strayed to his chin and idled at his beard, his eyes wintry despite the heat of the classroom.

'You have a long road ahead of you, Master Lucien.'

Lucien nodded and chewed his lip, his mind a savage churn of possibilities.

21

Into Madness

HOUSE CONTADINO

– *Febbraio* 315

Lucien sneaked down the stairs as silently as his boots would allow, the worn leather soles doing much to deaden the sound as long as he stayed off his heels.

Keep your weight on the balls of your feet, Master Lucien.

So many times had he heard that instruction from D'arzenta and Mistress Corvo. It had taken him a long time to get his footwork right for each of the disciplines. Lucien descended the stairwell with a dancer's grace, not giving a thought to his own apartment two floors below Anea's. He wanted only to reach the *sanatorio*. And Rafaela.

Demesne was a muted place. It seemed as if every possibe vignette and drama were playing out behind closed doors. Lucien wondered what else had occurred during his short time away. If Golia had decided to kill the other Orfani then what hope was there for the rest of the citizens? No one was sacred. Not Dino. Not Festo. Not Rafaela. Lucien worried for Virmyre and Camelia – he hoped they'd reached safety, if any safety could be found.

Lost in his thoughts he didn't notice her, hands clutched to her chest in mute agony. As ever, she wore her customary black, making her one with the shadows. If she hadn't gasped fitfully he may have missed her altogether.

'Who's there?'

She flinched.

'Mistress Corvo?'

She gazed at him, eyes wide, mouth pressed together into a

thin line, lips almost bloodless. Her hands looked skeletal and pale.

'They said you . . .'

Lucien waited. Careful to keep his hand away from the hilt of his sword.

'They said you killed them.'

She looked more cadaverous than usual in the meagre light of the corridor. Lucien said nothing.

'They said you killed all of them,' she stammered, 'Poor Dino, poor Festo.' She suppressed a sob. 'There are men everywhere. Armed men. You'll be caught no matter what you do to me.'

'I don't know who killed them, only that it wasn't me.'

'Lies,' she hissed, suddenly more sure of herself. 'You've always been trouble. A stain on House Contadino. Such a wicked boy. So much disobedience.'

'There's more going on here than either of us know about.'

'More lies!' She pressed her back to the wall and began to wail.

'Professore Russo is in Anea's chamber. You should go to her.'

She nodded, but he knew she agreed simply to be spared. He was, after all, the outcast *strega*, notorious killer of Demesne. Or so Giancarlo would have everyone believe.

'Don't tell a soul you've seen me. Understand?'

A frantic nod of the head. She was dissembling of course, sure to blurt her discovery to anyone with the wit to listen. He left her trembling where he'd found her, sour disgust uncoiling on his tongue.

And then he was outside the windowless room where he'd brought the Majordomo the day he collapsed. He tested the handle on instinct. The door was locked, and nothing could be heard within. And if the door had been locked the day of the collapse? Would he have still discovered the Domo for an Orfano? So much of life in Demesne rested on doors being open, closed, locked. Portals of wood, stone and sometimes truth. Lucien shrugged, untangling himself from thoughts like clinging cobwebs, continuing on his way.

The Contadino kitchen's back door was unguarded. He

hesitated in the porch, exhausted and afraid, fearing he'd run into someone else. He could ill afford the time. The fog still strangled the castle, the moon an indistinct glow high above. Silent feet carried him through the courtyard, eyes taking in every corner, expecting each door to release squads of sleep-muddled guards.

He emerged outside the castle, fog roiling sinuously as if alive. Guards on rooftops called to each other, the shouts forlorn and muted by the mist. Lucien walked steadily, head held high. He had no need to skulk here; he could let the night do its work and not draw attention to himself by sneaking. He'd look like any other shadowy figure in the night, perhaps mistaken for a *sergente* with the sword belted at his hip. It was quite dark now, the chill settling into his clothes quickly. His fingers grew numb. He found himself clenching his hands for warmth. The long grass clutched and whipped at his boots. He hammered on the doors of the *sanatorio* with one fist. No one answered. The iron-studded double doors remained closed to him.

Lucien slid around the building's broad circumference, tracking through fog that stirred in eddies around his feet. He made his way to a place where he might climb without being spotted. Hands sought out gaps in the stone and then he was ten feet, twenty feet from the ground. The many narrow windows were all barred with cold black iron. Wood he could kick in, but the crossed bars made the *sanatorio* inviolate.

There was another way.

He grinned to himself as climbed, the motion natural and pleasing to him. They'd imagined they could keep him out, keep him from Rafaela. Small chance of that. Finally he arrived at his location, a stained-glass window, age and guano adding a patina of filth to the once brightly coloured glass. He hung from the finely carved lintel that extended out over the window, tapping out individual panes with the hilt of his knife. Twice he had to stop for fear of losing his grip and falling to his death. Eventually he kicked in the soft lead framework and dragged himself inside.

The chapel had not seen any visitors for a very long time. Lucien lit stubby candles sitting on a wide table. His sleeves collected thick dust like ashes, his footprints looked as if left in shallow grey snow. The panes he had dislodged decorated the floor, gaudy gems gleaming in the candlelight. A shadow loomed at the corner of his eye, making him draw his sword on instinct. Spinning, he confronted the stranger. A woman clutched her child, head bowed almost fearfully. Lucien let out a taut breath.

Something about the statue unsettled him.

Had his own mother seen out her days in the *sanatorio*? Might she be alive still? Would he encounter her tonight and yet pass her over, not knowing the bond that existed between them?

These thoughts stilled his feet, questions he'd kept locked down in an oubliette of his own. Curiosities too painful to consider, denied even the balm of closure, if such a thing existed.

And there was the issue of his father. This thought provoked a swell of unease. He flinched, shaking off the speculation, and regarded his surroundings anew.

Four pews sat in the centre of the room coated in yet more of the deep dust. A lectern stood empty near the table, the brass dull, the book long since burned. Lucien took one of the thick candles and exited the chapel. He was unsure why such a place still existed since the king had forbidden religious worship. The ban had been imposed during one of his more eccentric episodes, over a hundred years ago, before he'd gone into seclusion. Some artefacts remained, but certain texts had been expunged completely.

The corridor extended out to his left and right, no doubt making a circle. All the sconces stood empty, the walls thick with wax drippings. And there was the smell. A thick miasma of unwashed bodies, the acrid reek of spent bladders. There were other smells mixed into the foulness. The metallic tang of blood, the mouldering of food and possibly even spoiled meat. All was filth and decay.

He approached the first cell, anxious at what he'd find. The *sanatorio* had haunted his nightmares almost as long as he could remember, but the phantoms inside had always remained as shadows, off limits to his imagination and his nightmares. Now he was exploring the dark confines first hand. The candlelight, although poor, revealed to him a solitary person. He thought her a boy or man at first. Her hair had been shorn a uniform length, her body was emaciated and thin. Only a simple shift provided any dignity, although the garment was wretched and dirty. Lucien called out to her, but she failed to acknowledge him. Sitting on the cold stone floor, her back to the wall, she stared at her feet. A thin line of spittle emerged from her mouth. She made no effort to wipe it away. Lucien stepped back, shaken.

He hurried on, looking in each cell with bated breath. Every dank chamber told the same awful story. Here and there cells stood empty, awaiting more of the Majordomo's abductees. All the prisoners looked similar in the dim light, stripped of their hair, their identities, their dignity.

Their sanity.

His confusion solidified into frustration, then to anger. He wanted to hurt someone very much. He descended the spiral staircase at the centre of the building and resumed his search on the next floor. Each cell here multiplied the wickedness of the floor above. Lucien was appalled by the number of abductions but also by his own long silence. He'd been complicit through inaction. With long shadows haunting his every step, he arrived at a cell from which issued the faintest sound, a lullaby.

And one he recognised

> Stella, stellina,
> La notte si avvicina.
> La fiamma traballa.
> La mucca nella stalla.
> La mucca e il vitello,
> La pecora e l'agnello,
> La chioccia con il pulcino,
> Ognuno ha il suo bambino,
> Ognuno ha la sua mamma,
> E tutti fanno la nanna

Lucien sheathed his sword and held up the candle with a trembling hand. The golden light shone through the barred window of the cell door. Another shaven-headed woman crouched in the corner. Not as thin as the rest, she wore a skirt of rich scarlet. Her legs were drawn up to her chest, her forehead resting on her knees. She was shaking.

'Rafaela?' he whispered, his voice harsh.

Bright hazel eyes looked up, wide and hopeful. Lucien felt his stomach shrink. Her beautiful hair, all gone. He couldn't breathe.

'What have they done to you?'

She stood, crossing the cell on naked dirty feet, pushed shivering hands through the bars to stroke his face. Tears tumbled down her cheeks.

'Lucien.'

'I'm getting you out of here,' he said, anger seething hotly in his veins. 'I'll find the keys. I'll be right back. I promise.'

She nodded mutely, too consumed with relief to attempt speech.

Lucien didn't need to search far.

The jailer stood just ten feet away, a fearful expression frozen on his face. His hair was shot through with white, but his face looked much younger. A few days' stubble covered his pockmarked cheeks. The backs of his hands were heavily scarred. Lucien couldn't remember ever seeing him before, another one of the Majordomo's secret cogs.

'Unlock the cell.' The words were shocking and loud in the crypt-like silence of the *sanatorio*.

'I can't do that. Only the Majordomo puts them in and takes them out.' His voice was reedy and high, the knot in his throat bobbing in a scrawny neck

'Unlock this cell now.' Lucien eyed the thick bundle of keys hanging from a large silvery loop, then met the jailer's furtive stare, drawing his sword.

'I won't ask you again.'

The jailer turned to flee. Lucien dropped the candle and lunged after him. The blade swung awkwardly, the confined corridor hampering his strike. A small cut appeared on the jailer's shoulder, the ragged sackcloth of his crude shift soaking up the blood.

'*Figlio di puttana!* Give me the keys!'

The jailer managed a few panicked steps then fell. Lucien fell on him instantly, straddling his chest. Dropping the sword, he punched the jailer again and again. The man went limp under the onslaught, face a battered mess. Lucien lurched to his feet, wrenching the keys from him as he went. He retrieved his sword and the candle and thought about giving the man a quick death. The tip of his sword hovered over the man's throat before Lucien calmed himself. Better the Domo's accomplice stand trial, if only for the families of all the lost girls.

The keys were a seemingly numberless series of blackened metal. Each one failed to fit into the lock on Rafaela's door or refused to turn. Frantic moments passed, fraying his nerves. Lucien began to worry the key he needed was somehow absent.

Then a satisfying click.

Rafaela's eyes looked at him through the bars, not daring to believe it. The door creaked open. And then the buzzing of flies reached Lucien's ears. He turned, candle in one hand, keys in the other, dreading what would come next.

'The exile returns,' droned the Majordomo. He held up a lantern in one hand, shedding sombre light over his charcoal-grey robes. His mouth was downturned and grim. Flies darted about and hovered near the opening of his cowl, adding to the nasal drone of Demesne's custodian.

Lucien didn't have time to draw his sword, his hands full of candle and keys. The first strike from the Majordomo's staff stamped into his chest, knocking him sprawling. He feared for his ribs, wheezing loud in the gloomy corridor. The Domo came on, looming over him, staff feinting and thrusting, quick, quick and then slow. Heavy strikes smacked from the stone walls as Lucien dodged under them, throwing himself back. He was being driven away from Rafaela's cell. The thought of this infuriated him and he lunged for the sword. Again the Domo thrust the butt of the staff into his chest, sending him reeling, slumping into the wall before ducking and rolling forward to avoid another crushing blow of the heavy oak. Winded and desperate, Lucien drew his knife, only to look up in time to receive a blow to the face.

What surprised him were the stairs.

Somehow the Domo had driven him back, directing him to the spiral staircase. He slithered and rolled, bumping down them, fingers struggling for purchase, trying to stop his descent. His head impacted on stone. He went limp.

The double doors of the *sanatorio* were open. A dozen men in House Fontein livery stood over him, some with weapons drawn, others holding lanterns. All looked incredulous. The Majordomo appeared at the bottom of the staircase, lantern in hand, staff scraping on the flagstones. It was as if he had never fought.

'This is Lucien, killer of the Orfani, arsonist, plotter.'

Lucien raised his head weakly, hiding his dagger inside his jacket.

'Take him to the oubliette,' ordered the Domo, slamming his staff against the floor for emphasis.

A few of the men gasped, but a few more smiled wickedly. Some laughed aloud. Lucien was grasped by calloused uncaring hands and taken to the very lowest levels of Demesne. His vision took in the stars above, then tracked back to the *sanatorio* itself, where Rafaela remained, once more behind a locked door.

22

Antigone, Achilles, and Agamemnon

Lucien had done everything right, he was sure of it, and yet a feeling of sickness remained. An uncoiling, nameless thing, it was yet another worry he could do without. The morning had been consumed with wordless fretting. He could find no relief. Not in books, or in training, or his studies. A brief trip to the kitchens had seen him scurrying back to his apartment, anxious and afeared. There was simply no escaping the fact.

Perseus was dying.

Lucien crouched in the armchair, one hand pressed to his mouth. The drake had hardly been the most demonstrative of pets, but he couldn't bear the idea of being without him. He'd fed him and nurtured him and been mindful to keep the reptile warm. Often he let the drake have the run of the apartment. Perseus would perch on the back of the couch while he read, or spend hours sunning himself in the window on warmer days. Inside the glass tank the cataphract drake lay still, looking uncomfortably bloated. The dun-brown scales were a healthy hue, the onyx eyes bright and alert, yet the drake refused to move. Lucien had changed his water, deposited crickets nearby, but no movement. The reptile looked different somehow, changed imperceptibly. Even the addition of a granite rock and small lamb skull had not aroused any interest. The drake sat perfectly immobile, soft belly submerged in the sand. Even blinking seemed a chore to the creature. How long did reptiles live anyway? And how much more life would this one cling to?

Lucien had dispatched Dino to find Virmyre and waited, nervously chewing his black fingernails. Dino had become a frequent visitor since the drake's arrival, fascinated by the reptile, quietly jealous of such a prize. Lucien found the younger Orfano amusing company, which is not to say they did not have their disagreements. The name of the drake had been Dino's suggestion, and he was thrilled when Lucien had agreed. Dino insisted on bringing mythology books from the House Erudito, smuggling them past Simonetti, the Archivist. Lucien had failed to read any of them, content to trust his young friend. Perseus had been a formidable warrior according to the younger Orfano, and that was good enough for Lucien.

Virmyre arrived without his teaching robe, attired in a heavy coat and grey britches. Lucien recalled the day he'd run away to the cemetery, how the *professore* had spent long moments in communion with his wife. He looked much as he did that day, windswept with a trace of unhappiness in the set of his eyes. Dino had followed as best he could, struggling to keep pace. He stumbled through the doorway out of breath and wide-eyed with anxiety. Virmyre swept his pale blue gaze from one boy to the other before exclaiming, 'You two look more alike every day. If it wasn't for the age gap I'd swear you were twins.'

Lucien scowled. He'd recently turned fourteen and had no wish to be compared to Dino, who was barely eight. Lucien was long resigned to the younger Orfano's desire to emulate his every affectation. He'd tried deterring him, but was secretly glad when he failed.

'And what appears to be the problem?' Virmyre reached into the tank slowly.

'Perseus just sits still all day. He doesn't move, he hasn't touched his water. He ignores the crickets I put in the tank. I don't know what to do.'

'Change the food perhaps?'

'I tried nematodes, but they dried up before he'd even look at them.'

'And you've kept your apartment warm, I trust?'

Lucien nodded and chewed his lip. Virmyre, never one to sully his features with an expression, looked as if he might break into a smile. Lucien realised he was holding his breath. Dino had grasped hold of the armchair, staring around the side of it with an expression so serious it verged on comical. Virmyre held up the drake, who didn't curl into a hoop, as was its usual tactic when being handled. The *professore* probed at the reptile with one careful finger, the corners of his mouth turned down, struggling not to smile

'I think I've determined the nature of the problem,' he said.

'What? What's wrong with him?'

'He's having a slight problem with pregnancy.' A flicker of amusement.

'He's pregnant?' mumbled Dino.

'Perseus is a girl?' said Lucien, failing to hide the disdain in his voice.

Dino dropped to his knees and dissolved into giggles, then gave up the pretence entirely, slumping to the floor and howling with laughter.

'Perseus, the unfortunately named,' said Virmyre, 'is a female and likely to give birth very soon, quite possibly in the next few hours.'

'I don't want a female reptile. Can't you give it to Anea? I bet she'd love to have a drake.'

'She's rather taken with her new kitten actually,' replied Virmyre, placing Perseus back in the tank with the utmost care. 'And I'm not sure kittens and drakes are terribly compatible.'

Dino was almost crying with laughter by now.

'Why did you give me a female lizard?' Lucien sneered, visibly nettled by Dino's mirth.

'I didn't think to sex her,' Virmyre rumbled in his rich baritone, 'nor did I predict you'd be so squeamish, Master Lucien.'

'I'll have her,' said Dino breathlessly. He pushed himself to his feet and flicked hair out of his face.

'You're not old enough,' snapped Lucien. 'I guess I'd better look after them. No one else knows as much about cataphract drakes as I do.'

'Quite. You're a veritable bastion of knowledge when it comes to the order of reptiles,' said Virmyre.

Lucien blushed and chewed his lip again. Virmyre said nothing more and swept from the room.

'You're an idiot,' muttered Dino. 'I'm going to see Festo.' He poked his tongue out, then flicked his fingertips from under his chin for good measure.

Lucien continued to crouch in his armchair, a gargoyle in his slate-grey jacket and britches. He caught sight of himself in the reflection of the glass tank and shivered. The drake sat motionless, full of potential. How many tiny lives would emerge? Would they be males or females? He considered giving one to Dino before discarding the idea.

Lucien drowsed in the chair, idly leafing through one of Dino's many hardbacks on mythology, the paper pleasing to the touch, the leather jacket reassuring. His new-found interest for the subject made the wait more bearable. He settled on Antigone to replace the now inapt Perseus, purely because he liked the sound of it. A knock at the door surprised him and the book hit the floor with a thud. He lurched out of the chair and spun round, scabbard in hand. Camelia entered the room, bringing a tray of hot food and a jug of water. Her blonde hair was a mess and she was rosy-cheeked, humming to herself pleasantly.

'I heard the news. Seems I'm not the only one expecting.' She beamed at Lucien and he smiled back, not knowing what to say. Camelia's generous hourglass figure was noticeably more rounded. She positively radiated contentment and vitality. The cook eased herself onto the couch and set the tray aside.

'I brought you some dinner. I guessed you'd not want to leave her. Never know when they might appear, eh? You must be excited.'

'Of course,' he managed, helping himself to some bread. 'How did you know?'

'Dino came down and told me all about it.'

Lucien forced another smile and poured a glass of water. He remembered Camelia at the last moment and offered it to her before filling another.

'Thank you,' she replied 'What have you been up to today?'

'Not much.' He sat beside her on the couch. 'I found a new name for the drake. I've decided on Antigone.'

'And the little ones?'

'I don't know. I like Achilles and Agamemnon.'

'You didn't get past the *A* section of the index, did you?'

'Ah. No, I didn't.' He gave a shrug. 'But Achilles *was* invincible.'

'Oh well, in that case...' Camelia smiled and ruffled his hair, a gesture that would surely be abandoned soon; he was much too old for that sort of thing now.

'And you'll give one of the babies to Dino.' This in a tone that didn't invite refusal. Lucien knew it all too well.

'Of course,' he managed and forced a smile. His eyes caught the wedding ring on her finger, a slim band of gold. It seemed she'd been married only months before the House Contadino kitchens were filled with congratulations. The buzzing of gossip about her pregnancy had been a welcome respite from the darker rumours that circulated Demesne. Lucien felt spectacularly left out. He stared at the offending bump, the tiny unborn usurper.

'Have you chosen a name yet?' he asked. He'd seen adults ask the same question and assumed it was customary.

'Not yet, we're still deciding. Would you like to feel it?'

Lucien knelt down on the rug, holding forth a tentative hand. Camelia smiled, folding his hand in her own, pressing it against her abdomen. He was just beginning to get bored when he felt something push back through the elastic confines of her stomach.

'That's disgusting!' he blurted. Camelia burst into a rich chuckle and tears appeared at the corners of her eyes.

'Sorry. I mean, ah, it took me by surprise. Did it hurt? Are you unwell?'

'No, it didn't hurt. You are funny, Lucien.'

He fell silent and noticed the drake had rolled over onto her side. He sprang up from the floor and pressed his fingers against the glass.

'Camelia. Look, she's...ah...'

'Gone into labour,' she supplied. With great effort Camelia knelt down next to him and they watched a tiny face appear from the drake's soft underside.

'Strange, isn't it?' breathed Lucien. 'Most reptiles lay eggs but these ones are different.'

The infant drake slithered out of its mother and lay panting on the warm sand. It was slick and wet, each scale perfect and tiny. Antigone seemed to be ignoring the newborn.

'Perhaps she'll only have one. Professore Virmyre said they never have more than two.'

'Just as well,' said Camelia. 'So is that one Achilles or Agamemnon?'

Lucien considered this for a moment and scratched his hair. He chewed his lip thoughtfully.

'Achilles wasn't really invulnerable, was he?'

'I'm afraid not. He had a weak spot on his heel.'

'Maybe I should call that one Agamemnon then.'

Seconds later another tiny face appeared. Antigone then scurried away behind a rock, leaving the two juveniles to dry out. After a moment or two the mother returned, feeding ripped-up portions of a cricket to the newborn. Neither seemed to be in the mood to eat. Lucien and Camelia watched the tiny creatures with wordless reverence, then she told him to get ready for bed.

'How long will you be away for, you know, after your baby comes?'

'Oh, probably about a year and a half.'

'A year and a half?' He surprised himself with how loud his voice was. 'Why so long?'

'Babies need a lot of looking after. You were the same when we first got you.'

Lucien climbed into bed; he'd absent-mindedly taken the mythology book with him. He slipped it under the pillow meaning to read it after Camelia left.

'Did you know Antigone was born out of an incestuous relationship? Her father Oedipus accidentally slept with his own mother.' He was sitting up in bed, doing his best not to yawn.

'I've heard of Oedipus, but I never realised he had a daughter. That sounds very confusing for everyone.' She folded up his suit and hung it in his closet, then retrieved his boots from where he'd kicked them off, placing them neatly under the mantelpiece.

'Do you think that's what happened with me?' Lucien said in a small voice. Camelia turned to him, then approached the bed. She sat down with eyes full of concern.

'I don't know Lucien, I honestly don't.'

'But it would make a certain kind of sense, wouldn't it? You said yourself, it would be confusing for everyone. The best way to solve the problem would be to get rid of the baby.'

'Lucien, you can't spend your time thinking about this type of thing. It'll do you no good.'

'But I do think about it.'

'All I know is that I'm glad I met you, Lucien.' She smoothed back his hair from his forehead. 'Every day you grow up a little bit more, and I'm proud to have helped make that happen.' She smiled. 'Not to say you don't have a few rough edges, mind.'

He smiled and tried a laugh, but tears arrived instead. He blinked them away.

'Will you still talk to me, you know, after the baby comes?'

'Of course I will, foolish boy. You'll be like an older brother, no doubt. Or an uncle at any rate.' She leaned forward and clutched him tightly. Lucien couldn't help another sob escaping.

'Why didn't my mother want to keep me the way you want to keep your baby, Camelia? It doesn't make any sense.'

'No, my beautiful boy, it doesn't,' she whispered, still holding him.

'Do you think I'll ever meet her?'

'I wouldn't pin any hopes on it. Hush now, go to sleep. Don't spend the night worrying at it.'

He cried some more, tiring himself with the effort of his upset, before exhaustion overtook him. Camelia remained until the candle flames were noticeably lower before making her way out. She brushed away tears of her own, pulling the door closed behind her.

23

The Fall

HOUSE FONTEIN

– *Febbraio* 315

They carried him from the *sanatorio* to the King's Keep. Ten of them at first, rough hands like manacles on his limbs. His head throbbed from where it had struck the steps during his tumble-down descent. Terrible pain emanated from his chest where the Majordomo had struck him. His eyes wouldn't focus, snatches of vision coming to him sometimes blurry, other times with jagged intensity. The distance between Lucien and Ella grew with every step the guards took.

His heart sank.

The men carrying him spat and cursed, calling him a 'filthy Orfano', '*strega*', '*buco del culo*', '*figlio di puttana*' and worse. He'd heard all the insults before of course, just never to his face. The age of the Orfano was over, and Golia was on course to be its lone survivor.

The curving corridor of King's Keep merged into another part of the castle. Ten men became eight, then two more peeled off for other duties. Two more stopped as they passed through what Lucien thought he recognised as an armoury in House Fontein. His mind lurched and drifted, struggling to maintain lucidity. There was a low murmuring, subdued congratulations, then quiet crowded in once more. Now it was just four men carrying him. He was still limp, mind foggy, body unresponsive despite his wishes to the contrary. The corridors were almost pitch-black in this part of Demesne. Strange that he should be carried by four men now. Four men. Eight legs. Like a spider. He was the mindless body being stolen away by marching limbs, ever onward.

Everyone knew about the oubliette. Mothers mentioned it to scare children into obedience; criminals were cast down into it, never to be seen again. As infamous as it was mysterious, few knew where the entrance to the oubliette lay, only the most trusted of House Fontein or those set to discover what lurked beneath. Just as Lucien's head was clearing he was placed on his feet. He swayed a moment, then the rough hands held him fast. He looked down at the front of his jacket. The knife remained lodged in the lining. For the moment.

Guido, the *capo de custodia*, stood to one side, regarding a rusting grille set in the floor. He'd foregone his usual livery for a suit of sombre black.

'Do you remember what you said to me the day of the duke's funeral?' the *capo* asked, a smirk playing on his lips. The two guards held Lucien firm, arms pinioned behind his back.

'All of our conversations are so riveting I have trouble discerning one from the other.'

The *capo* stiffened, lips curling into a sneer.

'You told me you'd chop my head off.'

'Really?' said Lucien casually. 'That doesn't sound like me. You must have been *very* naughty that day.' One of the guards at the door of the chamber failed to stifle his amusement. A laugh escaped him before he had the sense to feign a coughing fit. The *capo* glowered at the man, then wrenched up the grille. He cast it to one side of the room where it hit the floor with a bell-like clang.

Lucien took stock of his situation. They were below House Fontein. In a basement under the bustle of the kitchens and the silence of the pantries. Two guards on the door, two holding him fast, and the smug face of the *capo* in front of him. There was no way he could overpower all of them. The knife inside his jacket was slowly cutting through the lining, shredding the silk, threatening to fall out at any moment. Before him, four feet wide and yawning darkness, was the entrance to the oubliette.

And oblivion.

'Say hello to Salvaza for me, next time you're balls deep in her.' Lucien winked at the *capo*. Using Lady Prospero's first name was bound to rile him.

'She can't wait to be rid of you,' grated Guido from between clenched teeth. 'Giancarlo's assassins have put paid to almost all of you degenerate Orfano filth. Only Golia remains now, and he won't last for ever.'

Lucien suppressed a grimace. He'd not needed a reminder of Dino and Festo's deaths. Still, interesting to learn Lady Prospero's ambitions were not aligned with the Majordomo's schemes.

'Good luck trying to separate Giancarlo from his favourite animal. I think you'll come unstuck there, Guido.'

'Throw him in,' grated the *capo*. 'I'm sick of the sight of him.'

And with that Lucien was cast down into the darkness.

He had at various times of his life tried to picture what the oubliette might be like. He'd read various accounts of such places in his ghost stories and dreadfuls. What followed was much more subtle than he could have imagined.

The fall lasted agonising seconds, terminating in fetid water. The mud beneath it clung to him like clay. For a moment he was submerged, the filthy water seeping into his ears and washing over his eyes. He gagged, gulping a mouthful, then another, then pushing himself to the surface, hacking and spluttering. Wet to the skin, he struggled to stand, flailing, failing to find his footing. A taste in his mouth registered itself, like the scent of the air before a summer storm and yet...

Shattered furniture bobbed on the foul water, food scraps like flotsam on the rank tide. All about were shadowy presences, pressed up against the walls, ash-grey outlines drawn on the darkness itself. He checked himself and found nothing broken. The knife hadn't bitten into him under his jacket. It seemed like a strange place to keep a knife, as if he'd been hiding it. He wondered where he'd left his sword. The stagnant water lapped over the top of his boots, swilling around his toes, chilling him. Above came the sound of the metal grille being hefted back into place. Tiny clicks signalled padlocks securing his fate. He'd done something wrong, something to warrant being thrown down here, but try as he might he couldn't think what. He dimly remembered a stable on fire and a stallion screaming, flames consuming it as it ran through the night. And there had been the secret graveyard of course. Perhaps he'd been trespassing. Above him, the sounds of the *capo* and the guards receded into the distance, echoes down hollow corridors becoming more faint with each second.

The rib-vaulted ceiling arched above him, just beyond his reach. He stood in a nimbus of light which cascaded down through the grille. One of the guards had seen fit to leave a lantern in the chamber above. The oil would not last for ever, then he'd be plunged into a deeper darkness. He'd been expecting a cramped and chaotic cell full of the doomed, instead he found a warren-like layer of Demesne he'd not known existed. Additional chambers led away from the one he stood in, visible through broad peaked archways. Cobwebs hung from the corners of the room, like bedsheets left to dry. All around was the sickly reek of decay.

The light from the lantern above dipped and wavered. There couldn't be much oil left. And yet he needed to be free, he needed to get to the building outside, the place where they kept the insane. He groped about for the name of it, his mind as dark as the chamber he found himself in.

Nothing.

He couldn't recall it, only that leering stone faces looked down from the roof. There was someone locked inside he wanted to see very much. Someone locked inside, just as he was locked inside. Rafaela. He'd been trying to save Rafaela. He called out her name in the darkness, hoping the sound of it would wake his cloudy mind.

As the light above grew dimmer, Lucien sank to his knees, feeling the mud ooze and cling. The shadows at the edges of the room crept forward hesitantly, managing to move through the water without disturbing it. Cautiously, Lucien reached for the hilt of the knife. He'd not be able to fight all of them, but if he could make an example of one them he might stand a chance. They surrounded him entirely, at least a dozen, lurking at the edge of the lantern light as it shone down through the grille. Their curiosity and impatience were tangible.

Finally they swarmed forward, pressing up against him. Lucien struggled not to cry out. Hands poked and teased at his hair; fingers pinched at the fabric of his jacket. Guttural voices exchanged syllables and hisses. They wore hooded half-cloaks for the most part. Any trousers they owned had rotted away below the knee. Many of them were hunched, either with age or deformity, it was difficult to tell. Emaciated arms bore claw-like hands, broken nails blackened by the mire. Each one of the shadows was an echo of the Majordomo. Here a strong jaw. Another with thin and downturned lips. All of them had the Domo's skeletal hands and kept their eyes hidden beneath cowls. The robes were a uniform ash-grey. Lucien wondered what else they shared with the Domo.

The prisoners' interest in the newcomer waned. Lucien was left alone, the nimbus fading, the lantern oil nearly spent. Hope was extinguished, tiny increments of time slipping away. He'd told Rafaela's father he'd find her. Or had he just dreamed that part? It was so very difficult to remember. The shadows cast by the grille above became indistinct and diffuse. The other prisoners congregated in small groups, finding patches of earth above the water. Others lurked in corners pawing and groping each other, consensually or otherwise.

'Rafaela,' he said again, his voice wavering. Around him the prisoners looked up and paused what they were doing.

'Rafaela,' he said again, weakly now, no more than a croak. Above the light dimmed further. The world grew dark.

'Ella,' he droned. And in his voice he heard the dreary monotone of the Majordomo himself. Turning down the novitiate had been a poor decision, he realised.

'Ella,' he whispered. He couldn't remember why he hadn't accepted the position. The Domo was involved in something he'd not cared for. If he'd become the Domo's novice the girl in the madhouse would be safe. The girl in the madhouse. What was her name?

Her name.

Her name was Ra...

Above him the light winked out.

*

'It was coming from this direction,' said a voice. A tiny spark of hope kindled inside the Orfano. That voice. He knew that voice. Older than himself certainly, full of dependability.

'I think he's here, my lady, where they threw him,' said the man. The lady, whoever she was, decided not to answer.

The water rippled and swirled around the Orfano – someone was coming closer. Tiny waves of scum and filth washed over him. He was still slumped down on his knees, jaw slack, idiot gaze staring blankly at the darkness.

'Looks like he's had a good mouthful or two of the water. We'll have to hope it's not permanent.'

The Orfano had heard that voice before but could not place it. It was a voice from his childhood. Something about cider? He couldn't organise or focus his attention. His thoughts flapped and hopped like agitated birds, never settling.

'Lucien?'

Lucien. That was a nice name. He wondered who it belonged to. With a name like that a man could be important and respected. A man like that might live in his own apartment and have fine swords crafted for him.

'Lucien, my boy.' Calloused hands grabbed his head and searched his scalp roughly.

'Lucien, I know it's you – you haven't got any ears.'

He cried out in shock, then fell back in the water, away from the hands in the darkness.

'My ... my ears?'

'You never had any, boy. You're Lucien "Sinistro" di Fontein, and you haven't got any ears. That's why you grow your hair long, like me,' said the voice from childhood.

Lucien breathed, with each intake of air he came back to himself.

'I am ... Lucien "Sinistro" di Fontein.' He had lived in an apartment. He had owned finely crafted swords. Another breath. It was Golia that had set fire to the stables by accident, Viscount Contadino's prize horse immolated. He'd not been trespassing in the graveyard, rather he'd been shown it by another outcast Orfano. He pushed himself to his feet. The Domo had thrown him down here. He was an exile, returned to Demesne to . . . He dragged in another shuddering breath. The building outside was called the *sanatorio*, the girl, Rafaela. Beautiful Rafaela. Taken by mistake, instead of her sister, just turned eighteen.

'I am Lucien, although I don't care too much for House Fontein these days.'

'I'll say,' grunted the voice in the darkness.

'Franco?'

'Yes, it's me. They threw me down here after the testing. After you refused to kill me. I thought Giancarlo would do for me himself, but you really shook him. Tell me, how long have I been down here?'

'Two days, going on for three now.' Lucien couldn't see him, the darkness was total, but there were worse people to be locked up with. The farmer with the shoulder-length iron-grey hair. He owned a farm and a cider press, always had a kind word for the awkward Orfano who scampered and lurked at the House Contadino kitchens.

'It's good you've regained your wits, boy. The water does strange things down here,' said Franco.

'Is anyone else here with you?'

'Anea is right beside me,' said Franco, sounding pleased with himself. She was thrown in earlier. Don't ask me how much earlier.'

'Anea? Where?'

'Right here, boy. She's not in the habit of saying too much.'

A hand slipped into Lucien's own, small but strong, the fingers long and clever. A body pressed against his in the darkness, then an arm slipped around his waist. The body was slight; the body was Anea. He felt a surge of relief pass through him and hugged her back.

'You're unharmed. I looked for you in the *sanatorio*. They have Rafaela in there.'

Her hand squeezed his in the darkness. She was alive, if only to starve to death in the oubliette, or be forced to drink the water and forget herself.

'We're the last of the Orfani now,' murmured Lucien, 'except for Golia, but he's no more than Giancarlo's hound. I don't know what the Majordomo is planning, but I know I need to stop it.'

'I admire your optimism,' replied Franco.

'I have to try. I can't leave her in there.'

Anea hugged him closer. It wasn't the embrace he'd shared with Rafaela, having more in common with the way he'd held Camelia, the way she'd held him when he was smaller.

'We're the last of the Orfani now,' he repeated sadly.

Anea said nothing.

'Not quite the last, not exactly,' said a voice from above the grille. A lantern light shone down through the rusted bars, illuminating the three prisoners in golden light.

24

The Poisonous Missive

HOUSE CONTADINO

– Augusto 312

Lucien would always remember the night when Demesne was no longer safe. Not for himself. Not for any of the Orfani. The fights in the classrooms, the scuffles in abandoned corridors, the posturing and insults all paled into insignificance after the shocking events of that terrible summer evening.

Virmyre's warning in the classroom had not gone unheeded. Almost a year had passed since that tense conversation, and the path that lay before him remained obscure. The only certainty was that Golia would make a play for power, and Lucien's survival would depend on allies, which he had precious few of. Try as he might, he could not see what shape the forthcoming conflict might take, or how he could plan to survive it. Assassination was the obvious danger, but whether it would be delivered by blade or poison was yet to be seen.

The summer's day had been sultry. The air felt solid, unbreathable, no breeze or relief from the sun. He'd forgone dinner in the main hall that evening, instead taking bread, cheese and apples with some farmers. They'd brought their carts to Demesne, loaded down with produce: sacks of corn, crates of apples and a trio of barrels. Rafaela checked on him, making sure he wasn't being a nuisance. The ruddy-cheeked and weathered men fed Lucien small amounts of cider. The oldest of them, Franco, told him he'd grow up to be a fine young man. Franco had forearms larger than Lucien's thighs and iron-grey hair running to his shoulders. He was a cheerful type, able to take disappointments in his stride, and Lucien had never seen him angry. The Orfano smiled at them and nibbled on cheese, enjoying their camaraderie. He was less interested in growing up to be a 'fine young man' than he was in simply growing ears. If only it were that easy. Puberty had ushered in a broadening of the shoulders, the beginnings of stubble and a few extra inches of height, but the puckered holes on each side of his head would not enjoy any miraculous metamorphosis. The farmers left, carts creaking as they were drawn back to hamlets or homesteads departed hours earlier. Franco waved cheerfully over his shoulder with one meaty hand. Lucien watched the men leave until they became dots on the horizon, then headed into House Contadino.

A tension lingered in the air long after sunset, the dwellers within Demesne's walls longing for a thunderstorm to clear the charged atmosphere. Lucien lay awake with his sheets rucked around his ankles, skin grown clammy with the night's duration. He washed his face and hands in the basin to cool himself. Small chance of that. Deep below, a long-case clock announced midnight in muted chimes, the sound reverberating through the corridors of House Contadino.

That's when he heard it. Indistinct at first, then more loudly in the darkness. In seconds he was on his feet, sword drawn from its sheath, the obsidian blade invisible in the darkness. He was long past discarding the weapon in the armchair at the end of each day. The weapon slept at his side, another consequence of Virmyre's warning.

He crept out to the sitting room, bare feet silent on the rugs that covered the stone floor. The sound came again. Rustling, scratching. His pulse quickened as he looked around. The windows were open, but no raven had gained entrance. Lucien retreated back into his bedroom, lighting a lantern, fearful the sound would bring a cloaked assassin into view at any moment. He entered the sitting room again, emboldened by the illumination. Shadows haunted the corners of the chamber and the drake uncoiled in the glass tank. He wondered if rats had found a way in and looked down at the floors. A scrap of parchment had appeared underneath the door to the corridor. The gap was not large so delivery had been difficult.

He hesitated a moment before retrieving the note, then

retreated to his bed. The sword lay unsheathed across the pillows as his fingers teased the missive open. A worn key dropped into his lap as he unfolded the paper, ignored in his haste to read the contents. The handwriting was neat and fine, clearly a scholarly hand. The parchment looked much like the quality of paper Virmyre gave to his students. Lucien calmed himself and read.

Lucien,

Please come at once, this very night, to my chambers. I must discuss with you a plan I have for Golia. By now you must realise we will not survive if he gains any measure of standing within Demesne. I plan to poison the oaf and save the skin of all the Orfani.

Find a key to my chambers inside, so you may enter without undue fuss.

Yours,

Anea

It stood to reason of course. If Virmyre had warned Lucien of the forthcoming danger, then there was every chance he'd have given the same speech to Anea. Where Lucien had struggled to comprehend his survival, Anea had formulated a plan. A way to deal with Golia without recourse to arms.

Lucien waited in the lamplight a moment. It seemed odd that she'd written down her intentions for Golia. Such a declaration committed to paper was a dangerous thing, unless of course she trusted Lucien completely. He waited there for long seconds, heart racing in his chest, key in one hand, Anea's poisonous missive in the other, if indeed the words were hers.

His eyes scanned the text one more time. The signature looked uneven, rushed perhaps. If the note was a forgery he could be the instrument of Anea's downfall. And his own. All these thoughts raced and spun. He'd go to her. But only after burning the note.

House Contadino was shrouded in darkness, and only the ticking of the clock breached the silence, measuring the hours until the next sweltering day. Lucien crept along the passage, ascending the spiral staircase with care, the light from his lantern washing along walls, filtering over the floor ahead of him. The smell of the burned parchment still lingered in his nostrils. Had he dreamed the letter? He looked down and found the key in a sweating palm. He knew he must press on.

Anea's door stood before him. All this time spent as uneasy rivals, now changed by unexpected complicity. The key was suddenly heavy, his fingers thick and uncooperative. The lock *clunked*, thunder in the silence of the night. Lucien winced, then pushed open the door, entering and closing it quickly. Anea's room looked much like his own, the bedroom situated to the left of the sitting room. He thought it strange no candles were lit. Stranger still embers in the fireplace glowed with a ruddy light, making the already humid night unbearable. Sweat prickled at his brow; his neck was slick to the touch.

The connecting door stood ajar. Lucien slipped through and into Anea's bedchamber. He could hear her now, breath gusting lightly with each exhalation. Fast asleep and rolled on her side, she'd pushed the sheets pushed down to her waist. A silvery nightshirt covered her slender torso, arms bare and alabaster. Lucien called out, gently so as not to startle her. She remained soundly asleep.

He drew closer, suddenly aware she was without her veil. The candlelight lingered on her pale face, growing stronger as he approached. And then Lucien stopped breathing, staring in sickened fascination. He'd imaged frail bow lips and a small pointed chin if he ever admitted to thinking about her at all. In fact the truth was far from delicate or beautiful. Anea had a gaping hole where her mouth should be, flanked on each side by insect-like mandibles. Her lower jaw was missing, and stunted human teeth peaked from her gum line. From above the tip of her nose she looked like any other girl of eleven years. Yet the bottom half of her face was as nightmarish and twisted as anything in Virmyre's specimen jars.

Anea's eyes fluttered, then flicked open. She flinched and sat up, one hand gesturing toward the door emphatically, index finger issuing her silent command. Her other hand drew the sheets up, past her shoulders, past her mouth. Her green eyes were now shimmering with tears, shoulders shaking with upset. Lucien spread his hands in apology.

'I'm ... I'm sorry. I came as you asked. In your note. You asked me to come? You sent me the key.'

He felt terrible, withdrawing to the sitting room. She was still gesturing as he left her, the pointed finger now accusatory, no longer indicating the direction of his departure. He stood in the sitting room, trying to regain his composure, mind racing. A deep pang of shame swelled inside, shame for being so pre-occupied about his ears when Anea's plight was far worse. He took a deep breath, set down the key on a side table and made to leave.

But the door was locked.

He'd not locked it. He *knew* he'd not locked it. And then came the sickening realisation that they were in trouble.

The room was brighter than it had cause to be, the fire in the hearth now roaring, wood crackling and snapping in the heat. He could smell lamp oil on the air, aware of a thin veil of smoke obscuring the ceiling. A trail of fire sprang up from the hearth leading to the drapes at the windows. Another trail of flame reached out, this time grasping at the couch. Fingers of flame danced on the fabric, giving off jet smoke.

Lucien blew out the lamp and set it down, attempting to unlock the door. The keyhole was blocked from the other side.

They were trapped.

Behind him the heat intensified. Cursing, he rammed the key into the hole, conscious that the couch was now ablaze at one end. Yellow flames were licking at the window, glass tinkled from leading, now soft in the heat.

Anea appeared, one hand covering her face, her green eyes furious and brow creased.

'Someone's locked us in.' Lucien looked over his shoulder at the burning room. He had to admire the efficiency. Orange light danced across the surface of the walls as the furniture smouldered, burning fitfully. A pall of smoke weighed heavily on the air above them, thickening with each passing moment. Lucien's skin tightened in the heat. He worried the keyhole some more before Anea tugged at his sleeve, leading him back into the bedroom. The sitting room was thoroughly alight now. Lucien closed the bedroom door to buy them precious seconds. Anea stumbled around her room, a wretched wheezing sound issuing from her misshapen mouth.

Lucien knelt on her bed as the fire roared next door. Smoke was filtering into the bedroom from a gap above the door. He ripped the sheets in half, then tied them end to end, knotting them tightly. Anea saw the sense of his plan, fetching more sheets from a chest at the end of the bed. Lucien opened the windows and gulped down lungfuls of cool air. Suddenly, the storm arrived, edging in from the west. A cacophony like a hammer blow rolled in from the coastline, a slower angry rumble following after. Lucien tied the improvised rope to the bed as smoke poured into the bedroom, the door shuddering under the onslaught of the flames. The top half of the room was now a poisonous stew of fumes.

Anea looked down at the drop, some forty feet and more. She looked at Lucien and shook her head. The door to the bedroom disintegrated, falling away from the hinges. A wash of heat rolled over them. The rug on the floor kindled immediately, the sheepskin adding to the cloying smoke.

'I'll go first. You'll be fine. Just wrap the rope around your wrist like this and take it slowly. Brace your feet against the castle.'

Lucien loved climbing. Unless of course there was the possibility another Orfano might suddenly lose her grip, tumbling down onto him. Still, he'd rather risk a fall from over forty feet than be found a charred corpse come the morning. Lucien could have made short work of the climb down; instead he opted to match Anea's pace, looking up and coaxing her on with words of encouragement when she faltered. They inched down the makeshift rope, the inches adding up to feet, the feet bringing them closer to the safety of the ground. Lucien picked up the pace and dropped the last ten feet, landing and rolling, cat-like, just as D'arzenta had taught him. He looked up. A plume of roiling black poured from Anea's window. If the fire had consumed the apartment then the bed itself was alight, and the rope was tied to the...

Instinctively Lucien took a step back and held out his arms as the rope came away from the windowsill. Anea released a strangled yelp. She fell, hands clawing at the air, legs pedalling beneath her nightgown.

Seconds later Lucien found himself flat on his back, his left wrist aching. Anea was sitting nearby, her legs draw up to her chest, head down, weeping onto her knees. Lucien drew his knife and cut a sleeve from his own nightshirt, fashioning a veil. Anea took it, blinking away tears. Once the fabric was tied across her face she composed herself. They sat, watching the orange flames lick the windowsill, listening to the faint tinkle of glass as the remaining fixtures surrendered to the heat.

Lucien explained about the note and the key, apologised again for startling her. Anea listened, not looking at him, gaze fixed on her toes. She extended a hand, and when Lucien didn't respond she pointed at his dagger. He handed it to her warily. No need to fear, she just needed a tool to scratch her words into the dust.

Golia?

'I can't be sure.' He chewed his lip. 'I think it's safe to assume it's Golia. Dino and Festo are much too young. There's an older Orfano too, but I'm certain she never leaves her rooms.'

Anea spent long moments working the knife at the hard earth.

Whoever it was, they meant to eliminate both of us in one strike. They're not stupid. Or if they are stupid, they're receiving instruction.

Lucien stared at her in the darkness. This was the most protracted conversation he'd had with her. He was already admiring her deduction. However, this ruse possessed too much nuance and subtlety to be a scheme devised by Golia. He wondered if they had underestimated House Fontein's favourite student. The vanguard of the storm had reached Demesne now, occasional spots of rain flickering down in the night, threatening more to come. Lucien pulled Anea to her feet gently, leading her to the House Contadino kitchens.

There would be a lot of explaining to do come the morning.

25

Disobedience

THE OUBLIETTE

– Febbraio 315

Lucien, Franco and Anea gazed up at the grille, baffled. They were rank with the oubliette's foulness, their clothes ruined, hair matted with effluent. Above them came the sound of metal on metal, scraping and scoring, then a faint click. The process was repeated before the rusty grille was pulled to one side. There was a strained grunt; a dull clang followed. A rope slithered down, splashing into the water. The three prisoners regarded each other breathless with disbelief. One by one they emerged into the light, blinking, gasping down lungfuls of air, free of Demesne's underworld. Before them stood Dino, a tiny smile playing on his lips.

He was dressed in a charcoal-grey suit, the sleeves showing scarlet silk through tailored slashes. Achilles perched on his shoulder, all jagged dun-brown scales and beady black eyes. Dino grasped the sword cane in his right hand, a covered lantern in his left. Lucien swept him up and hugged him so hard the smaller boy squawked.

'Get off me, you're covered in shit,' said Dino. 'And mind Achilles, you great ass,' Lucien released him, continuing to stare as if the younger boy might disappear like a figment. Dino set down the lantern, then pulled something from an inside pocket. He handed a leather-bound journal and a pencil to Anea. She took it from him gratefully, pausing to embrace him. Franco voiced his thanks, and Dino replied with his usual lazy salute. Anea was already writing something down. She turned to Lucien.

The inscription in the book simply read *Russo?*

203

'As far as I know, she's in your apartment, locked in the bedroom,' he replied. 'I stopped two guards from hammering down the door. She was safe when I left her.' He swallowed uneasily. Any number of guardsmen could have revisited Anea's apartment since he'd left, preying on Russo easily, shocked and numb as she was. He turned to Dino, still struggling to believe the truth of it.

'Everyone said you'd been killed in your sleep.'

'I haven't slept in my own bed in years.' The smaller boy shrugged. 'Not since the fire at Anea's apartment. I'm not stupid.' He pouted. 'There's a small storeroom in a tower nearby. I've made it quite cosy.'

'But the guards—'

'They did kill someone.' Dino's grey eyes were filled with regret. 'Someone I've been letting use my apartment for some time now. He was stone dead when I got there. It was quick.' The young Orfano plucked at his lip. 'I hope it was quick,' he whispered.

'Who was it?' pressed Lucien.

'A baker's apprentice from the Erudito kitchens, his name was...' Dino swallowed and looked away.

'It can't be helped, boy,' said Franco, laying one meaty hand on the Orfano's shoulder. 'These are dark times. We'd best leave here before we're discovered.'

'Where do we go?' asked Dino. 'We're the most wanted people in Landfall.'

Anea scratched down something in her journal and proffered it to them.

House Erudito. Virmyre.

They set out slowly, Dino scouting ahead. Of all of them he looked least like an escaped prisoner, although the drake on his shoulder and expensive tailoring made him conspicuous. Dino returned to them after several minutes of squatting in the darkness of a rarely used stairwell. Only the odd cat hunting mice dwelled in the corridors here. He led them to a side door of the House Fontein kitchens. It was midnight now. Nothing stirred outside the castle, and the muted stars looked cold and white. Grasses tugged at their boots, which still leaked fetid water from the oubliette. The chilly air and the pounding of their hearts kept them alert. Gladly they entered the warmer corridors of House Erudito.

But only after Dino had disposed of the guard on duty.

The tip of his sword cane entered the man's skull, finding the soft depression below his ear. The guard writhed, went into spasm, collapsed.

'It's not right for you be so good at killing so young,' grunted Franco.

'There's much that's not right,' replied Dino, wiping the blood from the blade with a rag.

Franco took the dead guard's halberd and his clothes, glad to be free of the stink of the oubliette. Silence pressed down on the small gatehouse. They waited. No one investigated the noises. No one was expecting any trouble, not with Anea and Lucien disposed of and the remaining Orfani dead. They entered House Erudito, Virmyre's safety foremost in their minds. Franco followed last, clutching the halberd to his chest.

The classroom was a ruin. The cat shark, Virmyre's pride and joy, lay in a pool of shattered glass and pungent preservative. Once graceful and lithe, the creature was merely meat now, decomposing sadly. Lucien looked around, disgusted. All the curios and oddments had been scattered or broken. Books had been ripped and torn. There was evidence of an attempt at arson, but the fire raiser hadn't taken sufficient care, and the blaze had failed to take hold. Desks had been overturned, stools smashed. Lucien clenched his fists and chewed his lip, then let out a stream of invective.

'Well, he's not here,' said Dino, 'and he's not in the oubliette.'

'Let's try his apartment,' said Lucien, afraid of what they might find. The four hurried through night-shrouded corridors, Dino's lantern throwing long and sinister shadows along the walls.

They arrived at Virmyre's door just as Angelicola was letting himself out. He looked more ragged than usual, wisps of his messy grey hair falling into his face. His jacket was ripped, his eyes puffy, dark. The *dottore* froze, a horrified expression seeping in behind his eyes. The Orfani before him had truly become the things of ghost stories and witchcraft. Lucien in particular looked the essence of a vengeful revenant; Anea appeared no better. Dino held up the lantern, looking the rumpled *dottore* in the eye. Achilles gazed balefully at the old man.

'Dino?' choked Angelicola.

'Spare me.' The youngest of the Orfani rolled his eyes. 'You never liked us. So don't tell me how glad you are I'm still drawing breath.'

Lucien was impressed by how much venom the boy injected into each word.

'Is Virmyre here?' asked Franco. The *dottore* looked up, as if seeing him for the first time.

'What? Oh, yes. He's in his rooms. He's rather unwell. Giancarlo... Well, you can see for yourselves. He gave a brief awkward bow, then made his excuses and disappeared into the darkness.

'That bastard needs a bath and a new tailor,' muttered Dino.

'He's not the only one,' deadpanned Lucien. Anea pushed past them and turned the handle, opening the door.

They entered to find Virmyre lying on a couch, eyes shut, breathing hard. His jacket had been slung over a chair, one boot had found its way under his dining table, the other remained on his foot, unbuckled. Three wine bottles, now empty, had been discarded on the floor, one of them smashed. A glass rested on its side, the contents soaking into the cream rug.

'*Porca troia,*' mumbled Franco.

Virmyre's shirt was stained, although how much was blood and how much was red wine was academic. His right eye was swollen shut, bottom lip split. Stubble adorned his cheeks, making his usually immaculate goatee indistinct. His hair was matted with blood in places.

'That's it,' he slurred to no one in particular. 'All done now. Doomed to a life of teaching idiot *nobili*, and doing the requisite amount of arse-kissing to avoid being murdered in the night. Murdered,' he repeated in a harsh whisper.

'You'd best find some water,' said Franco. 'He's as drunk as a lord.'

'Two lords, most likely,' replied Dino.

Franco positioned himself inside the door, keeping watch on the corridor beyond. He'd taken to the uniform of the dead guardsman quickly. Lucien noticed he handled the halberd in a competent fashion – perhaps there was more to the old farmer. Anea walked the room, taking in the vast numbers of books, her gaze settling on the sword resting above the mantelpiece. She tugged Lucien's sleeve and pointed.

Dino tried to make Virmyre drink some water, which went badly.

'Get off me! Can't a man be drunk once in a while? I ask you. Tonight of all nights.'

'We're not dead,' said Lucien impatiently. Virmyre lurched upright, eyes wide open as if woken from a terrible dream.

'Lucien? *Porca misèria!* How? Anea? I don't understand.'

Lucien looked into Virmyre's face. He'd been made to suffer, but even Giancarlo wouldn't dare assassinate eminent members of House Erudito. Killing Orfani was one thing, but eliminating household staff would invite reprisals. A beating was message enough.

'Nice rooms,' said Lucien, realising he'd never entered Virmyre's apartment before. 'Shame about the wine stain on the rug.'

The *professore* shuffled his feet, taking a moment to compose himself. There was a dreadful moment when Lucien thought he might lose his stomach, but Virmyre remained standing, if somewhat green.

'Go, get some new clothes on,' said Virmyre. 'You'll catch your death in those sodden things.' He gestured to his bedroom. 'I'll send for an undertaker, and we can arrange a cremation for those dreadful rags.'

He lurched a few feet and gestured at Dino comically.

'Why can't you be more like him? He's got a nice suit. He's got a drake on his shoulder. He's got a sword cane. Really, Lucien, you've let the side down. This getting-thrown-into-the-oubliette business is beneath you.'

Lucien exchanged looks with Anea, who in spite of everything was struggling to contain her laughter. Her shoulders shook soundlessly. Lucien went through into the bedroom and after some searching around found some clothes that nearly fit him. The riding boots were perfect. He emerged back into the sitting room to discover Virmyre lecturing the others passionately about influenza and pneumonia. Anea looked out from under a blanket in which she had been bundled up in an expert fashion.

'I don't suppose you still have that horse?' said Virmyre.

'Don't ask,' replied Lucien, remembering the roan. 'Why do you have a sword above your mantelpiece?'

Franco looked round at this, clearly as interested as anyone else. Dino had perched in an armchair nearby, looking exhausted.

'I wasn't always a teacher. It may trouble you to know that I, too, was young once. I was the son of a farmer on the Contadino estate. I received a scholarship for the academy at House Fontein. But I hated it. Whenever I had any free time I'd sneak off to lessons with House Erudito. They chased me off at first. Then they let me in as long as I sat at the back and kept my mouth shut. A few years of that and I was offered a job as an assistant.' Virmyre slumped down on the couch. 'I suppose you want to borrow the bloody thing.' He gestured at the sword.

'The thought had crossed my mind,' said Lucien.

'You owe me a horse.'

'I do.'

'And the clothes you're wearing.'

'True enough.'

'Promise me you'll get that lovely girl out of the *sanatorio*.'

Lucien met Virmyre's gaze.

'I promise,' he replied, taking the sword down from the mantelpiece. It was dusty and needed sharpening. He turned to Franco.

'A favour?'

'Name it, my boy.'

'Look after our drunken friend here. Don't let him leave the room.'

'I'm drunk, not deaf, you insolent swine,' slurred Virmyre.

'I'm right here.' He made to stand, then slumped back on the couch and passed out.

Anea shook Dino gently by the shoulder and showed him something in her journal. He nodded his head, rising to his feet and rolling his shoulders.

'Where are you two going?' Lucien asked peevishly. He was having a hard time keeping everyone he cared about from harm.

'We're going to Anea's apartment to get Professore Russo,' said Dino.

'But—'

'We'll be fine,' the younger boy said. 'House Contadino rarely has any guards on duty. Besides, they think we're all dead, or under lock and key. Or both.'

'Can't you wait here?' Lucien was annoyed now. 'Just until I get back?'

Anea stood in front of him, green eyes glowering above the veil.

'Look,' said Dino. 'I'm not standing here all night refereeing an argument between you two. She wants to get Russo and I'm going with her. Besides, where are you going? I just rescued you, and now you're dashing off to get captured again. Or killed.'

'It would seem Dino has a point,' said Franco with a slow smile.

'Fine,' said Lucien. 'Do what you like. Just meet me here afterwards. Please?'

Dino nodded; Anea relaxed.

'Where are you going anyway?' pressed Franco.

'I'm going to see the king. I'm betting he's the only one with a spare set of keys to the *sanatorio*. Without those I can't get to Rafaela. They'll have blocked up the window I smashed in by now. I won't get in that way again.'

'The king?' said Dino, growing pale.

'It's not like I have a choice,' replied Lucien. 'Besides, he's an old man. How much trouble can he be?' He clutched at the hilt of Virmyre's sword, more to stop his hands shaking than out of any reassurance he might gain from being armed.

Anea stepped forward and hugged Lucien, before taking Dino by the hand and heading out the door. Dino had turned the lantern down to avoid attention.

'You ready for this?' Franco asked Lucien.

'I need to get her back.'

'That you do, boy. That you do. Go on then – time's wasting.'

Lucien exited Virmyre's room, fumbling, hands held out like a blind man. His eyes adjusted to the dark and he set off, his toes sliding over the flagstones. Once or twice he paused at junctions, wary of sounds coming from deep in the castle. Nervous sweat broke out and quickly chilled, leaving him cold. He pressed on, coming to the circuitous corridor of the King's Keep, the many ribs and supports casting shadows in the lantern light. Lucien looked around, puzzled. There were never this many lanterns lit in the King's Keep. He rounded the curve of the corridor to where the great double doors to the king's chambers awaited him. Statue-still, head bowed, clutching his staff with both hands, was the Majordomo. His ashen robes covered him from head to toe; only his emaciated hands and jutting chin were visible. A miasma of flies enveloped him, their droning audible.

'Ah, Lucien. Such a shame you won't die. You're the very model of disobedience – something I intend to beat out of you this very night.'

Lucien flinched, the need to run back to Virmyre's room overtaking him. His defeat in the *sanatorio* had been simple work for the Domo, and he was barely recovered from it. The Domo chuckled. It was a filthy, unpleasant sound that filled the corridor. It was the pompous laughter of one who thought victory assured.

Lucien's blood pounded, roaring in his ears.

'Disobedience? I'll show you disobedience. I'm just getting started.'

He drew Virmyre's sword, a snarl twisting his lips.

26

After the Fire

LUCIEN'S APARTMENT

– Augusto 312

Lucien was unable to explain why he'd been present in Anea's apartment when the fire broke out. Giancarlo, D'arzenta, Ruggeri, the *capo*, Mistress Corvo, Virmyre and Russo had all been roused from their beds. They presided over the lengthy interrogation of the two soot-stained and shivering Orfani, eyes narrow with suspicion. Lucien had never seen so many people crowded into his sitting room, feeling grateful his apartment had been spared from the flames.

Dottore Angelicola was also present, fussing over them in a brusque fashion. His untamed eyebrows were drawn together in a furious frown. He managed to look more slovenly than usual. Lucien noticed that Virmyre kept his distance from the ragged tousled-haired man. Finally Angelicola declared the Orfani in good health and went on his way. His muttering that he 'had better things to attend to than spoilt pyromaniac witchlings' could be heard in the corridor long after his departure. Rafaela stood near the doorway, attempting to be invisible. Not difficult as the teaching staff tended to ignore the more menial house staff.

House Contadino had been evacuated and bleary-eyed servants pressed into service as a human chain. Buckets from all over Demesne sloshed water as they were passed, hand over hand, to extinguish the smouldering remains of Anea's apartment. Anea had battened down her distress with a steely-eyed fury. She stood as if she were at sword practice, weight on the balls of her feet, her tiny hands clenched into fists.

'Is it not possible that Lucien did in fact go to Anea's

apartment to start the fire,' said Giancarlo, 'and then became trapped when the blaze took hold.'

This drew a startled gasp from Mistress Corvo. Anea stamped her foot and glowered at the instructor with unrestrained venom. Her green eyes were especially piercing, red-rimmed from smoke, tears and frustration. She scribbled down a riposte to Giancarlo's accusation on a scrap of paper and passed it to Russo.

'She says if it had not been for Lucien she would most certainly be dead. Furthermore, she views this incident as "nothing short of an attack on her person" and would ask you to not make baseless allegations.'

The room fell silent and the air around Anea crackled with tension. She still wore the makeshift veil Lucien had fashioned from his sleeve. Attired in dirt and grime, Lucien thought she resembled the unquiet dead of his horror stories, then realised he looked much the same.

'It seems to me that if Lucien was not there to burn Anea's apartment then perhaps he was there for another reason. To conspire, for instance.'

The other instructors and teaching staff shuffled their feet. D'arzenta folded his arms and looked away. Russo flicked her auburn hair over one shoulder and flashed a warning glare at Giancarlo, who chose to ignore it.

'Oh, come on,' said Russo. 'You need to set aside this vendetta against Lucien and start acting like a *superiore*.'

'And I would remind you to act like a woman, one who knows her place.'

'My *place* is bringing enlightenment and education, something you wouldn't know about.'

Giancarlo bristled. Russo held his gaze and threw up her chin defiantly, placing her hands on her hips.

'You would do well to confine your opinions to the class-room,' said Giancarlo quietly, 'where they are welcome, Mistress Russo.'

'That's *Professore* Russo to you.' The room had become taut with the exchange.

'You would be more able to build a case if some proof of

this conspiracy could be acquired, Superiore.' This last came from the darkness of the doorway, the corridor beyond unlit. Detaching himself from the shadows, solidifying in the light, the Majordomo stepped inside. Rafaela flinched as the grey-wrapped functionary entered the room. Flies followed in his wake, trailing him lazily.

'This is ridiculous,' rumbled Virmyre. 'Lucien is fourteen, Anea only eleven. Are you suggesting two children are fomenting rebellion? Pah! More likely it was for entirely more romantic reasons. Have you all forgotten what it is like to be in the first flush of puberty?' He stared around accusingly at the assembled staff, who stiffened with embarrassment. Lucien had a hard time imagining any of them succumbing to lust.

'Oh, good heavens,' whined Mistress Corvo. She fanned herself, struggling to breathe in a bravura of histrionics. 'How much more of this sham?' Her beady eyes blinked several times as she realised she'd spoken slightly louder than she intended.

Giancarlo was not so easily deterred, and Lucien's apartment was searched with the Majordomo assenting. Lucien allowed himself a smile of satisfaction. Whoever sent the note had depended on him to keep it. He'd at least been possessed of enough wit to burn the damning letter.

Finally he was allowed back into his room. Anea on the other hand was given temporary quarters in House Erudito, under guard. They were both confined to their rooms for a week, although no specific reason was given for their punishment.

The following day Lucien lay on his couch reading an old novel, trying not to think about the wreckage of Anea's apartment. Or her face. The corridors of House Contadino were full of commotion and the cursing of workmen. Artisans were tramping to and from Anea's rooms two floors above. The long process of redecoration was already under way. Rumours were already circulating about the exacting nature of the silent Orfano.

Bright sunlight shone through the latticed windows of Lucien's sitting room, and it was almost impossible to remain in dour spirits. The first day of his polite imprisonment was largely a farce. He received more visitors that day than at any other time in his life. The guard on duty, forgetting his strict instructions from Giancarlo, was bribed with a platter of good things from the kitchens.

D'arzenta appeared first, conducting an entire conversation without mentioning the fire or Anea once. The *maestro di spada* set Lucien a number of exercises that could be done during his confinement. Then D'arzenta departed without fuss or sentiment. But Lucien wouldn't remain alone for long.

Virmyre and Russo appeared on the pretext of checking the health of the drakes. That they brought water, wine, good bread, unsalted butter and a selection of olives rather betrayed their cover story. Lucien smiled cheerfully throughout the impromptu picnic, showing off his favourite books to his teachers. Both carefully avoided asking him why he'd been in Anea's room, and Russo assured him that the silent Orfano was recovering from the ordeal.

Lucien was sitting in the high-backed armchair feeding dead crickets to Antigone, Agamemnon and Achilles when Rafaela entered. Antigone had taken up her usual perch on his right shoulder, looking down imperiously on her offspring. Achilles' drab olive and sepia form was entwined about Lucien's right leg. The drake stared around balefully, champing on a mouthful of insect in a mechanical fashion.

'Well, aren't you all cosy?' Rafaela flashed Lucien a grin.

'There are worse punishments, I suppose.'

'Are you well? I didn't get the chance to ask you this morning. I still can't believe you climbed all the way down from Anea's room using bed sheets as rope. You must be mad.'

'Probably. Still, it was that or be burned alive. I'm only glad we didn't fall and break our necks.'

'So, are you going to give Dino one of your drakes? It seems unfair that you should have three and he have none.'

'Hmmm, I suppose I could,' he said. 'Trouble is, I like all them of them. Giving any of them up would be difficult. Especially Antigone, I love her the most.'

Rafaela stared at him a moment, quite still, and then resumed hanging up the clean shirts she had brought from the laundry.

'So, are you going to tell me what last night was about? The whole of Demesne has broken out in a rash of gossip. I've not heard anything like it since Camelia got pregnant before her wedding day.'

Lucien rolled his eyes and went back to feeding the drakes. Camelia would no doubt hear about the fire in due course – she was currently at her family's cottage following the birth of her son.

'I'll assume not then, Master Lucien?' Rafaela said, pouting slightly.

'If I tell you, do you promise to take me at my word and not tell a soul?'

Her eyes narrowed: clearly she'd not expected him to confide in her.

'Of course.' Rafaela closed the door to his apartment and locked it, then sat on the couch, hands clasped in her lap. Lucien thought she looked tense.

'Say it,' said Lucien, his eyes grave.

'Say what?'

'Say "I promise."' He tried out his most commanding tone, spoiled by Antigone climbing atop his head at precisely that moment.

'Very well,' she sighed. 'I promise.'

Lucien told her in hushed tones how the note had arrived, complete with the key, and why he'd gone to Anea's rooms. He edited out the exact contents of the missive and also the terrible sight of Anea's face. He owed her that much.

'I'm sure they got there before I did. They must have saturated the couch and curtains with lamp oil, then remained close by to bank up the fire. Perhaps they even started it while I was in her bedroom. Bastards.'

'You think it was more than one?' whispered Rafaela.

'Difficult to know. Clearly they didn't count on us climbing out the window.'

A knock at the door caused them both to jump. Lucien felt his pulse loud in his ears. He was beginning to lose his appetite for unannounced visitors. Rafaela stood and moved to the door, but before she could turn the key Lucien laid one hand on her shoulder. She looked back to find him gripping his scabbard, eyes full of wariness. He pressed an index finger to his lips. They waited. The time stretched painfully as Lucien's mind invented situations that included his assassination. If the Majordomo was out there he'd rather not open the door. The knock came again. Louder and more insistent. The door handle rattled as the person on the other side tested it.

'Oh, for goodness' sake.'

'Camelia?' Rafaela unlocked the door to find the cook with her son in the crook of her arm. Camelia stared at them both, adopting a cool expression.

'And just what exactly was keeping you two from opening the door when I knocked the first time?'

'Fear of assassination,' Lucien said casually. He threw his sword onto the couch and crossed his arms, but only to stop his hands from shaking. He wasn't sure where the paranoia had sprung from but had no wish to experience it again. It was then he noticed Rafaela blushing.

'What?' he asked.

'Nothing.' She shook her head. Lucien realised the nature of Camelia's insinuation.

'You'd better come in or the drakes will escape and end up dying in the corridors,' he said as thoughts of Rafaela danced in his mind.

Camelia entered and Rafaela soon forgot her blushes, helping the cook settle her newborn son on the couch. Camelia looked healthy, if tired in the way of new mothers, more happy than Lucien could ever remember her. This gnawed on his nerves for reasons he couldn't fully articulate.

'Can't you find a home for this?' said Rafaela, handing him the weapon. 'I'm sick of nearly sitting on the thing.' Lucien took it from her and stood mutely as the women fussed over the tiny boy. Rafaela began asking questions about the birth and ignored Lucien entirely. Camelia launched into a rather graphic and unsettling account of her labour. Lucien decided it was precisely that moment he needed to shelve some books that had been lurking near the couch. Then he decided the books would be best stored in his bedroom, absenting himself entirely.

*

'What was that about?'

Lucien looked up. His trousers were covered in dust and books were scattered across the floor. It was shaping up to be a big re-ordering of his collection. Rafaela was in the doorway, anger sketched on her features.

'What was what about?'

'Being so rude to Camelia. She came to see you.'

'What? Has she left already?' He stood up and brushed himself off. There was a lot of dust.

'You've been here for over an hour. Yes, she's gone, and she wasn't very happy.' Rafaela's usually warm hazel eyes flashed with annoyance.

'Sorry, I lost track of the time.'

'You didn't even ask her what her son's name was.'

Lucien bit his lip and scratched his hair, suddenly very warm. The events of the last twenty-four hours crashed down on him: the fire, Giancarlo's accusation and finally Camelia bringing her son. His felt his lip tremble and hated himself for it. He tried to speak but the words stuck in his throat. Rafaela crossed the room and wrapped her arms around him. No longer angry, her expression was now one of concern.

'You're shaking,' she whispered. He nodded back, unable to speak.

'I'm sorry. It's the fire, isn't it? No wonder you're acting strangely. Anyone else would be exactly the same.' She squeezed him a little tighter.

He broke the embrace. 'It's not that. Well, partly it's that. But...' A sigh. 'It's Camelia. She's never here any more, and now she's got the baby she's no need for me.' He looked away and chewed his lip before continuing, 'She has her own son now.'

'It's not like that,' said Rafaela. 'She'll always have time for you. But you can't run and hide just because things haven't turned out like you wanted. And besides, I'm still here, aren't I?' She squeezed his hand, her skin soft and warm.

Lucien studied the floor intently. Rafaela stepped forward, pushing his face against the soft junction of her neck and shoulder. His arms found her waist, faltering at first. Then her hand gently smoothed the hair on the back of his head. He was suddenly beset by a riot of feelings, mainly fear of the fire, but also loss. He knew he was being irrational about Camelia's new life. And there was Anea of course, and her secret, which he had resolved to protect. There was also something else. A yearning.

He was suddenly aware of Rafaela in a way that had only been hinted at before. The smell of her hair was intoxicating, the way his arms felt wrapped about her. How was he nearly as tall as her? When had that happened? She brushed her lips against his temple, softer than anything he'd known.

'It'll be all right, Lucien. I promise. Camelia will be back soon. But you have to allow for things to change.'

He looked at her, their faces inches apart. His mind reeled with the thought of her lips brushing against his own. He shivered, willing himself to discover that sensation.

But she broke away, slowly but firmly. There was a shadow of mistrust in her eyes.

'Don't go now,' he said, but the words tripped, stumbling on his teeth and tongue.

'I have things to do. I should go.' She eyed him, full of wariness, and left without another word. He got no sleep that night, wondering at the moment that had passed between them. He chided himself for driving her away, painfully aware he needed to see her again soon and feel her arms around him again.

27

The Domo's Apprentice

KING'S KEEP

– Febbraio 315

Lucien ran forward, remembering all the times he'd shrunk in the presence of Demesne's most trusted servant. The long hours fearing the Domo's visits to his apartment as a child. Every occasion the gaunt man had haunted his nightmares. The countless abducted women, Navilia among them, the starved and the lost. The outcast Orfani killed quietly, out of sight. Then the jarring recollection of the Domo sweeping him out of the *sanatorio* like vermin, sending him sprawling down the stairs, away from Rafaela. The sword in his hand cried out for violence, he would not deny it.

He swung, blind rage taking him off balance, leaving him open. His lips had peeled back from his teeth in a snarl of reckless fury. The Domo responded with short jabs from the butt of his staff, forcing Lucien back, blunting his momentum. The silent roar of his rage drowned out any pain the Domo inflicted. Lucien swore, then blinked, coughed. The ever-present flies were thick in the air, thicker than he had realised in the darkness. They were a barely seen vapour, a drone of wings around him. The cloud of tiny bodies swarmed over the Domo's opponent, the gaunt man apparently immune to their interference. Lucien batted and wiped his face. He was sure there was something in his mouth, writhing, crawling. The sound of them filled his ears. He faltered.

The Domo stepped forward, opening with light, probing attacks, striking at unprotected shins, stabbing at knees with the butt of the staff. Lucien parried, the weight of the steel blade unfamiliar, his wounded shoulder tiring. He searched in vain for some clue where the next attack might come from, but the Domo's face was inscrutable. The chin jutted out as if made from granite, the mouth was an unmoving line. Lucien knew all too well what lay hidden beneath the hood. What he lacked was a way to read his opponent.

Suddenly he was pressed back against the wall, the Domo towering over him, feinting and striking, yet out of reach of his own attacks. Lucien coughed, feeling as if the flies had invaded the deep places of his lungs, were in his ears, in his throat, threatening to consume him from inside. With sparse room to parry, he wrenched a lantern from the wall, throwing it down at the feet of the Domo. The glass shattered, metal door sprang open. Lantern oil spilled across the flagstones, soaking up into the ash-grey vestments of the King's steward. The Domo gave a grunt of irritation, tried to step back. Too late. The lantern had remained stubbornly alight.

A wordless howl escaped the warden's lips as his robes caught. Flies singed, spiralling down to the floor. The Domo staggered back, stumbling into the wall, ricocheted back into the centre of the corridor, where he clawed at himself. The skeleton-thin hands beat at the flames, wrenched at the fabric. Lucien looked on aghast. The memory of Anea's apartment burned brightly in his mind. The smell of oil, the mindless panic, the terrible heat. The descent from the window and the taste of smoke in the back of his throat.

Amid the inferno the Domo dragged off his garments, ripping them with desperation when they would not come loose. Finally free, he drew himself up to his full height, the true awfulness of his frame revealed. The spines on his forearms looked a brittle, shining midnight-blue. The four vestigial arms set into his chest curled about one another, pathetic and twisted. His frame was stooped yet taut with ropes of muscle straining beneath the pallid skin. His sex was a stunted thing, half-formed at best. The Domo's mouth was a curve of cruelty, six eyes regarding Lucien with insect-like indifference. Beside him the pile of rags continued to flame and smoulder.

Burned and soot-stained, the Domo sprang forward, horribly fast, the staff drawn back to strike. Lucien acted purely on instinct, every parry, every sidestep, every feint and strike he'd ever learned now the product of reaction alone. The Majordomo's assault was relentless. Lucien wove the sword around himself in a nimbus of steel, the blade flashing in the lantern light with each sweep, but the staff slipped through his defences. He gasped in dismay as the staff cracked against his ribs, then he felt his knee go numb as it was smashed on one side. Next his right shoulder was buffeted, sending him back, hammering into the wall behind. The impact numbed his left arm, leaving him unable to parry. The butt of the staff slammed into Lucien's forehead. The ceiling above spun and pitched around. Lanterns hanging from pitons on the walls trailed light across his vision, to be replaced by tiny sparks of white dancing before his eyes. He found himself with his cheek resting on the cool flagstones of the corridor.

He tried to speak.

Then nothing.

Lucien blinked, his breathing shallow and faint. He didn't know how long he'd been unconscious. Flies with scorched wings scuttled around him.

'I could have given you everything,' droned the Majordomo, somewhere out of sight. 'Golia was only ever meant to be a puppet, someone we could use to scare the populace – and the houses – into obedience. As the new Majordomo you could have had whatever you wanted. You would have been the real power in Demesne.'

Lucien rolled onto his back. His body was a choir of pain, the various wounds and bruises competing in volume. All the voices discordant. He tried to concentrate.

'Me? Majordomo?'

'You would have been responsible for the day-to-day running of Demesne, for the entire island, all the people of Landfall.' The Domo paused, drawing in a wheezing breath. 'This role does not come without certain advantages. If one has the mind to exploit them.'

The Domo was standing across the corridor from him, wearing a ragged kilt he'd fashioned for himself out of the ruins of his robes. Somehow the rope belt had survived the flames. His staff rested on the floor, clutched in soot-stained hands, the end sunk in a crack between the flagstones.

'Your own tower. Rafaela. Anea. Stephania. Whoever you wanted. All the tailors at your beck and call, the finest meals, the finest swords, the rarest books. Anything you wanted. You, Lucien, you could have shaped Demesne.' The Domo coughed, a prolonged racking that left him speechless. Spittle emerged flecked with black, stretched, dripped to the flagstones. The Domo took a moment to compose himself.

'You were never going to offer me your position,' Lucien sneered.

'Then who? Anea? Hardly a public speaker. I don't have the luxury of time. I can't wait for Dino to grow up. You were always the perfect choice. Why else do you think I intervened at your testing?'

'I see,' mumbled Lucien.

'Think of it. You would have been able to influence every house. Replace that idiot *capo de custodia*, suggest a new *professore* to Maestro Cherubini. Push for better wages for the farmers – whatever you desired. You and Golia were supposed to herald a new age after three centuries of the king's insanity.'

Lucien coughed, propping himself up on his elbows, then slithered away from the Domo. He slumped against the wall, head lolling to one side, dizziness lapping against him in nauseous waves.

'You were supposed to be a new beginning for these old stones,' continued the Domo, a mourning tone in his flat voice. 'Instead you only sought to pull them down around you. I'm not sure why I expected different: angry children only ever seek to destroy.'

'Rafaela,' murmured Lucien, sounding drunk even to himself. The Domo remained silent, his horrific visage looking down at the crumpled Orfano.

'If I become your novice, will you set her free?'

The Domo paused; the vestigial arms on his chest twitched and writhed. Fingers on a skeletal hand flickered in agitation

222

before returning to stillness. The only sound in the corridor was of laboured breathing, a deathly wheeze.

'You're too disobedient, Lucien. You have no thought for anyone or anything outside your own desires. You're incapable of taking instruction.'

'My own tower, you said?'

'Yes. Wherever you wanted to live in Demesne.'

'I could take instruction in return for my own tower.'

'Perhaps. But you threw that chance away. I blame Giancarlo. He was always too keen to encourage this competition between you and Golia. This childish feud, this vendetta. Ridiculous. And Anea—' the Domo's mouth twisted in disgust '—is next to worthless. I ordered Golia to start that fire in her apartment, but he let Giancarlo in on the plan. Before I knew it they had found a way to eliminate both of you at the same time.'

Lucien looked up at the Domo. He'd always suspected of course, but hearing the admission shook him.

'But you survived, found a way out. And not only did you save yourself, but you saved Anea too. That's when I realised how dangerous you were. You would have been a perfect Majordomo.'

'And you'll put an end to the king?'

'Of course,' said the Domo sourly. 'His madness bleeds into the countryside, pollutes everything. Everyone.'

'And the abductions will stop?'

'Of course. Without the king there is no need for them to continue.'

'I can set aside my disobedience if the abductions stop.'

The Domo considered this, hand straying to his great jaw, his many eyes blinking at different times. He remained silent.

'If you can persuade Golia to enter into this . . . this arrangement, I can become the Domo you've always planned for.' Lucien struggled to his feet, hoping he didn't pass out. It took him a while to stand, visibly shaking with the effort. The Domo didn't move, didn't speak. His six mismatched eyes gave away nothing. The silence was stifling.

'Perhaps all is not lost,' droned the Domo, finally. Lucien allowed a flicker of a smile to cross his features.

'With the right sort of robes, no one need know it's me. It can be our secret.'

'We may need to *remove* Giancarlo.' The Domo added a weight to the word that spoke volumes.

'I'd happily perform that task – to prove my loyalty, of course.'

'Yes. I can see how this could work,' replied the Domo, 'possibly better than I could have hoped.'

'My own tower, and Rafaela safe and sound. That's all I ask.'

'I'm sure we can agree on satisfactory terms.'

'And Dino and Anea given titles?'

'As you wish. Although titles rarely mean power, as you will soon learn.'

'There is one small problem,' said Lucien, eyes narrowing.

'Which is?' grunted the Domo.

'All the women you've taken, all the lives you've wrecked, the pain you've caused.'

The Domo blinked, six eyes filled with confusion, saying nothing.

'Crimes like that can't go unpunished.'

Lucien's blade was already moving, but not toward the Domo, rather the staff as it stood vertically before him. The sword smashed into the wood, held fast by the crack in the floor. The noise was like one of Virmyre's chemical detonations. Suddenly the Domo found himself clutching three feet of oak staff instead of six. The sundered end toppled to the floor and rolled away into the darkness.

Lucien snarled and pressed in, unleashing a series of slashes and strikes that D'arzenta would have been proud of. The Domo fell back, pitifully trying to turn the blows aside, emasculated, clutching his broken staff. Cuts appeared in the Domo's flesh, bleeding clear fluid that turned pale blue. Lucien forced them from his mind and pressed on.

'Stop this, Lucien.' The Domo's voice wavered. 'We are brothers.'

Lucien didn't pause, didn't want to hear the words, didn't want to unravel the lies spilling from the Domo's lips.

'Be quiet.'

'You and I are Orfani.'

'Be quiet!'

'Just as Dino and Golia are.' He staggered back, wheezing, holding out a placating hand. 'Anea too. We are all the king's children.'

'BE QUIET!' snarled Lucien, and the sword flickered through the Domo's arm at the elbow.

The hand spun away, severed, forearm trailing, hit the wall and came to rest on the floor, the blood transparent. The Domo hissed, his dry lips pulled back from his yellowing teeth in a dreadful rictus. He swung hard at Lucien's face with the remains of his staff. Lucien dropped to one knee to avoid the crushing blow, using the momentum to slash at the Domo. The blade passed through the steward's leg. Pain jolted through Lucien's arms. The Domo looked down, mouth gaping, then he pitched over, landing hard and jarring, the staff clattering on the stone floor.

'It's like pulling the legs from a spider,' whispered Lucien in sick fascination. 'You don't die, just keep crawling.' The Domo gazed up at Lucien, cold fury in his many eyes.

'Finish it, you bastard child!' It was the first time Lucien had ever heard the Majordomo shout.

'Give me the key,' growled Lucien, desperately wanting to plunge his blade into the Domo's chest, keen to rid Landfall of his presence once and for all. The Domo responded by swinging the remnants of the staff at his knee. Lucien stepped back and parried on instinct, his blade sliding under the wood, severing the Domo's other hand at the wrist.

His howling filled the corridor, subsiding into cursing, then unintelligible sounds that might have been the old tongue.

'Give me the key,' whispered Lucien, sickened at the carnage. The floor was awash with pale blue blood.

Slowly, tremulously, the atrophied arms that crossed the Domo's chest unfolded. Clutched in one tiny deformed hand was the blackened key. It was a cruel thing, two-pronged and bearing jagged teeth. Lucien reached down warily, snatching it away. The Domo wheezed and cursed quietly under his breath, a furious catechism.

'Finish it! Finish it, you hateful child.'

'I've meted out more than enough death. I'm sick of it. No reason why you should get such an easy way out.'

'They'll hunt you down. You'll die for the murder of the Orfani.'

Lucien smiled. 'Too bad Dino survived.'

The thin lips opened, the face, so unreadable all these years, aghast.

'You failed, Domo.'

'But...'

'It was Dino who rescued Anea and I from the oubliette. You underestimated him.'

'I don't understand.' Lucien almost felt sorry for the hideous creature at his feet, shorn of limbs and now his towering self-assurance.

'Dino had a double. He hasn't slept in his own room since the night of the fire you ordered to kill Anea.'

The Domo said nothing, watching with impotent rage as Lucien walked away to stand beneath the heavily decorated arch leading to the king's chambers. A moment's hesitation, then he was pushing the key into the hole – a turn, a click. The sound of chains scraping against metal filled his ears. The ancient wood opened inward, scuffing on the worn flagstones. Lucien took a moment to free another lantern from its hook on the wall.

'You will not survive this night, Lucien, if you pass through that door.'

Lucien looked at the ruin of a man, a grotesque, bleeding blue and convulsing. 'You're a monster,' he said sadly.

'Greater monsters than I await you.'

Lucien turned his back and entered the king's chambers. The doors boomed shut behind him just seconds later, drowning out the stream of curses the Majordomo uttered in his wake.

28

Prospero's Politics

HOUSE FONTEIN

– Febbraio 313

The sound of Lucien's boot heels reverberated down the stark corridors of House Contadino. He wore a midnight-blue doublet, brass buttons gleaming dimly in the sparse lantern light of Demesne's passages. Rafaela followed at his shoulder, wearing a sober grey bodice laced at the front. A matching skirt reached her ankles, moving in graceful sweeps and swishes. The cream blouse revealed her supple neck and the smooth olive skin of her shoulders. Dark brown tresses fell in ringlets on each side of her face, the rest of her hair tucked under a richly embroidered cap.

Lucien's thoughts lingered on the night he had wanted to kiss her, over a year and half ago now. He revisited that memory more than he was keen to admit. But the awkwardness of that embrace had been smoothed over with the passage of time. Ella had quickly resumed her unique role as maid, friend and confidante.

'I'm not sure why you want to see this through,' she whispered. 'It's not like Giancarlo is going to welcome you with open arms.'

'I've just turned sixteen so I can apply for adoption. You know that.'

'But you don't have to apply to House Fontein.'

'I've dreamed of being a soldier in House Fontein for as long as I can remember,' he replied.

Rafaela snorted behind him, failing to mask her disdain. He stopped abruptly and turned to face her. Her hazel eyes were full of mischief until she saw the angry expression on his face.

'What? What's so funny?'

'Well, you own a *lot* of books for an aspiring soldier. I doubt Golia sits around reading stories and feeding drakes.'

'Are you saying I'm not good enough?'

'No, of course not—' she pursed her lips thoughtfully '—just, well, you don't seem like a natural soldier. There's a bit more poetry to you than that.'

Lucien fell into silence. In one simple sentence she had calmed him, reining in his petulance. *Poetry . . . ?* His shoulders slumped a fraction.

'And after the way they've treated you all this time, are you sure House Fontein is the best place for you?'

'I'm sorry,' he mumbled. 'I'm on edge, that's all.'

'Just make sure this is what you really want, Lucien,' she said quietly, smoothing down his collar. 'Orfani are given choices that most folk only dream about.'

They stood at the gateway where House Contadino joined the King's Keep. All that separated him from achieving his most cherished goal was several metres of sprawling corridor, twenty minutes, and the Rite of Adoption.

'But Golia is House Fontein. I'm always being compared to him. What else am I supposed to do?'

'Virmyre isn't a soldier—' she shrugged '—and he's a perfect gentleman. Or he would be if he ever let himself smile.'

'But I'm an Orfano.'

'And what of the other Orfani, those in the past? Perhaps they thought the way you do now? Where are they?'

Lucien looked around, painfully aware Rafaela was breaching one of Demesne's taboos. The fate of previous generation's Orfani remained unspoken.

'Suppose they all trained as soldiers?' she continued. 'What if all that training bought them was an early death?'

'I can't back down now.'

'I know; I'm just saying you're not Golia. What's good for him may not suit you.'

She leaned forward. For a second Lucien's heart stopped in his chest – it was as if time itself had slowed to a crawl. He tried to swallow and couldn't. Rafaela rested her fingertips lightly on his shoulders and then raised herself onto her toes, kissing him gently on the forehead. Disappointment settled about him like a damp coat. He bowed his head so she wouldn't see his downcast expression.

'Come on,' she said, taking his arm. 'We'll be late.'

As it turned out, lateness was the least of Lucien's worries.

The House Fontein chapel was crowded with every functionary who could claim any standing. Pages and messengers, soldiers and *sergenti*, artisans and aides all shuffled their feet, waiting in the chill air. The minor houses – Marco, Datini, Di Toro, Elemosina, Sciaparelli, Allatamento, Martello and even House Albero – had representatives present. Archivist Simonetti favoured Lucien with a nod and a smile. The sun streamed through the stained-glass windows, casting snatches of multicoloured light over the throng. The pews of the rarely used room had been pushed aside. The guests stood expectantly, some elbowing their way forward for the best vantage point.

The three noble families were present. Lucien bowed to each in turn. Rafaela presented Duchess Fontein with a bouquet of flowers as was the custom. Anea was present in a splendid white gown that left her arms and shoulders bare. A huge ultramarine headdress swept back from her forehead, decorated with gold thread. Her veil and shawl were made from the same fabric, intricately embroidered. She was far more regal than any of the ladies of the court despite being just thirteen. Lucien bowed politely and she curtseyed in return, drawing raised eyebrows from the assembled nobles. A wash of half-whispered comments issued through the crowd. Duke and Duchess Prospero in particular exchanged concerned glances.

Dino had also gained entrance, standing with Rafaela, who was beaming a bright and generous smile. Dino flicked a lazy salute and Lucien matched it, a smile twisting his lips. Festo stood beside him, a small smile playing on his lips, his thatch of unruly hair smoothed down. Of all the Orfani he was the most handsome.

Virmyre and Russo headed the contingent of dusty teachers, resembling a murder of stuffed crows in their black gowns. Dottore Angelicola lurked near the House Erudito teaching staff, complaining just loudly enough to be heard over the din of the crowd. Lucien approached and grabbed him by his large aquiline nose, pulling him into the centre of the chamber. Conversations died in throats and all eyes turned to the upstart Orfano.

'If you spoil today for me with your incessant whining I'll take you outside and kill you myself,' growled Lucien. 'Do you understand?'

For every startled gasp there was a peal of unrestrained laughter. It appeared the *dottore* had fewer friends in Demesne that Lucien had imagined. Angelicola fell silent, blanching in the face of Lucien's threat. Behind them the Majordomo cleared his throat, smashing the foot of his staff against the floor, signalling his readiness for the ceremony. Lucien released the *dottore*, who did his best to look affronted under his bushy eyebrows. He pressed his fingers tenderly to his beaky nose and retreated into the congregation.

The Domo stood beneath the pulpit of the chapel, his great staff of office clutched in his near-skeletal fingers, gaunt frame swathed in splendid crimson. It was a welcome change to the mass of moth-eaten rags he usually wore. D'arzenta and Ruggeri stood beside him.

Giancarlo was conspicuously absent.

Lucien broke protocol a moment to turn his back on the Majordomo, searching the masses for Giancarlo's slab-like visage. Realisation of his absence crept through the assembly; a susurrus of whispering became an audible muttering.

Lucien forced himself to turn back to the Domo, biting down his frustration. The crowd fell silent, the soporific drone of Demesne's chief steward lulling them into a stupor. Lucien remained painfully alert, his throat dry, pulse hammering with indignation. Not a soul living within the crumbling walls would take today's Rite of Adoption seriously. The edict would be as hollow and meaningless as the chapel they stood in.

Dino stepped forward and presented Lucien with a bouquet of lilies, a symbol that his old name was now dead. Then Anea stepped forward, gracefully offering him a smaller posy of snowdrops. Lucien bowed, took the flowers. They were fake of course, made from coloured glass. His mind strayed to the night he'd been presented with the porcelain ears, then recoiled and refocused.

Finally, after Lucien had felt the last of his patience run out, D'arzenta and Ruggeri stepped forward, each tying a sash of silk around his arm above the elbow. D'arzenta's sash was black velvet, while Ruggeri tied on a sash of scarlet. Lucien saluted his instructors, bowed to the Majordomo and turned to the audience, who had roused themselves in order to applaud. He nodded politely to the few people he could bear to make eye contact with, failing to produce any sort of smile. The whole event had been a sham. He stalked from the chamber and headed directly back to House Contadino, leaving a near-silent chapel to decipher what had happened.

He was slumped in his armchair when they came, still brooding and cursing from the humiliation at the Rite. The snowdrops lay forgotten on the mantel. He almost ignored the knock on the door, then called out he was not receiving visitors. The sound came again, the door opened. Rafaela slipped in, gesturing frantically to him to get up.

'What? What are you doing? I said I'm not receiv—'

'It's not me visiting,' she replied, 'it's Duke and Duchess Prospero. Why are your boots in the fireplace?'

'Because I threw them there.' He frowned, refusing to rise from the armchair.

'Stand up. And for goodness' sake, grow up. If you don't make yourself presentable I'll resign this very minute.' There was nothing in her tone to suggest she was bluffing. Lucien climbed into his boots, pushing a small pile of books under the couch before whispering a quick apology. Rafaela opened the door and his guests entered the apartment.

They were an odd pair. Duke Stephano of House Prospero was barely five foot seven and as round as a barrel. He possessed a chin so weak as to be an extension of his blubbery neck. His finery, if it could be referred to as such, looked distinctly threadbare and dusty. Any hair he had possessed was now but a memory; a liver-spotted pate told of his advancing age.

Lucien placed him in his late sixties. Duchess Prospero stood six inches over her husband, her corsetry exaggerating an hourglass figure. A fine black gown exposed her supple shoulders and décolletage to a scandalous degree. Her hair was piled atop her head, an abundance of lustrous curls and coils.

Lucien bowed, Rafaela curtseyed and closed the door. There was an awkward moment of silence. All the etiquette Lucien had ever learned fled his mind. He realised he was blushing furiously.

'Please, take a seat,' he indicated the couch. Agamemnon glowered before slinking off to the floor.

'What fascinating pets you have, Master Lucien,' purred Duchess Prospero.

'Thank you.' Lucien shot an anxious glance at Rafaela, who remained calm and composed. 'Would either of you care for a drink?'

'That would be the very thing! A very *fine* thing!' boomed the duke and sat down with a thump on the couch. Rafaela curtseyed again and headed off to the kitchens to seek refreshments.

'So, this is an unexpected visit,' managed Lucien, hoping his uneasy grin wouldn't be misconstrued as a grimace.

'Yes, I suppose it is,' said the duchess. She and leaned forward as she sat down, and her neckline plunged even further. Lucien busied himself coaxing Antigone from under the armchair. The drake scaled his arm and took up her usual perch on his right shoulder. Lucien looked up and locked his gaze on the bulk of Duke Prospero, away from the heaving bosom of his wife.

'We came to say how sorry we are that House Fontein saw fit to slight you in such a despicable way.' Lucien guessed His Grace was partially deaf in one or both ears. There was simply no accounting for why he shouted so loudly.

'Yes,' said the duchess, 'that business with Master Giancarlo's attendance—'

'Or lack of,' said the duke.

'—was most unbecoming of a house with the prestige of Fontein.'

'Quite,' said the duke, and patted his wife's hand. Lucien

noted the way the duke's eyes lingered on his wife's lips. Not the gaze of adoration, rather one of understanding. Lucien guessed the duke read her lips.

'That's very kind of you, and doubly so to visit me,' said Lucien, charmed and baffled in equal measure. No lord or lady had ever paid him the slightest attention except when he was in trouble, and yet here he was with the rulers of House Prospero discussing the latest scandal.

Rafaela appeared with a silver tray loaded with three glasses and two bottles of wine. She set them out, flicking a glance at Lucien with a raised eyebrow. He smiled back at her and she retreated to the doorway after the mandatory curtsey. The duchess sampled her wine and made a breathy, satisfied sound before turning her attention back to Lucien.

'Stephano and I were keen to discover whether you had any romantic ambitions.'

Lucien, who had been halfway through his first sip of a particularly pleasing Barolo, spluttered, then choked and finally swallowed. He stared blinking at Duchess Prospero, who continued as if nothing had happened. 'It's been quite some time since an Orfano has been in a position to wed. We suspect you might be the first.'

'Assuming Golia doesn't have his eye on someone, eh?' rumbled the duke with a leery grin.

'How dreadful,' whispered the duchess. 'I pity the poor girl who finds herself shackled to that dullard.' She covered her mouth in mock dismay. 'Oh, forgive me for being so uncouth. It's not my place to speak in such a way of the king's chosen.' She smiled unapologetically and fluttered her eyelashes.

Lucien beamed back and waved the breach of etiquette aside. He was far more interested in how Rafaela had stiffened. Her eyes were directed toward her feet, hands clasped in the small of her back. Antigone fidgeted on his shoulder but continued her vigil.

'So, do you?' bawled the duke.

'Do I what?' said Lucien, tearing his eyes away from Rafaela.

'Have any romantic aspirations?' pressed Duchess Prospero.

'One such as you could position himself to enjoy the benefits of an alliance with any of the great houses,' continued the duke.

'Ah, I see,' said Lucien, resting one elbow on his armchair and pressing a thumb against the point of his eye tooth. 'I hadn't really given it any thought, to be honest. I'm a bit young to get married.'

'Nonsense,' exclaimed Duchess Prospero, eyes suddenly full of a manic energy. 'Why, I myself was married at just sixteen.'

'You do realise I've only just turned sixteen?'

'Why of course, my lovely boy,' boomed the duke, causing Lucien to flinch. 'That's why we're here.'

Lucien sipped his wine and tried to grasp on to something, anything he could say. His mind remained resolutely blank.

'Forgive me for being so forward again, Master Lucien,' said Duchess Prospero, fanning herself. 'You must think me dreadful. But I must ask, is there any truth to the rumour you were found in Mistress Anea's apartment?'

Lucien sat back back in the armchair and pressed his thumb against his tooth again. Antigone blinked but remained on his shoulder.

'Yes, someone tried to assassinate her. With fire.'

The duke and duchess gasped. The duke looked shocked. Duchess Prospero however had the look of someone hearing corroboration of what she already thought.

'I rescued her.'

'Oh, bravo!' boomed the duke, clapping great meaty hands together. 'Bravo, my splendid boy. Dashing.'

'Very dashing,' agreed the duchess.

They all took a moment to drink their wine.

'So, there's no truth that you and the most mysterious of the Orfani are engaged in a secret affair?' The duchess had become less animated, like a cat just before it pounces. Lucien regarded her a moment and narrowed his eyes.

'It wouldn't be very secret if I told you, would it?'

Duchess Prospero glowered. The duke, who clearly hadn't heard Lucien's retort, continued beaming his cheerful smile. Rafaela was still as straight as a blade, eyes downcast.

'However,' continued Lucien in a voice loud enough for even

234

Duke Prospero to hear, 'Anea is just thirteen. We're friends. Anything else would be unseemly.' He smiled and the duchess softened. 'Friends united by the fact that we are both Orfani, which is much less fun than people imagine.' Lucien couldn't cover the bitterness in his voice.

The duke and duchess sipped their wine, nodding sagely.

'If I might impose upon your greater knowledge of the history of Demesne,' said Lucien, 'is there any previous record of an Orfano marrying into the houses?'

'None my boy! None at all,' said the duke. 'All the Orfani have been too strange and misshapen to even entertain the idea of it.'

'There's also the high mortality rate,' said the duchess. 'Something a political marriage might insulate you from.'

Lucien met Duchess Prospero's eyes, realising just how much steel lay beneath her breathless amiability.

'Well, you've certainly given me a great deal to think about. I'm afraid I have to feed the drakes now, but I hope we can reconvene again soon.'

'Yes, that would be most proper, my splendid boy,' shouted the duke so loudly even the duchess shrank away from him.

They left in due course, the duke ambling out in his threadbare suit, the duchess a riot of brocade and velvet. Lucien set about feeding the drakes their usual meal of crickets.

'Well,' he said aloud, mostly to himself, 'I've no idea what that was about.' Antigone had no answers for him and bit in half a still-wriggling cricket. Rafaela gathered the silver tray and made it to the door before turning to him.

'You do know that Duke Prospero has a daughter, don't you?'

'Of course. She's ten or maybe eleven,' replied Lucien, intent on the drakes, who had gathered around him.

'Actually she turned fifteen back in August. You'd know if you'd bothered to attend the party you were invited to.'

Lucien looked up at her and shrugged his shoulders, shaking his head, eyes blank.

'Really? I don't think I've ever met her. Does she have a name?'

Rafaela exited, the door slammed behind her, causing Lucien to swear.

'What in nine hells has got into her?' he said to the empty room. The drakes, now fed, slunk off with full bellies. Lucien sat back in his armchair and opened a book. He managed to get through a paragraph before leaping to his feet, the book hitting the floor with a thump.

'*Che cazzo?* They can't possibly . . . I can't get married. I'm only sixteen.'

29

Stranded and Blind

KING'S KEEP

– Febbraio 315

Lucien stepped into the gloom, lantern held before him. There was a stillness here that demanded silence. Not a silence born of respect, but of awe. He'd not known such an absence of sound since the morning he woke in the mausoleum of House Prospero. Black and white flagstones ran in neat rows, a chequerboard covered in a blanket of dust, undisturbed but for a single path swept clean by the robes of the Majordomo. The walls were painted a sickly red, the carmine shade of blood newly spilled. Suspended from the ceiling was a single eight-sided lantern. The light it shed guttered, the flame flickering, dying. The corridor was long, leading him to a staircase. He grasped his own lantern more fervently and ascended, passing through a wide arched doorway to find himself surrounded by bookshelves. Floor to ceiling. Heavy leather-bound tomes nestled beside each other. Lucien approached, his curiosity piqued, but was only able to decipher fragments of the many titles. They were written in the old tongue or another language entirely. He dared to fetch a few down from their resting places. From the illustrations, biology seemed to be the mainstay of the collection. Here was a book on physiology, another on the pregnancy cycles of mammals, another on insect species.

Lucien stalked down the aisles between countless works before finding an exit. A spiral staircase made of stone, its bannister of polished beech, coiled upwards. He climbed, trying not to make a sound, wondering what lay beyond the spiral. The dust he disturbed took to the air, motes spectral and torpid.

Another pair of doors greeted him, left ajar, inches apart.

The lantern light fell on flecks of crimson which adorned the wood around black iron handles. Further down, a smeared bloody handprint testified to the king's wickedness. Lucien pushed against the doors, cursing under his breath as the hinges moaned a mourning creak. He passed into the chamber with a growing sense of repugnance.

A wave of revulsion overtook him, a deep emotion of the senses. The room appeared to be carpeted, but something was amiss. Feeling more than the now familiar unease, Lucien was sure something was profoundly wrong in this chamber. Lucien lowered the lantern, still not comprehending what lay before him. The lantern was at a level with his knees before he made sense of the writhing jumble beneath his feet. The floor was alive with the scramble of innumerable spiders. Larger longer-limbed grey members of the order stalked over their kin, occasionally snatching one, making it disappear between ravenous mandibles. Other varieties simply hobbled and scuttled, adding their mass to the endless shifting underfoot. Lucien wondered why the smaller species didn't use their weight of numbers to bring down their predatory kin. By now the scurrying tide was climbing up past his ankles. Small mercy he wore Virmyre's knee-length riding boots. He pressed on, wondering what abominations he would find.

Many feet away a huge object sat at the centre of the chamber, indistinct. Lucien crept toward it, braving the arachnid tide as it swirled and eddied around him. Each step was a dreadful massacre. Finally, the lantern light fell on his prize. He'd been expecting a table. Instead he found an ornate bed, the largest he had ever seen, fully four times the size of his own. The bed was as wide as it was disgusting. Mildew spread and spoiled the once-pristine sheets. Stains of rust-brown and jaundice-yellow spread like bruises. And there was the smell. Lucien gagged at the ammonia reek and stepped away retching. It was then he realised he was not alone.

At the cardinal points the circular room featured alcoves, reached through decorative arches supported by delicate clusters of colonnettes. Each apse was a deep enclave of night, and yet in one something had reflected the lantern light, a sharp glint drawing his eye. He drew his blade and advanced with caution, breath shallow and constricted. He could never have imagined what greeted him.

They sat on four exquisite wooden chairs, regarding him from behind blackened glass spectacles. Each nursed an instrument in long-fingered hands. He'd not seen them since the day of the Domo's collapse seven years ago. He remembered them distinctly. A quartet of dusty musicians dressed in out-of-fashion clothes, led into the king's chambers to play. Each had worn jet spectacles, concealing their blindness. How jealous he'd been of them that day, made privy to Landfall's greatest mystery while he had been forced to remain in the corridor outside.

They were of course quite dead now, their clothes, their very essence, undone by decay. Only mute grinning skulls kept him company in the darkness. Lucien approached, wondering if they had been made prisoners, but none of the skeletons wore shackles. Perhaps rope, which had succumbed to the same decomposition as their flesh? Lucien tried to imagine what it must have been like to sit in the solitude of blindness, waiting for the Majordomo to lead them away from their audience with the king. Waiting, starving.

He'd drawn close to the nearest of them now, his mind teasing at the cause of their death. His breath was bated, his entire being coiled like a spring. One of the larger spiders emerged from an eye socket, appearing from behind the blackened spectacles. It scuttled over the waxy yellow pate and down the spine. Lucien flinched and swore, dropping the lantern. It fell like a meteor in the darkness. The silence was shattered abruptly. He feared the flame within would flicker and die, leaving him stranded and blind. The carpet of spiders retreated, their twilight cavalcade illuminated by the yellow glow. Fortune smiled – the flame inside remaining resolute and alive. Lucien snatched the lantern up, breathing a sigh of relief. He edged away from the long-forgotten musicians, picking his way across the room with tentative steps. The soles of his boots were now slick with crushed thoraxes and abdomens. He circled the decaying bed, closing the distance on the next alcove, apprehension threatening to overwhelm him.

The stairs were wooden and clung to the curving wall of the alcove with a ramshackle tenacity. The steps disappeared up, mahogany-brown but for a coat of the all-pervading dust. He took the first flight, eight steps in total, before coming to a landing. The king's bedchamber must be two storeys high.

'Probably to accommodate his swollen ego,' muttered Lucien. It was good to hear his own voice, insurance against the drowning silence.

He took the next eight steps and spied an immense chandelier he'd not noticed earlier. It hung over the broad expanse of the bed, glittering in the meagre light. Shards of amethyst glass hung like wicked crystal knives. Any candles that had once been placed in the structure had been consumed, the wax existing only as drippings. It was simply a crystalline constellation looking down on the king's festering resting place.

Lucien pressed on, willing the stairs not to collapse. Sweat sheened his palms as he clutched the hilt of the sword, his other hand grasping fretfully at the lantern. The flights of stairs and landings continued until he found himself before double doors. They were scrawled over with formulae, the handwriting erratic. Light escaped beneath the doors and shone like a miniature sun through a keyhole. Lucien set down the battered lantern and tried the handles. They turned with rusty reluctance. He pushed against the wood and, taking a deep breath, stepped through, willing his shaking hands to calm themselves.

He was in the laboratory he'd discovered the night he'd been up on the rooftops of Demesne. The cupola he'd stared down from was at the centre of the ceiling, windows looking out onto night. The room was eight sided, eight benches surrounding a hollow octagon in the centre. Each was piled high with water-stained glass containers or books with long-broken spines. Pages lay scattered on the floor, clustering about table legs, screwed up and discarded in one corner. The sconces on the walls were all empty and starlight filtered in from the cupola above. Lucien closed with the nearest of the benches, discovering a withered organ suspended in a cloudy yellow fluid. The piece was ruddy red, but he failed to identify it or which animal had surrendered it. The glass container had a scrap of parchment pinned to the cork lid bearing a single word and a date, but the ink was so faded Lucien could make no sense of it. Other containers on the benches held increasingly grisly trophies. Here an adult hand, there a drake skeleton, not an ounce of flesh on the bones. Lucien spent minutes lost inside this museum of the grotesque, not daring to linger on any exhibit too long.

Until he arrived at the head.

The cloudy preservative made it difficult to discern the man's age, but he was younger than Virmyre, possibly younger than D'arzenta. His hair had become a congealed mass. The jaw hung slack, the teeth inside brown or blackened. Two strands of unknown material tethered the severed cranium to the container's base. Lucien could not tear his eyes away. He felt his heart hammering in his chest, breath refusing to come. His grip slackened on the hilt of the sword. It was then the head in the specimen jar opened its eyes.

Lucien stumbled back, a strangled cry escaping his lips. He crashed into another bench, unsettling another of the awful containers. The bench rocked, a flare of pain seared through his ribs, and a specimen jar crashed to the floor. A cloud of dust rose, filling the air with particles, causing him to cough. His boots were awash with fouled preservative, but that was a small concern compared to what followed. Clawing its way out of the shattered glass of its former prison, the thing emerged, wet and gasping, then righted itself.

Lucien stared in astonishment. The creature before him resembled a spider only in locomotion. Eight legs, pink and vivid, reached out from an oval corpus. Lucien blinked, then realised the object with eight spindly legs was a human head, oversized and unlovely. Bright blue eyes and a hooked nose adorned the front of the corrupted skull; the mouth opened but the scream was a silent one. For a few moments Lucien and the head faced each other, stunned silence and revulsion heavy on the air between them. Then, sensing much-longed-for freedom was now in its grasp, the head ran blindly.

Lucien lashed out at the abomination, only succeeding in scoring a deep groove in the leg of the nearest bench. The eight-legged thing ran backwards, blue eyes staring accusingly at Lucien, who fought between chasing the creature down and stunned abhorrence. He found himself rooted to the spot, watching the king's aberration escape the confines of the laboratory. It clattered down the stairs and still Lucien was unable to move. When the sounds of scuttling had receded he simply existed in the silence that followed, afeared of what would come next.

How many more of the king's twisted experiments would he be forced to endure? he wondered. His eyes swam in and out of focus, finally settling on a patchwork of parchment pinned to the wall. Lucien searched the sprawling script, grateful for something, anything, to occupy his mind. The parchment had a vast tree drawn upon it, and every branch that reached out from the trunk bore a name and split into finer twigs. After a minute or two Lucien realised the pictorial was governed by certain rules. The branches were all named after women. The thick branches also bore dates, all rendered in a legible hand. The names, male and female, on the further extremities of the branches were accompanied by a variety of details including house designations. Talents and aptitudes were recorded in succinct remarks. The general health of each was recorded as well as any defects. It was a family tree of sorts, he decided, but one that mentioned only mothers and their offspring. Lucien was pressed up against the parchment now, his fingers running across the paper, hoping to absorb some clue through the very membrane of his skin. It was then that he located Golia's name. Then his own. And Anea's.

The room spun.

He felt light-headed. His lungs refused much-needed air. He bent double, head between his knees, willing himself not to pass out. Gradually he returned to his upright position, but not before noticing one detail he'd missed before. At the base of the tree, at the point where the trunk met an unsketched earth, was a crown. Dazed and willing himself to close his eyes, Lucien looked up, finding a branch drawn in a wavering hand, the ink blacker, scribed more recently. The surname da Costa. The first name Salvaggia. The date just two nights past.

Speechless and shaken, the Orfano stepped away as if in a dream, exiting the laboratory in a fugue state. Lucien felt his mind clutch and seize at the evidence in front of him, failing to acknowledge a terrible truth he could not escape from. He staggered down the staircase, supporting himself with the rail, with the wall, retrieving the lantern subconsciously. The wood groaned and complained under his footfalls but held fast. It was as he passed the rotting putrescence of the king's bed that he heard his name. Lucien turned with an unfocused gaze, eyes searching the gaping maw of the alcove, opposite the resting place of the musicians. Existing at the edge of the illumination was the face of an old man, deeply lined and ashen.

'You should not be here,' whispered the king.

Lucien stared back wordlessly.

30

Tegenaria Duellica

LUCIEN'S APARTMENT

– Maggio 313

'That's dreadful,' complained Stephania as Achilles bit the head off a cricket. The insect's legs continued to pedal the empty air until the drake consumed it entirely. 'Are they always like this?'

Lucien nodded, eying her intently. She was the image of her mother, just coming into her birthright of an hourglass figure the equal of Duchess Prospero's. It was for the best that she had not acquired any of her father's features. She shared her mother's taste in gowns, although decidedly less provocative. Her coiffed hair was always immaculate, matched by flawless olive skin. Many of the bravos of House Fontein spoke of lusting for her.

Lucien idly wondered which of his parents' attributes stared back at him from the looking glass. Did he share any aspect of their temperaments? Or any of their intellectual gifts? He'd never know, he realised, masking his loss in front of Stephania, who remained oblivious.

'And my mother thought I'd be interested in this?' She pouted and looked away to the windows, shuddering theatrically. Lucien plucked at his lip, not knowing what to say.

'Do you know the *capo*?' she asked brightly.

'I think I insulted him once. Isn't he—'

'Very good-looking,' interrupted Stephania, suddenly serious. Lucien shrugged his shoulders and stole a glance at Rafaela, who stood by the door into his apartment from the corridor. She refused to meet his eye. As Lucien's appointed maid, she was required to act as chaperone. Stephania's own maid perused Lucien's bookshelves, ignoring everyone.

'He's an accomplished horseman too,' added Stephania.

'I'd heard he was a rider,' said Lucien, but Dino was too young to understand the joke and Stephania chose to ignore it. Rafaela at least let slip a smile.

'Mother said I was to invite you over for supper tomorrow evening,' added Stephania.

Lucien nodded. He'd done his best to avoid Duke and Duchess Prospero, who he'd dubbed Lady Voluptus Insanus. Rafaela had given up on even the pretence of upbraiding him for the dreadful nickname, frequently laughing along with his wicked observations. Barely a day passed when he wasn't invited for coffee during the afternoon or a late supper. At first these meetings had been with Duchess Prospero, who had grilled him on many subjects unrelated to anything meaningful – in Lucien's opinion. After a month, or possibly two – he'd lost track – the duchess had introduced her daughter. Lucien had tried every feint and ruse to escape these appointments, but the duchess was undeterred and implacable.

Finally the duchess suggested Stephania should visit Lucien on the pretext of seeing the drakes. The duchess had even managed to bend D'arzenta to her will, prevailing on him to cancel Lucien's lesson planned for that afternoon. Lucien had retaliated by inviting Dino along.

'I would have preferred it if we could be alone together,' Stephania whispered. 'I don't feel like I know you at all. You're so ... strange.'

When it was clear Lucien had no answer for her she rose, crossing to the windows to look at Landfall. He felt a pang of sympathy – she looked lonely silhouetted against the daylight.

'You know I'm only here in exchange for Achilles, don't you?' whispered Dino, his grey eyes serious beneath the sweep of his overgrown fringe.

'Just promise to stay until she's gone,' hissed Lucien. Stephania had already been in the apartment for thirty minutes and possible topics of conversation were dwindling. Lucien was desperate for any gambit that might lead to an exchange in which Stephania didn't insist on speaking of her parents. He now knew her lineage extensively, and not by choice.

A heavy knock sounded at Lucien's door and he swore under his breath.

'Who's that?' asked Dino.

Stephania turned as Lucien got to his feet. She forced a small smile onto her lips and he returned it.

'Sorry. I wasn't expecting anyone else,' he said and realised he meant it.

'I hope it's not the Domo,' she said.

Lucien grinned. 'I couldn't agree more.'

Rafaela opened the door and bobbed a curtsey. She had worn her hair down today, rich coils of untamed chocolate-brown falling around her face. Lucien would have given anything in that moment to be alone with her.

Virmyre entered, wearing the usual impassive expression on his fine features. He thanked Rafaela, then nodded curtly to each of the boys. A distinctly puzzled look possessed him for a moment as he caught sight of the Lady Stephania Prospero, before he remarked, 'Ah, yes, I'd heard something was afoot.'

Lucien was unsure if this was meant for him, or simply Virmyre thinking aloud. The *professore* carried a small card box, neatly tied with string, which he set down on the couch.

'If we might be excused, Professore?' said Rafaela. He nodded again and the maids left the room. Lucien's gaze lingered on Rafaela as she left.

'Master Lucien, Master Dino, my lady.' Virmyre bowed to the assembled nobility. 'I'm afraid we have a problem of the utmost seriousness.'

'Excellent,' said Lucien, then checked to see if Stephania had heard him. If she had it didn't matter; she was far more intent on what the stony-faced scholar had to say.

'As you are no doubt aware, it is summer, and that of course means the many spiders that inhabit Landfall have set themselves but one goal: entering Demesne to feed on the great numbers of flies that live here. Even now they have begun a mass assault to take these very walls.'

Lucien sighed. 'Spiders? Really?' He slumped on the couch.

'Indeed,' said Virmyre with characteristic intensity. 'We are positively invaded by the brutes: *Tegenaria duellica*, *Cheira-canthium* and of course the *Tegenaria domestica*.'

'I asked my maid take one from my bath this morning,' said Stephania. 'The poor girl all but fled the room.'

'It is a problem for those who suffer from arachnophobia, is it not?' continued Virmyre, his hands clasped behind his back, a common pose when he lectured.

'Lots of people have that in Demesne,' said Dino. 'It's as if the whole castle has nightmares about the little fuckers.' He looked around a moment to see if he would be reprimanded. Virmyre said nothing, only raised an eyebrow. Lucien laughed. Hearing Dino swear was one of life's pleasures, especially on the rare occasions he got the context correct. Stephania covered her own smile behind a hand, catching Lucien's eye. She giggled and looked away.

'All is not lost,' continued Virmyre. 'Our very good friends the cataphract drakes love to dine on our great enemy.'

'Perhaps I should get one for my apartment,' said Stephania, looking at Lucien. 'Perhaps you could visit me and give me advice.'

'Of course,' said Lucien, and found himself rewarded with a smile.

'But not Achilles, he's mine!' said Dino urgently, 'Lucien said I could have him if I—'

'Be quiet, Dino,' said Lucien, glaring. The younger Orfano fell silent.

The drakes roused themselves from their various hiding places in Lucien's apartment, scuttling across the blue rug that dominated the centre of the sitting room. Tan and drab-olive bodies grew taut waiting for the box to be opened, black eyes watchful and alert.

'What's in the box then?' Lucien said, keen to change the subject.

'Spiders of course,' said Virmyre with a hint of peevishness.

'Urgh! Disgusting,' exclaimed Dino, and hurriedly set about untying it. The spiders emerged the moment the lid was removed. Lucien suppressed a shudder. Virmyre had been busy: there was a feast of scuttling legs and fat round torsos. Dino stood regarding the scene, open-mouthed in wonder, grey eyes unusually bright.

Achilles, Agamemnon and Antigone spent the next twenty minutes scampering around after their eight-legged prey. It was a massacre.

'I don't think I've ever seen them so animated,' said Lucien. He'd shucked off his boots and was sitting, knees drawn up to his chest, on the couch.

'Wooagh! Achilles just got *two* in one bite!' Dino on the other hand had no problem about staying close to the action, and was following the drakes around on his hands and knees, providing an enthusiastic commentary.

'Chomp! Chomp!'

Stephania giggled from behind her fan, amused at the younger boy's antics. Her eyes always returned to Lucien, and he felt himself begin to blush under her repeated gaze.

'So, is there a point to this?' said Lucien after a few minutes.

'Simply to prove that some creatures, spiders in particular, have a strong effect on people,' replied Virmyre, who had seated himself in the armchair and laced his fingers in front of his chin. 'However, Lady Stephania remains resolutely calm.'

'They're not very big, are they?' She flashed another smile.

'And yourself, Lucien?' asked the *professore*. Dino whooped in delight behind the couch. Another arachnid fatality.

'I'm wondering if I'm going to wake up tonight and find a vengeful spider hanging over my bed as punishment for all this.' He gestured at the drakes, who were still hunting. 'Maybe I'll call it Damocles.'

They sat in Lucien's sitting room until the spiders had made good their escape or succumbed to the predations of the drakes. Dino then cradled the drowsing Achilles and marched from the room with his chin held high, not saying a word, prize finally claimed.

'And I think I will take this opportunity to take my leave,' said Virmyre. 'I can trust you not to trespass on Lady Stephania's dignity, Lucien.'

The Orfano blushed so hard it felt as if he'd been set on

fire. The room felt curiously empty without Virmyre. Lucien struggled for words.

'I sometimes hear people talking about how annoying their brothers are, and find myself sympathising. Dino, I mean.' He gestured toward the door, indicating the departed Orfano.

'Don't be too hard on him,' said Stephania. 'He's very fond of you.'

'Me?'

'Well, he's hardly going to warm to Golia, is he? And Anea is somewhat... distant.'

'He copies everything I do. The clothes I wear, the way I fight, owning a drake. It's maddening.'

'It must be such hard work being a good influence.'

'Very funny,' he replied, surprised to discover he liked her teasing.

'What a terrible burden, Master Lucien,' she said in a passable imitation of Virmyre. He burst into laughter at that and she joined him. They were at either end of the couch, the space between them taut. Lucien plucked at the string of the now-empty box.

'I'm sorry Giancarlo spoiled your Rite of Adoption,' said Stephania finally.

'Thank you. I should never have gone through with it. I was told not to, in fact.' His mind conjured up Rafaela in the corridor, kissing him on the forehead. Stephania reached across and laid one hand on his own, and his thoughts were dragged from that longing memory to the unfolding present.

'I know what it's like to be alone,' she said, 'and weighed down with expectations.'

Lucien blinked.

'I may not be Orfano, but I can imagine. I have no siblings. Like you.'

He shrugged awkwardly, tried for a smile, feeling a sting of unhappiness.

'Fucking Giancarlo,' he grunted. Stephania smiled.

'What will you do? About Giancarlo, I mean? Everyone's talking about it.'

'There's not much I can do. Duke Fontein backs his every

move. Giancarlo obviously wants Golia in a position of power, maybe even to be crowned king.'

Her hand still rested lightly on his, her skin soft and warm. Somehow she'd edged closer without him noticing. She smelled good. He relaxed into the softness of the couch, anxiety draining out of him.

'You don't have to remain a Fontein, you know,' she said. 'There are other houses, houses with more commercial influence.' A slow smile creased her lips, her insinuation clear. He found himself smiling in response.

'I spent sixteen years trying to join a house that didn't really want me. I must be mad. I've still no clue why they accepted.'

'The Domo insisted,' said Stephania, a look of victory in her eyes. 'We have spies in House Fontein. You've no idea how useful a friend I could be.'

'I think I'm starting to understand.'

She had edged closer and now sat beside him, her thigh resting against his. He found himself gazing at her collarbones, delicate beneath the olive skin. The curve of her breasts beneath the gown was intensely pleasing.

'What do you want to do?' she almost whispered.

Beyond the latticed windows the sun had begun to set, staining the sky vermilion. Lucien responded to the growing darkness by getting up and lighting the candles on the mantelpiece. He blew out the match and regarded the burned and twisted wood. He turned to find her gazing at him, an inviting smile playing about her lips. She had arrived as a guest received on sufferance but had since revealed herself in a new light.

'How could I know what I want?' He shrugged and smiled rueful. 'I'm only sixteen.'

Stephania stood and crossed the room. She stroked the side of his face with a tender hand. A shiver of pleasure passed over him. It was rare that anyone touched him.

'I've watched you struggle for a long time, watched your defeats and humiliations. And you've always picked yourself up and continued. Sometimes it's taken you a while, but you've never given in.'

'I . . .' He had no words for her.

'Just remember, there are other houses than Fontein, houses much keener to invite Orfani into their ranks.'

And then her lips were brushing his, like butterfly wings, so quickly the kiss had ended before he registered it.

'I should get back. Don't worry about escorting me; I'm quite capable of finding my way. Not that you'd know it the way my father acts.'

Lucien was still reeling from the kiss, and her touch.

'It was good to finally meet you – properly, I mean,' he said, feeling foolish.

She crossed to the door, blew him a kiss, bobbed a mock curtsey and disappeared, leaving him alone in the sitting room.

He spent long minutes thinking on what she had said, watching the sunset. Her invitation had been compelling, her sympathy welcome, her compliments apparently genuine. He extinguished the candles, retiring to his bedroom as possibilities swirled through his mind. He followed skeins of causality, looked for consequences, wondered at futures. Tiredness enfolded him as he undressed. He threw his clothes over the chair. He'd not the energy to hang them in his closet or even draw the curtains.

Finally he placed the two remaining drakes in the great glass tank. They eyed him with inscrutable onyx eyes, then scampered away to coil about one another. The bed was comfortable, the sheets fresh, and yet he stared at the ceiling, knowing sleep would arrive unwillingly at best. The clock in the hall measured out insomnia in the *ticks* and *tocks* of hollow seconds, each pregnant with possibilities. Restless, he got out of bed to check the corners of the bedroom for spiders. He muttered, 'Damocles,' under his breath before settling down again. Outside, the sun finished its descent but the air remained charged and close. Lucien watched the stars come out one by one and wondered where his mother could be. He was awake a long time, not succumbing to sleep until a purple star appeared in the darkened firmament.

31

A Rhapsody of Flesh

KING'S KEEP

– *Febbraio* 315

'I told them it would take time,' said the king in a reasonable, educated tone. His voice was a rich basso which carried across the room easily. His bulbous head was bald with a heavy brow that immersed his eyes in shadow. 'I told them it could take hundreds of years. But for every breakthrough, I fear I forget something I discovered in an earlier age.'

Lucien remained, mesmerised by the king's reverie despite desperately wanting to flee. He was unsure if the king was addressing him or just thinking aloud.

'And the Domo. He thinks me unaware of the various poisonings and assassinations. He thinks I don't know how he schemes and plots. He thinks Landfall will be his.' The king, still a disembodied head in the darkness, a face at the edge of the lantern light, regarded the floor. A moment of pensive silence followed. 'He wants to inherit all of my hard work, yet chooses not to help me. He is an ungrateful son. I appear to be cursed by ungrateful progeny. No matter. I can make more. I will have perfection, even though I am far from that destination myself.'

The king stepped forward into the light, still muttering to himself. All of the laboratory's horrors paled in the presence of Demesne's ruler. His body suspended from eight legs that sprouted from his back. Each limb began in a swollen mass of gross muscle and ended in a mottled scythe blade. Lesions and split skin glistened sickly, chitin showing underneath. His human legs had atrophied, hanging useless from his pelvis, like his sex. His arms by contrast looked strong and powerful with long-fingered hands. Thick tines emerged from his forearms, shining midnight-blue. He was naked except for a heavy chain hung around his thick neck, pregnant with veins. Keys, hanging from the chain in a profusion of black metal spikes, glinted in the light.

'I am not all that I was once was,' said the king mildly. 'I can't remember the last time I wore the outline of a common man.'

Lucien struggled to breathe.

'What have you done?'

'An improvement here, an improvement there. I'm afraid I rather lost track. And my legs aren't what they used to be.' The king indicated his withered human limbs. 'So I made some new ones.'

'Why spider's legs? Why spiders at all?'

'A good question.' The monstrosity paused to reflect. 'The spider knows patience, but can also create whole worlds, worlds of webs and tunnels. Strands of possibility. And there is poison of course.'

The king drew closer. Lucien struggled to guess how tall he was on those scabrous columns of chitin. Twelve feet at least.

'No good creating if you can't also destroy,' said the King.

A scythe-blade limb stepped closer, followed by another and yet more.

'I suppose I shall have to put my work to one side in order to retain my throne. How tiresome.'

Lucien was edging back now, his feet sweeping through the carpet of spiders as one foot followed the other. The floor still roiled with the endless orgy of tiny limbs, but Lucien was transfixed by the once-man in front of him.

'Of course I shall need to have new clothes made. I can't be naked in public. It simply won't do. That would be dé-classé.' The king laughed, revealing needle-sharp teeth between darkened lips. 'I suppose I could make clothes illegal. No, no. That wouldn't make me popular at all, especially during winter.'

Lucien continued to retreat, unable to tear his eyes away from the monstrous form, nor ignore the fractured soliloquy. The lantern light shrank back from the king, the darkness swallowing up his aberrant form. Only his head was still visible, hanging in the air like a baleful moon, white and pitted.

'And now you've blundered your way into my web, and I will have to eat you, my little Orfano. Such sweet, sweet meat.'

The king laughed again, the sound twisting Lucien's guts. He struggled not to drop the lantern and sword, desperate to clap his hands over his ears.

'I wouldn't really eat you, of course. I'm not a monster.' This weirdly indignant. 'The very idea of it is repugnant to me. I'm not Saturn.'

Lucien's retreat had led him to the alcove where the musicians mouldered. His elbow jerked into a corpse. The violin hit the floor before the body did, a discordant *twang* flaring briefly before being swallowed by a clatter of bones. Lucien stared down, trying to make sense of what he was seeing. Fine black twine held the bones together, emerging from joints and the top of the skull. The twine extended over the back of the chair, where it was tied to a wooden cross with neat knots.

'You made a marionette from a corpse,' he whispered.

'Wonderful, isn't it?'

'You made a marionette from a corpse.' His voice was louder now. Lucien looked up at the king, who had edged closer, his arachnid forelegs visible at the edge of the lantern's nimbus.

The monstrosity clasped his hands together in a display of delight. 'Aren't they fantastic?' His eyes glittered. 'Would you like to play with one?'

'That's all we are to you – marionettes. Toys. Amusements.' The last word curdled on the air between them, and even the silence couldn't swallow Lucien's seething disdain.

'Well, I *am* the king, you insolent boy.'

Lucien felt the hot rush of his anger, the quickening of his blood. Adrenaline flooded his senses, harsh in the back of his throat.

'I'm not your boy.'

The blade passed through an arachnid foreleg just above a knuckle. There was a sickening crack of chitin, and the deed was done before Lucien had decided how to follow up his initial strike. The king reared up on his four hind legs, a dismal shout escaping his purpled lips. The severed limb crashed to the floor wetly.

Lucien dodged to his left as the other foreleg was thrust forward, spear-like. A member of the long-dead quartet was shattered into a jumble of bones, the chair beneath him smashed into driftwood. Lucien struck again, but the blade did no more than leave a deep groove in rancid chitin. A grunt, and the monster backed up, allowing Lucien to escape the alcove.

Reduced to one foreleg, the king lunged forward, stabbing out a series of attacks. Lucien parried two, dodged the next, then ducked under another before retreating. It was impossible to determine how the next attack would come, or the angle the king would strike from. Lucien swiped at the stabbing leg, blade failing to bite into the armoured limb. Unrelenting, the king continued his assault, six limbs propelling him forward, the seventh continuing to thrust at the Orfano. The severed stump gouted clear blood, leaving a trail of blue gore across the chamber.

Lucien laboured to keep the light up. Bearing a knife or shield in his right hand was one thing, but the unfamiliar weight of the lantern was slowing him, taking him off balance. He eyed the dripping stump, hoping the king would bleed out and crash to the flagstones in a confusion of limbs. Small chance of that.

'I think it's time I took a more visible role in the ruling of Demesne,' said the king. 'I'll start by executing the current crop of Orfani. That should make my point quite neatly.'

Lucien parried a blow. The sword shook in his hand. He wondered if Dino and Anea were safe. He wondered if anyone could be safe again.

'It wouldn't be the first time I've had to deadhead the roses.'

Distracted by the king's ravings, Lucien almost failed to see the swipe directed at his head. He dropped to his knees, rolling forward, finding himself underneath the king's suspended body. His grip on both the lantern and the sword faltered but he clung to them fearfully. The light sputtered, flickering back to brightness a second later. Lucien thrust up, but his blade skidded from hard chitin plates beneath the human skin. He

255

swore and rolled again, emerging behind his opponent. The king stamped at the floor furiously. One steely pointed leg crashed down between Lucien's boots; another narrowly missed his hip. The Orfano floundered a moment, off balance, then lost his footing. The sword skittered away across the floor from nerveless fingers – he'd smashed his elbow.

'And the Domo will have to go too. He's outlived his usefulness, wouldn't you say? Time for retirement.'

A strange falsetto sound floated down to Lucien. He realised the king was giggling, the sound of a mind snapped. Somehow he managed to keep the lantern aloft. The spiders clambered over his supine form in seconds, threatening to engulf him. The king continued stamping down with his chitin legs, forcing Lucien away from Virmyre's sword.

'After all I've done for you,' bellowed the king. 'All the education, all the resources, the bloodlines, the research!'

Lucien had just regained his feet when the king's remaining foreleg slapped him across the chest, knocking the wind out of him. He fell to his knees.

'After all the training, all the advantages at your disposal.'

Another leg thrust down, missing Lucien's thigh by scant inches.

'I'm very disappointed in you, Lucien di Fontein,' said the king, then burst into a gale of hysterical laughter.

Lucien staggered to his feet and fell back several feet before opening the small door on the side of the lantern. He hefted the light, then threw it at the chandelier with a desperate grunt. The king followed the arc of the fluttering light as it sailed through the darkness, up over the lip of the great circle of glass. The lantern crashed into the gilded wooden frame, settling on the upper side of the gaudy construction. Oil spilled from it before catching fire. The king swore in the old tongue.

Suddenly the chamber was flooded with light. Every shard and blade of glass reflected and diffused the flames. Lucien blinked into the fierce glare. The smell of scorched wood and rope filled the air. Lucien forced himself to keep his eyes open, struggling to take in the true horror of the king. The monstrosity of his madness was laid bare: every twisted limb, every cruel lesion and tear in his rotting flesh, each crude spine jutting from his forearms. The king was a rhapsody of abused meat. Muscles that had no business being tied together strained against their impossible biology. Skin had putrefied and fallen away. It was the work of a mind trapped in flesh and wanting to reinvent itself. To escape itself. It was the work of a mind that had manifested the true depths of its depravity.

The spiders on the floor scattered to the darkness, leaving Lucien alone with the ruler of Demesne. The king held up his hands to his face, screeching. He staggered to the bed, sinking his fingers into fetid covers, pulling them up over his head like a cowl. The still-sitting musicians stared out from behind their spectacles in silent judgement. The king flailed and swore under the sheets, still holding one arm up to his eyes, a seethe of writhing limbs. In his agony he mounted the bed, trying to take some measure of comfort from it despite the blinding light raining from above. Lucien circled the thrashing king to retrieve Virmyre's blade, unsure of how to press his advantage. If he didn't strike now he might not survive a second engagement, and yet the king's torso had proved all but impregnable. Lucien despaired, but hefted the sword and prepared to charge. It was then the chandelier ripped free of the roof and plummeted onto the bed below.

There was a split second of wet chopping as glass sank into flesh before the chandelier exploded across the floor. A moment of silence followed, then a terrible wheezing emanated from the ruin on the bed. Shuddering breath dragged into punctured lungs. The smell of singeing flesh drifted on the air. Lucien advanced, stepping onto the bed, avoiding the small tongues of flame that licked and seared at the king. The bedding was afire; he wouldn't have long.

'The keys,' he grated from clenched teeth.

'*Vai al diavolo!*' The king rocked violently, but the wooden frame of the chandelier held him fast. He struggled harder. A glass blade sank deep into an exposed joint. The king howled.

'Give me the keys,' said Lucien. The tongues of fire were congregating now, not licking but consuming the bed. It was a matter of seconds before the ruin of the king and the chandelier became a conflagration.

'You were always the weakest,' spat the king, eyes full of hate, 'the most pitiful, the most guileless. We should have killed you at—'

'Fuck you then.'

The impact of the strike shuddered up the length of Lucien's arm, causing new agony in the old wound. The king's head spun off the thick stump of his neck, rolling away across the chamber floor, a look of anguish frozen on the pitted features. Lucien scooped the chain from the corpse, ignoring the blue gore jetting from the jugular. The remaining seven limbs twitched in dreadful spasms, then slumped and sprawled across the huge bed. Lucien vaulted over the rising fire, taking a few seconds to beat out an insistent flame on his sleeve. He wrapped the chain of precious keys around his right wrist and stumbled away. The flames rose, a bonfire of the grotesque, forcing him to retreat further. Heat intensified, filling the room with the terrible stench of charred flesh. Lucien took a moment to wonder if there would be anything left after the fire had done its work, or if anyone would believe him when he tried to explain what he had seen. His thoughts turned to Rafaela. He turned away from the cremation, seeing the flames dancing on the dark lenses of the violinists.

'I'm sorry,' he said, flipping them a salute and disappearing into the gloom of the king's library. He ran past the books and out into the curving corridor beyond with a single word on his lips.

Rafaela.

32

The Unquiet Dead

HOUSE CONTADINO COURTYARD

– Augusto 313

Lucien let the heat of the sun suffuse him. Sweat coursed from him freely; his arms ached with the effort of swinging the blade and bearing the shield. Blood pumped heavily in his veins, rich with vigour. The air smelled sweet, the faintest of breezes tugging at his hair. D'arzenta stood before him.

Lucien was grinning. His instructor had decided to teach outside. They'd cleared a fighting circle in the Contadino courtyard and marked it with broken cobblestones borrowed from the stonemason's workshop. A small crowd had gathered to watch the Orfano duel with the *maestro*. Dino stood nearby, clutching Achilles to his chest proudly. The drake stared over the younger Orfano's shoulder, uninterested in the clang and scuffle of the duel.

'Again!' bellowed D'arzenta, and launched into a series of strikes. The blade ricocheted from Lucien's shield, barely audible above the din of the crowd, who variously cheered or chanted the Orfano's name. The student struck back with a series of deft jabs and thrusts, forcing the instructor to go on the defensive, losing ground until he was at the limits of the circle. D'arzenta waited until the conclusion seemed inevitable, then sidestepped, striking Lucien across the back of the head. Fortunately, he'd used the flat of the blade.

'And that's how you get killed, Master Lucien.' D'arzenta smiled and shook his head slowly. 'Reckless. Impatient. Enough for today. You've fought hard and fought well. For the most part.' Lucien clutched the back of his head but couldn't help a rueful smile. He'd gone from over-cautious novice to

259

hot-headed adept. Something flickered behind D'arzenta's eyes. Lucien turned around on instinct.

Golia stood proudly attired in his usual sleeveless voluminous tunic. The quills on his forearms looked thicker than Lucien remembered, his bulk more imposing. The sheer weight of his presence fell like a shadow across the courtyard. The kitchen staff and pages of House Contadino recoiled from the Orfano.

'Perhaps if you've finished dancing with the fairy boy you can dance with me, D'arzenta.' Golia spat on the ground, drawing his steel blade from his scabbard. He'd faced his final test some eighteen months ago. Lucien eyed the weapon jealously, aware he was vulnerable with only a ceramic sword to defend himself. The shield would not last long, not against Golia.

'The only lesson you'll get from me today is one on manners,' replied D'arzenta. 'Why don't you run back to Giancarlo like the miserable cur you are. I'm sure his boots need polishing.'

The crowd erupted in a rash of gasps and murmuring. No one including Lucien had ever heard D'arzenta deliver such a scathing dismissal. Golia grinned, the thick cords of his lips pulling back from broad teeth. There was nothing about him that was in any way small. It was at that moment that Lucien spotted the family entering the courtyard. Everyone followed his gaze. Even Golia turned his great head and observed the ragged band as they stumbled toward them. A man, a woman and a boy of around sixteen. A girl at the edge of puberty followed them. All were tear-stained and tired. Their clothes were distressed from the journey and they stood hollow-cheeked and unblinking.

'Somebody get some water and a bench,' yelled Lucien. The kitchen staff setting about their orders, he strode across the courtyard, past Golia, and presented himself with a short bow. He immediately felt ridiculous and gauche, too formal.

'What happened?' he asked. D'arzenta appeared at his elbow and waited for their answer.

'Our daughter . . .' replied the man. He was grey from fringe to nape and hadn't seen a razor in days. His voice sounded rough and unvarnished. Lucien realised the man hadn't stopped on purpose but was unable to continue, his mouth twisted in agony as if the words themselves tortured him.

'They come and took my oldest sister, didn't they?' said the boy angrily. He squared up to Lucien. 'You sent your filthy guards to snatch her in the night.'

Lucien fell back a step, the vehemence of the boy's accusation staggering. D'arzenta held out placating hands and opened his mouth to speak.

'We are beset by a revenant.' Not D'arzenta's words. The droning nasal tone of the Majordomo called out across the courtyard. Above them, standing on a vine-choked balcony, the imposing figure of the Domo seemed like a cemetery angel, ash-grey robes completing the illusion.

'What's that then?' snarled the boy, anger dimmed by the Domo's sudden appearance.

'A revenant,' said the Domo, 'is an unquiet dead soul, come back to cause havoc among the living. He lives in the woods beyond the graveyard. We will hunt him down.'

'Why does the revenant only steal eighteen-year-old girls?' shouted the boy at the retreating form of the Domo. He was nearly shaking with fury, his eyes fixed on the now-empty balcony.

Lucien stepped forward, placing himself in front of the woman, who had a look of far-away suffering in her eyes. She appeared to be only vaguely aware of the situation unfolding around her, unseeing, unhearing.

'I'm sorry to have to ask, but—' Lucien drew in a breath '—did your daughter have any problems?' He touched two fingers to his temple, tapping twice. The woman didn't answer but instead looked at her feet.

Her husband scowled. Finally he replied, words thick with emotion, 'No, never. Nothing like that. She was a good girl. She wanted to . . .' He broke down, slumping onto his wife, resting his head on her shoulder as if it were a great weight. Lucien turned away from the family, hurrying inside, stomach knotted. He thought of Nardo and Navilia, knowing immediately what he must do.

*

261

Feigning disinterest in the incident was the hardest part. Lucien stayed in his rooms and told Rafaela to spread the rumour his was violently ill. Food poisoning. Camelia wouldn't thank him for such a slanderous deception, but he was hard pressed to think of anything else. Every dining hall in each of the four houses was buzzing with speculation that night. Rafaela absented herself, looking tired and drawn. She'd barely said a word since she'd heard the news, performing her chores in a fugue. Navilia's disappearance was a reopened wound, and Lucien would have given anything to console her. Instead he waited for darkness.

The night refused its summons. The sun set reluctantly, the horizon remaining afire despite Lucien's wishes to the contrary. He locked his door and made a slumbering mannequin of himself with spare pillows under his sheets. He scattered a handful of crickets into the glass tank to keep the drakes fed as it was possible he wouldn't return before the following day. The prospect of failing to return was a frightening one, but not unrealistic. Dino would undoubtedly come to the drakes' rescue. Lucien dragged a finger down the glass; the drakes looked back with unblinking black eyes.

And then he was out of the window, not letting fear dull his desire, nor caution contain his curiosity. The tenacious vines that grew on Demesne's walls served his needs more perfectly than any rope. But before he could climb down, he had to climb up.

Anea's startled face appeared at her window after a few tense seconds. He guessed she was attaching her veil and was quietly grateful. She opened the window, brow creased in silent question. Lucien sat himself on the sill, glad to take his weight off his arms. The sword hanging from his hip wasn't making the ordeal any easier.

'I'm off to the *sanatorio*,' he said simply, 'There's something amiss.'

He recounted seeing Giancarlo and the Majordomo spiriting a woman into the *sanatorio* the night he'd been roused by the raven. Anea sat still, listening, her head bowed, green eyes unreadable. Lucien told her of the Domo's explanation – the endemic madness that supposedly afflicted Demesne.

'I don't believe it,' he said bitterly. 'Not a word. There's a pattern here. Every few years the same thing: an eighteen-year-old woman disappears and no one sees her again.'

Anea retreated into her bedroom, returning with her battered book. She scribbled a message: *I'll wait for you to return. Tell me what you see. Go now and be careful.*

Lucien descended the stony face of the castle feeling unnaturally calm. He noted the fall would most likely kill him, but this was a minor consideration compared to the compulsion of his curiosity. His hands and feet picked their way through the masonry as if he made this journey every day of his life. Divesting himself of the Domo's secret had lifted a weight he'd been struggling to carry all these years. Now there was a surge of hope, a lightening of the spirit. In Anea he had a confidante, an ally. He continued downward, grasping the ancient vines. Ivy leaves stroked him, blood-red and apple-green. The sky overhead was now bruise-purple, dark blue creeping along the eastern horizon. The few clouds looked ethereal and unreal in the twilight. Lucien imagined them as shades arrived early, awkward and waiting for the haunting hours.

He reached the ground, shoulders and arms alive with exertion, heart beating a steady tempo in his chest. He noted the stillness. The landscape stretched out from him in a patchwork of fields and neatly ordered hedgerows. Clusters of trees watched over the graveyard in the distance, supposed home of the Domo's revenant.

He ran, eyes fixed to the ground, holding his breath in anticipation, waiting for the piercing shout that would lead to his discovery. No one called out. Onward, across the yellowing grasses of the untamed meadow between House Contadino and the *sanatorio*. Onward, under the watchful gaze of Anea, far up at her window. He wondered how many women had been dragged across this expanse. How many loyal citizens of Demesne discarded here under the pretence of madness?

He reached the *sanatorio*, heart a muffled drum, the sound thick in his ears, heightening the sense of danger. His mind drifted to the many times Virmyre had made him run the circumference of Demesne. He'd need to thank him for that. The doors of the miniature citadel stood in front of him, stained vermilion, sickly and visceral in the dying light. The iron banding and studs lent further brooding weight to the imposing portal. And beneath his feet the cracked flagstone where a roof tile had fallen all those years before. A physical scar, one that assured him the events had not been a figment of a young boy's imagination.

Lucien followed the broad sweep of the circular building until he came to the spindly tower. The taller of the two constructions leaned heavily on the main building. He picked his way up the vertical ravine where the two met, fingers like pitons, searching out every depression and crease in the grey stone. It was almost too easy. The ground simply fell away from him, the wall moving smoothly under his hands, under his boots. Upwards he climbed, not daring to look through the barred windows for fear of what might be waiting in the darkness. Once or twice he thought he discerned a muffled moan or stifled whimpering, but the sounds were at the very limit of his hearing.

He reached the top, hauling himself over the cornice and rolling onto his side. Thick clinging moss cradled him. No cry of alarm had sought him out, and yet he waited long minutes until the darkness offered more of itself. Overhead the first stars revealed their beauty, joining him on his lonely vigil. More clouds materialised, the breeze gaining a bite that had been absent before. No matter; he'd dressed for the task ahead, knowing all too well how cold it was in the company of gargoyles. Finally he sat up, but slowly so as not to attract attention. His sculpted companions were at the roof's edges, maintaining their eternal watch over the land, and he was not the only living creature on the gently sloping conical roof. At the apex perched a raven, inky black in contrast to the terracotta tiles. It stared at Lucien for long seconds, then turned its tail to him, fussing at its wing feathers.

'You again.' Lucien knew it could be any of the ravens which haunted Demesne, but his belief in coincidence was stronger.

'You wanted me to see them that night, didn't you?' The raven gazed at him balefully, then blinked a few times and looked away. 'You wanted me to unearth their secret.' The raven gave a half-hearted squawk and resumed cleaning itself. Lucien huddled next to a gargoyle, finding the very spot he'd clung to the last time he'd lurked here. The raven did likewise, an adjacent gargoyle's head providing a perch.

Time idled, and if the day had been slow to draw to an end then the dawn was equally tardy. More than once Lucien woke to find a length of spittle lining his sleeve, his buttocks numb, fingers cold. He contemplated returning to bed. Perhaps they weren't bringing her tonight. Perhaps he slept through their passing. It was possible they'd delivered her the night previous. He picked at the possibilities like a scab, then fell asleep as the horizon became lucent with amber and gold.

The raven squawked and flapped its wings. Lucien jolted awake, nearly pitching over the edge. He clutched the gargoyle for support, swearing softly under his breath. The dark bird produced a torrent of guano, staining the gargoyle's face white and black. Lucien wrinkled his nose.

'I really need to improve the company I keep,' he muttered, attempting to stand. His legs were stiff and refused his commands. He sat awkwardly, massaging feeling back into his feet, pulling his boots off when patience failed him. Sensation flooded back in waves of pain.

He almost didn't see them.

They were a silent procession: the girl slumped over Giancarlo's broad shoulder like a sack of grain, the Domo leading, his oak staff stabbing down into the withered grass of the meadow. Lucien stared, unable to breathe. Giancarlo was absorbed. The business of putting one booted foot in front of the other consumed him. The Domo picked his way across the field, seemingly blind, yet nimble in his long-limbed way. Dew had saturated the hem of his robe, which had darkened to charcoal-grey as far as the knee. They drew closer and Lucien slid onto his side, merging with the rooftop, daring himself to hang his head over the side.

Closer now, and Lucien was sure a dark mist of flies trailed the Domo, following lazy orbits around the cowled dignitary. The girl had a sack over her head, and her wrists were tied with heavy rope. The gaunt man battered at the door three times with his staff, and then they were gone, disappeared inside the *sanatorio*'s unknown depths.

Lucien fled.

The calm ordinariness of the girl's delivery had unmanned him. He'd been expecting resistance, had hoped for a desperate escape. Instead the whole scene had played out in chilling silence.

The grass conspired to slow him. Lucien pressed on harder, anger and disgust hot at the back of his throat. As soon as he reached the grey walls of Demesne his flight continued vertically, at much the same pace. His mind was full of questions that burned, while his gut was full of disappointment. A tiny spark had existed that wanted to believe the Domo's story of women driven to madness. Wanted to believe the fiction he'd been told. He'd not admitted such a spark could exist until it had been snuffed out.

Before he knew it, he was staring in through Anea's window, aching fingers gripping the cold stone. She was asleep in the vast fabric of her bed. Panic crawled up his spine. His arms were tiring, and yet he was terrified that if he knocked too loudly others would hear him. He squeezed himself onto the window ledge, feeling too large for the narrow sliver of stone. He looked below, regretting the glance immediately. The fall would snap him, and yet the prospect of climbing back down was a daunting one. He stared at the squat form of the *sanatario*, which appeared no less imposing for the sun's first rays. He shivered, wretched and despairing.

The window beside him opened. Anea waved him in, eyes, jade-green in the candlelight, full of concern. He climbed in, staggering as he jumped to the floor, turning to face her, shocked agony on his features. Anea stared back, hair falling about her face in a wave of pale yellow. Lucien smothered himself in it, clutching at her. She stiffened, her whole body going taut. Cautiously, she raised one hand to his head, smoothing down his wind-tousled hair. The embrace continued for many minutes, he silently shaking his grief out into the ropes and braids of her tresses, she remaining stiff-limbed, painfully self-conscious in his arms. Finally he released her and they sat down cross-legged on the floor as he dried his eyes on his jacket sleeves. Lucien couldn't meet her eyes, addressing his boots instead.

'They're taking women. They're taking them and I don't know why.'

He detached his scabbard from his belt, placing it across his knees.

'They're taking women, and I don't know if I can stop them.'

33

Among Gargoyles

HOUSE CONTADINO

– *Febbraio* 315

Lucien emerged into the corridor of King's Keep hollow-eyed and gaunt with shock. He looked around at the carnage. The Majordomo's severed limbs lay in congealing pools of blue blood. No sign of his inhuman strength remained in the hands. Pale and withered, they resembled diseased offcuts, as if specimens in the king's laboratory. Lucien hoped the museum of horrors might be consumed by fire, just as the perpetrator of those experiments had been.

The stench of burned meat and singed hair lingered in the corridor like a curse. The Domo's staff lay shattered on the floor, the amber headpiece glinting like a jaundiced eye, but he was nowhere to be seen. Lucien struggled to comprehend how the man had escaped, or even survived the sundering of three limbs. He had no wish to make death his constant companion, and yet the opportunity to end the Domo had fled. He doubted a second chance would present itself. His only priority now was Rafaela.

Keys jingled in the darkness, hanging from the king's chain, now wrapped around his forearm. His left hand grasped Virmyre's sword while he yanked a lantern from a sconce with his right. The darkness receded ahead of him, cowering, falling away to reveal locked portals and empty corridors. Once or twice he saw people at a distance, like phantoms. They drifted away, disappearing around corners beyond the range of the light and his curiosity. Doors closed and were locked. Tension clung to him like a cobweb until he reached the more familiar environs of House Contadino.

Nothing stirred here; even the cats had given up their nocturnal hunting. He pressed on, knees bruised, arms aching, ribs twingeing when he breathed too deeply. He was almost at the kitchens when he heard the commotion.

'Get away. I don't know anything about it.' A young voice. Maybe a few years older than himself, he guessed.

'We just want to ask some questions.' Older, grizzled, drunk. The last word distinctly threatening.

'Reckon if anyone knows where he is, you do. What with being a messenger an' all.' Another voice, much softer.

'Get away from me.'

Lucien traced the voices to the sitting room near the kitchens. Light flickered from underneath the door and down the side. Left ajar. Lucien would not refuse the invitation.

'I've not seen him since he left. The Majordomo had him thrown in the oubliette. Isn't that enough?' It was Nardo, the House Contadino messenger. Navilia's brother.

'Perhaps you should go in too,' said the older voice. 'You Contadini have always been too close to that filthy *strega*. Reckon it's time you paid for that.'

Lucien felt a new surge of anger, but it was a cold thing, not the heated fury that had consumed him when facing the Domo. He kicked open the door. It slammed against the wall, rattling on its hinges. Everyone turned to face him. Lucien's sword was held out in first position, its tip lurking near the nearest guard's exposed throat. Eyes widened in shock as they recognised him, changing to terror as they took in the sight. He was smeared with blue blood, clothes ragged and ripped from his encounters, face streaked with dirt, purple bruises flourishing beneath the grime.

'Gentlemen,' he said in a harsh whisper before calmly setting the lantern down on a dresser near the door. The sword at the guardsman's throat moved not an inch. The guards had cornered Nardo, but were armed only with knives. The messenger had crumpled to the floor, back pressed to the wall. He looked tired and dirty; his cheek was bloodied, the eye above starting to bruise. He nodded to the Orfano.

The nearest guard had his eyes fixed on the point of the

sword just inches from his jugular. He was a downy-cheeked sort, barely eighteen summers, the corner of his mouth a riot of sores. His accomplice was an older man bearing a slash across his cheekbone that had been sewn up badly, making him squint in one eye.

'I think it's time you both retired from House Fontein and took up something more useful. Farming perhaps.'

'Y-yes, Master Lucien,' said the younger guard in a falsetto. His boots began to fill with piss.

'Go. The Fuck. Away.'

The man left, his knife clattering to the floor. He struggled past Lucien, looking both apologetic and awkward as he went. The sound of his footsteps receded in the distance. Lucien's eyes remained locked on the older guard, who hadn't moved. His fist grew tight on the hilt of the knife as he squared up to Lucien, mouth a sour curve, arrogant and pugnacious.

'I serve the king,' growled the man, the scar twisting on his face. Lucien ignored him.

'Stand up, Nardo.' The messenger dragged himself to his feet, brushed himself down. 'It was the Majordomo who had your sister abducted, on the orders of the king.'

Nardo stared back wordlessly. He swallowed, then nodded.

'I'm sorry. But I thought you should know.'

The messenger knelt down and retrieved the discarded knife.

'Squads of guards from House Fontein were sent out under cover of darkness. Sent to abduct girls around their eighteenth birthday. Guards like this one.'

'I wasn't no part of that business,' blustered the scarred man. His face grew scarlet, uncertain eyes turning to Nardo, then back to the *strega* who held him at swordpoint. Sweat beaded on his forehead.

'I swear I didn't go with them. They asked me but I refused.'

'You refused an order from Giancarlo?' Lucien raised an eyebrow. 'And the Majordomo?'

'That's right. I stood up to them.'

'What a hero,' sneered Lucien. He slapped the man's knuckles with the flat of his blade leaving him nursing numbed fingers.

The knife fell and embedded itself in the floorboards with a gentle *thud*.

'He's all yours, Nardo.' Lucien backed out of the room and closed the door. The guard began to beg, his voice becoming high-pitched, then incoherent. Suddenly the sounds stopped. What Nardo had done wouldn't bring Navilia back, but it would have to do.

The night sky was smeared with an amber light where it met the land. The mist had a luminous quality as the sun crept closer to the horizon. At first Lucien thought he was hallucinating or his eyes were playing tricks with the dawn. Figures drifted in the meadow between Demesne and the *sanatorio*, awful shades half seen, the very images of the things that haunted his stories, creatures from dark tales. The unquiet dead.

But they were not dead.

The doors to the *sanatorio* had been unlocked. And not just the doors but the cells too. The shaven-headed women had stumbled out into the breaking dawn, legs stick-thin and unsteady. Some simply gazed at the stars above as they were extinguished by the coming of the sun. Others lurched and staggered, hunched over and heedless of anyone around them. A few clutched at companions only they could see or batted away invisible persecutors. Grubby shifts like burial shrouds concealed their sparse frames. Lucien staggered on, exhaustion weighing on his heels. Rafaela was not among them. His pulse raced, mouth turning dry.

The doors of the *sanatorio* yawned open, the arched portal revealing nothing but darkness within. Lucien looked at the chain of keys wrapped around his forearm with disgust. He'd faced the king for nothing. The call of ravens reached him as he picked his way through the meadow of withered women, past unseeing gazes. A few noticed him and tried to mouth words but none came. The awful silence remained unbroken.

Inside the *sanatorio*, sprawled on the floor, was Dottore Angelicola, his right eye darkened by bruising, hair tousled and wild, trousers wet with dew. Keys lay discarded on the floor nearby. He was rocking back and forth keening to himself like a child. Cradled in his arms was a haggard woman close to death. If she was aware of Angelicola's distress she didn't show it: her eyes remained blank and rheum-grey. Her hands were lifeless claws in her lap.

'Just for a while, they said. Oh yes.'

Lucien wasn't sure the *dottore* had seen him. He stood at the doorway and listened.

'You and your pretty wife can live for ever, they said, Oh yes. Such a pretty wife.'

The *dottore* sobbed and sobbed, only stopping to cough and shudder.

'And all you have to do is deliver the babies in the *sanatorio*. Such pretty babies. And such unfortunate women. Oh yes. So pretty.'

Lucien gripped the hilt of his sword. He was certain Angelicola's confession would be more than he could bear to hear.

'But those pretty babies weren't pretty at all. They lied. I pulled those creatures from the wombs of women, cutting them out when I had to. Filthy Orfani, foul *streghe* every one.' The *dottore* had settled into a conspiratorial whisper, the woman in his arms a captive audience.

'But we won't let those dreadful vermin take over, will we? Not even that thug Golia. No, we're much too clever. Aren't we? Oh yes.'

The *dottore* pressed his forehead against the woman's own.

'I don't know why I'm telling you these things. Your mind snapped twenty years ago.' He laughed hysterically, almost screeching. Lucien wondered if he'd sampled his own morphine.

'Dottore.'

Angelicola looked up as if he'd just woken from a dream. He drew in a shuddering breath.

'L-lucien?'

'Care to tell me what in the nine hells is going on?'

'I-I set them free.'

'You had keys to this place the whole time?'

The wild-haired *dottore* nodded.

'*Porcia misèria!* I could have stolen them from you and been spared meeting the king.'

'The king?' Horror seeped in behind Angelicola's eyes. 'H-how is he?'

'Dead. Which is what you're going to be if you don't give me an answer.'

The *dottore* squealed and scrambled away from him. The corpse-like woman fell to the flagstones, her head hitting the floor with a dull *smack*.

'Where is Rafaela?'

'I've not seen her. I swear. Golia brought me here. He made me give him the keys. He said he was . . . looking for someone.' The *dottore*'s eyes filled with understanding. Lucien felt his stomach clench. 'Lucien. I'm—'

'Where?' Barely restrained violence.

'I don't know.' Angelicola choked back a sob. 'Lucien, finish this. Finish me, I beg you.' His eyes were brimming.

Lucien ignored him, pressing on into the *sanatorio*. His mind was blank, feet seeking out the stone steps that would take him higher, legs protesting underneath him. It was cold in the heart of the *sanatorio*, and he felt the chill all too keenly. Running from cell to cell, he searched each and every one, scoured the corridors, ignoring the smell of bodies and piss. His every exhalation was transformed. A single-word prayer, a chant.

Rafaela, Rafaela, Rafaela.

Only emptiness greeted him. Here a sodden pile of rags, there a mouldering mattress or a pail of excrement. The *sanatorio* was deserted. Lucien despaired. He screamed in fury, throwing his lantern against the wall in pure rage. It hit the floor and leaked oil for a few seconds before the liquid spluttered into life. Fire bloomed.

He was still shaking with anger when he spotted it – a ladder lit by the bright glow of the broken lantern. He followed the wooden steps up, then realised they were attached to the wall with metal pitons. Above him was a trapdoor that could only lead to the rooftop and the ring of gargoyles that looked out across the countryside.

Lucien sheathed his sword and scrambled onto the bottom rungs, nearly losing his footing in his haste. He scaled the ladder quickly, pushing against the trapdoor, flinging it back.

Morning light flooded in, making him squint. He climbed up, drawing his sword on instinct as soon as he gained his feet. The women still drifted in the meadow below: they stumbled on, arms outstretched, moaning faintly to themselves. Lucien glanced at them only briefly before turning his attention to the presence at the edge of his vision. His mouth went dry.

Golia stood with a rope in his hand, a rope terminating at a hangman's noose, looped over Rafaela's neck. She was tight-lipped with fear, her eyes pressed shut. More rope bound her wrists together in front of her. Mercifully she looked unhurt.

The largest of the Orfano was dressed for *La Festa*. His suit was immaculate, his shirt brilliant white. Only the sword in his hand and the dagger hilt protruding from each boot disclosed his agenda. And the crude leash about Rafaela's neck.

'They were going to make me king.'

'I know.'

'Giancarlo and the Domo. They were going to make *me* king.'

'That's right.'

'And you couldn't stand it, could you?' Golia snorted. 'That they chose me and not you.'

'I don't want to be king, Golia.'

'They chose me, Lucien, *me*.'

'There's a lot more going on in Demesne than you know. We—'

'No more words, Lucien. Everyone speaks of how clever you are. Well all the clever words in the world aren't going to help now, are they?'

He tugged on the rope, causing Rafaela to flap and flounder. She clawed at the rope.

Lucien took a step forward. 'Please.'

'Don't even think about trying anything clever.' Golia grinned without humour. 'I'll kick her over the side.' He flicked his eyes to the edge of the roof. Lucien saw the rope passed through Golia's hand and was tied around one of the gargoyles.

'Don't do this, Golia.' He held out one hand. 'You can still be king.'

'I've seen you.' Lucien wondered if Golia was drunk. 'Getting all cosy with Dino and Anea. Plotting to get rid of me. Think you're so clever, don't you, Lucien?' He looked down at the rope in his hand and smiled sadly. 'I don't want to be king either.' He released a great sigh. 'I just want to kill you, kill you and all your clever words.' He looked down at Rafaela. 'I don't even care about this *porca puttana*: I just wanted to see you squirm.'

Golia dropped the rope and drew his sword, advancing toward Lucien across the rooftop of the *sanatorio*, his eyes flat, showing nothing. Dawn light flashed from the blade.

34

Until Someone Dies

HOUSE FONTEIN GREAT HALL

– Ottobre 314

Lucien always approached *La Festa del Ringraziamento* with trepidation. The night the porcelain ears shattered on the floor had haunted his every public appearance since. Despite this nagging memory quite a different creature prepared to enter the grand hall of House Fontein five years later. He was dressed in a severe suit of black damask, trousers bearing a stripe down the seam of each leg in House Fontein scarlet. His matching shirt was immaculate. A kerchief in his jacket pocket completed the ensemble. Determined not to be unarmed yet mindful of etiquette, a sword cane had been commissioned especially. He'd wasted an afternoon in a forgotten practice room, drawing the blade over and over, working through his forms. The weapon was, he'd decided, exquisite. And completely illegal of course. Orfani weren't allowed metal blades until they turned eighteen. He rolled his shoulders, working the tension out, taking a moment to compose himself before the doors of the grand hall.

It had been just over a year since his vigil on the rooftop of the *sanatorio*. Now seventeen, the speculation surrounding him was rampant. Who would he marry and what would he do after his final testing? Would he in fact survive at all, or would Golia move against him? His occasional assignations with Stephania had become common knowledge, adding further fuel to the fires of gossip that swept through Demesne. Anea had remained resolutely unreachable, consumed with study and assignations of her own. These were rumoured to be political in nature, and Russo was now a fixture at Anea's side. The silent Orfano was crafting an agenda, but Lucien had yet to discover her intent.

The doors opened and the steward announced him to the room. Even Golia's hulking presence at *La Festa* couldn't dim his confidence. The guests turned to him, some whispering behind fans, others nodding respectfully. Far too few of the last. He took care to keep his expression neutral, knowing he was given to scowling when under scrutiny. Camelia had chided him often.

Dino fell in beside him with a sour look, Achilles on his shoulder, scaly and imperious. A servant wound his way through the crowd toward them, bringing a tray of wine-filled glasses.

'Where the hell have you been?' whispered the younger Orfano, brow furrowed.

'Getting dressed. There's no rush. *La Festa* lasts all night.'

'Duchess Prospero has been asking after you. Every ten minutes, without fail.' Dino lowered his voice. 'She's as mad as a box of frogs, you know.'

'Keep your voice down; she's heading this way. And why the hell did you bring Achilles?'

Dino said nothing, shifting his gaze to the trio of figures that stepped through the parted crowd. The hall buzzed, thrumming with small talk and speculation.

Lucien doubted Duchess Prospero could have traversed the short distance alone. The nearly-deaf duke supported her as she towered over him, a gratuitous amount of décolletage on display. Stephania followed in a matching dress, demure compared to the confection of her mother. The effect was of seeing two twins separated by a span of twenty years and a watering-down of values.

'Now I know what a migraine feels like,' whispered Lucien.

'What *does* a migraine feel like? asked Dino.

'You should know – you've already been talking to her.'

Dino coughed laughter into his wine glass, displacing most of it onto the floor. Servants scurried about him as he made his apologies. Duchess Prospero turned to the string quartet and gave them the signal after the requisite pleasantries were exchanged. Lucien bowed to Stephania. She took his hand and smiled. The dance was under way. There was a faint trace of red wine on her lips. His mind flashed back to the day she'd kissed him by the mantelpiece. There'd been no repeat of that event, but she'd blessed him with her smile freely and often.

'New dress?'

'Yes,' she replied, sounding weary. 'Not exactly what I had in mind, but you know what mother is like.'

'Insistent.'

'That's a nice word for it.' Stephania smiled again. Lucien couldn't help joining her.

'And how is life as a member of the feared Fontein?' A common enquiry. 'I notice you've yet to take an apartment with them.'

'I grew up in House Contadino. And besides, assassinating me there would cause political problems for Duke Fontein.'

'Sound thinking,' she agreed.

'I find I sleep easier when I'm not under the same roof as Golia.'

'Ever consider that you might sleep more easily under the Prospero roof?'

He was used to this. She enjoyed being bold, speaking in a manner designed to shock.

'It's crossed my mind a few times.' She returned his smile, eyes lingering on his face. Her overtures were enchanting, even exciting, yet he lacked the motivation to make their joining an official one. Something held him back from surrendering to her completely.

Lucien padded through the gavotte easily. So easily in fact he had time to take in the other guests. Only the Majordomo was conspicuous by his absence. And Rafaela. She'd not have received an invitation, but it was an unspoken courtesy that the maids of Orfani were allowed to attend. Stephania cleared her throat, drawing his attention.

'I think Mother will press you for a decision soon,' she said casually. Lucien had been expecting this.

'We're still so young,' he mumbled, more to himself. They turned and bowed to each other, and the dance dragged on.

'How do you feel about that?'

'Well, I'm glad it's not Golia.' She smiled again. 'And Dino is much too young. I suppose I could make do with someone like you.' She raised an eyebrow. Lucien forced another grin. Damned by faint praise. Again.

'You don't have to marry an Orfano,' he replied. 'You do know that?'

'Who do you suggest?' Her smile slipped, an edge in her voice. 'Not exactly a wealth of men in Demesne, is there? Not of my status, anyway.'

'Is there someone you want, someone you find yourself thinking of?' His eyes searched the crowd for Rafaela.

'It doesn't work like that,' she said, all trace of her previous good humour now departed. 'Not for my mother, and not for me.'

Lucien took in her face, the corners of her eyes narrowed with the barest hint of anguish.

'Besides,' she said, 'we might grow to love each other. Perhaps if we gave each other a chance, something might flourish. At the very least we might be friends.'

He regarded the fuchsia-clad girl for a moment. Hers was an optimism rooted in resignation, someone trying to make the best of a situation she had no control over. He respected her for that, he realised. The music drew to a close. Lucien bowed while Stephania smiled from behind a fan before bobbing a polite curtsey. She melting into the crowd, rejoining her coterie. He watched her go, the swish and sway of hips in rich fabric distracting.

We might grow to love each other – was such a thing even possible?

Lucien retired to the side of the room, folding his arms and leaning on one of the many pillars. A tap on the shoulder brought him face to face with Anea. Lucien found himself at a loss for words. People nearby moved away, whispering behind fluttering fans, exchanging knowing glances. Vestiges of old gossip and rumour kindled and took flame around them.

She was wearing the same outfit she had worn at his Rite of Adoption. The white dress had been let out slightly to accommodate the ripening of her figure. Her headdress looked more splendid than he remembered it, matching the ultramarine veil she wore across her nose and mouth. Gold thread conspired to make her green eyes look more piercing that usual. She held out her book, opened to a page bisected by single line of her handwriting: *Are you just going to roll over like a dog and marry the first girl they throw at you?*

Lucien raised his eyebrows and blinked.

She flicked the page over where more script lay in wait: *I can think of far better things to be doing than maintaining the status quo. Can't you?*

Mistress Corvo interrupted them, clucking and cooing.

'Anea, darling, I have the *capo* here for you. Won't you dance with him?'

Anea glanced at Lucien, eyes hard as jade, before allowing Guido to take her hand. The *capo de custodia* led her onto the dance floor. Was there a hint of resignation in the set of his shoulders? Where was the smirk that all-too-frequently perched on his lips? Lucien watched them dance, sipping wine and giving Dino single-syllable responses He ignored Mistress Corvo entirely as she provided a commentary. Sadness descended about him. He realised the *capo* would not dance with Anea if he knew what lay beneath the veil. Still, there was much about Anea that was lovely. Lovely yet furious. The stiffness of her steps betrayed the full extent of her indignation. Her gaze flickered back to Lucien. The eye contact caused her to misstep, angering her further.

'Well, if it isn't the most pathetic weakling in all of Demesne.' Golia's voice came from behind them, very close. Dino turned and staggered back a step, awed by the sheer physical presence of the older Orfano.

'Fuck. Off. Golia,' said Lucien, each word a study in boredom, not bothering to face his tormentor. His left hand tightened on the handle of the sword cane, drawing the blade an inch from its scabbard. Mistress Corvo uttered a pained exclamation. She hurried away, blacks skirts rustling around emaciated legs. The conversation in the grand hall fell silent even as the quartet continued playing, ignorant of the unfolding confrontation. Guests stared as the mood curdled around the Orfani.

There was a handful of uncomfortable seconds and then Dino spoke: 'He's gone.'

The tension around them dissipated; the taut crowd relaxed, resuming their chatting.

'Will it always be like this?' asked Dino, staring after Golia, who pressed his way through the courtiers.

'Only until someone dies.'

'That might be sooner than any of us think,' said the younger boy, the sweep of the music threatening to drown his words.

Duke Prospero approached, smiling amiably. He wore a powdered wig, as ridiculous as it was hideously out of date. Lucien suspected him to be the worse for drink, judging by his gait.

'Lucien, my boy,' he boomed cheerily. Stephania stood on the other side of the room, surrounded by House Prospero functionaries. She gazed at Lucien over the top of her fan. It was not contentment in her eyes, he realised, but hope. Lucien and Dino bowed to the duke.

'Are you enjoying the party?' asked Lucien.

'I'll say. A very fine time indeed!' Lucien couldn't help flashing a lopsided grin at Dino, who had to look away from the tipsy duke for fear he be consumed by laughter. Suddenly Lucien felt the great weight of the duke's arm around his shoulders. The wine on his breath was pungent. Guests raised eyebrows at the display. Physical contact between nobles was uncommon, between men it was unthinkable.

'You'll take care of her, m'boy. Tell me you'll take care of her?'

Lucien looked at the duke. He'd whispered, and in that whisper had been the tiniest of cracks in a facade. Where was the almost-deaf duke he knew so well? Where was the jovial and stentorian leader of House Prospero?

'Tell me you'll take care of her. You two have a chance I never had. You're the same age. Don't make the mistake I did. Her mother cats around with that insipid *capo* and thinks I don't know. But I do.' Bloodshot eyes brimmed with drunken tears. 'I do.'

'Duke Prospero, I'm so sorry,' Lucien replied, voice hushed. 'I had no idea.'

'Don't worry about me, m'boy. But by the love of all that's righteous, look after my sweet Stephania.' He cleared his throat, clearly embarrassed, blinking back tears, tremulous lips stained with wine.

'She'll be fine, my lord.'

Duke Prospero lurched away, wig slipping from his head as he departed, the hairpiece on the floor behind him, a chorus of laughter rising at his passing. A page snatched the wig from the floor and crammed it onto his head, mimicking Prospero's drunken amble. The sorry form of the duke located a side door and exited into the dark corridors beyond, oblivious.

The *capo* sidled over to Duchess Prospero as soon as the music stopped, leaving Anea alone. The party was in full swing now, but Anea might just well have been stranded on a deserted island at that cruel moment. Lucien recalled the time he had left her after they had first danced. The night of the porcelain ears.

'Dino, go to Anea. Escort her. Be sure to walk her back to her room at the end of the night.'

'Why me?' he muttered. Achilles flicked out a tongue and flexed his claws on Dino's epaulette.

'Because I'm leaving.' Lucien fixed him with a stern look. 'Take this.' He held out the sword cane. 'If anyone lifts a finger against either of you, kill him.' Dino stared at the weapon as if it were made of solid gold. Lucien was struggling to keep his temper. There seemed to be nothing about Demesne that didn't sicken him in some way.

'Go to her, Dino. Do it now.' Then Lucien followed the duke through the side door.

For a large drunk man unsteady on his feet, the duke did an admirable disappearing act. Lucien sought him for many minutes, eventually calling at his chambers. The page on duty shrugged his shoulders, telling him he had assumed the duke was still at *La Festa*. Lucien sighed, troubled by thoughts of the future as he began the journey back to House Contadino. Inevitably he and Stephania would tire of each other, remaining wed in name only, pursuing intrigues and infidelities as diversions. It was clear to him now why the nobles were so unhappy. Political marriages bore sour fruit.

He arrived outside his apartment. A cold wind gusted down the corridor; shutters clapped and boomed in the distance. He shivered, pulling the collar of his jacket closer around his neck and drawing his chin down to his chest to ward off the chill. Golden light emerged from under the door.

His door.

Someone awaited him in his apartment. Giving the sword cane to Dino now seemed like a very foolish decision. One that could cost him his life.

35

An Unkindness

THE *SANATORIO*

– Febbraio 315

Lucien knew he was in trouble. Golia had a distinct height and weight advantage and always played to his strengths, raining blows on his opponents like hammer strikes. He was master of the overhead cut. No finesse, just punishment, the sword reduced to a club.

But not today.

Golia circled him, then thrust and followed up with a series of attacks, testing Lucien's defences. He stepped in close, using his dagger in lethal jabs, or else parrying Lucien's ripostes with casual ease. The sound of blade on blade pierced the still morning air. The roof of the *sanatorio* was uneven, the roof tiles threatening to trip the duelling Orfani at any moment.

Lucien was distracted by Rafaela. She tugged and strained at the knots in the rope to no effect. His shoulder ached, continuing to pain him long after the initial wound. Lack of sleep and scores of bruises and abrasions had worn him down. Lucien suspected Golia knew he had little left. He'd draw out the fight, waiting for Lucien to tire. With exhaustion would come mistakes. They circled and struck. Lucien parried and Golia pressed his advantage, pushing him back to the edge of the roof. Lucien dodged sideways and slashed at the back of his opponent's head, just as D'arzenta had done the day they'd trained in the Contadino courtyard. Golia bent double at the waist to avoid the strike, then withdrew with a grunt, his momentum broken.

A raven alighted on the head of a gargoyle, cawing loudly. Golia snatched a sidelong glance, and Lucien thrust his blade forward, keen to capitalise on the distraction. Golia swept his sword across his torso, a clumsy move not helped by the uncertain footing. He stumbled slightly, batting Lucien's thrust aside.

Another raven descended and perched, eyeing the duellists with a piercing gaze. The black bird joined its mournful din with that of the first, who was still hectoring Golia. More ravens appeared, settling on stony heads and flapping. Still more positioned themselves on hunched shoulders, adding their voices to the throng. The Gargoyles were soon indistinct under black wings. Accusatory eyes followed Golia's every move.

The Orfani fought on, grunting with exertion, dripping sweat, snarling curses. Their blades rang out, drawing the attention of the *sanatorio* inmates in the meadow. Lucien noticed a change in Golia. The larger Orfano couldn't keep his eyes from the ravens, who glared and harangued him stridently. He was ashen.

Golia was afraid of birds.

Lucien waited for the next sidelong glance and then unleashed an attack of his own, not aimed at Golia directly but the dagger he clutched in his left hand. There was a clash of metal on metal followed by a gasp. The short blade skittered across the roof, coming to rest at the feet of a gargoyle. Golia stared down at his empty hand, making a fist and then clutching the numb fingers to his chest.

'They chose me!' he roared, hefting the sword over his head. Lucien stepped away from a blow that would have broken his collarbone or more likely have split him from neck to sternum. The sword crashed into the roof tiles, which jumped from the rafters in fragments. 'I'll be king. Not you. Not Dino.' Golia was eying Lucien with naked hatred.

Lucien took advantage of the lull, knowing it was of small consequence. He was spent and needed a good deal more than just a few seconds' respite. Golia hefted his sword and came on, calm again. They danced like this for many minutes. To Lucien it felt like hours: his muscles were turning to lead, his feet dragging. Golia would circle then lunge, the steel racing ahead of him, threatening to split Lucien's skull in two. Lucien dodged time and again, moving as nimbly as the sloping roof would allow. Again and again Golia brought his sword down in savage arcs, forcing him back with the sheer ferocity of each strike.

Lucien's mind wandered to the Majordomo and the many people the official had lied to. The people he'd manipulated to do his bidding. The gravedigger, Angelicola, Giancarlo; the list went on and on. Golia was no different, lacking the insight to realise he was being played like a piece on a board. He was a blunt instrument, nothing more.

There was a pause as Lucien sidestepped again and Golia staggered from a combination of fatigue and uneven footing. The ravens called out as Lucien turned his blade and brought it down with a great slap across Golia's right wrist. The hulking Orfano howled and Lucien desperately hoped he'd fractured the bones. His prayers were answered.

Golia dropped his sword, filling the air around him with curses. Lucien extended his blade, feeling unsteady, the strength in his arms beginning to fail.

'It's done. You're unarmed.'

Golia continued to curse expansively in the old tongue.

'Have the intelligence to surrender at least,' said Lucien, exasperation creeping into his voice.

'I don't need a sword to deal with vermin like you,' grunted Golia, and shucked off his jacket. The shirt beneath was sleeveless, leaving his heavily muscled arms free. Shiny blue spines arced back toward his elbows from brawny forearms. He threw the jacket at Lucien, who parried on instinct. The fabric wrapped itself around the steel, then Golia was bearing down on him, charging across the roof of the *sanatorio*.

Lucien freed the blade from the tangle of the jacket, turning to strike at the oncoming Orfano. Too late. Dashed to the tiles, the air driven from his lungs, he watched Virmyre's sword go rattling across the roof and over the edge to fall to the meadow below.

Golia was astride him, hands clutching at his throat, pressing down with implacable force. His huge hands fitting easily around Lucien's slender neck.

'Not. So. Clever. Now,' grated Golia from clenched teeth.

The edges of Lucien's vision swam and began to grow dark. He clawed weakly at the hands around his throat, but Golia had always been bigger, stronger. He reached down for the dagger tucked in his boot but found nothing. He remembered the other outcast Orfano, how he'd wheezed and spluttered with Lucien's dagger in his throat. No such reprieve today. The ravens were shrieking now, flapping and hopping on their stony perches like a demented black-robed choir. Golia was shouting, but Lucien could only hear a dim roar. Everything seemed far away.

Suddenly the pressure stopped and he dragged down a lungful of air, pushing himself to his elbows. Golia was clutching his throat. Rafaela stood behind him, the rope that had bound her wrists now a garrotte. She was red-faced with the strain, her eyes shut tight with the effort. Golia slammed an elbow into her stomach. She bent double a moment, then sprawled across the roof, collapsed in pain.

Lucien reached out for Golia's sword. The hilt was just within reach of his right hand. He writhed underneath the hulking mass of the larger man, feeling the leather-bound hilt under his fingertips.

He didn't see Golia slash down, plunging his spines into his unprotected neck. Lucien coughed and drew in a shuddering gasp.

Golia withdrew his arm and leaned back, roaring into the sky, 'Not so clever now!'

Lucien coughed, clutching at the spread of piercing wounds. He felt like Golia's hands were still around his throat, pressing down, stifling him with panic.

'Poison.' Golia laughed, cradling Lucien's head between his hands in a mockery of affection. He pressed his forehead to Lucien's own, his face filling the Orfano's field of vision.

'I bested you, you pathetic weakling. You'll be dead in minutes.'

Golia sat back, looking supremely proud of himself. Lucien's throat continued to swell. He was making a dreadful noise, like an ancient pair of bellows.

'Giancarlo always said I'd best you. He always said you were weak.'

Lucien stared at the spines that curved from Golia's forearms. Dino, Golia, the Majordomo, even the king, all of them had blue spines, and yet he'd lacked the wit to discover how dangerous they were. He clawed at his neck, knowing it was too late. Golia hawked and spat on Lucien's jacket, then plastered on a manic grin. He barked out more cruel laughter, then a jolt passed through him. Golia looked down at the red knife tip protruding from his chest. His eyes widened, straining to look over his shoulder to see what Lucien had already seen.

Rafaela stood over them, smeared dirt and shorn hair making her almost unrecognisable. One hand had snaked around Golia's neck; the other was working the knife into his lungs. Golia sighed and a whimper escaped with it. She clung to him, withdrawing the blade and thrusting again. There was a wet sound. Golia opened his mouth to protest, and a trickle of blood escaped from the corner. He turned his head back to Lucien, blood-rimmed smile twisting his mouth.

'No matter,' he wheezed. 'Sinistro will still die. No one survives that much poison.'

Lucien clutched at his throat, willing cool air to seep down into his lungs. He was beginning to grow faint.

'No one survives that much poison,' repeated Golia. A terminal cough rattled through him.

'You're wrong,' said Rafaela, holding Golia close. 'Lucien is immune.'

Golia stared up her, brow creased and incredulous. He opened his mouth to speak, but only scarlet emerged from his lips.

'You think I'm some stupid girl from the countryside? A maid who washes bed sheets and hangs up clothes?'

Lucien drew in a gasp, the pressure at his throat beginning to lessen.

'How?' whispered Golia.

'Dino has the same spines. I've been feeding Lucien tiny amounts of poison since he was ten.' She whispered this into his ear, as close as a lover, hand clutching the blade still thrust into his broad back.

Golia released a grunt; more blood trickled down his chin, spattering on his chest. Rafaela stood back, and he crashed down onto his side, the knife still embedded in his back. He was bleeding freely, his eyes growing dim.

'You won't ever call me *porca puttana* again, you sack of shit,' said Rafaela.

Lucien pulled himself to his knees, still wheezing, and Rafaela helped him to his feet. They stared for at each other a moment before embracing, arms holding tight with fierce intensity. Neither daring to let go.

Trembling, Lucien looked her in the eye. 'You've been poisoning me for eight years?'

'Just a bit.' She shrugged. 'Every morning.'

'You've been poisoning me *every day* for the last eight years?'

'Not when I had a day off.' She smiled. 'I can't be everywhere at once, you know.'

'How did you know Dino's poison would immunise me from Golia's spines?'

She hesitated. 'I didn't.'

'Oh,' said Lucien, then ran a hand across the puncture wounds in his throat.

'I was going to be king,' wheezed Golia, blood and spittle leaking from his mouth. Lucien looked down and felt a wave of sadness overtake him.

'Yes, you were, but only in name. The Domo had other plans. I'm sorry, Golia. Everyone you ever trusted lied to you.'

The elder Orfano looked up at Lucien, gritted his teeth against the pain.

'I always hated you,' he hissed. And then the light went from his eyes like a candle snuffed.

They stood, staring at the crumpled form of Golia, the pair of them spattered with his blood, each certain there had been no other possible outcome. It didn't make either of them feel any better.

The stillness of the morning returned; even the unkindness of ravens had fallen silent, dark-eyed witnesses to a duel, a failed poisoning, a brutal ending. Offering no comment, they kept their stony perches and stared at the reunited couple. Lucien pushed his fingers into Rafaela's hand, then led her to the trapdoor. He breathed deeply, daring himself to believe she was safe again.

One of the ravens cawed loudly, causing Lucien to turn, releasing Rafaela's hand with reluctance. She descended into the darkness of the empty *sanatorio*. One of the birds detached itself from the rest and hopped down, settling on the hilt of Golia's sword. It cawed again, flapping its wings. Lucien crossed the rooftop and stooped to retrieve the blade. The raven took to wing and the rest of the birds followed suit, exploding from the rooftop in a scattering of daybreak silhouettes.

Lucien had a feeling he'd need a sword again before the day was done.

36

After La Festa

Lucien crossed the corridor and unhooked a lantern from the wall, imagining Golia waiting in his apartment. The older Orfano would be brooding on his coarse dismissal at *La Festa* no doubt, keen to avenge the slight or put matters to rest for all time. Lucien stepped inside, all too aware he was unarmed. At first he thought the sitting room untouched, then noticed the fire had been banked up. New wood had been brought in for the pile. The ruddy light imbued the room with a hellish cast, putting him in mind of Anea's apartment the night of the fire. He needed no reminder of that event. The panic and choking fumes revisited him as dreams only rarely, but vividly all the same.

He took up a dagger he'd left on the sideboard, knowing it would be little help if Golia were in his chamber armed with a sword. No sound greeted him; only darkness showed beneath the bedroom door. He pressed the absence of one ear to it, hearing nothing except the racing of his heart.

The door creaked open.

Waiting for him in the twilight was Rafaela, slumped on the bed, her boots discarded on the floor. Thick coils of hair covered her face and splayed out across the cream linen. He approached, hands shaking. Would she wake? Had Golia killed her and left the body where Lucien couldn't help but find it?

'Lucien?' she mumbled through a smile, eyes heavy lidded, teased open by the lantern light.

'Yes, it's me.' He concealed the knife so not to startle her. 'What are you doing here?'

'I only sat for a minute.' She brushed her hair away from her face, smile deepening. 'I must have fallen asleep. Looks like I missed *La Festa*.'

'Not quite. I left early. If you want, we could still make the end.'

He set the lantern down on the floor, noticing the bottle of Barolo, half full. She looked at him, propped up on one elbow, her bodice slightly unlaced, her blouse rucked and untucked, lips stained a darker red.

'Looks like you've been having a party of your own,' he said, raising an eyebrow. She shrugged, regarding him from the corner of one eye.

'Might be more fun now that you're here.'

He picked up the bottle and took a swig, then stood and kicked off his boots beside hers. His jacket was cast off next, slung in the direction of the wardrobe. All this was done under the watchful gaze of her hazel eyes. He felt them linger on him, not unpleasantly.

'You look out of sorts,' she said.

A brief nod of his head, an unhappy curve of the mouth. He sat on the bed, fingers kneading his temples before looking back to her.

'The older I get, the less things make sense.'

'It seems to work that way,' she replied. 'I thought you'd discovered that truth a long time ago.'

'I did, but...' He faltered, looking at the palms of his hands as if he might find his fortune told in the whorls and creases of his skin. Some clue. Anything. 'This place. I can't stand it. Anea baffles me; Golia is a constant threat; Duchess Prospero is...'

'Wearing out all the men under twenty-five?' Rafaela grinned.

'Just the *capo*, as far as I'm aware.' He returned her smile, letting it take him over. She always found a way to make him smile. She always had. His thoughts turned to Prospero. 'The duke spoke to me tonight. He looked so broken. Like he'd bet everything and managed to walk away with nothing but his shirt.'

'There are people in Landfall who enjoy much less.'

Lucien nodded at the truth of this before continuing.

'He was drunk, of course. But he knows about the *capo* and the duchess. It was awful. He knows, and there's nothing he can do about it. They married for political reasons and now what?'

'I had no idea you were so fond of him.'

'I'm not.' Lucien shrugged, surprised at the strength of his own reaction. 'Not really. But seeing him like that ... He whispered to me to look after his daughter.'

'And will you?' Rafaela had pushed herself up and swung her legs over the side of the bed.

'He meant—'

'I know what he meant.'

He shrugged and swallowed, a surge of emotion forcing its way up from his chest until his eyes were prickling with the force of it. Rafaela pressed close to him, her lips drawn into a pout, brow creased with the beginnings of a question.

'What else did he say?'

Lucien shrugged, 'All he really wanted was ... Never mind.'

'It's very sweet of you to care about him, but he never acknowledged you before the Rite of Adoption. Try not to let it worry you.'

She was so close he could almost taste the wine on her breath. Other traces teased at his senses – the sleep-warm smell of her skin, her hair. Her eyes, ever a pleasing hazel, looked green and cat-like by lantern light.

'Why are you in my room tonight, Rafaela?'

She met his eyes for a second, then leaned forward, lips brushing his. Impossibly soft. One hand stroked the side of his face as she continued to kiss him tenderly. The world pitched sideways a fraction, perhaps the entire universe. His skin flushed and sensation flooded through his body, suddenly blood-warm and delirious. He'd wanted her for ever, at first not even knowing the name of his longing or how to satisfy it. And now here in this moment, this unexpected moment, she'd come to him.

'I don't understand,' he murmured. 'When did you start—'

'Since Navilia,' she said, eyes downcast. 'You were so determined that day, so brave. You've always been brave. And the Rite of Adoption. You wanted to be House Fontein for so long, so passionately. I would have done anything that day to see a smile on your face.'

'I don't care for House Fontein any more; there's something else I want . . .'

'I know.' Her voice was barely a whisper, then she was kissing him again with the trace of wine on her tongue, he in turn kissing her neck, losing himself in the soft fragrance of her hair, unlacing her bodice with trembling fingers, heart pounding. His buttons were suddenly apart, dress shirt pulled over the top of his head, revealing supple shoulders crossed with scars. She smiled again, mouth pressed to his as he ran his fingers through her rich ringlets.

'Wait,' he said, then stooped over the side of the bed to retrieve the lamp and made to blow it out.

'Don't do that,' she said. 'I want to see you; I want to remember everything.'

Lucien set the lamp back on the floor, then turned to her. 'How will this work? I mean, you and me?'

'There won't be a you and me, Lucien. There can't be.' A flash of defiance in her eyes now, something he'd never seen before. 'Except for tonight.'

'But—'

'Nothing. You'll be married off soon, and I'll not be a mistress. I deserve better. And so does she.'

'We could run away?'

'They'll kill you if you don't marry. Everyone knows it.'

She wriggled off the bed. Her skirt and small clothes fell to the floor, leaving her in just a blouse, eyes twinkling. Her naked legs were olive-brown, the curve of her calves exciting him, the soft sweep of her thighs enchanting.

'How do I look?'

'Luminous.' He swallowed, unsure, uncertain, almost painfully. 'How do we do this?' he whispered.

She summoned him with a crooked finger. He stood, pressing

his body against hers, feeling her bite his lower lip. And then her tongue was brushing his, her arms crossing over her body, removing her blouse, his fingers tracing the soft swells of her breasts. And now she was tugging down his britches, grasping him, fingers entwined about his girth. His own fingers ranged lower, she guiding him to the soft enticing folds, tight curls tickling his flesh.

'That's it,' she breathed. 'Gently.' Her own hand commanding his to make tiny circles, the callouses of his fingers pressing against the sweet bud of her sex. They stood like that for long minutes, she guiding him with one hand, gently tugging at him with the other. Her breaths came shorter, faster, her guidance more insistent, until she bucked her hips, her knees bending with the power of it. She let out a throaty murmur of pleasure.

'Get on the bed, lie back.' Her smile was pure mischief and delight. He obeyed, freeing himself of his britches as he went, feeling ridiculous. He'd not been naked in front of anyone since childhood. She didn't give him long to dwell on his self-consciousness, straddling him, pressing one finger to his lips. He breathed in her rich musk and found himself besotted. Her hand curled around the shaft of him and he stifled a grunt before her mouth locked on his once more. And then the perfect velvet slickness of her sex enveloped him.

They both gasped.

Lucien was tremulous, breathless.

She eased back onto his hips, the mischief on her face now mixed with hunger, his own expression shock and wonderment.

'That's it,' she breathed, rising and falling, taking more of him, then kissing him again, harder now as his hands savoured the contours of hip and waist, ample breast and hardened nipple.

'Teeth,' she managed between laboured gasps.

'Softly.' She flinched, laughed. 'They're sensitive.'

'Sorry,' he mumbled, face aflame.

'It's fine. Yes, like that.'

She took all of him, riding harder, his hands working her hips, his own rising to meet hers.

'Just. Stay. Still,' she managed, her motion becoming a

crescendo, earthy moans escaping her lips as she ground down against him, the movements becoming short. A jagged insistent compulsion. A shudder passed through her, hands clutching at his shoulders. He thought she said his name but she might have been growling. Her hair trailed down over his face.

Everything stopped.

She let out a long, throaty laugh.

'Is that...? Are you...?'

'Fine,' she breathed into his ear, 'I'm fine,' a sleepy smile of satisfaction on her perfect lips.

Then there was some small commotion as she wriggled underneath him. He suddenly found himself on his knees, leaning over her, savouring every line and contour. They began to kiss and he found himself inside again, led by her clever fingers.

'I've wanted you for so long,' he breathed into her ear. She said nothing, her smile alone worth countless words. Her legs angled higher, her ankles hooking in the small of his back, ushering him deeper.

A sudden burst of laughter shook through him.

'What?' She didn't stop, entwined legs still urging him on.

'I just can't believe it.'

Her smile was dizzying, fingertips trailing pleasure across his scalp, his back, dragging down the toned curves of his arms. He increased the tempo, excited by the moans now freely escaping her lips.

'Harder,' she whispered, eyes now closed, lost in pleasure.

And then an ache sweeter than anything he had ever known, building, expanding. Breath came only as short gasps; speech fled him, time slowed.

And then he was shuddering into her, every muscle tense and suddenly weak, leaving him collapsed over her, buried in the coils of her hair.

'I lo—'

'Don't say it, Lucien. Please.'

His chest became leaden. Was she rejecting him? And now, like this?

'I don't underst—'

'Just.' She drew warm fingertips down his face, an index finger tracing his lips. The slightest shimmer of teardrops appeared at the corners of her eyes. 'Please, let's enjoy each other. But don't say that. You'll break my heart.'

37

Beyond Shattered

THE GREAT HALL OF HOUSE ERUDITO

– *Febbraio* 315

The grand hall of House Erudito had been one of the last additions to the complex that was Demesne. Erudito was the youngest of the four houses, formed at the express wish of the king, and less a branch of nobility, more a caste of the finest and most learned minds. Erudito was everything the king cared for and all he aspired to. The grand hall by extension was a perfect study of the king's ego and narcissism, made all the more strange by his increasingly reclusive behaviour. His absence from Demesne was total by the time the craftsmen filed out, work complete.

Black diamonds and cream squares tiled the floor, meticulously waxed and polished by the household staff. A triptych of the king in a saintly robe stared down from the frescoed ceiling fifty feet above. In the first of the pictures he stood over the shipwrecks of legend, a yellow nimbus circling his head. The second picture showed him overseeing swarthy men at work on the foundations of King's Keep. The third section showed the king's coronation, the nimbus at his head now supplemented by a silver crown. The triptych was usually overlooked in favour of the splendour of the floor-to-ceiling stained-glass window. Another rendering of the king looked down in benevolence upon the room, cherubs fluttering at his shoulders, wolfhounds flanking his heels. In his left hand he held a sword, in his right a sheaf of wheat. Fertile fields and the outline of Demesne stood in the background. The craftsmanship was breathtaking, the composition of the image immaculate, the angle of the window perfect for catching the rays of the rising sun.

Except no one was paying attention to the window because they were arguing heatedly among themselves. Lucien wasn't sure if Rafaela was supporting him, or vice versa; he only knew they'd dragged themselves through the winding corridors of Demesne trying to find everyone. They looked on with weary detachment as the throng occupying the hall squabbled and bickered.

Angelicola sprawled on the floor like a drunk, his face in his hands, while Duchess Prospero and Stephania seethed at each other nearby. The *capo de custodia* looked on impotently as mother and daughter aired their grievances.

Elsewhere Giancarlo argued with Lord and Lady Contadino. Massimo lurked at the viscount's shoulder, his eyes fixed on Giancarlo's student, Carmine. The youths' hands rested on the hilts of their swords, quietly threatening, violence waiting to be let off the leash.

Nardo, struggling to get at Duke and Duchess Fontein, was being restrained by a clutch of farmers. The elderly pair looked on aghast as the messenger shouted accusations of their complicity in his sister's abduction.

Mistress Corvo, for want of inclusion in the drama, was scolding Virmyre for being drunk. Russo, on the other hand, was keeping six guardsmen at bay with her acid tongue. The guards seemed intent on arresting Franco a second time, and mostly likely would have if not for Dino and Anea, who flanked Russo with crossed arms and sullen expressions.

Adding to the uproar were a smattering of aides and officials, notaries and even domestic staff from various households. Nobles from minor houses had also come, apparently just to watch and wary of being drawn in. D'arzenta and Ruggeri stood off to one side, keeping their own counsel, both dressed formally yet armed. Maestro Cherubini stood with them, a pained expression on his round face. He wrung his hands above his large stomach, rings glittering on chubby fingers.

The noise began to subside.

Voice by voice, each accuser or defender fell silent, each argument discarded, each slight forgotten. All eyes turned toward the two figures in the doorway. Lucien realised he'd not taken the scabbard from Golia's corpse and so was not able to sheath the sword. He'd been holding one blade or another for so long now it felt like a natural extension of him. One he was keen to be free of.

Giancarlo stood on a chair at the opposite end of the room. 'There he is. The exile. Guards, arrest him at once and we can lay this business to rest.'

The guards advanced, but very slowly. Whatever they'd heard about Lucien in the last two days filled them with trepidation.

' "This business"?' said Lucien, surprised at the strength in his own voice. Every eye rested on him, every ear bent toward him. 'Let me tell you about the "business" of Demesne.'

The guards faltered, their curiosity piqued. Some looked back at Giancarlo but most focused their attention at the gore-slicked Orfano standing before them. The hall was quiet except for Dottore Angelicola, who sobbed into his hands quietly.

'You stand accused of the murder of four Orfani and a litany of other crimes.' Giancarlo remained on the chair, looking ridiculous and pugnacious in equal measure.

'It would have been five Orfani, wouldn't it, Giancarlo? Except Dino didn't die that night. He had a decoy in his bed. Anea you simply threw in the oubliette. No stomach for killing women, eh? I'd been exiled by that point, to be hunted down in the countryside, out of sight.'

'Lies,' snapped Giancarlo. 'I don't know what you're talking about.'

Lucien removed his arm from around Rafaela's shoulder and tried to stand up a bit straighter. The pain of his wounds showed on his face. Rafaela nodded her encouragement.

'There's much that goes on in the countryside, out of sight,' said Lucien, turning to the members of the crowd closest to him. 'The Domo sent men to capture Salvaggia, Rafaela's sister.' He pointed at the shorn woman in the dirty shift. 'But they took the wrong woman. That's why I came back.'

All eyes turned to Rafaela, who stared at Giancarlo with unbridled disgust. People gasped as they recognised her. Lucien limped forward a few steps, the crowd parting in front of him, rapt.

'And it's not the first time a girl has gone missing around her eighteenth birthday, is it? Nardo's sister Navilia was taken some years back.'

The messenger set his eyes on Giancarlo, his face ashen.

'In fact,' continued Lucien, 'I'd say these abductions occur every three years or so.'

'Silence!' Roared the *superiore* from the chair. 'I said arrest him.'

But the guards still didn't move.

'All so the king can carry out his monstrous experiments.' Lucien limped forward, his gaze locked on Giancarlo's panicked eyes.

'This is treason!' spluttered the *superiore*. 'The king's name will not be defamed in such a way.'

'The king is dead,' said Lucien. The hall filled with the sound of gasping. Mistress Corvo and Duchess Prospero fanned themselves and played at feeling faint. Someone fetched the dance teacher a chair and she all but collapsed into it.

'I said arrest him,' thundered Giancarlo, now red-faced with fury. The guards roused themselves and pushed through the crowd, but when they arrived in front of Lucien they found their path blocked. D'arzenta and Ruggeri had both drawn steel and were adopting stances of casual violence. Lord Contadino stood alongside them, sword in hand. Not a ceremonial blade, Lucien noted. Massimo was as ever at his master's elbow, his own finely crafted blade drawn, looking as if he wanted to fight all six guards single-handed. Dino had drawn the sword from the cane and was sighting down the length of the weapon at the guard in front of him, a cool sneer on his lips. Anea had wrested the halberd from Franco and stood closest of all to Lucien, green eyes narrowed above her veil. She ignored the guards, eyes intent on Giancarlo, who withered under her accusing gaze. Nardo joined them, bearing only a knife but bristling with tear-stained ferocity.

'This is a coup,' shouted Giancarlo, his voice breaking.

'No.' Lucien's smile was thin and bitter. 'You were the one attempting a coup. You wanted to install Golia as your puppet king on orders from the Majordomo.'

'What is this about, Lucien?' said Virmyre. 'What experiments has the king been doing?'

'I'm not sure about the experiments themselves, only that the results of those experiments stand before you. The Orfano. The king has been trying to breed an heir according to some insane design of his own. The Majordomo decided it was going to be Golia.'

'And he will make a fine king,' said Giancarlo.

'No—' Lucien shook his head sadly '—he won't.'

The blood drained from Giancarlo's face. 'You ... you killed Golia?'

'He took Rafaela hostage on the roof of the *sanatorio*. But you already know that because you gave him the order.'

Giancarlo shook his head, wanting to unhear the words. 'You killed him?'

'Actually it was me,' said Rafaela defiantly, reddened hands testament to the fact.

Giancarlo's shoulders slumped and he laid his trembling hand on the hilt of his sword. Lucien turned back to Virmyre.

'Some of the Orfani were so twisted, so deformed, they stood no chance of a normal life. I found one living on the rooftops, no doubt stealing food to survive. Another lived behind the graveyard; yet more are imprisoned in the oubliette. The Orfani's mothers were sent to the *sanatorio* to rot in obscurity. The Domo had the perfect cover if any escaped and tried to explain: he'd say they were afflicted by madness, had imagined all of it.'

Angelicola stopped his sobbing at this point. He looked up at Lucien with a pained look in his eyes.

'There's your proof.' Lucien pointed his sword at the broken *dottore*. 'His mind's gone with the strain of delivering the king's bastards.'

'If anyone's mind has gone, it is yours, Master Lucien,' spluttered Giancarlo.

Lucien and his ring of protectors had advanced up the room. The guards opposing them had melted back into the crowd, unsure of who was in control any more. Lucien was now only feet away from Giancarlo, who surrendered his vantage point on the chair.

'My mind is just fine,' replied Lucien. 'You've spent most of your life trying to break my spirit, even kill me, but my mind is perfectly intact, I can assure you. I unravelled the king's sick scheme and now the Majordomo is finished.' Lucien limped closer. 'You're the last of them, Superiore. The last of the conspirators.' He pointed with one finger. 'You had me exiled and I will have satisfaction.'

Giancarlo took a half-step back. He smiled and drew his sword.

'You can't possibly think to defeat me. Look at you – you're half-dead. You'll never best me with a blade, you *strega* bastard.'

He was right of course. Lucien *was* half dead. The testing, the fight on the rooftop, the horsemen on the road, his beating at the hands of Raul da Costa's idiot son-in-law. All of these exchanges had cost him dearly. His body was a litany of abrasions and cuts; he was attired in a motley of bruises and dried blood. Facing the Domo not once but twice had all but broken him, and then he'd fought the king and been poisoned by Golia.

He was beyond shattered.

And there was the small issue that he'd never once bested the *superiore*, not with a blade at least.

Lucien threw up a parry, turning aside a thrust from the *superiore*, saw the hatred in his eyes.

'You're a liar!' bellowed Giancarlo. Lucien's fingers weakened on the hilt of his sword as the blades met. The weapon had been Golia's; the *superiore* knew it all too well.

'You're a murderer!' Another blow. No finesse, just manic intensity.

The unfamiliar blade all but tumbled from Lucien's grasp. Lucien thrust, not content just to react.

'You're a *strega*!'

A deafening clang. Golia's blade spun across the tiles. Lucien looked down at his hand, the fingers numb. He was almost too tired to be afeared, too exhausted to be shocked. His legs betrayed him and he fell, waiting for the killing blow, one arm held up, a pitiful shield. Giancarlo grinned and lunged in.

The *superiore*'s body collapsed to the floor.

There was a wet thud as his head landed a few feet away, coming to rest at the feet of Mistress Corvo, who fainted clean away, dissolving from her chair, a collection of limbs in black.

All eyes turned.

Anea stood glowering at everyone, Franco's halberd in her hands. She threw it down with naked disgust, before conjuring her book, then scribbled a message. Virmyre approached her and accepted the book, clearing his throat. A pause, then a raised eyebrow. He turned to her. She nodded in response to his enquiring stare.

'Lady Anea Erudito wishes it to be known that the next person to use the word *strega* will, and I quote, "have their fucking head cut off".'

There were no dissenting voices.

Lucien pushed himself to his feet despite gravity's best efforts to retain him.

Virmyre extended a hand. 'I see you've lost my sword.'

'I dropped it off a roof.'

'From anyone else, Lucien, from anyone else . . .' A flicker of amusement.

'What *did* happen to the horse?'

'Best you don't know.' Lucien turned to Anea. 'It seems I owe you my life.'

Anea, as ever, said nothing, just inclined her head.

'Perhaps we can get on with the business of caring for the women of the *sanatorio*,' said Virmyre, but the calm was short lived.

There was a second of quiet and then Carmine launched himself at Lucien, a snarl curling his lips. Carmine, the last of Giancarlo's protégés, continuing his master's vendetta. Unarmed as he was, Lucien could do nothing to protect himself. Anea made to snatch up the discarded halberd, but she was too late to defend the threatened Orfano a second time. Everyone stared in horror. A sword flashed in the sunlight and fell with lethal inevitability. Lucien regarded it with a detached disregard, too stunned to move.

Carmine shuddered as the tip of Dino's blade punctured his throat. The momentum carried him further onto Dino's blade. It slid from the back of his neck, a sleek red length of steel. The young boy clutched the sword cane Lucien had given him at *La Festa* with a dreadful intensity. Carmine tried to cough, but no sound escaped his lips, just a trickle of blood. Slowly he sank to his knees, his eyes set disbelievingly on the hilt, now just inches away from his chin. People nearby moaned in disgust, turning away appalled.

'Stupid,' said Dino, and withdrew the sword in a fluid motion. Carmine clutched his neck, but the blood jetted through the gaps in his fingers. He fell face down, expiring at Dino's feet, who cleaned the blade on a rag and turned to Lucien before giving him a lazy salute.

Lucien nodded. 'I'm glad you kept that thing.'

'So am I,' replied Dino, sheathing the weapon with a flourish.

'If you ever want to give it back ...'

'Highly unlikely,' said the younger Orfano.

'Is it over?' asked Virmyre.

'I hope so,' said Russo. 'There's not many of us left.'

Stephania was holding a kerchief up to her face and trying to disguise the fact she was crying. The *capo* was desperately trying to make himself invisible. D'arzenta and Ruggeri re-sheathed their swords. Tension ebbed from the room.

Lucien breathed heavily. Silence crowded in behind him. He felt the weight of the last two days drag at every muscle. His vision wavered a moment and then his gaze fell on Rafaela. He walked toward her, glad not to have a weapon at hand for once.

'But ... but what now?' asked Duchess Prospero.

Lucien turned to her, his face impassive.

'Demesne has been abducting people for hundreds of years. I think it's time you starting giving something back.'

A few of the nobles spluttered in the beginnings of outrage but were quickly silenced by Lucien's flinty gaze.

'I'm leaving her in charge,' he said, pointing at Anea. 'It will be unfortunate if I have to come back.'

38

The Duke's Funeral

The day after *La Festa* brought a deluge of questions, many of which would remain unanswered. Some for mere hours, others for all time. Lucien stood in the arch of the House Contadino gatehouse, watching the grey skies unleash wave after wave of hazy raindrops. He clasped a mug of coffee to his chest, lost in thought. Virmyre found him, joining him in the rain-slicked silence. Nothing needed to be said. Together they watched the lightning fracture the horizon, listened to the rumble and boom. Staff went about their morning chores, some of them suffering from the previous night's excesses, all of them keeping their voices to a hush.

Death had visited Demesne again.

Dino appeared turned out in black, clutching Lucien's sword cane. His eyes were red-rimmed, his face grey and unwell. Even Achilles, perched on his shoulder, wore a small black sash around his neck. Lucien thought it looked ridiculous but said nothing. Virmyre nodded to the Orfano politely.

'We found him at the bottom of the stairs,' said Dino, voice not more than a whisper. Lucien blinked a few times and stared at the boy.

'What did you say?'

'We found him, Duke Prospero, at the bottom of the stairs. He must have hit every one of them on the way down. He was a mess.'

'I thought Dottore Angelicola discovered him?'

'No.' Dino shook his head. 'After you left *La Festa*, Anea wanted to leave too. I escorted her back to her rooms, just as you asked me. It was still early so I went back. Lady Stephania spoke to me. She was a little drunk at that point. She wanted to show me her pony.'

'Her pony?' Lucien exchanged puzzled glances with Virmyre.

'She was drunk. She was talking about her pony and . . . anyway, we left the party to go to the stables. She said she knew a short cut, a stairwell in House Prospero. That's where we found him.' Dino shivered and looked down at his feet. The wind shrieked around the towers of Demesne, across an army of battlements, haranguing rusted weathervanes.

'I'm so sorry, Dino. Did you get any sleep?'

'There's more,' said the boy with a touch of defiance, daring himself not to cry, Lucien guessed. Virmyre stared at the boy, one hand straying to his beard.

'Stephania wanted to come to you after we found him. I brought her to your apartment. The door was open so we went into the sitting room.'

Lucien felt himself grow pale. His stomach became a tight knot.

Dino glanced at Virmyre for an instant, then continued. 'When it was obvious you were unavailable we left, but she's very upset.'

'How is Lady Stephania today?' asked Virmyre. If he caught the unspoken moment between the Orfani he did not show it.

'Not good. Not good at all. She's refusing to speak to her mother. She says her father threw himself down those stairs because of the business with the *capo*.'

'The duke was drunk. He got lost and he fell,' said Lucien angrily. 'He'd never commit suicide. He'd never abandon Stephania.' But even as he uttered the words he faltered, remembering how broken and despairing the old man had sounded.

'It doesn't really matter now, does it?' said Virmyre. 'He could have had a heart attack or just dropped dead on the spot – he might even have been pushed. We'll never know.'

They stood unspeaking as blacker clouds heaved themselves across the sky, presaging a twilight darkness. Drain pipes gurgled and gutters ran like miniature rivers all across the rooftops of Demesne. The blocky form of the *sanatorio* was just discernible in the distance, visible through a veil of rain.

'I should take Achilles back inside,' said Dino. The drake had curled up and looked miserable. 'I came to return this.' He proffered the sword cane to Lucien, barely concealing his distaste.

'Keep it. Seems to me you earned it last night.'

'I don't see how: the duke's dead.'

'I didn't ask to you to protect the duke.' Lucien emptied the dregs of his coffee onto the cobbles and gave Dino a hard stare. The younger Orfano shrugged and turned away, leaving without another word.

'Anything you'd like to tell me?' rumbled Virmyre.

Lucien shook his head, watching the puddles in the courtyard ripple as the rain fell, imagining the scent of Rafaela.

The funeral took place a week later, coming to be regarded as the most awkward event in living memory. The rain had fallen steadily since that bleak morning, making the trip to the cemetery an ordeal for anyone who couldn't get a seat on a cart or carriage. At the graveside the mourners huddled under stiff parasols of waxed black canvas. The artisans of House Prospero had worked tirelessly to prepare them. The duke had his faults but was unanimously loved by his workers, Lucien wondered if they'd remain as productive under Duchess Prospero.

The high wall that surrounded the final resting place of Demesne's nobility seemed lower than Lucien remembered it. A few more stones had come loose since the day he'd run away, only to be brought back by Virmyre, and everywhere was the insistent cling of ivy, seeking to undermine the barrier between living and dead. It looked to be succeeding. The copse of cypress trees rustled, bending in the wind like old men. No one had repaired the gates, and so they remained rusted in place, weeds binding them to the ground. Lucien had arrived early and hunched down under his own parasol beside them, watching the other mourners approach.

Anea and Dino arrived first. Dino kept off the rain with a parasol as Anea held his arm. She was huddled in a great fur cloak and met Lucien's eyes reluctantly. Dino had been conspicuously absent since he'd attempted to return the sword cane. The two Orfani headed into the cemetery without a word. Lucien took this as a signal to wait outside a moment longer.

Virmyre and Russo arrived, representing the teaching faculty. They nodded to Lucien, exchanging a few words with him before passing through the gates. Lucien realised he could count the number of people he could trust on one hand, but he was grateful that Virmyre was among them.

Duchess Prospero was attended by a smattering of pages. Her aide was a new girl with bright blonde hair braided into a severe plait that drooped over her shoulder in the rain. Lady Prospero smiled tightly at Lucien but swept past him, keen to get the ceremony over.

The Majordomo arrived, unfolding his lank frame from a carriage. He moved with lurching, arthritic grace. The damp had invaded his joints and he rested heavily on his staff. He was splendid in formal crimson robes, now wet and muddy to the ankle. If the Domo saw Lucien he didn't show it, instead making his way straight into the graveyard.

The *capo* followed, leading a guard of honour that seemed as redundant as it was in bad taste. Duke Prospero had never been a fighting man, and it was unlikely he'd have wanted the *capo* within fifty miles of his funeral. The soldiers marched past, keeping their gazes frozen ahead of them. Lucien scowled and pushed his fingers through damp hair.

Everyone present had someone to stand with.

Everyone except Lady Stephania, who arrived by carriage. Alone. Lucien approached her with a tightness in his chest.

'Hello,' he said in a low voice, feeling abashed. Stephania nodded to him, her mouth pinched, brow set hard.

'Where are they burying him?' No grave had been dug as far as Lucien could see. He doubted digging a grave in these conditions was even possible. Stephania extended an arm, pointing to a sepulchre at the back of the cemetery. They walked toward it, boots crunching on the gravel path.

'About *La Festa*—' He got no further.

'I really don't care, Lucien,' she said icily. 'I don't care who she is, if you love her, if you're going to bed her again or even if you prefer men. We're getting married, and that's all there is to it. I'm going to take control of House Prospero before my mother makes us a complete laughing stock. And you're going to help me.'

Lucien concentrated on the ground. The rain beat a staccato on the fabric of his parasol. He chewed his lip. 'I'm not sure this is going to work, Stephania.'

'I don't see you have any choice. Giancarlo and Golia are dying to find a reason to get rid of you. Permanently. By becoming Duke Prospero you'd make their lives hell. They wouldn't dare try and kill you for fear of the other three houses uniting against them.'

They were close to the sepulchre now. People were shaking the rain from their parasols and squeezing into the gloomy interior. The Majordomo waited with a scroll unfurled in front of him.

'You'll marry me, Lucien. You'll marry me if you want to live. And you'll help me teach my mother a lesson. What you do at night is your own concern, but I *will* want an heir at some point, so try not to catch anything.'

Her brown eyes ran him through before she turned on her heel and entered the sepulchre, leaving him drowning in uncertainty outside.

After the ceremony the mourners filed out, glad to be away. Stephania exchanged a few brief words with the Majordomo as the sombre gathering dispersed. If Duchess Prospero had any feelings about her husband's passing she did not show them. No one stepped forward to offer her condolences, instead addressing Stephania. The mourners crossed the cemetery, picking their way through overgrown grasses and broken masonry, back to the convoy of carts and carriages. Coachmen shouted, whips cracked, and the procession headed back to Demesne – back to the beating heart of Landfall and the strange edicts of the reclusive king.

Lucien remained. He leaned against the cold stone of the

sepulchre, lingering on Stephania's words, turning them over in his mind. She was correct of course. Politically, her thinking was sound. Only by aligning with each other might they survive. There was a dreadful hardness to her. It were as if she were someone else, someone new. As if the flirtatious girl at *La Festa* had surely fallen down the stairs with her father. Lucien wondered how excruciating it must have been for her to stand in his sitting room, hearing him abed with Rafaela. How terrible for her to have sought him in her hour of need, only to find him in the arms of another. He cursed Dino for bringing her to his apartments, knowing even as he did that Dino was blameless.

A shadow detached itself from the trees, no more than an outline in grey. It approached quickly, bearing no parasol, blurred and indistinct due to the falling rain. Lucien drew his blade on instinct. He'd welcome a fight. Someone who could hurt him. Someone he could hurt. Anything to prove he had some choices left in his life. Anything but the twisting skeins of politics and intrigue.

Capo de Custodia Guido di Fontein emerged from the gloom, hair plastered to his pretty face, clothes sodden. Despite this he wore a ridiculous grin. He stopped a dozen feet away from Lucien, beyond the range of his blade. He rested a hand on the hilt of his sword and took a moment to catch his breath.

'Master Lucien, you appear to have missed your ride back to House Contadino.'

'I was just enjoying the weather.'

'You have peculiar tastes, if you don't mind me saying so.'

'Actually I do.' Lucien still hadn't sheathed his sword. No reason to make it easy for the empty-headed noble.

'We've not really had a chance to talk recently,'

'It seems I'm still entitled to small mercies.'

'I had to discipline one of my men yesterday.' The *capo* smiled, relishing this, like the final moves of a chess game. Lucien didn't reply, merely raised an eyebrow and nodded to show he was still listening.

'I caught him gossiping. It seems your maid was seen leaving House Contadino early the morning after *La Festa*.'

Check, thought Lucien.

Perhaps she left something at home. She lives out on the estate,' replied Lucien. He tightened his grip on his sword.

'The guard in question is an observant sort. He couldn't help noticing she was wearing the same attire she had worn on the previous day.' *Checkmate.*

Lucien let it hang between them. The rain was beginning to slacken.

'I can't say I'm concerned by such things. If your man is so interested in dresses perhaps you should buy him one.'

The *capo* clapped his hands slowly in mock applause.

'What do you want, Guido?'

'You will address as me as Capo,' he snapped.

'Work hard to earn that title, did you?'

'Did you work hard to earn yours, Orfano?'

'I didn't ask to be born Orfano; there are days I'd rather be anything but.'

Silence crowded about the cemetery and the *capo* shivered.

'Duchess Prospero would prefer it if you declined any invitation to marriage from Lady Stephania.'

'Really?' Lucien almost laughed. 'The duchess has been actively campaigning for many months for that very thing.'

'She would prefer it if you declined any—'

'Or she'll tell every one in the four houses that *she thinks* I bedded my maid on *La Festa.*'

'I can see Virmyre has trained your intellect to be razor sharp.'

'It's not the only thing I own that's razor sharp,' replied Lucien, rolling his shoulders and flicking rainwater from the blade. 'Tell Her Highness I'll think about it.'

'What?' The *capo* looked less sure of himself. Lucien guessed Duchess Prospero had coached him, but she'd not rehearsed him in what to say in the event Lucien didn't yield. He stepped forward, eyes like flint, hatred aching out of every pore. How he'd love to cut this popinjay down where he stood. For the duke. For Stephania. For himself.

'Tell her I'm not going to be blackmailed with half-truths and might-have-beens. Tell her she's going to need a bit more than a hung-over guard crowing about a maid. Tell her that after the death of her husband it would be respectful for her to retire from public life for few weeks.'

The *capo* stood with his mouth open.

'Now get the fuck out of here before I chop your head off,' growled Lucien. He spun the sword in his hand, keen to use it on the soaking fop. The *capo* fled, falling twice before he made the safety of the cemetery gates.

Lucien sneered after the fleeing figure, annoyed at anyone thinking he might be cowed with such paltry threats. His marriage to Stephania seemed all but inevitable now, but his reason to refuse it wouldn't be blackmail. It would be Rafaela.

39

Coda

THE OLD *SANATORIO*

– Febbraio 316

Lucien sat in bed, his hair tousled, sleep crusted at the corners of his eyes, last night's sweat faint and salty on his skin. Rafaela stood at the window, her scarlet skirt hanging from her hips, shoulders bare. Lucien admired the curve of her spine, the sweep of her back, her olive skin soft and inviting. Her hair had grown back but had yet to reach her shoulders.

'What happened that night in the King's Keep?' The words had come unbidden, the thought leaving his mouth unconsciously. She stiffened but said nothing. He waited, chewing his lip, regretting the question.

'You're asking me that, now, a year later?' Her eyes remained fixed on the world outside, her voice hushed.

'Yes, I suppose I am.'

'Seems a strange time to discuss that. I'd been doing my best to forget.'

'Me too.'

He waited, wanting her to fill the silence, unsure he'd like what would come next. She remained at the window, ribcage rising and falling with the passage of breath. He knew every inch of her now. They'd been insatiable at first, their passion a hunger that had been denied far too long. The nine months since they'd been together had been heady, but the shadow of Rafaela's night in King's Keep had always darkened their time together.

'I should have asked sooner, but I was scared—'

'Scared?' She looked at him over her shoulder. 'You didn't seem very scared when you fought Golia, or Giancarlo. Were

314

you scared when you killed the king?' Her eyes had none of their characteristic warmth, while her arms were folded across her stomach.

'Of course I was scared when I fought, but it was a different kind of fear. When you walk into a fight you face your opponent and then you walk away. Or you don't. But the truth? No one walks away from the truth.'

She softened at this, sitting at the end of the bed, folding her hands into her lap neatly. She addressed the floor, her gaze unfocused, remembering the night of her abduction.

'He didn't touch me, if that's what you're asking.'

'I—'

'He *didn't* touch me. He said I was no use to him. I was so scared. He said I was barren and too old.' She pressed one hand to her mouth and swallowed, then took a breath. 'He sniffed me like a dog, said I had a scent of sickness about me. He ridiculed me for not being able to bear children.'

Lucien attempted to speak, but she silenced him with an outstretched palm, eyes locked on the floor in front of her.

'And then they took me to the *sanatorio*. And I was so glad, so grateful. Sitting there in the dark I realised how many girls, how many women, hadn't had my luck. Every Orfani in Demesne is a testament to the king's wickedness. Every Orfani is a marker for a life ruined, a woman preyed on.'

Lucien felt the familiar wave of guilt that washed over him at times like these. Being well acquainted with the feeling didn't make it any easier to bear. The king had used devices to deliver his seed, but in the end his rape was as repellent as any other.

She paused. Her eyes hadn't left the floor. Lucien watched her profile, the tightness in the jaw, the tension in her smooth shoulders. Her hands clutched at one another.

'And I felt guilty,' she whispered, 'guilty that I should be spared something so horrible, so awful, when all those other women had suffered and were driven insane.'

'I should have asked sooner,' he said, shifting until he was kneeling next to her on the bed. She looked up at him at last, tears bright in her eyes and tracking down the soft curves of her face.

'No, I'm sorry. I could have started this conversation – should have started it. I hoped it would go away, be forgotten about. But nothing ever goes away, does it?'

Warm hands found each other. They looked down at the union of their entwined fingers.

'Perhaps it's for the best,' said Lucien. 'Who knows what any child of mine might look like. Simply birthing an Orfano might kill you.' He chewed at his lip. 'I couldn't bear it. I nearly lost you once; I'll not see you in danger again.'

A smile touched her soft lips, and then she leaned forward and pressed her mouth to his. They sat together for silent minutes, heads at peace on each other's shoulders, arms wrapped firmly around one another.

'Come on, time to get up. You've a big day ahead of you.'

'Don't say that; you sound like my nanny used to.'

'Uncanny, isn't it?'

'You'd like her.' He grinned. 'Attractive, funny, smart. Kind too.'

'Too bad she's already taken.'

A knock came at the door.

'You're late,' came a peeved voice from the other side. Unmistakably Dino.

When Lucien had washed and dressed, he found the younger Orfano outside. He was taller now, hair cut short in a rakish sort of way, and festooned with daggers. He'd adopted a suit of pale grey since Demesne's reformation and taken to wearing his boots unbuckled, sword cane clutched in one hand, lacquered and polished.

'You know, you've had all year to get under her skirt, and now when you're summoned, you're *still* at it.' Dino shook his head and rolled his eyes.

'One is not "at it" with a woman like Rafaela.'

'Sleeping in, were we, my lord?'

'You'll be the same one day.' Lucien grinned. 'Just you wait and see.'

'I doubt it.'

*

316

They walked in silence for a moment. Dino had often visited the *sanatorio*, which Lucien had claimed for himself, turning the place into a school. The previous tenants had been moved to a new *sanatorio* nearer the coast with better conditions and a score of nurses. Banners the colour of newly turned earth flapped and rippled in the wind behind them, suspended from each of the gargoyles on the building's roof. Seven triangles in turquoise ran down the left side of each flag, a device of Lucien's own design.

'How's it going in there?' Lucien gestured to Demesne. He'd not been back in a year, busying himself with the school and Rafaela. The corridors held memories he was in no rush to revisit.

'It's all piss and vinegar,' replied Dino casually. 'Anea has curtailed House Fontein's influence somewhat. The guards answer directly to her. Duke and Duchess Fontein have attracted a clique of blacksmiths and armourers, most of whom they had to poach from House Prospero. They still have the *Maestri di Spada*. They're an academy and an armoury now, nothing more.' He smiled at the older Orfano before continuing.

'Duchess Prospero is up in arms of course. The *capo de custodia* looks like he can't tell his arse from his elbow. Nothing new there. And there's talk of a new Majordomo being appointed.'

'Sounds like something you could do,' said Lucien, waiting for the riposte.

'Not likely,' replied Dino. 'I'm only thirteen. Besides, look what happened to the last one.'

'Good point.'

They were outside Demesne now, not any of the houses but the gates of King's Keep itself. A triumphal arch led from the gates to the exterior doors of the keep.

'Don't think I've ever passed this way before.'

'Probably as a good a day to do so as any. Long live the king.' Dino laughed. There was a flicker of movement at one of the narrow windows two floors up, and then the mighty wooden doors were opening outwards, pushed by teams of men, each four strong.

'All this for me?'

'They call you the Jack of Ravens now,' said Dino.

'And what do they call you?'

'Well, Virmyre calls me "that bastard Orfano who swears too much", but it'll never catch on.'

'He could shorten it to "bastard".'

'Yes,' said Dino, 'and I could shorten his life expectancy. And yours.'

'I've heard you're the quite the prodigy.'

'I know the hilt from the blade. I find that helps.'

'Such modesty in one so young.'

'Shut up, Lucien.'

The doormen bowed and the man and boy entered the yawning portal. It was a vast and ornate threshold with six colonnettes on each side, each sporting a raven etched in stone. New additions since the king's demise. No sooner had they passed under the arch than the doors were drawn shut again.

The circuitous corridor was barely recognisable. Oil lamps lit every alcove and new tiles had been laid in turquoise and white, Anea's house colours. The doors to the king's chambers had been replaced and painted white. Outside stood a hooded figure in deep crimson, clutching a silver staff. Lucien fought down a shudder of grim remembrance. The Majordomo had worn similar robes the day he'd been sworn in as a Fontein. And at Duke Prospero's funeral.

A slender hand reached up to draw back the hood, revealing Russo's oval face.

Dino let out a low whistle. 'I guess I should have seen that coming.'

'Surprised?' she asked.

He shrugged. 'Just glad she didn't ask me to do it.'

'Hello, Lucien.' Russo smiled warmly

'Anea found you a new job then, did she?'

'You're not afraid of women on top, are you, Lucien?'

'Not at all, just ask Rafaela.'

Dino rolled his eyes. 'Can we go now?'

Russo turned to the gates, producing the two-pronged key that Lucien had wrested from the old Majordomo. Some things hadn't changed after all. They entered the library, where Virmyre leafed through an old tome while he waited for them.

'Remarkable,' he whispered to himself.

'Find anything interesting?' asked Lucien.

'Interesting?' Virmyre turned to the Orfano. 'Everything in this library is interesting, Lucien. There are things written here we couldn't have imagined.'

'How have you been keeping?'

'Good. Anea has been keeping me busy.'

'Don't you mean Lady Diaspora?' Anea had made a lot of changes in the last year, most notably reinventing herself.

'Come on, she's waiting,' pressed Russo.

The king's chamber had been transformed, the laboratory on the upper level dismantled. White drapes cascaded from the ceiling, running down the walls. The floor had been tiled, polished and waxed. It was a place of light and beauty now. Three score nobles stood and preened. Duchess Prospero whispered to Lady Allatamento. Lucien ignored her, nodding politely to Stephania instead. Stephania returned a tight smile and looked away, fanning herself.

'She hates me, doesn't she?'

'It's not your fault, but she's not exactly drowning in suitors.'

The *capo* glowered at the Orfani as they passed. Lucien smiled cheerfully back.

'Didn't he throw you in the oubliette?' enquired Dino.

'I'd forgotten that minor detail.'

'We could still arrest him, you know.'

'I *wish* you would arrest him,' grumbled Virmyre.

'*You* could still arrest him,' said Lucien. 'I don't live here any more, remember?'

'I'm just saying. I don't like him,' added Dino.

'Another thing we all have in common,' said Virmyre.

In front of them was Araneae Oscuro Diaspora, ruler of Demesne and all of sixteen years old. There was no throne or sceptre, no crown or tiara, not even a banner to proclaim her authority. She'd carefully avoided the trappings of power while wielding it absolutely. A pair of pageboys lurked nearby, but there was meagre evidence that she was the island's ruler. Her turquoise gown was belted by a white silk sash which matched her veil and gloves.

Russo joined Anea, nodding politely to her. 'Lady Diaspora welcomes you back to Demesne, where you have been sorely missed.'

Anea's eyes flickered with amusement above her veil. Smiles and greetings were exchanged and then the group retired up the staircase that led to the gallery. Below them the nobles muttered and seethed.

'I see the Orfani are as popular with the *nobili* as ever,' said Lucien, remembering a time he might have been tempted to spit over the railings.

'They're anxious,' said Russo, her staff tapping out a regular rhythm on the wooden floor. 'They know that taking power from House Fontein is just the start.'

'The Contadini don't care much for the other houses,' said Virmyre. 'They might prove useful in the years ahead.'

Anea took Lucien by the hand and led him to an alcove off the dome. Sunlight streamed in around them. He looked down, unable to believe this was the same place he'd confronted the king. Russo, Virmyre and Dino waited at the railing, talking between themselves.

In the alcove was a plinth carved from pure white marble, a rosewood box four feet long resting on it. Lucien instinctively knew what it was. He turned to Anea and she nodded, her eyes filled with happiness. He reached forward and undid the brass clasps, lifting the lid reverently. Inside was a replica of the blade he'd carried into his final testing, perfect in every way. It could have been the same blade. He ran his fingers over the smooth ceramic and looked at Anea.

'It's beautiful.' He lifted the weapon out of the case, remembering how Giancarlo had destroyed the previous incarnation. He returned the blade to its case.

Anea brought a notebook out from one of her sleeves, turning to a page marked with a black ribbon. Lucien looked down at the words she'd prepared for him: *I wanted you to have these also.*

320

She circled the plinth and stooped, retrieving a smaller rose-wood box. Lucien waited, unsure of what to expect. He took the container and opened it, feeling his throat grow thick with emotion. Inside were the porcelain ears that Raul da Costa had made him when he was twelve. They were smaller than he remembered them. Pitiful and yet perfect somehow, despite their ruin.

'You kept them all this time,' he breathed. 'You kept them even though I was awful to you, or neglected you or failed you.'

She hurriedly wrote something in her book, then turned it to him: *You never failed me. You saved me. We saved each other. And from now on I think I'd like to call you brother.*

Lucien lent forward and kissed her on the forehead.

'You know, if we accept that we're brother and sister, we have to accept Dino as part of this too.'

Anea cocked her head to one side, taking a moment to write a response: *A girl can never have too many brothers.*

She took a moment to scratch down something else in the book: *What do we call you now?*

'I think I'd like to be Lord Marino from now on.'

'Lord Marino?' interrupted Russo. 'What sort of name is that?'

'You'll see,' said Lucien with a slow smile. 'You'll see.'

Acknowledgements
Or the Real Dramatis Personae

HOUSE PATRICK

Duchess Szalkai
who never told me to get a proper job or a haircut

***Margravio* Patrick**
provider of encouragement and praise

Squires Perry and Shurin
friends, educators, encouragers, enthusiasm monsters

Viscount and Viscountess Odd
providers of shelter to waifs and strays

Lord Morgan and Lord Bailey
generous gentlemen

***Maestro di Spada* Andrew James**
an intellect matched only by kindness

Master of Scribes Tom Pollock
a comrade in arms

Archivist Julie Crisp
who knows a thing or two about books, throws good shapes

Matt Rowan, Lizzie Barrett and Matt Lyons
test readers and providers of wise counsel

HOUSE GOLLANCZ

Chief Archivist of Landfall Simon Spanton
champion of the *Orfani*

Exemplar Gillian Redfearn
wielder of red pens and longbows

Faithful Messengers
Jon Weir, Sophie Calder

Captains of the Watch
Charlie Panayiotou, Jen McMenemy and all at Gollancz

Agent extraordinaire Juliet Mushens
tiny, leopard-print tornado

INFLUENCES OF ESPECIAL IMPORTANCE

Frank Herbert's *Dune*, Mervyn Peake's *Gormenghast*, and all of Joe Abercrombie's output. Not forgetting Jon Courtenay Grimwood's *Assassini* trilogy, Scott Lynch's Gentlemen Bastards and *Use of Weapons* by Iain M. Banks. I'd be remiss for failing to mention Chris Wooding, Steph Swainston, Richard Morgan, China Miéville and M. John Harrison.

BRINGING NEWS FROM OUR WORLDS TO YOURS . . .

Want your news daily?

The Gollancz blog has instant updates on the hottest SF and Fantasy books.

Prefer your updates monthly?

Sign up for our in-depth newsletter.

www.gollancz.co.uk

Follow us 🐦 @gollancz

Find us 📘 facebook.com/GollanczPublishing

Classic SF as you've never read it before.

Visit the SF Gateway to find out more!

www.sfgateway.com